KAZUO ISHIGURO

THE REMAINS OF THE DAY

Cornelsen

Kazuo Ishiguro
The Remains of the Day

Herausgegeben von:
Peter Freienstein
Dr. Paul Maloney

Verlagsredaktion: Neil Porter

Technische Umsetzung: Peter Richter

Umschlagillustrationen:
© Cinetext Bildarchiv

complete original text

Herausgeber der *Cornelsen Senior English Library:*
Prof. Dr. Albert-Reiner Glaap

http://www.cornelsen.de

1. Auflage Druck 4 3 2 1 Jahr 08 07 06 05

Alle Drucke dieser Auflage sind inhaltlich unverändert und können im Unterricht nebeneinander verwendet werden.

Druck: Druckhaus Berlin-Mitte

ISBN 3-464-31088-4

Bestellnummer 310884

Gedruckt auf säurefreiem Papier, umweltschonend hergestellt aus chlorfrei gebleichten Faserstoffen.

CONTENTS

The Remains of the Day
5

Prologue: July 1956
Darlington Hall
5

Day One –Evening
Salisbury
23

Day Two – Morning
Salisbury
47

Day Two – Afternoon
Mortimer's Pond, Dorset
107

Day Three – Morning
Taunton, Somerset
123

Day Three – Evening
Moscombe, near Tavistock, Devon
137

Day Four – Afternoon
Little Compton, Cornwall
189

Day Six – Evening
Weymouth
213

The Author
228

In Memory of Mrs Lenore Marshall

Abbreviations

adj	adjective	jdm./jdn.	jemandem/en
adv	adverb	n	noun
AE	American English	p., pp.	page, pages
cf.	confer; see	pl	plural
derog	derogatory	sb.	somebody
e.g.	exempli gratia; for example	sl	slang
esp.	especially	sth.	something
etc.	et cetera; and so on	usu.	usually
i.e.	id est; in other words	v	verb
infml	informal		

The annotations are arranged chronologically: the first time a word is used is where you will find it explained. All pronunciations given are British English. An alphabetical list of all the annotated words can be found at **www.learnetix.de/bookshelf**.

As this novel can be regarded as a kind of monologue spoken by the butler Stevens, its language is largely determined by Stevens's attempt to imitate the mannerisms of upper-class English (most notably the use of the impersonal 'one' when he is talking about himself). For this reason, the register label 'formal' does not appear in the annotations, as it would apply to innumerable expressions used by the narrator.

PROLOGUE: JULY 1956

Darlington Hall

It seems increasingly likely that I really will undertake the expedition that has been preoccupying my imagination now for some days. An expedition, I should say, which I will undertake alone, in the comfort of Mr Farraday's Ford; an expedition which, as I foresee it, will take me through much of the finest countryside of England to the West Country, and may keep me away from Darlington Hall for as much as five or six days. The idea of such a journey came about, I should point out, from a most kind suggestion put to me by Mr Farraday himself one afternoon almost a fortnight ago, when I had been dusting the portraits in the library. In fact, as I recall, I was up on the step-ladder dusting the portrait of Viscount Wetherby when my employer had entered carrying a few volumes which he presumably wished returned to the shelves. On seeing my person, he took the opportunity to inform me that he had just that moment finalized plans to return to the United States for a period of five weeks between August and September. Having made this announcement, my employer put his volumes down on a table, seated himself on the *chaise-longue*, and stretched out his legs. It was then, gazing up at me, that he said.

'You realize, Stevens, I don't expect you to be locked up here in this house all the time I'm away. Why don't you take the car and drive off somewhere for a few days? You look like you could make good use of a break.'

Coming out of the blue as it did, I did not quite know how to reply to such a suggestion. I recall thanking him for his consideration, but quite probably I said nothing very definite for my employer went on:

'I'm serious, Stevens. I really think you should take a break. I'll foot the bill for the gas. You fellows, you're always locked up in these big houses helping out, how do you ever get to see around this beautiful country of yours?'

This was not the first time my employer had raised such a question; indeed, it seems to be something which genuinely troubles him. On this occasion, in fact, a reply of sorts did occur to me as I stood up

▷ **1** *increasingly:* more and more • *likely* (adj): probable **2** *preoccupy sb.:* jdn. beschäftigen **10** *recall sth.:* remember sth. **12** *presumably:* probably **14** *finalize sth.:* finish the last part of sth. (e.g. a plan) **18** *gaze at sb./sth.:* look at sb./sth. hard and steadily **24** *out of the blue:* unexpectedly **28** *foot the bill for sth.* (infml): pay for sth. • *gas* (AE): petrol **33** *a reply of sorts:* a reply that was not very good • *occur to sb.:* come into sb.'s mind

there on the ladder; a reply to the effect that those of our profession, although we did not see a great deal of the country in the sense of touring the countryside and visiting picturesque sites, did actually 'see' more of England than most, placed as we were in houses where the greatest ladies and gentlemen of the land gathered. Of course, I could not have expressed this view to Mr Farraday without embarking upon what might have seemed a presumptuous speech. I thus contented myself by saying simply:

'It has been my privilege to see the best of England over the years, sir, within these very walls.'

Mr Farraday did not seem to understand this statement, for he merely went on: 'I mean it, Stevens. It's wrong that a man can't get to see around his own country. Take my advice, get out of the house for a few days.'

As you might expect, I did not take Mr Farraday's suggestion at all seriously that afternoon, regarding it as just another instance of an American gentleman's unfamiliarity with what was and what was not commonly done in England. The fact that my attitude to this same suggestion underwent a change over the following days – indeed, that the notion of a trip to the West Country took an ever-increasing hold on my thoughts – is no doubt substantially attributable to – and why should I hide it? – the arrival of Miss Kenton's letter, her first in almost seven years if one discounts the Christmas cards. But let me make it immediately clear what I mean by this; what I mean to say is that Miss Kenton's letter set off a certain chain of ideas to do with professional matters here at Darlington Hall, and I would underline that it was a preoccupation with these very same professional matters that led me to consider anew my employer's kindly meant suggestion. But let me explain further.

The fact is, over the past few months, I have been responsible for a series of small errors in the carrying out of my duties. I should say that these errors have all been without exception quite trivial in themselves. Nevertheless, I think you will understand that to one not accustomed to committing such errors, this development was rather disturbing, and I did in fact begin to entertain all sorts of alarmist theories as to their cause. As so often in these situations, I had become blind to the obvious – that is, until my pondering over the implications of Miss Kenton's letter finally opened my eyes to the simple truth: that these small errors of recent months have derived from nothing more sinister than a faulty staff plan.

It is, of course, the responsibility of every butler to devote his utmost care in the devising of a staff plan. Who knows how many quarrels, false accusations, unnecessary dismissals, how many promising careers cut short can be attributed to a butler's slovenliness at the stage of drawing up the staff plan? Indeed, I can say I am in agreement with those who say that the ability to draw up a good staff plan is the cornerstone of any decent butler's skills. I have myself devised many staff plans over years, and I do not believe I am being unduly boastful if I say that very few ever needed amendment. And if in the present case the staff plan is at fault, blame can be laid at no one's door but my own. At the same time, it is only fair to point out that my task in this instance had been of an unusually difficult order.

What had occurred was this. Once the transactions were over – transactions which had taken this house out of the hands of the Darlington family after two centuries – Mr Farraday let it be known that he would not be taking up immediate residence here, but would spend a further four months concluding matters in the United States. In the meantime, however, he was most keen that the staff of his predecessor – a staff of which he had heard high praise – be retained at Darlington Hall. This 'staff' he referred to was, of course, nothing more than the skeleton team of six kept on by Lord Darlington's relatives to

▷ **1** *to the effect that:* saying that, meaning that **2** *sense* (n): the meaning a word has **3** *picturesque:* charming, attractive **7** *embark upon sth.:* start sth. • *presumptuous:* almost arrogant **12** *merely:* simply, only **17** *unfamiliarity with sth.:* ignorance of sth., lack of experience with sth. **20** *notion:* idea **21** *substantially:* very much • *attributable to sth.:* caused by sth. **23** *discount sth.* [- '-]: not include sth. **26** *matter:* Angelegenheit; • *underline sth.:* stress sth., emphasize sth. **28** *anew:* again but in a different way **35** *disturbing* (adj): making you worry • *entertain sth.:* think about sth. a lot **37** *ponder over sth.:* think over sth. deeply **38** *implication:* potential consequence **39–40** *derive from sth.:* be due to sth. **40** *sinister:* serious • *faulty:* having faults **42** *utmost:* greatest possible • *devise sth.:* create sth., work sth. out **43** *dismissal:* removal of an employee from a position of work **44** *cut sth. short:* stop sth. suddenly • *slovenliness:* negligence, carelessness **49** *unduly:* excessively • *boastful:* showing too much pride in yourself • *amendment:* change, improvement **50–51** *lay blame at sb.'s door:* hold sb. responsible for sth. **53** *transaction:* business of buying and selling **58** *keen* (adj): very interested, eager **59** *predecessor* ['priːdɪsesə]: (here) the previous owner • *retain sb./sth.:* keep sb./sth.

administer to the house up to and throughout the transactions; and I regret to report that once the purchase had been completed, there was little I could do for Mr Farraday to prevent all but Mrs Clements leaving for other employment. When I wrote to my new employer conveying my regrets at the situation, I received by reply from America instructions to recruit a new staff 'worthy of a grand old English house'. I immediately set about trying to fulfil Mr Farraday's wishes, but as you know, finding recruits of a satisfactory standard is no easy task nowadays, and although I was pleased to hire Rosemary and Agnes on Mrs Clements's recommendation, I had got no further by the time I came to have my first business meeting with Mr Farraday during the short preliminary visit he made to our shores in the spring of last year. It was on that occasion – in the strangely bare study of Darlington Hall – that Mr Farraday shook my hand for the first time, but by then we were hardly strangers to each other; quite aside from the matter of the staff, my new employer in several other instances had had occasion to call upon such qualities as it may be my good fortune to possess and found them to be, I would venture, dependable. So it was, I assume, that he felt immediately able to talk to me in a businesslike and trusting way, and by the end of our meeting, he had left me with the administration of a not inconsiderable sum to meet the costs of a wide range of preparations for his coming residency. In any case, my point is that it was during the course of this interview, when I raised the question of the difficulty of recruiting suitable staff in these times, that Mr Farraday, after a moment's reflection, made his request of me; that I do my best to draw up a staff plan – 'some sort of servant's rota' as he put it – by which this house might be run on the present staff of four – that is to say, Mrs Clements, the two young girls, and myself. This might, he appreciated, mean putting sections of the house 'under wraps', but would I bring all my experience and expertise to bear to ensure such losses were kept to a minimum? Recalling a time when I had had a staff of seventeen under me, and knowing how not so long ago a staff of twenty-eight had been employed here at Darlington Hall, the idea of devising a staff plan by which the same house would be run on a staff of four seemed, to say the least, daunting. Although I did my best not to, something of my scepticism must have betrayed itself, for Mr Farraday then added, as though for reassurance, that were it to prove necessary, then an additional member of staff could be hired. But he would be much obliged, he repeated, if I could 'give it a go with four'.

Now naturally, like many of us, I have a reluctance to change too much of the old ways. But there is no virtue at all in clinging as some do to tradition merely for its own sake. In this age of electricity and modern heating systems, there is no need at all to employ the sorts of numbers necessary even a generation ago. Indeed, it has actually been an idea of mine for some time that the retaining of unnecessary numbers simply for tradition's sake – resulting in employees having an unhealthy amount of time on their hands – has been an important factor in the sharp decline of professional standards. Furthermore, Mr Farraday had made it clear that he planned to hold only very rarely the sort of large social occasions Darlington Hall had seen frequently in the past. I did then go about the task Mr Farraday had set me with some dedication; I spent many hours working on the staff plan, and at least as many hours again thinking about it as I went about on other duties or as I lay awake after retiring. Whenever I believed I had come up with something, I probed it for every sort of oversight, tested it through from all angles. Finally, I came up with a plan which, while perhaps not exactly as Mr Farraday had requested, was the best, I felt sure, that was humanly possible. Almost all the attractive parts of the house could remain operative: the extensive servants' quarters – including the back corridor, the two still rooms and the old laundry – and the guest corridor up on the second floor would be dust-sheeted, leaving all the main ground-floor rooms and

▷ **1** *administer to sth.:* do the necessary work in sth. **6** *recruit sb.* [rɪ'kruːt]: hire sb. **8** *recruit* (n): (here) person who is to join or has just joined the staff **12** *preliminary:* initial, that is intended to prepare for sth. • *to our shores:* to our country **18** *venture* (v): dare to say • *dependable:* verlässlich **22** *residency:* permanent stay **26** *rota:* list that shows when each person in a group must do a particular job **29** *appreciate sth.:* understand sth. and realize that it is true • *put sth. under wraps* (infml): let sth. not be used any more **30** *bring sth. to bear:* use sth. • *expertise* [ˌekspɜː'tiːz]: expert knowledge • *ensure:* make sure **35** *daunting* [dɔːntɪŋ]: frightening **36** *betray sth.:* show or reveal sth. **37** *as though for reassurance:* as if sb. wanted to remove another person's fears or doubts **39** *much obliged:* very grateful **40** *reluctance:* unwillingness **41–42** *cling to sth.:* hold on to sth. tightly **42** *for its own sake:* because it is what it is **47** *an unhealthy amount of time on their hands:* too much free time **48** *decline* (n): act of getting worse **50** *social occasion:* meeting, gathering, party **52** *with some dedication:* seriously and energetically **55** *probe sth.:* check sth. very closely **56** *from all angles:* in all its aspects **57** *request sth.:* ask for sth. **60** *servants' quarters:* those parts of the house where the servants live • *still room:* Vorratskammer **61** *laundry:* room where clothes are washed and ironed **62** *dust-sheet sth.:* cover the furniture in sth. (esp. a room) with sheets to protect them from dust

a generous number of guest rooms. Admittedly, our present team of four would manage this programme only with reinforcement from some daily workers; my staff plan therefore took in the services of a gardener, to visit once a week, twice in the summer, and two cleaners, each to visit twice a week. The staff plan would, furthermore, for each of the four resident employees mean a radical altering of our respective customary duties. The two young girls, I predicted, would not find such changes so difficult to accommodate, but I did all I could to see that Mrs Clements suffered the least adjustments, to the extent that I undertook for myself a number of duties which you may consider most broad-minded of a butler to do.

Even now, I would not go so far as to say it is a bad staff plan; after all, it enables a staff of four to cover an unexpected amount of ground. But you will no doubt agree that the very best staff plans are those which give clear margins of error to allow for those days when an employee is ill or for one reason or another below par. In this particular case, of course, I had been set a slightly extraordinary task, but I had nevertheless not been neglectful to incorporate 'margins' wherever possible. I was especially conscious that any resistance there may be on the part of Mrs Clements, or the two girls, to the taking on of duties beyond their traditional boundaries would be compounded by any notion that their workloads had greatly increased. I had then, over those days of struggling with the staff plan, expended a significant amount of thought to ensuring that Mrs Clements and the girls, once they had got over their aversion to adopting these more 'eclectic' roles, would find the division of duties stimulating and unburdensome.

I fear, however, that in my anxiety to win the support of Mrs Clements and the girls, I did not perhaps assess quite as stringently my own limitations; and although my experience and customary caution in such matters prevented my giving myself more than I could actually carry out, I was perhaps negligent over this question of allowing myself a margin. It is not surprising then, if over several months, this oversight should reveal itself in these small but telling ways. In the end, I believe the matter to be no more complicated than this: I had given myself too much to do.

You may be amazed that such an obvious shortcoming to a staff plan should have continued to escape my notice, but then you will agree that such is often the way with matters one has given abiding thought to over a period of time; one is not struck by the truth until prompted quite accidentally by some external event. So it was in this instance; that is to say, my receiving the letter from Miss Kenton, containing as it did, along with its long, rather unrevealing passages, an unmistakable nostalgia for Darlington Hall, and – I am quite sure of this – distinct hints of her desire to return here, obliged me to see my staff plan afresh. Only then did it strike me that there was indeed a role that a further staff member could crucially play here; that it was, in fact, this very shortage that had been at the heart of all my recent troubles. And the more I considered it, the more obvious it became that Miss Kenton, with her great affection for this house, with her exemplary professionalism – the sort almost impossible to find nowadays – was just the factor needed to enable me to complete a fully satisfactory staff plan for Darlington Hall.

Having made such an analysis of the situation, it was not long before I found myself reconsidering Mr Farraday's kind suggestion of some days ago. For it had occurred to me that the proposed trip in the car could be put to good professional use; that is to say, I could drive to the West Country and call on Miss Kenton in passing, thus exploring at first hand the substance of her wish to return to employment here at Darlington Hall. I have, I should make clear, reread Miss Kenton's recent letter several times, and there is no possibility I am merely imagining the presence of these hints on her part.

For all that, I could not for some days quite bring myself to raise the matter again with Mr Farraday. There were, in any case, various

▷ **2** *reinforcement:* extra help or support **6** *altering* (n): change **7** *customary:* usual, normal • *predict sth.:* say sth. will happen in advance **8** *accommodate sth.:* get used to sth. **11** *broad-minded:* tolerant **15** *margins of error:* acceptance of what can be done if conditions are not ideal **16** *below par:* not as good as usual **18** *incorporate sth.:* include sth. **21** *boundary:* limit (of responsibility) **21–22** *be compounded by sth.:* be made stronger by sth. **24** *expend sth. to (*usu. *on) sth. else:* spend sth. (e.g. thought, time) on sth. else **25** *aversion to sth.:* dislike for sth. **26** *eclectic:* including a wide range **27** *unburdensome:* easy to cope with **29** *assess sth.* [-'-]: judge sth. • *stringent*: careful **31** *caution:* carefulness so as to avoid taking risks **32** *negligent over (*usu. *about) sth.:* not giving proper care or attention to sth. **34** *telling* (adj): revealing sth. without intending to **37** *shortcoming* (n): deficiency, weakness, fault **39** *abiding* (adj): enduring, lasting **40** *strike sb. (– struck – struck):* make sb. suddenly realize **41** *external:* (here) not related to his work as a butler **44** *nostalgia* [nɒ'stældʒə]: attitude of looking back with fondness to the past **45** *oblige sb.:* force sb. **47** *crucial:* significant, important **63** *for all that:* in spite of that

aspects to the matter I felt I needed to clarify to myself before proceeding further. There was, for instance, the question of cost. For even taking into account my employer's generous offer to 'foot the bill for the gas', the costs of such a trip might still come to a surprising amount considering such matters as accommodation, meals, and any small snacks I might partake of on my way. Then there was the question of what sorts of costume were appropriate on such a journey, and whether or not it was worth my while to invest in a new set of clothes. I am in the possession of a number of splendid suits, kindly passed on to me over the years by Lord Darlington himself, and by various guests who have stayed in this house and had reason to be pleased with the standard of service here. Many of these suits are, perhaps, too formal for the purposes of the proposed trip, or else rather old-fashioned these days. But then there is one lounge suit, passed on to me in 1931 or 1932 by Sir Edward Blair – practically brand new at the time and almost a perfect fit – which might well be appropriate for evenings in the lounge or dining room of any guest houses where I might lodge. What I do not possess, however, is any suitable travelling clothes – that is to say, clothes in which I might be seen driving the car – unless I were to don the suit passed on by the young Lord Chalmers during the war, which despite being clearly too small for me, might be considered ideal in terms of tone. I calculated finally that my savings would be able to meet all the costs I might incur, and in addition, might stretch to the purchase of a new costume. I hope you do not think me unduly vain with regard to this latter matter; it is just that one never knows when one might be obliged to give out that one is from Darlington Hall, and it is important that one be attired at such times in a manner worthy of one's position.

During this time, I also spent many minutes examining the road atlas, and perusing also the relevant volume of Mrs Jane Symons's *The Wonder of England*. If you are not familiar with Mrs Symon's books – a series running to seven volumes, each one concentrating on one region of the British Isles – I heartily recommend them. They were written during the thirties, but much of it would still be up to date – after all, I do not imagine German bombs have altered our countryside so significantly. Mrs Symons was, as a matter of fact, a frequent visitor to this house before the war; indeed, she was among the most popular as far as the staff were concerned due to the kind appreciation she never shied from showing. It was in those days, then, prompted by my natural admiration for the lady, that I had first taken to perusing her volumes in the library whenever I had an odd moment. Indeed, I recall that shortly after Miss Kenton's departure to Cornwall in 1936, myself never having been to that part of the country, I would often glance through Volume III of Mrs Symon's work, the volume which describes to readers the delights of Devon and Cornwall, complete with photographs and – to my mind even more evocative – a variety of artists' sketches of that region. It was thus that I had been able to gain some sense of the sort of place Miss Kenton had gone to live her married life. But this was, as I say, back in the thirties, when as I understand, Mrs Symons's books were being admired in houses up and down the country. I had not looked through those volumes for many years, until these recent developments led me to get down from the shelf the Devon and Cornwall volume once more. I studied all over again those marvellous descriptions and illustrations, and you can perhaps understand my growing excitement at the notion that I might now actually undertake a motoring trip myself around that same part of the country.

It seemed in the end there was little else to do but actually to raise the matter again with Mr Farraday. There was always the possibility, of course, that his suggestion of a fortnight ago may have been a whim of the moment, and he would no longer be approving of the idea. But from my observation of Mr Farraday over these months, he is not one of those gentlemen prone to that most irritating of traits in an employer – inconsistency. There was no reason to believe he would not be as enthusiastic as before about my proposed motoring trip – indeed, that he would not repeat his most kind offer to 'foot the bill for the gas'. Nevertheless, I considered most carefully what might be

▷ **6** *partake of sth.:* eat or drink sth. **7** *appropriate:* suitable **20** *don sth.:* wear sth. **24** *incur sth.:* have to pay sth. • *stretch to sth.:* be sufficient for sth. **26** *latter* (adj): letztere(r/s), zweite(r/s) **27** *give out sth.:* reveal sth. **28** *attired:* clothed **31** *peruse sth.* [pə'ru:z]: read or study sth. carefully **40** *appreciation* [əˌpri:ʃi'eɪʃn]: respect for good qualities • *shy from sth.:* not do sth. because you are too shy or embarrassed **42–43** *an odd moment:* a moment when sb. has free time **48** *evocative:* making you think of sth. in a pleasant way **49** *sense* (n): feeling **61–62** *a whim of the moment:* just a passing idea which is not to be taken seriously **62** *be approving of sth.:* show support for sth. **64** *prone to sth.:* likely to do sth. (usu. unpleasant) • *trait:* feature of sb.'s character **65** *inconsistency:* quality of changing your opinion regularly

the most opportune occasion to bring the matter up with him; for although I would not for one moment, as I say, suspect Mr Farraday of inconsistency, it nevertheless made sense not to broach the topic when he was preoccupied or distracted. A refusal in such circumstances may well not reflect my employer's true feelings on the matter, but once having sustained such a dismissal, I could not easily bring it up again. It was clear, then, that I had to choose my moment wisely.

In the end, I decided the most prudent moment in the day would be as I served afternoon tea in the drawing room. Mr Farraday will usually have just returned from his short walk on the downs at that point, so he is rarely engrossed in his reading or writing as he tends to be in the evenings. In fact, when I bring in the afternoon tea, Mr Farraday is inclined to close any book or periodical he has been reading, rise and stretch out his arms in front of the windows, as though in anticipation of conversation with me.

As it was, I believe my judgement proved quite sound on the question of timing; the fact that things turned out as they did is entirely attributable to an error of judgement in another direction altogether. That is to say, I did not take sufficient account of the fact that at that time of the day, what Mr Farraday enjoys is a conversation of a light-hearted, humorous sort. Knowing this to be his likely mood when I brought in the tea yesterday afternoon, and being aware of his general propensity to talk with me in a bantering tone at such moments, it would certainly have been wiser not to have mentioned Miss Kenton at all. But you will perhaps understand that there was a natural tendency on my part, in asking what was after all a generous favour from my employer, to hint that there was a good professional motive behind my request. So it was that in indicating my reasons for preferring the West Country for my motoring, instead of leaving it at mentioning several of the alluring details as conveyed by Mrs Symons's volume, I made the error of declaring that a former housekeeper of Darlington Hall was resident in that region. I suppose I must have been intending to explain to Mr Farraday how I would thus be able to explore an option which might prove the ideal solution to our present small problems here in this house. It was only after I had mentioned Miss Kenton that I suddenly realized how entirely inappropriate it would be for me to continue. Not only was I unable to be certain of Miss Kenton's desire to rejoin the staff here, I had not, of course, even discussed the question of additional staff with Mr Farraday since that first preliminary meeting over a year ago. To have continued pronouncing aloud my thoughts on the future of Darlington Hall would have been, to say the very least, presumptuous. I suspect, then, that I paused rather abruptly and looked a little awkward. In any case, Mr Farraday seized the opportunity to grin broadly at me and say with some deliberation.

'My, my, Stevens. A lady-friend. And at your age.'

This was a most embarrassing situation, one in which Lord Darlington would never have placed an employee. But then I do not mean to imply anything derogatory about Mr Farraday; he is, after all, an American gentleman and his ways are often very different. There is no question at all that he meant any harm; but you will no doubt appreciate how uncomfortable a situation this was for me.

'I'd never have figured you for such a lady's man, Stevens,' he went on. 'Keeps the spirit young, I guess. But then I really don't know it's right for me to be helping you with such dubious assignations.'

Naturally, I felt the temptation to deny immediately and unambiguously such motivations as my employer was imputing to me, but saw in time that to do so would be to rise to Mr Farraday's bait, and the situation would only become increasingly embarrassing. I therefore continued to stand there awkwardly, waiting for my employer to give me permission to undertake the motoring trip.

Embarrassing as those moments were for me, I would not wish to imply that I in any way blame Mr Farraday, who is in no sense

▷ **1** *the most opportune occasion:* the best time and situation to do sth. **3** *broach sth.:* begin to talk about sth. **4** *distracted* (adj): occupied with sth. else **6** *sustain such a dismissal:* (here) not be successful in achieving sth. **8** *prudent:* best-chosen **10** *the downs:* an area of open land with low hills **11** *engrossed in sth.* [ɪn'grəʊst]: so interested in sth. that you give it all your attention **13** *be inclined to do sth.:* have the tendency to do sth. **15** *in anticipation of sth.:* expecting or waiting for sth. **16** *sound* (adj): good, right **17** *entirely:* totally **23** *propensity:* tendency • *banter* (v): talk in a joking and playful way **30** *alluring* (adj): attractive **32** *be resident in sth.:* live in sth. (esp. an area) **37** *inappropriate:* not suitable **44** *awkward* ['ɔːkwəd]: embarrassed • *seize sth.* [siːz]: take sth. **45** *with some deliberation:* (here) in a way that is slow and well-thought out and for a particular reason **49** *derogatory:* insulting **50–51** *there is no question at all that ...:* it is certainly not the case that ... **51** *mean harm:* intend to insult sb. **53** *figure sb. for sth.* (AE): believe that sb. is sth. **55** *dubious:* slightly suspicious, having a bad reputation • *assignation:* secret romantic meeting **56–57** *unambiguously:* in a way as to leave no doubt **57** *impute sth. to sb.:* jdm. etwas zuschreiben **58** *rise to sb.'s bait:* fall into sb.'s trap

an unkind person; he was, I am sure, merely enjoying the sort of bantering which in the United States, no doubt, is a sign of a good, friendly understanding between employer and employee, indulged in as a kind of affectionate sport. Indeed, to put things into a proper perspective, I should point out that just such bantering on my new employer's part has characterized much of our relationship over these months – though I must confess, I remain rather unsure as to how I should respond. In fact, during my first days under Mr Farraday, I was once or twice quite astounded by some of the things he would say to me. For instance, I once had occasion to ask him if a certain gentleman expected at the house was likely to be accompanied by his wife.

'God help us if she does come,' Mr Farraday replied. 'Maybe you could keep her off our hands, Stevens. Maybe you could take her out to one of those stables around Mr Morgan's farm. Keep her entertained in all that hay. She may be just your type.'

For a moment or two, I had not an idea what my employer was saying. Then I realized he was making some sort of joke and endeavoured to smile appropriately, though I suspect some residue of my bewilderment, not to say shock, remained detectable in my expression.

Over the following days, however, I came to learn not to be surprised by such remarks from my employer, and would smile in the correct manner whenever I detected the bantering tone in his voice. Nevertheless, I could never be sure exactly what was required of me on these occasions. Perhaps I was expected to laugh heartily; or indeed, reciprocate with some remark of my own. This last possibility is one that has given me some concern over these months, and is something about which I still feel undecided. For it may well be that in America, it is all part of what is considered good professional service that an employee provide entertaining banter. In fact, I remember Mr Simpson, the landlord of the Ploughman's Arms, saying once that were he an American bartender, he would not be chatting to us in that friendly, but ever-courteous manner of his, but instead would be assaulting us with crude references to our vices and failings, calling us drunks and all manner of such names, in his attempt to fulfil the role expected of him by his customers. And I recall also some years ago, Mr Rayne, who travelled to America as valet to Sir Reginald Mauvis, remarking that a taxi driver in New York regularly addressed his fare in a manner which if repeated in London would end in some sort of fracas, if not in the fellow being frogmarched to the nearest police station.

It is quite possible, then, that my employer fully expects me to respond to his bantering in a like manner, and considers my failure to do so a form of negligence. This is, as I say, a matter which has given me much concern. But I must say this business of bantering is not a duty I feel I can ever discharge with enthusiasm. It is all very well, in these changing times, to adapt one's work to take in duties not traditionally within one's realm; but bantering is of another dimension altogether. For one thing, how would one know for sure that at any given moment a response of the bantering sort is truly what is expected? One need hardly dwell on the catastrophic possibility of uttering a bantering remark only to discover it wholly inappropriate.

I did though on one occasion not long ago, pluck up the courage to attempt the required sort of reply. I was serving Mr Farraday morning coffee in the breakfast room when he had said to me:

'I suppose it wasn't you making that crowing noise this morning, Stevens?'

My employer was referring, I realized, to a pair of gypsies gathering unwanted iron who had passed by earlier making their customary calls. As it happened, I had that same morning been giving thought to the dilemma of whether or not I was expected to reciprocate my employer's bantering, and had been seriously worried at how he might be viewing my repeated failure to respond to such openings. I therefore set about thinking of some witty reply; some statement which would still be safely inoffensive in the event of my having misjudged the situation. After a moment or two, I said:

▷ **3** *indulge in sth.:* do sth. in an enjoyable (and usu. incorrect) way **4** *affectionate:* friendly **7** *confess sth.:* admit to sth. **9** *astounded* (adj): surprised, shocked **18–19** *endeavour* (v): try very hard **19** *residue:* the part that is left after the main part has gone **20** *bewilderment:* confusion • *detectable:* visible **26** *reciprocate:* react in a similar way **32** *were he:* if he were **33** *ever-courteous:* always polite **34** *assault sb.:* attack sb. • *crude:* rude, primitive, offensive • *vice:* fault, bad habit **35** *failing* (n): weakness, fault **38** *valet* ['væleɪ]: a man's personal male servant **39** *fare:* (here) passenger(s) **40** *fracas* ['frækɑː]: noisy argument or fight **40–41** *frogmarch sb.:* force sb. to move forward with their arms held tightly together behind their back **46** *discharge sth.* [-'-]: carry sth. out **48** *realm* [relm]: area of responsibility **53–54** *pluck up the courage to do sth.:* make yourself do sth. even though you are uncertain **56** *crow* (v): make a noise like a cock (= Hahn) **58** *gypsy:* Zigeuner/in

'More like swallows than crows, I would have said, sir. From the migratory aspect.' And I followed this with a suitably modest smile to indicate without ambiguity that I had made a witticism, since I did not wish Mr Farraday to restrain any spontaneous mirth he felt out of a misplaced respectfulness.

Mr Farraday, however, simply looked up at me and said: 'I beg your pardon, Stevens?'

Only then did it occur to me that, of course, my witticism would not be easily appreciated by someone who was not aware that it was gypsies who had passed by. I could not see, then, how I might press on with this bantering; in fact, I decided it best to call a halt to the matter and, pretending to remember something I had urgently to attend to, excused myself, leaving my employer looking rather bemused.

It was, then, a most discouraging start to what may in fact be an entirely new sort of duty required of me; so discouraging that I must admit I have not really made further attempts along these lines. But at the same time, I cannot escape the feeling that Mr Farraday is not satisfied with my responses to his various banterings. Indeed, his increased persistence of late may even be my employer's way of urging me all the more to respond in a like-minded spirit. Be that as it may, since that first witticism concerning the gypsies, I have not been able to think of other such witticisms quickly enough.

Such difficulties as these tend to be all the more preoccupying nowadays because one does not have the means to discuss and corroborate views with one's fellow professionals in the way one once did. Not so long ago, if any such points of ambiguity arose regarding one's duties, one had the comfort of knowing that before long some fellow professional whose opinion one respected would be accompanying his employer to the house, and there would be ample opportunity to discuss the matter. And of course, in Lord Darlington's days, when ladies and gentlemen would often visit for many days on end, it was possible to develop a good understanding with visiting colleagues. Indeed, in those busy days, our servants' hall would often witness a gathering of some of the finest professionals in England talking late into the night by the warmth of the fire. And let me tell you, if you were to have come into our servants' hall on any of those evenings, you would not have heard mere gossip; more likely, you would have witnessed debates over the great affairs preoccupying our employers upstairs, or else over matters of import reported in the newspapers; and of course, as fellow professionals from all walks of life are wont to do when gathered together, we could be found discussing every aspect of our vocation. Sometimes, naturally, there would be strong disagreements, but more often than not, the atmosphere was dominated by a feeling of mutual respect. Perhaps I will convey a better idea of the tone of those evenings if I say that regular visitors included the likes of Mr Harry Graham, valet-butler to Sir James Chambers, and Mr John Donalds, valet to Mr Sydney Dickenson. And there were others less distinguished, perhaps, but whose lively presence made any visit memorable; for instance, Mr Wilkinson, valet-butler to Mr John Campbell, with his well-known repertoire of impersonations of prominent gentlemen; Mr Davidson from Easterly House, whose passion in debating a point could at times be as alarming to a stranger as his simple kindness at all other times was endearing; Mr Herman, valet to Mr John Henry Peters, whose extreme views no one could listen to passively, but whose distinctive belly-laugh and Yorkshire charm made him impossible to dislike. I could go on. There existed in those days a true camaraderie in our profession, whatever the small differences in our approach. We were all essentially cut from the same cloth, so to speak. Not the way it is today, when on the rare occasion an employee accompanies a guest here, he is likely to be some newcomer who has little to say about anything other than Association Football and who prefers to pass the evening not by the fire of the servants' hall, but drinking at the Ploughman's Arms – or indeed, as seems increasingly likely nowadays, at the Star Inn.

▷ **1** *swallow:* Schwalbe • *crow* (n): Krähe **2** *migratory* ['maɪgrətri]: moving from one place to another **3** *without ambiguity:* with absolute clarity • *witticism:* joke **4** *restrain sth.:* not to show sth. • *mirth:* happy laughter **5** *misplaced respectfulness:* respect that is at the time unnecessary **11** *call a halt to sth.:* stop sth. that has already started **12** *urgent:* that requires immediate attention or action **13** *bemused* (adj): confused **19** *persistence:* act of continually trying to do sth. • *of late:* recently **25** *corroborate sth.:* confirm sth. **30** *ample:* more than enough **32** *on end:* continuously **37** *gossip* (n): casual talk about other people's lives **39** *import:* importance **41** *from all walks of life:* from different types of jobs and different levels of society • *be wont to do:* usually do, be in the habit of doing **42** *vocation:* job, profession **44** *mutual respect:* respect for each other **48** *distinguished* (adj): respected because of their extremely high position or reputation **51** *impersonation:* imitation **54** *endearing* (adj): charming, attractive **56** *belly-laugh:* loud, uncontrolled laugh **58** *camaraderie:* feeling of friendliness towards each other

I mentioned a moment ago Mr Graham, the valet-butler to Sir James Chambers. In fact, some two months ago, I was most happy to learn that Sir James was to visit Darlington Hall. I looked forward to the visit not only because visitors from Lord Darlington's days are most rare now – Mr Farraday's circle, naturally, being quite different from his lordship's – but also because I presumed Mr Graham would accompany Sir James as of old, and I would thus be able to get his opinion on this question of bantering. I was, then, both surprised and disappointed to discover a day before the visit that Sir James would be coming alone. Furthermore, during Sir James's subsequent stay, I gathered that Mr Graham was no longer in Sir James's employ; indeed that Sir James no longer employed any full-time staff at all. I would like to have discovered what had become of Mr Graham, for although we had not known each other well, I would say we had got on on those occasions we had met. As it was, however, no suitable opportunity arose for me to gain such information. I must say I was rather disappointed, for I would like to have discussed the bantering question with him.

However, let me return to my original thread. I was obliged, as I was saying, to spend some uncomfortable minutes standing in the drawing room yesterday afternoon while Mr Farraday went about his bantering. I responded as usual by smiling slightly – sufficient at least to indicate that I was participating in some way with the good-humouredness with which he was carrying on – and waited to see if my employer's permission regarding the trip would be forthcoming. As I had anticipated, he gave his kind permission after not too great a delay, and furthermore, Mr Farraday was good enough to remember and reiterate his generous offer to 'foot the bill for the gas'.

So then, there seems little reason why I should not undertake my motoring trip to the West Country. I would of course have to write to Miss Kenton to tell her I might be passing by; I would also need to see to the matter of the costumes. Various other questions concerning arrangements here in the house during my absence will need to be settled. But all in all, I can see no genuine reason why I should not undertake this trip.

▷ **6** *presume:* believe **7** *as of old:* as in the past **10** *subsequent:* next **11** *be in sb.'s employ:* be working for sb. **18** *thread:* theme, topic **23** *carry on: behave or talk in a particular way* **24** *forthcoming* (adj): going to happen **25** *anticipate sth.:* expect sth. **27** *reiterate sth.:* repeat sth. **33** *genuine:* real

DAY ONE – EVENING

Salisbury

Tonight, I find myself here in a guest house in the city of Salisbury. The first day of my trip is now completed, and all in all, I must say I am quite satisfied. This expedition began this morning almost an hour later than I had planned, despite my having completed my packing and loaded the Ford with all the necessary items well before eight o'clock. What with Mrs Clements and the girls also gone for the week, I suppose I was very conscious of the fact that once I departed, Darlington Hall would stand empty for probably the first time this century – perhaps for the first time since the day it was built. It was an odd feeling and perhaps accounts for why I delayed my departure so long, wandering around the house many times over, checking one last time that all was in order.

It is hard to explain my feelings once I did finally set off. For the first twenty minutes or so of motoring, I cannot say I was seized by any excitement or anticipation at all. This was due, no doubt, to the fact that though I motored further and further from the house, I continued to find myself in surroundings with which I had at least a passing acquaintance. Now I had always supposed I had travelled very little, restricted as I am by my responsibilities in the house, but of course, over time, one does make various excursions for one professional reason or another, and it would seem I have become much more acquainted with those neighbouring districts than I had realized. For as I say, as I motored on in the sunshine towards the Berkshire border, I continued to be surprised by the familiarity of the country around me.

But then eventually the surroundings grew unrecognizable and I knew I had gone beyond all previous boundaries. I have heard people describe the moment, when setting sail in a ship, when one finally loses sight of the land. I imagine the experience of unease mixed with exhilaration often described in connection with this moment is very similar to what I felt in the Ford as the surroundings grew strange around me. This occurred just after I took a turning and found myself on a road curving around the edge of a hill. I could sense the steep drop to my left, though I could not see it due to the trees and thick

▷ **4** *despite sth.:* in spite of sth. **6** *what with …:* used to list reasons for sth. **15** *anticipation* [- - - '- -]: expectation **18** *passing* (adj): slight • *acquaintance:* knowledge, familiarity **20** *excursion:* trip **26** *eventually:* as time went on, finally **29** *unease:* feeling of uncertainty or unrest **30** *exhilaration:* joyful excitement **32** *occur:* happen **33** *steep:* rising or dropping quickly

foliage that lined the roadside. The feeling swept over me that I had truly left Darlington Hall behind, and I must confess I did feel a slight sense of alarm – a sense aggravated by the feeling that I was perhaps not on the correct road at all, but speeding off in totally the wrong direction into a wilderness. It was only the feeling of a moment, but it caused me to slow down. And even when I had assured myself I was on the right road, I felt compelled to stop the car a moment to take stock, as it were.

I decided to step out and stretch my legs a little and when I did so, I received a stronger impression than ever of being perched on the side of a hill. On one side of the road, thickets and small trees rose steeply, while on the other I could now glimpse through the foliage the distant countryside.

I believe I had walked a little way along the roadside, peering through the foliage hoping to get a better view, when I heard a voice behind me. Until this point, of course, I had believed myself quite alone and I turned in some surprise. A little way further up the road on the opposite side, I could see the start of a footpath, which disappeared steeply up into the thickets. Sitting on the large stone that marked this spot was a thin, white-haired man in a cloth cap, smoking his pipe. He called to me again and though I could not quite make out his words, I could see him gesturing for me to join him. For a moment, I took him for a vagrant, but then I saw he was just some local fellow enjoying the fresh air and summer sunshine, and saw no reason not to comply.

'Just wondering, sir,' he said, as I approached, 'how fit your legs were.'

'I beg your pardon?'

The fellow gestured up the footpath. 'You got to have a good pair of legs and a good pair of lungs to go up there. Me, I haven't got neither, so I stay down here. But if I was in better shape, I'd be sitting up there. There's a nice little spot up there, a bench and everything. And you won't get a better view anywhere in the whole of England.'

'If what you say is true,' I said, 'I think I'd rather stay here. I happen to be embarking on a motoring trip during the course of which I hope to see many splendid views. To see the best before I have properly begun would be somewhat premature.'

The fellow did not seem to understand me, for he simply said again: 'You won't see a better view in the whole of England. But I tell you, you need a good pair of legs and good pair of lungs.' Then he added: 'I can see you're in good shape for your age, sir. I'd say you could make your way up there, no trouble. I mean, even I can manage on a good day.'

I glanced up the path, which did look steep and rather rough.

'I'm telling you, sir, you'll be sorry if you don't take a walk up there. And you never know. A couple more years and it might be too late' – he gave a rather vulgar laugh – 'Better go on up while you still can.'

It occurs to me now that the man might just possibly have meant this in a humorous sort of way; that is to say, he intended it as a bantering remark. But this morning, I must say, I found it quite offensive and it may well have been the urge to demonstrate just how foolish his insinuation had been that caused me to set off up the footpath.

In any case, I am very glad I did so. Certainly, it was quite a strenuous walk – though I can say it failed to cause me any real difficulty – the path rising in zigzags up the hillside for a hundred yards or so. I then reached a small clearing, undoubtedly the spot the man had referred to. Here one was met by a bench – and indeed, by a most marvellous view over miles of the surrounding countryside.

What I saw was principally field upon field rolling off into the far distance. The land rose and fell gently, and the fields were bordered by hedges and trees. There were dots in some of the distant fields which I assumed to be sheep. To my right, almost on the horizon, I thought I could see the square tower of a church.

It was a fine feeling indeed to be standing up there like that, with the sound of summer all around one and a light breeze on one's face. And I believe it was then, looking on that view, that I began for the

▷ **1** *foliage:* bushes and trees **3** *aggravate sth.* ['- - -]: make sth. worse **6** *assure sb.:* make sb. feel that they are correct in what they are doing or thinking **7** *compel sb.* [- '-]: force or oblige sb. **7–8** *take stock:* examine your situation as a whole **10** *perched on sth.:* sitting on the edge of sth. **11** *thicket:* group of bushes growing closely together **12** *glimpse sth.:* see sth. briefly or with difficulty **22** *gesture* (v): use body language to convey a wish, etc. **23** *vagrant* ['veɪgrənt]: homeless person **25** *comply* [kəm'plaɪ]: do what you have been asked to do **26** *approach* (v): come or go nearer **36** *splendid:* beautiful and remarkable **37** *premature* ['premətʃə]: too early **44** *glance* (v): look briefly **52** *insinuation:* unpleasant thing that is said in an indirect way **55** *strenuous:* needing a lot of effort **57** *yard:* unit of length (ca. 0.9 m) • *clearing* (n): small area in the middle of the wood where there are no trees **60** *principally:* mostly **62** *hedge:* Hecke **63** *assume:* believe

first time to adopt a frame of mind appropriate for the journey before me. For it was then that I felt the first healthy flush of anticipation for the many interesting experiences I know these days ahead hold in store for me. And indeed, it was then that I felt a new resolve not to be daunted in respect to the one professional task I have entrusted myself with on this trip; that is to say, regarding Miss Kenton and our present staffing problems.

But that was this morning. This evening I found myself settled here in this comfortable guest house in a street not far from the centre of Salisbury. It is, I suppose, a relatively modest establishment, but very clean and perfectly adequate for my needs. The landlady, a woman of around forty or so, appears to regard me as a rather grand visitor on account of Mr Farraday's Ford and the high quality of my suit. This afternoon – I arrived in Salisbury at around three thirty – when I entered my address in her register as 'Darlington Hall', I could see her look at me with some trepidation, assuming no doubt that I was some gentleman used to such places as the Ritz or the Dorchester and that I would storm out of the guest house on being shown my room. She informed me that a double room at the front was available, though I was welcome to it for the price of a single.

I was then brought up to this room, in which, at that point of the day, the sun was lighting up the floral patterns of the wallpaper quite agreeably. There were twin beds and a pair of good-sized windows overlooking the street. On inquiring where the bathroom was, the woman told me in a timid voice that although it was the door facing mine, there would be no hot water available until after supper. I asked her to bring me up a pot of tea, and when she had gone, inspected the room further. The beds were perfectly clean and had been well made. The basin in the corner was also very clean. On looking out of the windows, one saw on the opposite side of the street a bakery displaying a variety of pastries, a chemist's shop and a barber's. Further along, one could see where the street passed over a round-backed bridge and on into more rural surroundings. I refreshed my face and hands with cold water at the basin, then seated myself on a hard-backed chair left near one of the windows to await my tea.

I would suppose it was shortly after four o'clock that I left the guest house and ventured out into the streets of Salisbury. The wide, airy nature of the streets here give the city a marvellously spacious feel, so that I found it most easy to spend some hours just strolling in the gently warm sunshine. Moreover, I discovered the city to be one of many charms; time and again, I found myself wandering past delightful rows of old timber-fronted houses, or crossing some little stone footbridge over one of the many streams that flow through the city. And of course, I did not fail to visit the fine cathedral, much praised by Mrs Symons in her volume. This august building was hardly difficult for me to locate, its looming spire being ever-visible wherever one goes in Salisbury. Indeed, as I was making my way back to the guest house this evening, I glanced back over my shoulder on a number of occasions and was met each time by a view of the sun setting behind that great spire.

And yet tonight, in the quiet of this room, I find that what really remains with me from this first day's travel is not Salisbury Cathedral, nor any of the other charming sights of this city, but rather that marvellous view encountered this morning of the rolling English countryside. Now I am quite prepared to believe that other countries can offer more obviously spectacular scenery. Indeed, I have seen in encyclopedias and the *National Geographic Magazine* breath-taking photographs of sights from various corners of the globe; magnificent canyons and waterfalls, raggedly beautiful mountains. It has never, of course, been my privilege to have seen such things at first hand, but I will nevertheless hazard this with some confidence: the English landscape at its finest – such as I saw it this morning – possesses a quality that the landscapes of other nations, however more superficially dramatic, inevitably fail to possess. It is, I believe, a quality that will mark out the English landscape to any

▷ **1** *frame of mind:* attitude, way of thinking about sth. **2** *flush of anticipation:* sudden feeling of expectation **3–4** *hold sth. in store for sb.:* etwas für jdn. bereithalten **4** *resolve* (n): strong determination to achieve sth. **5** *daunted* ['dɔːntɪd]: made afraid or less confident **10** *modest:* not luxurious, simple **16** *trepidation:* feeling of anxiety or fear **17** *the Ritz, the Dorchester:* luxurious London hotels **24** *inquire:* ask **31** *display sth.:* show sth. in a pleasant way **33** *rural* (adj): of the countryside **37** *venture out:* go out (esp. somewhere unknown) **38** *marvellous:* wonderful • *spacious* ['speɪʃiəs]: large and with lots of room, not narrow or crowded **39** *stroll* (v): walk in a slow and relaxed way **42** *timber-fronted house:* Fachwerkhaus **45** *august* [ɔː'gʌst] (adj): old and impressive **46** *looming* (adj): (here) high, easily seen • *spire:* Turmspitze **49** *occasion:* time **59** *magnificent:* impressive, beautiful **59** *ragged* (adj): having sharp contours **61** *hazard sth.:* dare to suggest sth. **64** *superficial:* oberflächlich • *inevitably:* (here) in every case

objective observer as the most deeply satisfying in the world, and this quality is probably best summed up by the term 'greatness'. For it is true, when I stood on that high ledge this morning and viewed the land before me, I distinctly felt that rare, yet unmistakable feeling – the feeling that one is in the presence of greatness. We call this land of ours *Great* Britain, and there may be those who believe this a somewhat immodest practice. Yet I would venture that the landscape of our country alone would justify the use of this lofty adjective.

And yet what precisely is this 'greatness'? Just where, or in what, does it lie? I am quite aware it would take a far wiser head than mine to answer such a question, but if I were forced to hazard a guess, I would say that it is the very lack of obvious drama or spectacle that sets the beauty of our land apart. What is pertinent is the calmness of that beauty, its sense of restraint. It is as though the land knows of its own beauty, of its own greatness, and feels no need to shout it. In comparison, the sorts of sights offered in such places as Africa and America, though undoubtedly very exciting, would, I am sure, strike the objective viewer as inferior on account of their unseemly demonstrativeness.

The whole question is very akin to the question that has caused much debate in our profession over the years: what is a 'great' butler? I can recall many hours of enjoyable discussion on this topic around the fire of the servants' hall at the end of a day. You will notice I say 'what' rather than 'who' is a great butler; for there was actually no serious dispute as to the identity of the men who set the standards amongst our generation. That is to say, I am talking of the likes of Mr Marshall of Charleville House, or Mr Lane of Bridewood. If you have ever had the privilege of meeting such men, you will no doubt know of the quality they possess to which I refer. But you will no doubt also understand what I mean when I say it is not at all easy to define just what this quality is.

Incidentally, now that I come to think further about it, it is not quite true to say there was no dispute as to who were the great butlers. What I should have said was that there was no serious dispute among professionals of quality who had any discernment in such matters. Of course, the servants' hall at Darlington Hall, like any servants' hall anywhere, was obliged to receive employees of varying degrees of intellect and perception, and I recall many a time having to bite my lip while some employee – and at times, I regret to say, members of my own staff – excitedly eulogized the likes of, say, Mr Jack Neighbours.

I have nothing against Mr Jack Neighbours, who sadly, I understand, was killed in the war. I mention him simply because his was a typical case. For two or three years in the mid-thirties. Mr Neighbours's name seemed to dominate conversations in every servants' hall in the land. As I say, at Darlington Hall too, many a visiting employee would bring the latest tales of Mr Neighbours's achievements, so that I and the likes of Mr Graham would have to share the frustrating experience of hearing anecdote after anecdote relating to him. And most frustrating of all would be having to witness at the conclusion of each such anecdote otherwise decent employees shaking their heads in wonder and uttering phrases like: 'That Mr Neighbours, he really is the best.'

Now I do not doubt that Mr Neighbours had good organizational skills; he did, I understand, mastermind a number of large occasions with conspicuous style. But at no stage did he ever approach the status of a great butler. I could have told you this at the height of his reputation, just as I could have predicted his downfall after a few short years in the limelight.

How often have you known it for the butler who is on everyone's lips one day as the greatest of his generation to be proved demonstrably within a few years to have been nothing of the sort? And yet those very same employees who once heaped praise on him will be too busy eulogizing some new figure to stop and examine their sense of judgement. The object of this sort of servants' hall talk is invariably some butler who has come to the fore quite suddenly through having been appointed by a prominent house, and who has perhaps man-

▷ **2** *term:* Begriff **3** *ledge:* natural platform on the edge of a hill or mountain **4** *distinct:* clear • *unmistakable:* easily recognized **7** *immodest:* too proud **8** *justify sth.:* provide a convincing reason for sth. • *lofty:* grand, elevated **13** *pertinent:* important to consider **14** *restraint:* quality of being reserved and quiet and not showing emotion **18** *unseemly:* improper, out of place • *demonstrativeness:* showiness **19** *akin:* similar, related **25** *the likes of sb.:* people like sb. **31** *incidentally:* by the way **34** *discernment:* the knowledge and ability to judge sth. well **37** *perception:* the ability to observe **39** *eulogize sb.* ['ju:lədʒaɪz]: praise sb. • *say:* for example **45** *tale:* (usu. entertaining) story **45–46** *achievement:* Leistung **47** *relating to sb.:* (here) about sb. **53** *mastermind sth.:* organize and manage sth. **54** *conspicuous:* noteworthy and striking; easily seen **55–56** *at the height of his reputation:* when he was most famous **57** *in the limelight:* in the public view **59–60** *demonstrably:* so that everyone recognizes it **63** *invariably:* always **64** *come to the fore:* become well-known

aged to pull off two or three large occasions with some success. There will then be all sorts of rumours buzzing through servants' halls up and down the country to the effect that he has been approached by this or that personage or that several of the highest houses are competing for his services with wildly high wages. And what has happened before a few years have passed? This same invincible figure has been held responsible for some blunder, or has for some other reason fallen out of favour with his employers, leaves the house where he came to fame and is never heard of again. Meanwhile, those same gossipers will have found yet some other newcomer about whom to enthuse. Visiting valets, I have found, are often the worst offenders, aspiring as they usually do to the position of butler with some urgency. They it is who tend to be always insisting this or that figure is the one to emulate, or repeating what some particular hero is said to have pronounced upon professional matters.

But then, of course, I hasten to add, there are many valets who would never dream of indulging in this sort of folly – who are, in fact, professionals of the highest discernment. When two or three such persons were gathered together at our servants' hall – I mean of the calibre of, say, Mr Graham, with whom now, sadly, I seem to have lost touch – we would have some of the most stimulating and intelligent debates on every aspect of our vocation. Indeed, today, those evenings rank amongst my fondest memories from those times.

But let me return to the question that is of genuine interest, this question we so enjoyed debating when our evenings were not spoiled by chatter from those who lacked any fundamental understanding of the profession; that is to say, the question '*what* is a great butler?'

To the best of my knowledge, for all the talk this question has engendered over the years, there have been very few attempts within the profession to formulate an official answer. The only instance that comes to mind is the attempt of the Hayes Society to devise criteria for membership. You may not be aware of the Hayes Society, for few talk of it these days. But in the twenties and the early thirties, it exerted a considerable influence over much of London and the Home Counties. In fact, many felt its power had become too great and thought it no bad thing when it was forced to close, I believe in 1932 or 1933.

The Hayes Society claimed to admit butlers of 'only the very first rank'. Much of the power and prestige it went on to gain derived from the fact that unlike other such organizations which have come and gone, it managed to keep its numbers extremely low, thus giving this claim some credibility. Membership, it was said, never at any point rose above thirty and much of the time remained closer to nine or ten. This, and the fact that the Hayes Society tended to be a rather secretive body, lent it much mystique for a time, ensuring that the pronouncements it occasionally issued on professional matters were received as though hewn on tablets of stone.

But one matter the Society resisted pronouncing on for some time was the question of its own criteria for membership. Pressure to have these announced steadily mounted, and in response to a series of letters published in *A Quarterly for the Gentleman's Gentleman*, the Society admitted that a prerequisite for membership was that 'an applicant be attached to a distinguished household'. 'Though of course,' the Society went on, 'this by itself is far from sufficient to satisfy requirements.' It was made clear, furthermore, that the Society did not regard the houses of businessmen or the 'newly rich' as 'distinguished', and in my opinion this piece of out-dated thinking crucially undermined any serious authority the Society may have

▷ **1** *pull sth. off* (infml): organize and get sth. done **2** *rumour:* Gerücht **5** *compete for sb./sth.:* fight over sb./sth. like in a competition **6** *invincible:* unbeatable **7** *blunder* (n): serious and obvious mistake **8** *fall out of favour with sb.:* lose sb.'s good opinion of you **10** *gossiper:* person who talks a lot about other people **11** *enthuse about sb.:* talk about sb. in an enthusiastic way **12** *offender:* person who does sth. wrong • *aspire to sth.:* try to get or achieve sth. **13** *urgency:* hurry **14** *emulate sb.:* try to behave like sb. who has a higher status **17** *folly:* stupidity, foolishness **23** *rank among(st) sth.:* be considered to be among sth. • *fond:* dear, enjoyable **25** *spoil sth.:* disturb or ruin sth. **26** *chatter* (n): trivial talk **28–29** *engender sth.:* bring sth. about, result in sth., create sth. **30** *instance:* example **31** *criterion* (pl *criteria*): thing that is necessary for sth. **34** *the Home Counties:* the counties (= Grafschaften) around London **41** *credibility:* Glaubwürdigkeit **44** *secretive:* not open about itself • *mystique:* aura of glamour and exclusivity • *ensure sth.:* result in sth. **45** *pronouncement:* statement • *occasionally:* from time to time • *issue sth.:* make sth. publicly known **46** *hewn on tablets of stone:* (here) written on flat stones (like the Ten Commandments given to Moses by God) **49** *mount* (v): grow stronger **51** *prerequisite* [ˌpriːˈrekwəsɪt] (n): condition that must be fulfilled **52** *applicant:* person who applies to become a member • *be attached to sth.:* (here) work in sth. • *a distinguished household:* a family or employer of high social standing **53** *sufficient:* adequate, enough **54** *satisfy requirements:* meet the necessary conditions **57** *undermine sth.:* make sth. less strong or convincing

achieved to arbitrate on standards in our profession. In response to further letters in *A Quarterly*, the Society justified its stance by saying that while it accepted some correspondents' views that certain butlers of excellent quality were to be found in the houses of businessmen, 'the assumption had to be that the houses of *true* ladies and gentlemen would not refrain long from acquiring the services of any such persons'. One had to be guided by the judgement of 'the true ladies and gentlemen', argued the Society, or else 'we may as well adopt the proprieties of Bolshevik Russia'. This provoked further controversy, and the pressure of letters continued to build up urging the Society to declare more fully its membership criteria. In the end, it was revealed in a brief letter to *A Quarterly* that in the view of the Society – and I will try and quote accurately from memory – 'the most crucial criterion is that the applicant be possessed of a dignity in keeping with his position. No applicant will satisfy requirements, whatever his level of accomplishment otherwise, if seen to fall short in this respect.'

For all my lack of enthusiasm for the Hayes Society, it is my belief that this particular pronouncement at least was founded on a significant truth. If one looks at these persons we agree are 'great' butlers, if one looks at, say, Mr Marshall or Mr Lane, it does seem to me that the factor which distinguishes them from those butlers who are merely extremely competent is most closely captured by this word 'dignity'.

Of course, this merely begs the further question: of what is 'dignity' comprised? And it was on this point that the likes of Mr Graham and I had some of our most interesting debates. Mr Graham would always take the view that this 'dignity' was something like a woman's beauty and it was thus pointless to attempt to analyse it. I, on the other hand, held the opinion that to draw such a parallel tended to demean the 'dignity' of the likes of Mr Marshall. Moreover, my main objection to Mr Graham's analogy was the implication that this 'dignity' was something one possessed or did not by a fluke of nature; and if one did not self-evidently have it, to strive after it would be as futile as an ugly woman trying to make herself beautiful. Now while I would accept that the majority of butlers may well discover ultimately that they do not have the capacity for it, I believe strongly that this 'dignity' is something one can meaningfully strive for throughout one's career. Those 'great' butlers like Mr Marshall who have it, I am sure, acquired it over many years of self-training and the careful absorbing of experience. In my view, then, it was rather defeatist from a vocational standpoint to adopt a stance like Mr Graham's.

In any case, for all Mr Graham's scepticism, I can remember he and I spending many evenings trying to put our fingers on the constitution of this 'dignity'. We never came to any agreement, but I can say for my part that I developed fairly firm ideas of my own on the matter during the course of such discussions, and they are by and large the beliefs I still hold today. I would like, if I may, to try and say here what I think this 'dignity' to be.

You will not dispute, I presume, that Mr Marshall of Charleville House and Mr Lane of Bridewood have been the two great butlers of recent times. Perhaps you might be persuaded that Mr Henderson of Branbury Castle also falls into this rare category. But you may think me merely biased if I say that my own father could in many ways be considered to rank with such men, and that his career is the one I have always scrutinized for a definition of 'dignity'. Yet it is my firm conviction that at the peak of his career at Loughborough House, my father was indeed the embodiment of 'dignity'.

I realize that if one looks at the matter objectively, one has to concede my father lacked various attributes one may normally expect

▷ **1** *arbitrate on sth.:* help to decide on sth. **2** *stance:* position, attitude **5** *assumption:* Annahme **6** *refrain from sth.:* hesitate to do sth. • *acquire sb./sth.:* get sb./sth. by offering money **9** *proprieties* [prəˈpraɪətiz]: manners, rules concerning behaviour • *Bolshevik Russia:* Russia after the communist revolution of 1917 • *provoke sth.:* lead to sth., result in sth. **10** *controversy:* lively debate or discussion **14** *be possessed of sth.:* possess sth., have sth. as a fundamental quality • *dignity:* Würde **14–15** *in keeping with sth.:* as is expected from sth. **16** *accomplishment:* Fähigkeit, Leistung • *fall short:* not be good enough **19** *founded on sth.:* based on sth. (solid and correct) **22** *distinguish sb./sth. from sb./sth. else:* jdn./etwas von jdm./etwas anderem unterscheiden bzw. abheben **23** *capture sth.:* describe sth. **24** *beg sth.:* lead to sth., raise sth. (esp. a question) **25** *comprise sth.:* form or make sth. **28** *pointless:* having no purpose, not worth doing **29** *demean sth.:* make sth. seem less important **30** *objection:* argument against sth. **31** *implication:* idea implied or contained in what you say **32** *fluke of nature:* Laune der Natur **33** *self-evident:* obvious to everyone • *strive after sth.:* attempt to acquire/get sth. • *futile:* vain, hopeless **35** *ultimately:* finally **36** *capacity:* ability **39** *absorb sth.:* gather or acquire sth. **40** *defeatist* (adj): without hope of success **43** *put our fingers on sth.:* really understand and describe sth. • *constitution:* (here) exact nature **49** *dispute sth.:* disagree with sth., argue against sth. **53** *biased* [ˈbaɪəst]: prejudiced, showing unfair favour to sb./sth. **55** *scrutinize sth.:* look at sth. closely **56** *at the peak of his career:* in his best time as a butler **57** *embodiment:* living symbol **59** *concede sth.:* etwas eingestehen

in a great butler. But those same absent attributes, I would argue, are every time those of a superficial and decorative order, attributes that are attractive, no doubt, as icing on the cake, but are not pertaining to what is really essential. I refer to things such as good accent and command of language, general knowledge on wide-ranging topics such as falconing or newt-mating – attributes none of which my father could have boasted. Furthermore, it must be remembered that my father was a butler of an earlier generation who began his career at a time when such attributes were not considered proper, let alone desirable in a butler. The obsessions with eloquence and general knowledge would appear to be ones that emerged with our generation, probably in the wake of Mr Marshall, when lesser men trying to emulate his greatness mistook the superficial for the essence. It is my view that our generation has been much too preoccupied with 'trimmings'; goodness knows how much time and energy has gone into the practising of accent and command of language, how many hours spent studying encyclopedias and volumes of 'Test Your Knowledge', when the time should have been spent mastering the basic fundamentals.

Though we must be careful not to attempt to deny the responsibility which ultimately lies with ourselves, it has to be said that certain employers have done much to encourage these sorts of trends. I am sorry to say this, but there would appear to have been a number of houses in recent times, some of the highest pedigree, which have tended to take a competitive attitude towards each other and have not been above 'showing off' to guests a butler's mastery of such trivial accomplishments. I have heard of various instances of a butler being displayed as a kind of performing monkey at a house party. In one regrettable case, which I myself witnessed, it had become an established sport in the house for guests to ring for the butler and put to him random questions of the order of, say, who had won the Derby in such and such a year, rather as one might to a Memory Man at the music hall.

My father, as I say, came of a generation mercifully free of such confusions of our professional values. And I would maintain that for all his limited command of English and his limited general knowledge, he not only knew all there was to know about how to run a house, he did in his prime come to acquire that 'dignity in keeping with his position', as the Hayes Society puts it. If I try, then, to describe to you what I believe made my father thus distinguished, I may in this way convey my idea of what 'dignity' is.

There was a certain story my father was fond of repeating over the years. I recall listening to him tell it to visitors when I was a child, and then later, when I was starting out as a footman under his supervision. I remember him relating it again the first time I returned to see him after gaining my first post as butler – to a Mr and Mrs Muggeridge in their relatively modest house in Allshot, Oxfordshire. Clearly the story meant much to him. My father's generation was not one accustomed to discussing and analysing in the way ours is and I believe the telling and retelling of this story was as close as my father ever came to reflecting critically on the profession he practised. As such, it gives a vital clue to his thinking.

The story was an apparently true one concerning a certain butler who had travelled with his employer to India and served there for many years maintaining amongst the native staff the same high standards he had commanded in England. One afternoon, evidently, this butler had entered the dining room to make sure all was well for dinner, when he noticed a tiger languishing beneath the dining table. The butler had left the dining room quietly, taking care to close the doors behind him, and proceeded calmly to the drawing room where his employer was taking tea with a number of visitors. There he

▷ **3** *icing* (n): Glasur **3–4** *pertain to sth.:* belong to sth., be essential for sth. **5** *command* (n): (hier) Beherrschung **6** *falconing* (n): use of trained falcons (= Falken) for hunting • *newt-mating* (n): Wassermolch-Zucht **10** *desirable:* wished for • *obsession with sth.:* excessive interest in sth. • *eloquence:* the art of talking elegantly and convincingly **11** *emerge:* appear (for the first time) **12** *in the wake of sb./sth.:* caused by and following sb./sth. **13** *mistake sth. for sth. else:* believe wrongly that sth. is sth. else **15** *trimmings* (pl): decoration • *goodness knows ...:* no one knows ... **24** *pedigree:* standing, reputation, status **26** *show sth. off:* show or present sth. merely to impress others **31** *random:* chosen for no special reason • *of the order of sth.:* concerning sth. • *Derby:* famous horse race **33** *music hall:* (in the 19th and early 20th centuries) theatre for popular entertainment **34** *mercifully:* fortunately **35** *maintain sth.:* hold the view that sth. is true, assert sth. **38** *in his prime:* at the top or summit of his career **42** *be fond of sb./sth.:* like or enjoy sb./sth. very much **44** *footman:* male servant below the rank of butler **45** *relate sth.:* tell sth. **49** *accustomed to sth.:* in the habit of doing sth. **52** *a vital clue to sth.:* an important key or piece of evidence to understanding sth. **53** *apparently:* anscheinend **55** *maintain sth.:* keep sth. at the same level, standard, etc. **56** *evidently:* apparently **58** *languish:* lie sleepily **60** *drawing room* (old use): living-room

attracted his employer's attention with a polite cough, then whispered in the latter's ear: 'I'm very sorry, sir, but there appears to be a tiger in the dining room. Perhaps you will permit the twelve-bores to be used?'

And according to legend, a few minutes later, the employer and his guests heard three gun shots. When the butler reappeared in the drawing room some time afterwards to refresh the teapots, the employer had inquired if all was well.

'Perfectly fine, thank you, sir,' had come the reply. 'Dinner will be served at the usual time and I am pleased to say there will be no discernible traces left of the recent occurrence by that time.'

This last phrase – 'no discernible traces left of the recent occurrence by that time' – my father would repeat with a laugh and shake his head admiringly. He neither claimed to know the butler's name, nor anyone who had known him, but he would always insist the event occurred just as he told it. In any case, it is of little importance whether or not this story is true; the significant thing is, of course, what it reveals concerning my father's ideals. For when I look back over his career, I can see with hindsight that he must have striven throughout his years somehow to *become* that butler of his story. And in my view, at the peak of his career, my father achieved his ambition. For although I am sure he never had the chance to encounter a tiger beneath the dining table, when I think over all that I know or have heard concerning him, I can think of at least several instances of his displaying in abundance that very quality he so admired in the butler of his story.

One such instance was related to me by Mr David Charles, of the Charles and Redding Company, who visited Darlington Hall from time to time during Lord Darlington's days. It was one evening when I happened to be valeting him, Mr Charles told me he had come across my father some years earlier while a guest at Loughborough House – the home of Mr John Silvers, the industrialist, where my father served for fifteen years at the height of his career. He had never been quite able to forget my father, Mr Charles told me, owing to an incident that occurred during that visit.

One afternoon, Mr Charles to his shame and regret had allowed himself to become inebriated in the company of two fellow guests – gentlemen I shall merely call Mr Smith and Mr Jones since they are likely to be still remembered in certain circles. After an hour or so of drinking these two gentlemen decided they wished to go for an afternoon drive around the local villages – a motor car around this time still being something of a novelty. They persuaded Mr Charles to accompany them, and since the chauffeur was on leave at that point, enlisted my father do drive the car.

Once they had set off, Mr Smith and Mr Jones, for all their being well into their middle years, proceeded to behave like schoolboys, singing coarse songs and making even coarser comments on all they saw from the window. Furthermore, these gentlemen had noticed on the local map three villages in the vicinity called Morphy, Saltash and Brigoon. Now I am not entirely sure these were the exact names, but the point was they reminded Mr Smith and Mr Jones of the music hall act, Murphy, Saltman and Brigid the Cat, of which you may have heard. Upon noticing this curious coincidence, the gentlemen then gained an ambition to visit the three villages in question – in honour, as it were, of the music hall artistes. According to Mr Charles, my father had duly driven to one village and was on the point of entering a second when either Mr Smith or Mr Jones noticed the village was Brigoon – that is to say the third, not the second, name of the sequence. They demanded angrily that my father turn the car immediately so that the villages could be visited 'in the correct order'. It so happened that this entailed doubling back a considerable way of the route, but, so Mr Charles assures me, my father accepted the request as though it were a perfectly reasonable one, and in general, continued to behave with immaculate courtesy.

But Mr Smith's and Mr Jones's attention had now been drawn to my father and no doubt rather bored with what the view outside had to offer, they proceeded to amuse themselves by shouting out unflattering remarks concerning my father's 'mistake'. Mr Charles

▷ **1** *with a polite cough:* indem er sich räusperte **2** *the latter:* der/die/das Letztere **3** *twelve-bores:* eine Art Jagdgewehr **10** *discernible traces:* noticeable marks • *occurrence:* event **18** *hindsight* ['haɪndsaɪt]: the understanding that sb. has of a situation after it has happened **24** *in abundance:* in great quantity **29** *valet sb.:* serve as a sb.'s valet (i.e. a personal servant) **36** *inebriated* [ɪ'ni:brieɪtɪd] (adj): drunk **41** *novelty:* thing that is new and exciting **42** *accompany sb.:* go with sb. • *on leave:* absent, not working **43** *enlist sb.:* tell sb. to do a job **46** *coarse* [kɔ:rs]: rude **48** *vicinity:* neighbourhood **53** *gain an ambition to do sth.:* decide very much to do sth. **60** *entail sth.:* involve sth., consist of sth. • *double back* (v): go back the way you have come **63** *immaculate:* perfect • *courtesy:* politeness **67** *unflattering* (adj): critical and nasty

remembered marvelling at how my father showed not one hint of discomfort or anger, but continued to drive with an expression balanced perfectly between personal dignity and readiness to oblige. My father's equanimity was not, however, allowed to last. For when they had wearied of hurling insults at my father's back, the two gentlemen began to discuss their host – that is to say, my father's employer, Mr John Silvers. The remarks grew ever more debased and treacherous so that Mr Charles – at least so he claimed – was obliged to intervene with the suggestion that such talk was bad form.

This view was contradicted with such energy that Mr Charles, quite aside from worrying he would become the next focus of the gentlemen's attraction, actually thought himself in danger of physical assault. But then suddenly, following a particularly heinous insinuation against his employer, my father brought the car to an abrupt halt. It was what happened next that had made such an indelible impression upon Mr Charles.

The rear door of the car opened and my father was observed to be standing there, a few steps back from the vehicle, gazing steadily into the interior. As Mr Charles described it, all three passengers seemed to be overcome as one by the realization of what an imposing physical force my father was. Indeed, he was a man of some six feet three inches, and his countenance, though reassuring while one knew he was intent on obliging, could seem extremely forbidding viewed in certain other contexts. According to Mr Charles, my father did not display any obvious anger. He had, it seemed, merely opened the door. And yet there was something so powerfully rebuking, and at the same time so unassailable about his figure looming over them that Mr Charles's two drunken companions seemed to cower back like small boys caught by the farmer in an act of stealing apples.

My father had proceeded to stand there for some moments, saying nothing, merely holding open the door. Eventually, either Mr Smith or Mr Jones had remarked: 'Are we not going on with the journey?'

My father did not reply, but continued to stand there silently, neither demanding disembarkation nor offering any clue as to his desires or intentions. I can well imagine how he must have looked that day, framed by the doorway of the vehicle, his dark, severe presence quite blotting out the effect of the gentle Hertfordshire scenery behind him. Those were, Mr Charles recalls, strangely unnerving moments during which he too, despite not having participated in the preceding behaviour, felt engulfed with guilt. The silence seemed to go on interminably, before either Mr Smith or Mr Jones found it in him to mutter: 'I suppose we were talking a little out of turn there. It won't happen again.'

A moment to consider this, then my father had closed the door gently, returned to the wheel and had proceeded to continue the tour of the three villages – a tour, Mr Charles assured me, that was completed thereafter in near silence.

Now that I have recalled this episode, another event from around that time in my father's career comes to mind which demonstrates perhaps even more impressively this special quality he came to possess. I should explain here that I am one of two brothers – and that my elder brother, Leonard, was killed during the South African War while I was still a boy. Naturally, my father would have felt this loss keenly; but to make matters worse the usual comfort a father has in these situations – that is, the notion that his son gave his life gloriously for king and country – was sullied by the fact that my brother had perished in a particularly infamous manoeuvre. Not only was it alleged that the manoeuvre had been a most un-British attack on civilian Boer settlements, overwhelming evidence emerged that it had been irresponsibly commanded with several floutings of

▷ **1** *marvel at sth.:* be very astonished at sth. **2** *discomfort:* feeling of being ill at ease **3** *readiness to oblige:* willingness to do what you have been asked to do **4** *equanimity:* stoical indifference and patience **5** *weary of sth.:* grow tired of sth. • *hurl sth.:* throw sth. **7** *debased* (adj): lacking all sense of what is proper **8** *treacherous:* lacking all sense of loyalty **9** *intervene:* interrupt **12–13** *physical assault:* violent attack **13** *heinous* ['heɪnəs]: very nasty or unpleasant **15** *indelible:* unforgettable, permanent **20** *as one:* all together at the same time • *imposing* (adj): impressive **22** *countenance:* facial expression • *reassuring* (adj): making you feel safe and protected **23** *forbidding* (adj): inspiring feelings of fear **26** *rebuke sb.:* express extreme criticism of sb. **27** *unassailable:* that cannot be attacked or defeated • *loom:* appear in a threatening way **28** *cower back:* zusammenkauern **34** *disembarkation:* act of getting out of a car **36** *severe:* (hier) threatening **37** *blot sth. out:* cover sth. completely **39** *unnerving* (adj): making sb. feel ill at ease **40** *preceding* (adj): that had just taken place • *engulfed with sth.:* full of sth. **41** *interminable:* endless **42** *mutter* (v): speak in a low, unclear voice **43** *out of turn* (infml): improperly **52** *South African War:* usually called the Boer War (1899–1902) **54** *keenly:* sharply **56** *sullied* (adj): spoiled, damaged **57** *perish:* die • *infamous* ['ɪnfəməs]: well-known for being bad or evil **58** *allege sth.:* say sth. (which cannot be proved) **59** *overwhelming evidence:* erdrückende Beweise **60** *flout sth.* [flaʊt]: ignore sth. on purpose in spite of knowing better

elementary military precautions, so that the men who had died – my brother among them – had died quite needlessly. In view of what I am about to relate, it would not be proper of me to identify the manoeuvre any more precisely, though you may well guess which one I am alluding to if I say that it caused something of an uproar at the time, adding significantly to the controversy the conflict as a whole was attracting. There had been calls for the removal, even the court-martialling, of the general concerned, but the army had defended the latter and he had been allowed to complete the campaign. What is less known is that at the close of the Southern African conflict, this same general had been discreetly retired, and he had then entered business, dealing in shipments from Southern Africa. I relate this because some ten years after the conflict, that is to say when the wounds of bereavement had only superficially healed, my father was called into Mr John Silvers's study to be told that this very same personage – I will call him simply 'the General' – was due to visit for a number of days to attend a house party, during which my father's employer hoped to lay the foundations of a lucrative business transaction. Mr Silvers, however, had remembered the significance the visit would have for my father, and had thus called him in to offer him the option of taking several days' leave for the duration of the General's stay.

My father's feelings towards the General were, naturally, those of utmost loathing; but he realized too that his employer's present business aspirations hung on the smooth running of the house party – which with some eighteen or so people expected would be no trifling affair. My father thus replied to the effect that while he was most grateful that his feelings had been taken into account, Mr Silvers could be assured that service would be provided to the usual standards.

As things turned out, my father's ordeal proved even worse than might have been predicted. For one thing, any hopes my father may have had that to meet the General in person would arouse a sense of respect or sympathy to leaven his feelings against him proved without foundation. The General was a portly, ugly man, his manners were not refined, and his talk was conspicuous for an eagerness to apply military similes to a very wide variety of matters. Worse was to come with the news that the gentleman had brought no valet, his usual man having fallen ill. This presented a delicate problem, another of the house guests being also without his valet, raising the question as to which guest should be allocated the butler as valet and who the footman. My father, appreciating his employer's position, volunteered immediately to take the General, and thus was obliged to suffer intimate proximity for four days with the man he detested. Meanwhile, the General, having no idea of my father's feelings, took full opportunity to relate anecdotes of his military accomplishments – as of course many military gentlemen are wont to do to their valets in the privacy of their rooms. Yet so well did my father hide his feelings, so professionally did he carry out his duties, that on his departure the General had actually complimented Mr John Silvers on the excellence of his butler and had left an unusually large tip in appreciation – which my father without hesitation asked his employer to donate to a charity.

I hope you will agree that in these two instances I have cited from his career – both of which I have had corroborated and believe to be accurate – my father not only manifests, but comes close to being the personification itself, of what the Hayes Society terms 'dignity in keeping with his position'. If one considers the difference between my father at such moments and a figure such as Mr Jack Neighbours even with the best of his technical flourishes, I believe one may begin to distinguish what it is that separates a 'great' butler from a merely competent one. We may now understand better, too, why my father

▷ **1** *precaution:* step normally taken to ensure safety **5** *allude to sth.:* refer to sth. indirectly • *uproar:* public outcry, scandal **7–8** *court-martial sb.:* put sb. on trial for misconduct before a military court **11** *discreet:* without arousing attention **12** *shipment:* goods that are transported from one country to another **14** *bereavement:* loss suffered through the death of a loved one **16** *personage:* well-known person **18** *lucrative:* promising financial gain, profitable **24** *loathing* (n): extreme hatred **25** *aspiration:* plan, goal • *hang on sth.:* be dependent on sth. **26–27** *no trifling affair:* not a simple task **31** *ordeal:* very unpleasant experience **34** *leaven sth.* ['levn]: make sth. less strong or painful **34–35** *proved without foundation:* (here) turned out not to be the case **35** *portly:* fat, heavy **36** *refined* (adj): polite, well-mannered • *conspicuous for sth.:* characterized by sth. **39** *delicate:* that needs to be dealt with in a careful or sensitive way **41** *allocate sb. to sb. else:* give sb. to sb. else for a special task **42–43** *volunteer* (v): offer to do sth. without being forced to do it **44** *intimate proximity:* state of being very close to sb. • *detest sb.:* hate sb. **51** *tip:* Trinkgeld **52–53** *donate sth. to a charity:* give sth. to an organization that supports good causes **54** *cite sth.:* mention sth. as an example **56** *manifest sth.:* display sth. clearly **60** *flourish* (n): gesture intended only for show

was so fond of the story of the butler who failed to panic on discovering a tiger under the dining table; it was because he knew instinctively that somewhere in this story lay the kernel of what true 'dignity' is. And let me now posit this: 'dignity' has to do crucially with a butler's ability not to abandon the professional being he inhabits. Lesser butlers will abandon their professional being for the private one at the least provocation. For such persons, being a butler is like playing some pantomime role; a small push, a slight stumble, and the façade will drop off to reveal the actor underneath. The great butlers are great by virtue of their ability to inhabit their professional role and inhabit it to the utmost; they will not be shaken out by external events, however surprising, alarming or vexing. They wear their professionalism as a decent gentleman will wear his suit: he will not let ruffians or circumstances tear it off him in the public gaze; he will discard it when, and only when, he wills to do so, and this will invariably be when he is entirely alone. It is, as I say, a matter of 'dignity'.

It is sometimes said that butlers only truly exist in England. Other countries, whatever title is actually used, have only manservants. I tend to believe this is true. Continentals are unable to be butlers because they are as a breed incapable of the emotional restraint which only the English race is capable of. Continentals – and by and large the Celts, as you will no doubt agree – are as a rule unable to control themselves in moments of strong emotion, and are thus unable to maintain a professional demeanour other than in the least challenging of situations. If I may return to my earlier metaphor – you will excuse my putting it so coarsely – they are like a man who will, at the slightest provocation, tear off his suit and his shirt and run about screaming. In a word, 'dignity' is beyond such persons. We English have an important advantage over foreigners in this respect and it is for this reason that when you think of a great butler, he is bound, almost by definition, to be an Englishman.

Of course, you may retort, as did Mr Graham whenever I expounded such a line during those enjoyable discussions by the fire, that if I am correct in what I am saying, one could recognize a great butler as such only after one had seen him perform under some severe test. And yet the truth is, we accept persons such as Mr Marshall or Mr Lane to be great, though most of us cannot claim to have ever scrutinized them under such conditions. I have to admit Mr Graham has a point here, but all I can say is that after one has been in the profession as long as one has, one is able to judge intuitively the depth of a man's professionalism without having to see it under pressure. Indeed, on the occasion one is fortunate enough to meet a great butler, far from experiencing any sceptical urge to demand a 'test', one is at a loss to imagine any situation which could ever dislodge a professionalism borne with such authority. In fact, I am sure it was an apprehension of this sort, penetrating even the thick haze created by alcohol, which reduced my father's passengers into a shamed silence that Sunday afternoon many years ago. It is with such men as it is with the English landscape seen at its best as I did this morning: when one encounters them, one simply knows one is in the presence of greatness.

There will always be, I realize, those who would claim that any attempt to analyse greatness as I have been doing is quite futile. 'You know when somebody's got it and you know when somebody hasn't,' Mr Graham's argument would always be. 'Beyond that there's nothing much you can say.' But I believe we have a duty not to be so defeatist in this matter. It is surely a professional responsibility for all of us to think deeply about these things so that each of us may better strive towards attaining 'dignity' for ourselves.

▷ **3** *kernel:* essence **4** *posit sth.:* claim sth. **5** *lesser* (adj): not so great **8** *stumble* (n): fall (usu. from walking or doing sth. carelessly) **9** *underneath:* below sth. **10** *by virtue of sth.:* due to sth. **11** *to the utmost:* to the highest degree **12** *vexing* (adj): annoying sb. or making sb. angry **14** *ruffian:* violent man • *in the public gaze:* in front of others **15** *discard sth.:* take sth. off, abandon sth., cast sth. aside **21** *breed:* race, type of person • *emotional restraint:* ability to keep your feelings to yourself **22–23** *by and large:* on the whole **25** *demeanour* [dɪ'miːnə]: the way that sb. behaves **27** *coarsely:* roughly, bluntly **31–32** *bound to be sth.:* certain to be sth. **33** *retort:* reply **34** *expound sth.:* explain sth. in detail • *line:* (here) argument that is carefully thought out **36–37** *perform under some severe test:* (here) behave in a very difficult situation **45** *be at a loss to do sth.*: be unable to do sth. • *dislodge sth.:* unsettle or disturb sth. **46** *borne with sth.:* carried (out) with sth. **47** *apprehension:* realization, insight, awareness • *penetrate sth.:* get or pass through sth. • *haze:* state of mind in which you are unable to think clearly **60** *attain sth.:* reach or achieve sth.

DAY TWO – MORNING

Salisbury

Strange beds have rarely agreed with me, and after only a short spell of somewhat troubled slumber, I awoke an hour or so ago. It was then still dark, and knowing I had a full day's motoring ahead of me, I made an attempt to return to sleep. This proved futile, and when I decided eventually to rise, it was still so dark that I was obliged to turn on the electric light in order to shave at the sink in the corner. But when having finished I switched it off again, I could see early daylight at the edges of the curtains.

When I parted them just a moment ago, the light outside was still very pale and something of a mist was affecting my view of the baker's shop and chemist's shop opposite. Indeed, following the street further along to where it runs over the little round-backed bridge, I could see the mist rising from the river, obscuring almost entirely one of the bridge-posts. There was not a soul to be seen, and apart from a hammering noise echoing from somewhere distant, and an occasional coughing in a room to the back of the house, there is still no sound to be heard. The landlady is clearly not yet up and about, suggesting there is little chance of her serving breakfast earlier than her declared time of seven thirty.

Now, in these quiet moments as I wait for the world about to awake, I find myself going over in my mind again passages from Miss Kenton's letter. Incidentally, I should before now have explained myself as regards my referring to 'Miss Kenton'. 'Miss Kenton' is properly speaking 'Mrs Benn' and has been for twenty years. However, because I knew her at close quarters only during her maiden years and have not seen her once since she went to the West Country to become 'Mrs Benn', you will perhaps excuse my impropriety in referring to her as I knew her, and in my mind have continued to call her throughout these years. Of course, her letter has given me extra cause to continue thinking of her as 'Miss Kenton', since it would seem, sadly, that her marriage is finally to come to an end. The letter does not make specific the details of the matter, as one would hardly expect it to do, but Miss Kenton states unambiguously that she has now, in fact, taken the step of moving out of Mr Benn's

▷ **1** *agree with sb.:* (here) make sb. feel comfortable or at ease **2** *spell* (n): short period of time • *slumber* (n): sleep **6** *sink* (n): Spülbecken **10** *mist:* Nebel • *affect sth.:* (here) disturb sth. **13** *obscure sth.:* make sth. difficult to see **19** *her declared time:* (here) the time she said she would do sth. **25** *at close quarters:* on a personal level **26** *maiden:* unmarried **28** *impropriety* [ˌɪmprəˈpraɪəti]: improper behaviour

house in Helston and is presently lodging with an acquaintance in the nearby village of Little Compton.

It is of course tragic that her marriage is now ending in failure. At this very moment, no doubt, she is pondering with regret decisions made in the far-off past that have now left her, deep in middle age, so alone and desolate. And it is easy to see how in such a frame of mind, the thought of returning to Darlington Hall would be a great comfort to her. Admittedly, she does not at any point in her letter state explicitly her desire to return; but that is the unmistakable message conveyed by the general nuance of many of the passages, imbued as they are with a deep nostalgia for her days at Darlington Hall. Of course, Miss Kenton cannot hope by returning at this stage ever to retrieve those lost years, and it will be my first duty to impress this upon her when we meet. I will have to point out how different things are now – that the days of working with a grand staff at one's beck and call will probably never return within our lifetime. But then Miss Kenton is an intelligent woman and she will have already realized these things. Indeed, all in all, I cannot see why the option of her returning to Darlington Hall and seeing out her working years there should not offer a very genuine consolation to a life that has come to be so dominated by a sense of waste.

And of course, from my own professional viewpoint, it is clear that even after a break of so many years, Miss Kenton would prove the perfect solution to the problem at present besetting us at Darlington Hall. In fact, by terming it a 'problem', I perhaps overstate the matter. I am referring, after all, to a series of very minor errors on my part and the course I am now pursuing is merely a means of pre-empting any 'problems' before one arises. It is true, these same trivial problems did cause me some anxiety at first, but once I had had time to diagnose them correctly as symptoms of nothing more than a straightforward staff shortage, I have refrained from giving them much thought. Miss Kenton's arrival, as I say, will put a permanent end to them.

But to return to her letter. It does at times reveal a certain despair over her present situation – a fact that is rather concerning. She begins one sentence: 'Although I have no idea how I shall usefully fill the remainder of my life …' And again, elsewhere, she writes: 'The rest of my life stretches out as an emptiness before me.' For the most part, though, as I have said, the tone is one of nostalgia. At one point, for instance, she writes:

'This whole incident put me in mind of Alice White. Do you remember her? In fact, I hardly imagine you could forget her. For myself, I am still haunted by those vowel sounds and those uniquely ungrammatical sentences only she could dream up! Have you any idea what became of her?'

I have not, as a matter of fact, though I must say it rather amused me to remember that exasperating housemaid – who in the end turned out to be one of the most devoted. At another point in her letter, Miss Kenton writes:

'I was so fond of that view from the second-floor bedrooms overlooking the lawn with the downs visible in the distance. Is it still like that? On summer evenings there was a sort of magical quality to that view and I will confess to you now I used to waste many precious minutes standing at one of those windows just enchanted by it.'

Then she goes on to add:

'If this is a painful memory, forgive me. But I will never forget that time we both watched your father walking back and forth in front of the summerhouse, looking down at the ground as though he hoped to find some precious jewel he had dropped there.'

It is something of a revelation that this memory from over thirty years ago should have remained with Miss Kenton as it has done with me. Indeed, it must have occurred on just one of those summer evenings she mentions, for I can recall distinctly climbing to the second landing and seeing before me a series of orange shafts from the sunset breaking the gloom of the corridor where each bedroom door stood ajar. And as I made my way past those bedrooms, I had seen through a doorway Miss Kenton's figure, silhouetted against a window, turn and call softly: 'Mr Stevens, if you have a moment.' As I entered, Miss Kenton had turned back to the window. Down below,

▷ **10** *nuance:* hidden meaning or feeling **10–11** *imbued with sth.:* full of sth. **13** *retrieve sth.:* win sth. back **15–16** *at sb.'s beck and call:* always ready to do what sb. wants **19** *see sth. out:* continue until the end of sth. **24** *beset sb.* [-'-]: trouble or disturb sb. **25** *term sth.:* call sth. by a particular name • *overstate the matter:* exaggerate **27** *pursue sth.:* follow sth. • *pre-empt sth.:* prevent sth. from happening **31** *refrain from sth.:* keep yourself from doing sth. **34** *concerning* (adj): that makes sb. worry **36** *remainder:* rest **37** *stretch out:* lie ahead **42** *be haunted by sth.* ['hɔːntɪd]: not be able to stop thinking about sth. **46** *exasperating* (adj): extremely annoying **47** *devoted* (adj): faithful **50** *lawn:* Rasen **53** *enchanted* (adj): delighted, filled with great pleasure **63** *landing* (n): the floor at the top of a set of stairs • *shaft:* (here) sunray **64** *gloom:* sombre and dark atmosphere **65** *ajar:* open

the shadows of the poplars were falling across the lawn. To the right of our view, the lawn sloped up a gentle embankment to where the summerhouse stood, and it was there my father's figure could be seen, pacing slowly with an air of preoccupation – indeed, as Miss Kenton puts it so well, 'as though he hoped to find some precious jewel he had dropped there.'

There are some very pertinent reasons why this memory has remained with me, as I wish to explain. Moreover, now that I come to think of it, it is perhaps not so surprising that it should also have made a deep impression on Miss Kenton given certain aspects of her relationship with my father during her early days at Darlington Hall.

Miss Kenton and my father had arrived at the house at more or less the same time – that is to say, the spring of 1922 – as a consequence of my losing at one stroke the precious housekeeper and under-butler. This had occurred due to these latter two persons deciding to marry one another and leave the profession. I have always found such liaisons a serious threat to the order in a house. Since that time, I have lost numerous more employees in such circumstances. Of course, one has to expect such things to occur amongst maids and footmen, and a good butler should always take this into account in his planning; but such marrying amongst more senior employees can have an extremely disruptive effect on work. Of course, if two members of the staff happen to fall in love and decide to marry, it would be churlish to be apportioning blame; but what I find a major irritation are those persons – and housekeepers are particularly guilty here – who have no genuine commitment to their profession and who are essentially going from post to post looking for romance. This sort of person is a blight on good professionalism.

But let me say immediately I do not have Miss Kenton in mind at all when I say this. Of course, she too eventually left my staff to get married, but I can vouch that during the time she worked as a housekeeper under me, she was nothing less than dedicated and never allowed her professional priorities to be distracted.

But I am digressing. I was explaining that we had fallen in need of a housekeeper and an under-butler at one and the same time and Miss Kenton had arrived – with unusually good references, I recall – to take up the former post. As it happened, my father had around this time come to the end of his distinguished service at Loughborough House with the death of his employer, Mr John Silvers, and had been at something of a loss for work and accommodation. Although he was still, of course, a professional of the highest class, he was now in his seventies and much ravaged by arthritis and other ailments. It was not at all certain, then, how he would fare against the younger breed of highly professionalized butlers looking for posts. In view of this, it seemed a reasonable solution to ask my father to bring his great experience and distinction to Darlington Hall.

As I remember it was one morning a little while after my father and Miss Kenton had joined the staff, I had been in my pantry, sitting at the table going through my paperwork, when I heard a knock on my door. I recall I was a little taken aback when Miss Kenton opened the door and entered before I had bidden her to do so. She came in holding a large vase of flowers and said with a smile:

'Mr Stevens, I thought these would brighten your parlour a little.'

'I beg your pardon, Miss Kenton?'

'It seemed such a pity your room should be so dark and cold, Mr Stevens, when it's such bright sunshine outside. I thought these would enliven things a little.'

'That's very kind of you, Miss Kenton.'

'It's a shame more sun doesn't get in here. The walls are even a little damp, are they not, Mr Stevens?'

I turned back to my accounts, saying: 'Merely condensation, I believe, Miss Kenton.'

▷ **1** *poplar:* Pappel **2** *slope up:* rise • *embankment:* flat area of ground that is higher than the rest **4** *pace* (v): walk in a slow and deliberate manner • *preoccupation:* total concentration **14** *at one stroke:* at the same time **22** *disruptive:* disturbing **24** *churlish:* rude, impolite • *apportion sth.:* give a share of sth. (among people) **26** *commitment:* willingness to work hard and give your energy to a particular prupose **28** *blight on sth.:* thing that has a bad effect on sth. **31** *vouch:* truly say **32** *dedicated* (adj): committed to her work **33** *allow your professional priorities to be distracted:* (here) allow sth. to come between you and your professional duties **34** *digress* [daɪ'gres]: move away from the main topic you are talking about **39–40** *be at loss for sth.:* not know what to do about sth. **42** *ravaged* (adj): (here) seriously affected • *ailment* ['eɪlmənt]: illness that is not very serious **43** *how he would fare against sb.:* (here) how he could compete with sb. **48** *pantry:* (here) small private workroom **50** *taken aback:* surprised, shocked **51** *bid (– bade – bidden) sb. to do sth.:* ask sb. to do sth. **53** *parlour* (old-fashioned): living room; (here) private workroom **57** *enliven sth.:* make sth. more attractive **60** *damp:* slightly and unpleasantly wet

She put her vase down on the table in front of me, then glancing around my pantry again said: 'If you wish, Mr Stevens, I might bring in some more cuttings for you.'

'Miss Kenton, I appreciate your kindness. But this is not a room of entertainment. I am happy to have distractions kept to a minimum.'

'But surely, Mr Stevens, there is no need to keep your room so stark and bereft of colour.'

'It has served me perfectly well this far as it is, Miss Kenton, though I appreciate your thoughts. In fact, since you are here, there was a certain matter I wished to raise with you.'

'Oh, really, Mr Stevens.'

'Yes, Miss Kenton, just a small matter. I happened to be walking past the kitchen yesterday when I heard you calling to someone named William.'

'Is that so, Mr Stevens?'

'Indeed, Miss Kenton. I did hear you call several times for "William". May I ask who it was you were addressing by that name?'

'Why, Mr Stevens, I should think I was addressing your father. There are no other Williams in this house, I take it.'

'It's an easy enough error to have made,' I said with a small smile. 'May I ask you in future, Miss Kenton, to address my father as "Mr Stevens"? If you are referring to him to a third party, then you may wish to call him "Mr Stevens senior" to distinguish him from myself. I'm most grateful, Miss Kenton.'

With that I turned back to my papers. But to my surprise, Miss Kenton did not take her leave. 'Excuse me, Mr Stevens,' she said after a moment.

'Yes, Miss Kenton.'

'I am afraid I am not quite clear what you are saying. I have in the past been accustomed to addressing under-servants by their Christian names and saw no reason to do otherwise in this house.'

'A most understandable error, Miss Kenton. However, if you will consider the situation for a moment, you may come to see the inappropriateness of someone such as yourself talking "down" to one such as my father.'

'I am still not clear what you are getting at, Mr Stevens. You say someone such as myself, but I am as far as I understand the housekeeper of this house, while your father is the under-butler.'

'He is of course in title the under-butler, as you say. But I am surprised your powers of observation have not already made it clear to you that he is in reality more than that. A great deal more.'

'No doubt I have been extremely unobservant, Mr Stevens. I had only observed that your father was an able under-butler and addressed him accordingly. It must indeed have been most galling for him to be so addressed by one such as I.'

'Miss Kenton, it is clear from your tone you simply have not observed my father. If you had done so, the inappropriateness of someone of your age and standing addressing him as "William" should have been self-evident to you.'

'Mr Stevens, I may not have been a housekeeper for long, but I would say that in the time I have been, my abilities have attracted some very generous remarks.'

'I do not doubt your competence for one moment, Miss Kenton. But a hundred things should have indicated to you that my father is a figure of unusual distinction from whom you may learn a wealth of things were you prepared to be more observant.'

'I am most indebted to you for your advice, Mr Stevens. So do please tell me, just what marvellous things might I learn from observing your father?'

'I would have thought it obvious to anyone with eyes, Miss Kenton.'

'But we have already established, have we not, that I am particularly deficient in that respect.'

'Miss Kenton, if you are under the impression you have already at your age perfected yourself, you will never rise to the heights you are no doubt capable of. I might point out, for instance, you are still often unsure of what goes where and which item is which.'

This seemed to take the wind out of Miss Kenton's sails somewhat. Indeed, for a moment, she looked a little upset. Then she said:

'I had a little difficulty on first arriving, but that is surely only normal.'

▷ **3** *cutting* (n): (here) flower that has been cut **6** *stark:* very simple and severe in appearance **7** *bereft of sth.:* completely without sth. **34** *talk down to sb.:* treat sb. as an inferior by what you say **42** *unobservant:* not able to notice things **44** *galling* ['gɔːlɪŋ] (adj): making sb. feel upset and angry **57** *indebted* (adj): very grateful **63** *deficient:* not good enough, imperfect

'Ah, there you are, Miss Kenton. If you had observed my father who arrived in this house a week after you did, you will have seen that his house knowledge is perfect and was so almost from the time he set foot in Darlington Hall.'

Miss Kenton seemed to think about this before saying a little sulkily:

'I am sure Mr Stevens senior is very good at his job, but I assure you, Mr Stevens, I am very good at mine. I will remember to address your father by his full title in future. Now, if you would please excuse me.'

After this encounter, Miss Kenton did not attempt to introduce further flowers into my pantry, and in general, I was pleased to observe, she went about settling in impressively. It was clear, furthermore, she was a housekeeper who took her work very seriously and in spite of her youth, she seemed to have no difficulty gaining the respect of her staff.

I noticed too that she was indeed proceeding to address my father as 'Mr Stevens'. However, one afternoon perhaps two weeks after our conversation in my pantry, I was doing something in the library when Miss Kenton came in and said:

'Excuse me, Mr Stevens. But if you are searching for your dust-pan, it is out in the hall.'

'I beg your pardon, Miss Kenton?'

'Your dust-pan, Mr Stevens. You've left it out here. Shall I bring it in for you?'

'Miss Kenton, I have not been using a dust-pan.'

'Ah, well, then forgive me, Mr Stevens. I naturally assumed you were using your dust-pan and had left it out in the hall. I am sorry to have disturbed you.'

She started to leave, but then turned at the doorway and said:

'Oh, Mr Stevens. I would return it myself but I have to go upstairs just now. I wonder if you will remember it?'

'Of course, Miss Kenton. Thank you for drawing attention to it.'

'It is quite all right, Mr Stevens.'

I listened to her footsteps cross the hall and start up the great staircase, then proceeded to the doorway myself. From the library doors, one has an unbroken view right across the entrance hall to the main doors of the house. Most conspicuously, in virtually the central spot of the otherwise empty and highly polished floor, lay the dust-pan Miss Kenton had alluded to.

It struck me as a trivial, but irritating error; the dust-pan would have been conspicuous not only from the five ground-floor doorways opening on to the hall, but also from the staircase and the first-floor balconies. I crossed the hall and had actually picked up the offending item before realizing its full implication; my father, I recalled, had been brushing the entrance hall a half-hour or so earlier. At first, I found it hard to credit such an error to my father. But I soon reminded myself that such trivial slips are liable to befall anyone from time to time, and my irritation soon turned to Miss Kenton for attempting to create such unwarranted fuss over the incident.

Then, not more than a week later, I was coming down the back corridor from the kitchen when Miss Kenton came out of her parlour and uttered a statement she had clearly been rehearsing; this was something to the effect that although she felt most uncomfortable drawing my attention to errors made by my staff, she and I had to work as a team, and she hoped I would not feel inhibited to do similarly should I notice errors made by female staff. She then went on to point out that several pieces of silver had been laid out for the dining room which bore clear remains of polish. The end of one fork had been practically black. I thanked her and she withdrew back into her parlour. It had been unnecessary, of course, for her to mention that the silver was one of my father's main responsibilities and one he took great pride in.

It is very possible there were a number of other instances of this sort which I have now forgotten. In any case, I recall things reaching something of a climax one grey and drizzly afternoon when I was in the billiard room attending to Lord Darlington's sporting trophies. Miss Kenton had entered and said from the door:

'Mr Stevens, I have just noticed something outside which puzzles me.'

▷ **5** *sulky:* eingeschnappt **12** *settle in:* become used to your new surroundings **20–21** *dust-pan:* Kehrschaufel **37** *virtually:* practically **38** *polished* (adj): shiny and clean **44** *item* ['aɪtəm]: thing • *its full implication:* what was really behind it, what it really meant **46** *credit sth. to sb.:* (here) blame sth. on sb. **47** *slip* (n): small mistake • *liable* ['laɪəbl] (adj): likely • *befall sb.*: happen to sb. **49** *unwarranted* (adj): unnecessary, exaggerated • *fuss* (n): too much worry or excitement **52** *utter sth.:* say sth. • *rehearse sth.* [rɪ'hɜːs]: practise sth. in advance **55** *inhibited* (adj): gehemmt **58** *bear sth. (– bore – borne):* show sth. • *remains* (pl): traces of sth. left over **65** *drizzly* (adj): characterized by a light steady rain **68** *puzzle sb.:* make sb. feel confused

'What is that, Miss Kenton?'

'Was it his lordship's wish that the Chinaman on the upstairs landing should be exchanged with the one outside this door?'

'The Chinaman, Miss Kenton?'

'Yes, Mr Stevens. The Chinaman normally on the landing you will now find outside this door.'

'I fear, Miss Kenton, that you are a little confused.'

'I do not believe I am confused at all, Mr Stevens. I make it my business to acquaint myself with where objects properly belong in a house. The Chinamen, I would suppose, were polished by someone then replaced incorrectly. If you are sceptical, Mr Stevens, perhaps you will care to step out here and observe for yourself.'

'Miss Kenton, I am occupied at present.'

'But, Mr Stevens, you do not appear to believe what I am saying. I am thus asking you to step outside this door and see for yourself.'

'Miss Kenton, I am busy just now and will attend to the matter shortly. It is hardly one of urgency.'

'You accept then, Mr Stevens, that I am not in error on this point.'

'I will accept nothing of the sort, Miss Kenton, until I have had the chance to deal with the matter. However, I am occupied at present.'

I turned back to my business, but Miss Kenton remained in the doorway observing me. Eventually, she said:

'I can see you will be finished very shortly, Mr Stevens. I will await you outside so that this matter may be finalized when you come out.'

'Miss Kenton, I believe you are according this matter an urgency it hardly merits.'

But Miss Kenton had departed, and sure enough, as I continued with my work, an occasional footstep or some other sound would serve to remind me she was still there outside the door. I decided therefore to occupy myself with some further tasks in the billiard room, assuming she would after a while see the ludicrousness of her position and leave. However, after some time had passed, and I had exhausted the tasks which could usefully be achieved with the implements I happened to have at hand, Miss Kenton was evidently still outside. Resolved not to waste further time on account of this childish affair, I contemplated departure via the French windows. A drawback to this plan was the weather – that is to say, several large puddles and patches of mud were in evidence – and the fact that one would need to return to the billiard room again at some point to bolt the French windows from the inside. Eventually, then, I decided the best strategy would be simply to stride out of the room very suddenly at a furious pace. I thus made my way as quietly as possible to a position from which I could execute such a march, and clutching my implements firmly about me, succeeded in propelling myself through the doorway and several paces down the corridor before a somewhat astonished Miss Kenton could recover her wits. This she did, however, rather rapidly and the next moment I found she had overtaken me and was standing before me, effectively barring my way.

'Mr Stevens, this is the incorrect Chinaman, would you not agree?'

'Miss Kenton, I am very busy. I am surprised you have nothing better to do than stand in corridors all day.'

'Mr Stevens, is that the correct Chinaman or is it not?'

'Miss Kenton, I would ask you to keep your voice down.'

'And I would ask you, Mr Stevens, to turn around and look at that Chinaman.'

'Miss Kenton, please keep your voice down. What would employees below think to hear us shouting at the top of our voices about what is and what is not the correct Chinaman?'

'The fact is, Mr Stevens, all the Chinamen in this house have been dirty for some time! And now, they are in incorrect positions!'

'Miss Kenton, you are being quite ridiculous. Now if you will be so good as to let me pass.'

'Mr Stevens, will you kindly look at the Chinaman behind you?'

'If it is so important to you, Miss Kenton, I will allow that the Chinaman behind me may well be incorrectly situated. But I must say I am at some loss as to why you should be so concerned with these most trivial of errors.'

▷ **2** *Chinaman:* large porcelain figure of a Chinese man **17** *of urgency:* requiring immediate attention **25** *accord sth. sth. else:* give sth. sth. else (e.g. a quality) **26** *merit sth.:* deserve sth. **31** *ludicrousness:* stupidity, foolishness **33** *exhaust sth.:* totally finish sth. **34** *implement:* tool, object for working with **35** *resolved* (adj): determined **36** *contemplate sth.:* think about sth. • *via* ['vaɪə] (prep): through • *French window:* pair of doors containing plates of glass which usu. open out on to a garden **37** *drawback:* disadvantage **39** *bolt sth.:* lock sth. (using a metal bar) **41** *stride out:* walk out with long hurried steps **42** *at a furious pace:* very quickly and energetically **43** *clutch sth.:* hold sth. tightly **44** *propel* [- '-]: move quickly **46** *recover your wits:* (hier) ihre Fassung wiedererlangen **48** *bar sb.'s way:* put yourself in sb.'s way

'These errors may be trivial in themselves, Mr Stevens, but you must yourself realize their larger significance.'

'Miss Kenton, I do not understand you. Now if you would kindly allow me to pass.'

'The fact is, Mr Stevens, your father is entrusted with far more than a man of his age can cope with.'

'Miss Kenton, you clearly have little idea of what you are suggesting.'

'Whatever your father was once, Mr Stevens, his powers are now greatly diminished. That is what these "trivial errors" as you call them really signify and if you do not heed them, it will not be long before your father commits an error of major proportions.'

'Miss Kenton, you are merely making yourself look foolish.'

'I am sorry, Mr Stevens, but I must go on. I believe there are many duties your father should now be relieved of. He should not, for one, be asked to go on carrying heavily laden trays. The way his hands tremble as he carries them into dinner is nothing short of alarming. It is surely only a matter of time before a tray falls from his hands on to a lady or gentleman's lap. And furthermore, Mr Stevens, and I am very sorry to say this, I have noticed your father's nose.'

'Have you indeed, Miss Kenton?'

'I regret to say I have, Mr Stevens. The evening before last I watched your father proceeding very slowly towards the dining room with his tray, and I am afraid I observed clearly a large drop on the end of his nose dangling over the soup bowls. I would not have thought such a style of waiting a great stimulant to appetite.'

But now that I think further about it, I am not sure Miss Kenton spoke quite so boldly that day. We did, of course, over the years of working closely together come to have some very frank exchanges, but the afternoon I am recalling was still early in our relationship and I cannot see even Miss Kenton having been so forward. I am not sure she could actually have gone so far as to say things like: 'these errors may be trivial in themselves, but you must yourself realize their larger significance'. In fact, now that I come to think of it, I have a feeling it may have been Lord Darlington himself who made that particular remark to me that time he called me into his study some two months after that exchange with Miss Kenton outside the billiard room. By that time, the situation as regards my father had changed significantly following his fall.

The study doors are those that face one as one comes down the great staircase. There is outside the study today a glass cabinet displaying various of Mr Farraday's ornaments, but throughout Lord Darlington's days, there stood at that spot a bookshelf containing many volumes of encyclopedia, including a complete set of the *Britannica*. It was a ploy of Lord Darlington's to stand at this shelf studying the spines of the encyclopedias as I came down the staircase, and sometimes, to increase the effect of an accidental meeting, he would actually pull out a volume and pretend to be engrossed as I completed my descent. Then, as I passed him, he would say: 'Oh, Stevens, there was something I meant to say to you.' And with that, he would wander back into his study, to all appearances still thoroughly engrossed in the volume held open in his hands. It was invariably embarrassment at what he was about to impart which made Lord Darlington adopt such an approach, and even once the study door was closed behind us, he would often stand by the window and make a show of consulting the encyclopedia throughout our conversation.

What I am now describing, incidentally, is one of many instances I could relate to you to underline Lord Darlington's essentially shy and modest nature. A great deal of nonsense has been spoken and written in recent years concerning his lordship and the prominent role he came to play in great affairs, and some utterly ignorant reports have had it that he was motivated by egotism or else arrogance. Let me say here that nothing could be further from the truth. It was completely contrary to Lord Darlington's natural tendencies to take such public stances as he came to do and I can say with conviction that his lordship was persuaded to overcome his more retiring side only through a deep sense of moral duty. Whatever may be said about his lordship these days – and the great majority of it is, as I say, utter nonsense – I can declare that he was a truly good man at heart, a

▷ **5** *be entrusted with sth.:* be responsible for sth. **9** *diminished* (adj): reduced **10** *signify sth.:* mean sth. • *heed sth.:* pay attention to sth. **11** *of major proportions:* important **14** *relieve sb. of sth.:* take sth. away from sb. **15** *laden* ['leɪdən] (adj): loaded with many things • *tray:* Tablett **16** *nothing short of alarming:* very alarming **24** *dangle:* hang or swing loosely **27** *bold:* dreist **28** *frank exchange:* open and direct talk in which the people involved have different views **30** *forward* (adj): too direct and confident **43** *volume:* Band **44** *ploy:* clever method **45** *spine:* back part of a book **50** *to all appearances:* as it seemed from the outside • *thoroughly:* deeply, totally, completely **52** *impart sth.:* tell sth. **65** *retiring* (adj): reserved, keeping in the background

gentleman through and through, and one I am today proud to have given my best years of service to.

On the particular afternoon to which I am referring, his lordship would still have been in his mid-fifties; but as I recall, his hair had greyed entirely and his tall slender figure already bore signs of the stoop that was to become so pronounced in his last years. He barely glanced up from his volume as he asked:

'Your father feeling better now, Stevens?'

'I'm glad to say he has made a full recovery, sir.'

'Jolly pleased to hear that. Jolly pleased.'

'Thank you, sir.'

'Look here, Stevens, have there been any – well – *signs* at all? I mean signs to tell us your father may be wishing his burden lightened somewhat? Apart from this business of him falling, I mean?'

'As I say, sir, my father appears to have made a full recovery and I believe he is still a person of considerable dependability. It is true one or two errors have been noticeable recently in the discharging of his duties, but these are in every case very trivial in nature.'

'But none of us wish to see anything of that sort happen ever again, do we? I mean, your father collapsing and all that.'

'Indeed not, sir.'

'And of course, if it can happen out on the lawn, it could happen anywhere. And at any time.'

'Yes, sir.'

'It could happen, say, during dinner while your father was waiting at table.'

'It is possible, sir.'

'Look here, Stevens, the first of the delegates will be arriving here in less than a fortnight.'

'We are well prepared, sir.'

'What happens within this house after that may have considerable repercussions.'

'Yes, sir.'

'I mean *considerable* repercussions. On the whole course Europe is taking. In view of the persons who will be present, I do not think I exaggerate.'

'No, sir.'

'Hardly the time for taking on avoidable hazards.'

'Indeed not, sir,'

'Look here, Stevens, there's no question of your father leaving us. You're simply being asked to reconsider his duties.' And it was then, I believe, that his lordship said as he looked down again into his volume and awkwardly fingered an entry: 'These errors may be trivial in themselves, Stevens, but you must yourself realize their larger significance. Your father's days of dependability are now passing. He must not be asked to perform tasks in any area where an error might jeopardize the success of our forthcoming conference.'

'Indeed not, sir. I fully understand.'

'Good. I'll leave you to think about it then, Stevens.'

Lord Darlington, I should say, had actually witnessed my father's fall of a week or so earlier. His lordship had been entertaining two guests, a young lady and gentleman, in the summerhouse, and had watched my father's approach across the lawn bearing a much welcome tray of refreshments. The lawn climbs a slope several yards in front of the summerhouse, and in those days, as today, four flagstones embedded into the grass served as steps by which to negotiate this climb. It was in the vicinity of these steps that my father fell, scattering the load on his tray – teapot, cups, saucers, sandwiches, cakes – across the area of grass at the top of the steps. By the time I had received the alarm and gone out, his lordship and his guests had laid my father on his side, a cushion and a rug from the summerhouse serving as pillow and blanket. My father was unconscious and his face looked an oddly grey colour. Dr Meredith had already been sent for, but his lordship was of the view that my father should be moved out of the sun before the doctor's arrival; consequently, a bath-chair arrived and with not a little difficulty, my

▷ **5** *slender:* slim **6** *stoop* (n): special posture in which a person stands with his or her shoulders sloped forward • *pronounced* (adj): evident, distinct, obvious • *barely:* hardly **10** jolly (adv; infml): very **13** *burden:* amount of work • *lighten sth.:* reduce sth. **16** *dependability:* reliability **25–26** *wait at table:* serve food, etc. at dinner **28** *delegate* ['delɪgət] (n): person at a conference who represents a group, country, etc. **32** *repercussion:* consequence **38** *hazard* (n): risk **40** *there's no question of sth. happening:* sth. is not going to happen **43** *entry:* item written in a list or a reference book **45** *be passing*: be going to end soon **47** *jeopardize sth.:* endanger sth., risk spoiling sth. **53** *bear sth. (– bore – borne):* carry sth. **56** *flagstone:* smooth flat piece of stone used for floors, paths, etc. • *embedded:* firmly fixed **57** *negotiate sth.:* succeed in getting past or over sth. difficult • *in the vicinity of sth.:* near sth. **58** *scatter sth.:* throw lots of sth. over a wide area **61** *cushion:* Kissen • *rug:* kleiner Teppich **66** *bath-chair:* wheelchair for ill or elderly people to lie in

father was transported into the house. By the time Dr Meredith arrived, he had revived considerably and the doctor soon left again making only vague statements to the effect that my father had perhaps been 'over-working'.

The whole episode was clearly a great embarrassment to my father, and by the time of that conversation in Lord Darlington's study, he had long since returned to busying himself as much as ever. The question of how one could broach the topic of reducing his responsibilities was not, then, an easy one. My difficulty was further compounded by the fact that for some years my father and I had tended – for some reason I have never really fathomed – to converse less and less. So much so that after his arrival at Darlington Hall, even the brief exchanges necessary to communicate information relating to work took place in an atmosphere of mutual embarrassment.

In the end, I judged the best option to be to talk in the privacy of his room, thus giving him the opportunity to ponder his new situation in solitude once I took my leave. The only times my father could be found in his room were first thing in the morning and last thing at night. Choosing the former, I climbed up to his small attic room at the top of the servants' wing early one morning and knocked gently.

I had rarely had reason to enter my father's room prior to this occasion and I was newly struck by the smallness and starkness of it. Indeed, I recall my impression at the time was of having stepped into a prison cell, but then this might have had as much to do with the pale early light as with the size of the room or the bareness of its walls. For my father had opened his curtains and was sitting, shaved and in full uniform, on the edge of his bed from where evidently he had been watching the sky turn to dawn. At least one assumed he had been watching the sky, there being little else to view from his small window other than roof-tiles and guttering. The oil lamp beside his bed had been extinguished, and when I saw my father glance disapprovingly at the lamp I had brought to guide me up the rickety staircase, I quickly lowered the wick. Having done this, I noticed all the more the effect of the pale light coming into the room and the way it lit up the edges of my father's craggy, lined, still awesome features.

'Ah,' I said, and gave a short laugh, 'I might have known Father would be up and ready for the day.'

'I've been up for the past three hours,' he said, looking me up and down rather coldly.

'I hope Father is not being kept awake by his arthritic troubles.'

'I get all the sleep I need.'

My father reached forward to the only chair in the room, a small wooden one, and placing both hands on its back brought himself to his feet. When I saw him stood upright before me, I could not be sure to what extent he was hunched over due to infirmity and what extent due to the habit of accommodating the steeply sloped ceilings of the room.

'I have come here to relate something to you, Father.'

'Then relate it briefly and concisely. I haven't all morning to listen to you chatter.'

'In that case, Father, I will come straight to the point.'

'Come to the point then and be done with it. Some of us have work to be getting on with.'

'Very well. Since you wish me to be brief, I will do my best to comply. The fact is, Father has become increasingly infirm. So much so that even the duties of an under-butler are now beyond his capabilities. His lordship is of the view, as indeed I am myself, that while Father is allowed to continue with his present round of duties, he represents an ever-present threat to the smooth running of this household, and in particular to next week's important international gathering.'

My father's face, in the half-light, betrayed no emotion whatsoever.

▷ **7** *busy yourself:* (here) occupy yourself with many duties **11** *fathom sth.:* find out about sth. **14** *mutual:* for both people concerned **17** *in solitude:* alone **19** *attic:* top floor of a house, immediately below the roof **21** *rarely:* seldom • *prior to sth.* ['praɪə]: before sth. **22** *struck* (adj): astonished, mildly shocked • *starkness:* comfortlessness **25** *bareness:* emptiness **30** *roof-tile:* Dachziegel • *guttering* (n): Regenrinne **31** *extinguish sth.:* put sth. (e.g. a light or fire) out • *disapproving* (adj): showing dislike **32** *rickety:* unstable **33** *wick:* Docht **35** *craggy:* with many deep lines • *lined* (adj): marked with wrinkles • *awesome* ['ɔːsəm]: very impressive so that you feel great admiration or respect **44** *upright:* standing straight **45** *hunched over* (adj): sloping forward with bent shoulders • *infirmity:* illness **46** *accommodate sth.:* adapt to sth. • *sloped* (adj): higher at one end than at the other **48** *concise:* giving only the necessary information, short and to thc point **49** *chatter* (v): talk quickly about things that are not serious or important **58** *ever-present:* that is always there • *threat* [θret]: danger • *smooth:* without problems **60** *gathering* (n): meeting

‘Principally,’ I continued, ‘it has been felt that Father should no longer be asked to wait at table, whether or not guests are present.’

‘I have waited at table every day for the last fifty-four years,’ my father remarked, his voice perfectly unhurried.

‘Furthermore, it has been decided that Father should not carry laden trays of any sort for even the shortest distances. In view of these limitations, and knowing Father’s esteem for conciseness, I have listed here the revised round of duties he will from now on be expected to perform.’

I felt disinclined actually to hand to him the piece of paper I was holding, and so put it down on the end of his bed. My father glanced at it then returned his gaze to me. There was still no trace of emotion discernible in his expression, and his hands on the back of the chair appeared perfectly relaxed. Hunched over or not, it was impossible not to be reminded of the sheer impact of his physical presence – the very same that had once reduced two drunken gentlemen to sobriety in the back of a car. Eventually, he said:

‘I only fell that time because of those steps. They’re crooked. Seamus should be told to put those right before someone else does the same thing.’

‘Indeed. In any case, may I be assured Father will study that sheet?’

‘Seamus should be told to put those steps right. Certainly before these gentlemen start arriving from Europe.’

‘Indeed. Well, Father, good morning.’

That summer evening referred to by Miss Kenton in her letter came very soon after that encounter – indeed, it may have been the evening of that same day. I cannot remember just what purpose had taken me up on to the top floor of the house to where the row of guest bedrooms line the corridor. But as I think I have said already, I can recall vividly the way the last of the daylight was coming through each open doorway and falling across the corridor in orange shafts. As I walked on past those unused bedrooms, Miss Kenton’s figure, a silhouette against a window within one of them, had called to me.

When one thinks about it, when one remembers the way Miss Kenton had repeatedly spoken to me of my father during those early days of her time at Darlington Hall, it is little wonder that the memory of that evening should have stayed with her all of these years. No doubt, she was feeling a certain sense of guilt as the two of us watched from our window my father's figure down below. The shadows of the poplar trees had fallen across much of the lawn, but the sun was still lighting up the far corner where the grass sloped up to the summer-house. My father could be seen standing by those four stone steps, deep in thought. A breeze was slightly disturbing his hair. Then, as we watched, he walked very slowly up the steps. At the top, he turned and came back down, a little faster. Turning once more, my father became still again for several seconds, contemplating the steps before him. Eventually, he climbed them a second time, very deliberately. This time he continued on across the grass until he had almost reached the summerhouse, then turned and came walking slowly back, his eyes never leaving the ground. In fact, I can describe his manner at that moment no better than the way Miss Kenton puts it in her letter; it was indeed 'as though he hoped to find some precious jewel he had dropped there.'

But I see I am becoming preoccupied with these memories and this is perhaps a little foolish. This present trip represents, after all, a rare opportunity for me to savour to the full the many splendours of the English countryside, and I know I shall greatly regret it later if I allow myself to become unduly diverted. In fact, I notice I have yet to record here anything of my journey to this city – aside from mentioning briefly that halt on the hillside road at the very start of it. This is an omission indeed, given how much I enjoyed yesterday's motoring.

I had planned the journey here to Salisbury with considerable care, avoiding almost entirely the major roads; the route might have seemed unnecessarily circuitous to some, but then it was one that enabled me to take in a fair number of the sights recommended by Mrs J. Symons in her excellent volumes, and I must say I was well pleased with it. For much of the time it took me through farmland,

▷ **7** *esteem for sth.:* appreciation of sth. **8** *revised* (adj): new and changed **10** *disinclined* (adj): not in the mood **13** *discernible:* visible **15** *sheer impact of sth.:* powerful impression created by sth. **16** *sobriety* [sə'braɪəti]: the state of not being drunk **18** *crooked* (adj): twisted, not straight and flat **48** *deliberately:* in a determined and concentrated way **57** *savour sth.:* enjoy sth. • *splendours* (pl): the beautiful and impressive features of sth. (esp. a place) **59** *divert sb.:* take sb.'s thoughts away from the main topic **62** *omission:* thing that has been left out or not mentioned **65** *circuitous* [sə'kjuːɪtəs]: long and not direct

amidst the pleasant aroma of meadows, and often I found myself slowing the Ford to a crawl to better appreciate a stream or a valley I was passing. But as I recall, I did not actually disembark again until I was quite near Salisbury.

On that occasion, I was moving down a long, straight road with wide meadows on either side of me. In fact, the land had become very open and flat at that point, enabling one to see a considerable distance in all directions, and the spire of Salisbury Cathedral had become visible on the skyline up ahead. A tranquil mood had come over me, and for this reason I believe I was again motoring very slowly – probably at no more than fifteen miles per hour. This was just as well, for I saw only just in time a hen crossing my path in the most leisurely manner. I brought the Ford to a halt only a foot or two from the fowl, which in turn ceased its journey, pausing there in the road in front of me. When after a moment it had not moved, I resorted to the car horn, but this had no effect other than to make the creature commence pecking at something on the ground. Rather exasperated, I began to get out and had one foot still on the running board when I heard a woman's voice call:

'Oh, I do beg your pardon, sir.'

Glancing round, I saw I had just passed on the roadside a farm cottage – from which a young woman in an apron, her attention no doubt aroused by the horn, had come running. Passing me, she swooped up the hen in her arms and proceeded to cradle it as she apologized to me again. When I assured her no harm had been done, she said:

'I do thank you for stopping and not running poor Nellie over. She's a good girl, provides us with the largest eggs you've ever seen. It's so good of you to stop. And you were probably in a hurry too.'

'Oh, I'm not in a hurry at all,' I said with a smile. 'For the first time in many a year, I'm able to take my time and I must say, it's rather an enjoyable experience. I'm just motoring for the pleasure of it, you see.'

'Oh, that's nice, sir. And you're on your way to Salisbury, I expect.'

'I am indeed. In fact, that's the cathedral we can see over there, isn't it? I'm told it's a splendid building.'

'Oh, it is, sir, it's very nice. Well, to tell you the truth, I hardly go to Salisbury myself, so I couldn't really say what it's like at close quarters. But I tell you, sir, day in day out we have a view of the steeple from here. Some days, it's too misty and it's like it's vanished altogether. But you can see for yourself, on a fine day like this, it's a nice sight.'

'Delightful.'

'I'm so grateful you didn't run over our Nellie, sir. Three years ago a tortoise of ours got killed like that and on just about this very spot. We were all very upset over that.'

'How very tragic,' I said, sombrely.

'Oh, it was, sir. Some people say we farm people get used to animals being hurt or killed, but that's just not true. My little boy cried for days. It's so good you stopped for Nellie, sir. If you'd care to come in for a cup of tea, now that you've got out and everything, you'd be most welcome. It would set you on your way.'

'That's most kind, but really, I feel I should continue. I'd like to reach Salisbury in good time to take a look at the city's many charms.'

'Indeed, sir. Well, thank you again.'

I set off again, maintaining for some reason – perhaps because I expected further farm creatures to wander across my path – my slow speed of before. I must say, something about this small encounter had put me in very good spirits; the simple kindness I had been thanked for, and the simple kindness I had been offered in return, caused me somehow to feel exceedingly uplifted about the whole enterprise facing me over these coming days. It was in such a mood, then, that I proceeded here to Salisbury.

But I feel I should return just a moment to the matter of my father; for it strikes me I may have given the impression earlier that I treated

▷ **1** *amidst* (prep): in the middle of • *meadow* ['medəʊ]: field with wild grass and flowers **2** *slow sth. to a crawl:* drive sth. (esp. a car) at a very slow speed **3** *disembark:* (here) get out of a car **9** *tranquil:* calm **13** *leisurely* (adj): done without hurrying **14** *fowl* [faʊl]: a bird (e.g. a chicken) kept by a farmer • *cease sth.:* stop sth. **15** *resort to sth.:* make use of sth. to achieve sth., often because there is no longer any other solution **16** *horn:* Hupe **17** *commence:* begin, start • *peck* (v): (esp of a chicken) make quick repeated movements with the beak to find food • *exasperated* (adj): annoyed and losing your patience **22** *cottage:* small house in the country • *apron* ['eɪprən]: Schürze **24** *swoop sth. up:* pick sth. up in a sudden and quick movement • *cradle sth.* ['kreɪdl]: hold sth. gently in your arms for protection **25** *no harm has been done:* no damage or injury has occured **39** *steeple:* tall pointed tower on the roof of a church **40** *misty:* neblig • *vanish:* disappear **47** *sombre:* sad and serious **51** *and everything:* and so on **54** *charm:* (here) attraction **61** *exceedingly:* extremely, very much • *uplifted* (adj): in a very good mood

him rather bluntly over his declining abilities. The fact is, there was little choice but to approach the matter as I did – as I am sure you will agree once I have explained the full context of those days. That is to say, the important international conference to take place at Darlington Hall was by then looming ahead of us, leaving little room for indulgence or 'beating about the bush'. It is important to be reminded, moreover, that although Darlington Hall was to witness many more events of equal gravity over the fifteen or so years that followed, that conference of March 1923 was the first of them; one was, one supposes, relatively inexperienced, and inclined to leave little to chance. In fact, I often look back to that conference and, for more than one reason, regard it as a turning point in my life. For one thing, I suppose I do regard it as the moment in my career when I truly came of age as a butler. That is not to say I consider I became necessarily, a 'great' butler; it is hardly for me, in any case, to make judgements of this sort. But should it be that anyone ever wished to posit that I have attained at least a little of that crucial quality of 'dignity' in the course of my career, such a person may wish to be directed towards that conference of March 1923 as representing the moment when I demonstrated I might have a capacity for such a quality. It was one of those events which at a crucial stage in one's development arrive to challenge and stretch one to the limit of one's ability and beyond, so that thereafter one has new standards by which to judge oneself. That conference was also memorable, of course, for other quite separate reasons, as I would like now to explain.

The conference of 1923 was the culmination of long planning on the part of Lord Darlington; indeed, in retrospect, one can see clearly how his lordship had been moving towards this point from three years or so before. As I recall, he had not been initially so preoccupied with the peace treaty when it was drawn up at the end of the Great War, and I think it is fair to say that his interest was prompted not so much by an analysis of the treaty, but by his friendship with Herr Karl-Heinz Bremann.

Herr Bremann first visited Darlington Hall very shortly after the war while still in his officer's uniform, and it was evident to any observer that he and Lord Darlington had struck up a close friendship. This did not surprise me, since one could see at a glance that Herr Bremann was a gentleman of great decency. He returned again, having left the German army, at fairly regular intervals during the following two years, and one could not help noticing with some alarm the deterioration he underwent from one visit to the next. His clothes became increasingly impoverished, his frame thinner; a hunted look appeared in his eyes, and on his last visits, he would spend long periods staring into space, oblivious of his lordship's presence or, sometimes, even of having been addressed. I would have concluded Herr Bremann was suffering from some serious illness, but for certain remarks his lordship made at that time assuring me this was not so.

It must have been towards the end of 1920 that Lord Darlington made the first of a number of trips to Berlin himself, and I can remember the profound effect it had on him. A heavy air of preoccupation hung over him for days after his return, and I recall once, in reply to my inquiring how he had enjoyed his trip, his remarking: 'Disturbing, Stevens. Deeply disturbing. It does us great discredit to treat a defeated foe like this. A complete break with the traditions of this country.'

But there is another memory that has remained with me very vividly in relation to this matter. Today, the old banqueting hall no longer contains a table and that spacious room, with its high and magnificent ceiling, serves Mr Farraday well as a sort of gallery. But in his lordship's day, that room was regularly required, as was the long table that occupied it, to seat thirty or more guests for dinner; in fact, the banqueting hall is so spacious that when necessity demanded to, further tables were added to the existing one to enable almost fifty to

▷ **1** *bluntly:* in a very direct way, without showing deep or kind feelings • *declining* (adj): becoming weaker **5** *ahead of us:* before us; (here) in the very near future **6** *indulgence:* Nachgiebigkeit, Nachsichtigkeit • *beat about the bush:* avoid coming to the point when you have sth. disagreeable to say **7** *witness sth.:* (here) be the place where sth. happens **8** *gravity:* importance **10–11** *leave little to chance:* plan as best you can **14** *come of age:* prove your worth, mature **15** *for me:* up to me **24** *memorable:* worth remembering, easy to remember **29** *initially:* at the beginning **30** *peace treaty:* the Treaty of Versailles (1919), which ended the Great War (i.e. the First World War) **31** *prompt sth.:* cause sth. **36** *strike up sth.:* form or establish sth. (e.g. a friendship) **38** *decency* ['di:snsi]: Anstand **39** *at fairly regular intervals:* in ziemlich regelmäßigen Abstände **41** *deterioration:* decline in wealth, health, etc. **42** *impoverished* (adj): worse and poorer in quality • *frame:* body **43** *hunted* (adj): gehetzt **44** *oblivious:*unaware **47** *but for sth.:* if it were not for sth. **54** *do sb. discredit:* damage sb.'s reputation **55** *foe* [fəʊ]: enemy **57** *banqueting hall:* large room in which formal dinners take place **59** *gallery:* place where works of art are hung

be seated. On normal days, of course, Lord Darlington took his meals, as does Mr Farraday today, in the more intimate atmosphere of the dining room, which is ideal for accommodating up to a dozen. But on that particular winter's night I am recollecting the dining room was for some reason out of use, and Lord Darlington was dining with a solitary guest – I believe it was Sir Richard Fox, a colleague from his lordship's Foreign Office days – in the vastness of the banqueting hall. You will no doubt agree that the hardest of situations as regards dinner-waiting is when there are just two diners present. I would myself much prefer to wait on just one diner, even if he were a total stranger. It is when there are two diners present, even when one of them is one's own employer, that one finds it most difficult to achieve that balance between attentiveness and the illusion of absence that is essential to good waiting; it is in this situation that one is rarely free of the suspicion that one's presence is inhibiting the conversation.

On that occasion, much of the room was in darkness, and the two gentlemen were sitting side by side midway down the table – it being much too broad to allow them to sit facing one another – within the pool of light cast by the candles on the table and the crackling hearth opposite. I decided to minimize my presence by standing in the shadows much further away from table than I might usually have done. Of course, this strategy had a distinct disadvantage in that each time I moved towards the light to serve the gentlemen, my advancing footsteps would echo long and loud before I reached the table, drawing attention to my impending arrival in the most ostentatious manner; but it did have the great merit of making my person only partially visible while I remained stationary. And it was as I was standing like that, in the shadows some distance from where the two gentlemen sat amidst those rows of empty chairs, that I heard Lord Darlington talk about Herr Bremann, his voice as calm and gentle as usual, somehow resounding with intensity around those great walls.

'He was my enemy,' he was saying, 'but he always behaved like a gentleman. We treated each other decently over six months of shelling each other. He was a gentleman doing his job and I bore him no malice. I said to him: "Look here, we're enemies now and I'll fight you with all I've got. But when this wretched business is over, we shan't have to be enemies any more and we'll have a drink together." Wretched thing is, this treaty is making a liar out of me. I mean to say,

I told him we wouldn't be enemies once it was all over. But how can I look him in the face and tell him that's turned out to be true?'

And it was a little later that same night that his lordship said with some gravity, shaking his head: 'I fought that war to preserve justice in this world. As far as I understood, I wasn't taking part in a vendetta against the German race.'

And when today one hears talk about his lordship, when one hears the sort of foolish speculations concerning his motives as one does all too frequently these days, I am pleased to recall the memory of that moment as he spoke those heartfelt words in the near-empty banqueting hall. Whatever complications arose in his lordship's course over subsequent years, I for one will never doubt that a desire to see 'justice in this world' lay at the heart of all his actions.

It was not long after that evening there came the sad news that Herr Bremann had shot himself in a train between Hamburg and Berlin. Naturally, his lordship was greatly distressed and immediately made plans to dispatch funds and commiserations to Frau Bremann. However, after several days of endeavour, in which I myself did my best to assist, his lordship was not able to discover the whereabouts of any of Herr Bremann's family. He had, it seemed, been homeless for some time and his family dispersed.

It is my belief that even without this tragic news, Lord Darlington would have set upon the course he took; his desire to see an end to injustice and suffering was too deeply ingrained in his nature

▷ **4** *recollect sth.:* (here) talk about sth. you remember **7** *Foreign Office:* (in GB) ministry for foreign affairs • *vastness:* extremely large space **13** *attentiveness:* concentration on taking care of sb.'s needs **15** *inhibit sth.:* prevent sth. from developing as well as it could **19** *crackle:* make the short sharp sound of sth. burning in a fire • *hearth* [hɑːð]: fireplace **25** *impending* (adj): (often of sth. unpleasant) going to happen very soon • *ostentatious:* (here) attracting other people's attention **26** *merit* (n): advantage **27** *stationary:* not moving **31** *resound* (v): echo **34** *shell sb.:* attack sb. with shells (= Granaten) **34–35** *bear sb. no malice:* not consider that sb. is doing sth. wrong or blame them for their actions **36** *wretched* ['retʃɪd]: very bad, terrible **42** *preserve sth.:* keep sth., maintain sth. **43** *vendetta:* long and violent fight in which you continually weaken your enemy **54** *distressed* (adj): extremely upset and shocked **55** *dispatch sth.:* send sth. • *funds* (pl): money • *commiserations* (pl): expression of sympathy to sb. who has lost a loved one **56** *endeavour* (n): effort **57** *the whereabouts:* the place where sb. is **59** *dispersed* (adj): separated and living in different places **62** *ingrained* (adj): firmly established

for him to have done otherwise. As it was, in the weeks that followed Herr Bremann's death, his lordship began to devote more and more hours to the matter of the crisis in Germany. Powerful and famous gentlemen became regular visitors to the house – including, I remember, figures such as Lord Daniels, Mr John Maynard Keynes, and Mr H.G. Wells, the renowned author, as well as others who, because they came 'off the record', I should not name here – and they and his lordship were often to be found locked in discussion for hours on end.

Some of the visitors were, in fact, so 'off the record' that I was instructed to make sure the staff did not learn their identities, or in some cases, even glimpse them. However – and I say this with some pride and gratitude – Lord Darlington never made any efforts to conceal things from my own eyes and ears; I can recall on numerous occasions, some personage breaking off in mid-sentence to glance warily towards my person, only for his lordship to say: 'Oh, that's all right. You can say anything in front of Stevens, I can assure you.'

Steadily, then, over the two years or so following Herr Bremann's death, his lordship, together with Sir David Cardinal, who became his closest ally during that time, succeeded in gathering together a broad alliance of figures who shared the conviction that the situation in Germany should not be allowed to persist. These were not only Britons and Germans, but also Belgians, French, Italians, Swiss; they were diplomats and political persons of high rank; distinguished clergymen; retired military gentlemen; writers and thinkers. Some were gentlemen who felt strongly, like his lordship himself, that fair play had not been done at Versailles and that it was immoral to go on punishing a nation for a war that was now over. Others, evidently, showed less concern for Germany or her inhabitants, but were of the opinion that the economic chaos of that country, if not halted, might spread with alarming rapidity to the world at large.

By the turn of 1922, his lordship was working with a clear goal in mind. This was to gather under the very roof of Darlington Hall the most influential of the gentlemen whose support had been won with a view to conducting an 'unofficial' international conference – a conference that would discuss the means by which the harshest terms of the Versailles treaty could be revised. To be worthwhile, any such conference would have to be of sufficient weight so that it could have a decisive effect on the 'official' international conferences – several of which had already taken place with the express purpose of reviewing the treaty, but which had succeeded in producing only confusion and bitterness. Our Prime Minister of that time, Mr Lloyd George, had called for another great conference to be held in Italy in the spring of 1922, and initially his lordship's aim was to organize a gathering at Darlington Hall with a view to ensuring a satisfactory outcome to this event. For all the hard work on his and Sir David's part, however, this proved too harsh a deadline; but then with Mr George's conference ending yet again in indecision, his lordship set his sights on a further great conference scheduled to take place in Switzerland that following year.

I can remember one morning around this time bringing Lord Darlington coffee in the breakfast room, and his saying to me as he folded *The Times* with some disgust: 'Frenchmen. Really, I mean to say, Stevens. Frenchmen.'

'Yes, sir.'

'And to think we have to be seen by the world to be arm in arm with them. One wishes for a good bath at the mere reminder.'

'Yes, sir.'

'Last time I was in Berlin, Stevens, Baron Overath, old friend of my father, came up and said: "Why do you do this to us? Don't you see we can't go on like this?" I was jolly well tempted to tell him it's those wretched Frenchmen. It's not the English way of carrying on, I wanted to say. But I suppose one can't do things like that. Mustn't speak ill of our dear allies.'

But the very fact that the French were the most intransigent as regards releasing Germany from the cruelties of the Versailles treaty

▷ **5** *John Maynard Keynes* (1883–1946): British economist **6** *H.G. Wells* (1866–1946): English writer and social thinker • *renowned* [rɪ'naʊnd] (adj): famous **9** *off the record:* unofficial, secret **13** *numerous:* many **15** *wary* ['weəri]: cautious, suspicious **19** *ally* ['ælaɪ]: person who helps and supports you to achieve sth. **20** *alliance* [ə'laɪəns]: group with similar ideas and plans **21** *persist:* continue in the same way **24** *clergyman:* priest or minister of the Christian church **30** *rapidity:* very fast movement **35** *harsh:* hard, tough **36** *revise sth.:* change sth. **39** *express* (adj): explicit, clearly and openly stated **41** *Lloyd George = David Lloyd George* (1863–1945): British Prime Minister (1916–1922) **44** *outcome* (n): result **46** *too harsh a deadline:* too early a date to do the necessary work beforehand successfully **48** *schedule sth.:* fix or plan sth. **52** *disgust* (n): strong feeling of dislike **56** *at the mere reminder:* when anyone mentions it **63** *speak ill of sb.:* say bad things about sb. **64** *intransigent:* unwilling to change their ideas **65** *release sb. from sth.:* free sb. from sth.

made all the more imperative the need to bring to the gathering at Darlington Hall at least one French gentleman with unambiguous influence over his country's foreign policy. Indeed, I heard several times his lordship express the view that without the participation of such a personage, any discussion on the topic of Germany would be little more than an indulgence. He and Sir David accordingly set upon this final crucial lap of their preparations and to witness the unswerving determination with which they persevered in the face of repeated frustrations was a humbling experience; countless letters and telegrams were dispatched and his lordship himself made three separate trips to Paris within the space of two months. Finally, having secured the agreement of a certain extremely illustrious Frenchman – I will merely call him 'M. Dupont' – to attend the gathering on a very strict 'off the record' basis, the date for the conference was set. That is to say, for that memorable March of 1923.

As this date grew ever nearer, the pressures on myself, though of an altogether more humble nature than those mounting on his lordship, were nevertheless not inconsequential. I was only too aware of the possibility that if any guest were to find his stay at Darlington Hall less than comfortable, this might have repercussions of unimaginable largeness. Moreover, my planning for the event was complicated by the uncertainty as to the numbers involved. The conference being of a very high level, the participants had been limited to just eighteen very distinguished gentlemen and two ladies – a German countess and the formidable Mrs Eleanor Austin, at the time still resident in Berlin; but each of these might reasonably bring secretaries, valets and interpreters, and there proved no way of ascertaining the precise number of such persons to expect. Furthermore, it became clear that a number of the parties would be arriving some time before the three days set aside for the conference, thus giving themselves time to prepare their ground and gauge the mood of fellow guests, though their exact arrival dates were, again, uncertain. It was clear then that the staff would not only have to work extremely hard, and be at their most alert, they would also have to be unusually flexible. In fact, I was for some time of the opinion that this huge challenge ahead of us could not be surmounted without my bringing in additional staff from outside. However, this option, quite aside from the misgivings his lordship was bound to have as regards gossip travelling, entailed my having to rely on unknown quantities just when a mistake could prove most costly. I thus set about preparing for the days ahead as, I imagine, a general might prepare for a battle: I devised with utmost care a special staff plan anticipating all sorts of eventualities; I analysed where our weakest points lay and set about making contingency plans to fall back upon in the event of these points giving way; I even gave the staff a military-style 'pep-talk', impressing upon them that, for all their having to work at an exhausting rate, they could feel great pride in discharging their duties over the days that lay ahead. 'History could well be made under this roof,' I told them. And they, knowing me to be one not prone to exaggerated statements, well understood that something of an extraordinary nature was impending.

You will understand then something of the climate prevailing around Darlington Hall by the time of my father's fall in front of the summerhouse – this occurring as it did just two weeks before the first of the conference guests were likely to arrive – and what I mean when I say there was little room for any 'beating about the bush'. My father did, in any case, rapidly discover a way to circumvent the limitations on his effectiveness implied by the stricture that he should carry no laden trays. The sight of his figure pushing a trolley loaded with cleaning utensils, mops, brushes arranged incongruously, though always tidily, around teapots, cups and saucers, so that it at times resembled a street-hawker's barrow, became a familiar one around

▷ **1** *imperative:* necessary **2** *unambiguous:* definite, clear, obvious **7** *lap:* part, section **8** *unswerving* (adj): very strong and never changing • *persevere:* continue trying to do sth. and work hard to achieve it **9** *humbling* (adj): making sb. feel humble **12** *illustrious:* famous **18** *inconsequential:* unimportant **25** *formidable:* very impressive • *resident* (adj): living in a particular place **27** *interpreter:* translator • *ascertain sth.* [ˌæsəˈteɪn]: find out about sth. **30** *set sth. aside for sth. else:* keep sth. (esp. time) for sth. particular **31** *gauge sth.* [geɪdʒ]: form a correct idea of sth., find out about sth. **34** *alert* (adj): always watchful and ready to act **36** *surmount sth.:* overcome sth., cope with sth. difficult **37** *misgiving* (n; usu. pl): feeling of doubt, mistrust or fear **40** *costly* (adj): harmful, disastrous **42** *anticipate sth.:* prepare for sth. that might happen in the future • *eventuality:* unexpected event that might happen **43** *contingency plan:* plan in order to deal with unexpected events that might happen **45** *pep-talk* (infml): a speech that is intended to encourage sb. to work harder and be full of confidence **51** *prevail:* exist **56** *circumvent sth.:* avoid sth. in a clever or dishonest way **57** *stricture:* a rule that limits you **59** *utensil:* tool **61** *street-hawker:* person who carries goods from place to place and tries to sell them • *barrow:* Karren

the house. Obviously he still could not avoid relinquishing his waiting duties in the dining room, but otherwise the trolley enabled him to accomplish a surprising amount. In fact, as the great challenge of the conference drew nearer, an astonishing change seemed to come over my father. It was almost as though some supernatural force possessed him, causing him to shed twenty years; his face lost much of the sunken look of recent times, and he went about his work with such youthful vigour that a stranger might have believed there were not one but several such figures pushing trolleys about the corridors of Darlington Hall.

As for Miss Kenton, I seem to remember the mounting tension of those days having a noticeable effect upon her. I recall, for instance, the occasion around that time I happened to encounter her in the back corridor. The back corridor, which serves as a sort of backbone to the staff's quarters of Darlington Hall, was always a rather cheerless affair due to the lack of daylight penetrating its considerable length. Even on a fine day, the corridor could be so dark that the effect was like walking through a tunnel. On that particular occasion, had I not recognized Miss Kenton's footsteps on the boards as she came towards me, I would have been able to identify her only from her outline. I paused at one of the few spots where a bright streak of light fell across the boards and, as she approached, said: 'Ah, Miss Kenton.'

'Yes, Mr Stevens?'

'Miss Kenton, I wonder if I may draw your attention to the fact that the bed linen for the upper floor will need to be ready by the day after tomorrow.'

'The matter is perfectly under control, Mr Stevens.'

'Ah, I'm very glad to hear it. It just struck me as a thought, that's all.'

I was about to continue on my way, but Miss Kenton did not move. Then she took one step more towards me so that a bar of light fell across her face and I could see the angry expression on it.

'Unfortunately, Mr Stevens, I am extremely busy now and I am finding I have barely a single moment to spare. If only I had as much spare time as you evidently do, then I would happily reciprocate by wandering about this house reminding *you* of tasks you have perfectly well in hand.'

'Now, Miss Kenton, there is no need to become so bad-tempered. I merely felt the need to satisfy myself that it had not escaped your attention ...'

'Mr Stevens, this is the fourth or fifth time in the past two days you have felt such a need. It is most curious to see that you have so much time on your hands that you are able to simply wander about this house bothering others with gratuitous comments.'

'Miss Kenton, if you for one moment believe I have time on my hands, that displays more clearly than ever your great inexperience. I trust that in years to come, you will gain a clearer picture of what occurs in a house like this.'

'You are perpetually talking of my "great inexperience", Mr Stevens, and yet you appear quite unable to point out any defect in my work. Otherwise I have no doubt you would have done so long ago and at some length. Now, I have much to be getting on with and would appreciate your not following me about and interrupting me like this. If you have so much time to spare, I suggest it might be more profitably spent taking some fresh air.'

She stamped past me and on down the corridor. Deciding it best to let the matter go no further, I continued on my way. I had almost reached the kitchen doorway when I heard the furious sounds of her footsteps coming back towards me again.

'In fact, Mr Stevens,' she called, 'I would ask you from now on not to speak to me directly at all.'

'Miss Kenton, whatever are you talking about?'

'If it is necessary to convey a message, I would ask you to do so through a messenger. Or else you may like to write a note and have it sent to me. Our working relationship, I am sure, would be made a great deal easier.'

'Miss Kenton ...'

'I am extremely busy, Mr Stevens. A written note if the message is at all complicated. Otherwise you may like to speak to Martha or Dorothy, or any members of the male staff you deem sufficiently trustworthy. Now I must return to my work and leave you to your wanderings.'

▷ **1** *relinquish sth.:* give sth. up, no longer do sth. **6** *shed twenty years:* (here) look twenty years younger **8** *vigour:* energy **15** *cheerless:* making you feel sad, bored or uncomfortable **21** *streak:* line **30** *bar:* narrow band **34** *reciprocate:* do sth. because a similar thing has been done to you **43** *gratuitous:* unasked for, superfluous **48** *perpetually:* all the time **69** *deem sb.:* consider sb. (to have a particular quality) **70** *trustworthy:* reliable

Irritating as Miss Kenton's behaviour was, I could not afford to give it much thought, for by then the first of the guests had arrived. The representatives from abroad were not expected for a further two or three days, but the three gentlemen referred to by his lordship as his 'home team' – two Foreign Office ministers attending very much 'off the record' and Sir David Cardinal – had come early to prepare the ground as thoroughly as possible. As ever, little was done to conceal anything from me as I went in and out of the various rooms in which these gentlemen sat deep in discussion, and I thus could not avoid gaining a certain impression of the general mood at this stage of the proceedings. Of course, his lordship and his colleagues were concerned to brief each other as accurately as possible on each one of the expected participants; but overwhelmingly, their concerns centred on a single figure – that of M. Dupont, the French gentleman – and on his likely sympathies and antipathies. Indeed, at one point, I believe I came into the smoking room and heard one of the gentlemen saying: 'The fate of Europe could actually hang on our ability to bring Dupont round on this point.'

It was in the midst of these preliminary discussions that his lordship entrusted me with a mission sufficiently unusual for it to have remained in my memory to this day, alongside those other more obviously unforgettable occurrences that were to take place during that remarkable week. Lord Darlington called me into his study, and I could see at once that he was in a state of some agitation. He seated himself at his desk and, as usual, resorted to holding open a book – this time it was *Who's Who* – turning a page to and fro.

'Oh, Stevens,' he began with a false air of nonchalance, but then seemed at a loss how to continue. I remained standing there ready to relieve his discomfort at the first opportunity. His lordship went on fingering his page for a moment, leaned forward to scrutinize an entry, then said: 'Stevens, I realize this is a somewhat irregular thing to ask you to do.'

'Sir?'

'It's just that one has so much of importance on one's mind just now.'

'I would be very glad to be of assistance, sir.'

'I'm sorry to bring up a thing like this, Stevens. I know you must be awfully busy yourself. But I can't see how on earth to make it go away.'

I waited a moment while Lord Darlington returned his attention to *Who's Who*. Then he said, without looking up: 'You are familiar, I take it, with the facts of life.'

'Sir?'

'The facts of life, Stevens. Birds, bees. You are familiar, aren't you?'

'I'm afraid I don't quite follow you, sir.'

'Let me put my cards on the table, Stevens. Sir David is a very old friend. And he's been invaluable in organizing the present conference. Without him, I dare say, we'd not have secured M. Dupont's agreement to come.'

'Indeed, sir.'

'However, Stevens, Sir David has his funny side. You may have noticed it yourself. He's brought his son, Reginald, with him. To act as secretary. The point is, he's engaged to be married. Young Reginald, I mean.'

'Yes, sir.'

'Sir David has been attempting to tell his son the facts of life for the last five years. The young man is now twenty-three.'

'Indeed, sir.'

'I'll get to the point, Stevens. I happen to be the young man's godfather. Accordingly, Sir David has requested that *I* convey to young Reginald the facts of life.'

'Indeed, sir.'

'Sir David himself finds the task rather daunting and suspects he will not accomplish it before Reginald's wedding day.'

'Indeed, sir.'

'The point is, Stevens, I'm terribly busy. Sir David should know that, but he's asked me none the less.' His lordship paused and went on studying his page.

▷ **12** *brief sb. on sth./sb.:* inform sb. in detail about sth./sb. **13** *participant:* person taking part in sth. • *overwhelmingly:* to a great extent **18** *bring sb. round on sth.:* convince sb. of sth. **24** *agitation:* nervous excitement **26** *Who's Who:* reference book containing information about all the important living people (esp. in Britain) • *to and fro:* hin und her, vor und zurück **27** *nonchalance:* calm behaviour that makes sb. appear unconcerned about sth. **29** *relieve sb.'s discomfort:* (here) help sb. overcome their uneasiness **31** *irregular:* unusual **36** *assistance:* help **46** *invaluable:* extremely useful **47** *I dare say:* I think, I imagine **59** *godfather:* Pate **63** *accomplish sth.:* achieve sth., manage to do sth.

'Do I understand, sir,' I said, 'that you wish *me* to convey the information to the young gentleman?'

'If you don't mind, Stevens. Be an awful lot off my mind. Sir David continues to ask me every couple of hours if I've done it yet.'

'I see, sir. It must be most trying under the present pressures.'

'Of course, this is far beyond the call of duty, Stevens.'

'I will do my best, sir. I may, however, have difficulty finding the appropriate moment to convey such information.'

'I'd be very grateful if you'd even try, Stevens. Awfully decent of you. Look here, there's no need to make a song and dance of it. Just convey the basic facts and be done with it. Simple approach is the best, that's my advice, Stevens.'

'Yes, sir. I shall do my best.'

'Jolly grateful to you, Stevens. Let me know how you get on.'

I was, as you might imagine, a little taken aback by this request and ordinarily the matter might have been one I would have spent some time pondering. Coming upon me as it did, however, in the midst of such a busy period, I could not afford to let it preoccupy me unduly, and I thus decided I should resolve it at the earliest opportunity. As I recall, then, it was only an hour or so after being first entrusted with the mission that I noticed the young Mr Cardinal alone in the library, sitting at one of the writing tables, absorbed in some documents. On studying the young gentleman closely, one could, as it were, appreciate the difficulty experienced by his lordship – and indeed, by the young gentleman's father. My employer's godson looked an earnest, scholarly young man, and one could see many fine qualities in his features; yet given the topic one wished to raise, one would have certainly preferred a lighter-hearted, even more frivolous sort of young gentleman. In any case, resolved to bring the whole matter to a satisfactory conclusion as quickly as possible, I proceeded further into the library, and stopping a little way from Mr Cardinal's writing desk, gave a cough.

'Excuse me, sir, but I have a message to convey to you.'

'Oh, really?' Mr Cardinal said eagerly, looking up from his papers. 'From Father?'

'Yes, sir. That is, effectively.'

'Just a minute.'

The young gentleman reached down to the attaché case at his feet and brought out a notebook and pencil. 'Fire away, Stevens.'

I coughed again and set my voice into as impersonal a tone as I could manage.

'Sir David wishes you to know, sir, that ladies and gentlemen differ in several key respects.'

I must have paused a little to form my next phrase, for Mr Cardinal gave a sigh and said: 'I'm only too aware of that, Stevens. Would you mind coming to the point?'

'You are aware, sir?'

'Father is perpetually underestimating me. I've done extensive reading and background work on this whole area.'

'Is that so, sir?'

'I've thought about virtually nothing else for the past month.'

'Really, sir. In that case, perhaps my message is rather redundant.'

'I can assure Father I'm well briefed indeed. This attaché case' – he nudged it with his foot – 'is chock-full of notes on every possible angle one can imagine.'

'Is that so, sir?'

'I really think I've thought through every permutation the human mind is capable of. I wish you'd reassure Father of that.'

'I will, sir.'

Mr Cardinal seemed to relax a little. He prodded once more his attaché case – which I felt inclined to keep my eyes averted from – and said: 'I suppose you've been wondering why I never let go of this case. Well, now you know. Imagine if the wrong person opened it.'

'That would be most awkward, sir.'

'That is, of course,' he said, sitting up again suddenly, 'unless Father has come up with an entirely new factor he wants me to think about.'

'I cannot imagine he has, sir.'

'No? Nothing more on this Dupont fellow?'

'I fear not, sir.'

▷ **5** *trying* (adj): annoying, difficult **22** *absorbed in sth.*: deeply interested in sth. so that you do not pay attention to anything else **26** *scholarly* (adj): having a lot of learning and enjoying studying **39** *fire away:* go ahead **48** *underestimate sb.*: think that sb. is not as good or clever as they really are • *extensive:* wide, a lot of **52** *redundant:* not necessary (because known already) **54** *nudge sth.*: push sth. gently **57** *permutation:* variation **60** *prod sth.*: push sth. with your finger **61** *keep your eyes averted from sth.*: not look at sth.

I did my best not to give away anything of my exasperation on discovering that a task I had thought all but behind me was in fact still there unassaulted before me. I believe I was collecting my thoughts for a renewed effort when the young gentleman suddenly rose to his feet and clutching his attaché case to his person, said: 'Well, I think I'll go and take a little fresh air. Thanks for your help, Stevens.'

It had been my intention to seek out a further interview with Mr Cardinal with minimum delay, but this proved to be impossible, owing largely to the arrival that same afternoon – some two days earlier than expected – of Mr Lewis, the American senator. I had been down in my pantry working through the supplies sheets, when I heard somewhere above my head the unmistakable sounds of motor cars pulling up in the courtyard. As I hastened to go upstairs, I happened to encounter Miss Kenton in the back corridor – the scene, of course, of our last disagreement – and it was perhaps this unhappy coincidence that encouraged her to maintain the childish behaviour she had adopted on that previous occasion. For when I inquired who it was that had arrived, Miss Kenton continued past me, stating simply: 'A message if it is urgent, Mr Stevens.' This was extremely annoying, but, of course, I had no choice but to hurry on upstairs.

My recollection of Mr Lewis is that of a gentleman of generous dimensions with a genial smile that rarely left his face. His early arrival was clearly something of an inconvenience to his lordship and his colleagues who had reckoned on a day or two more of privacy for their preparations. However, Mr Lewis's engagingly informal manner, and his statement at dinner that the United States 'would always stand on the side of justice and didn't mind admitting mistakes had been made at Versailles' seemed to do much to win the confidence of his lordship's 'home team'; as dinner progressed, the conversation had slowly but surely turned from topics such as the merits of Mr Lewis's native Pennsylvania back to the conference ahead, and by the time the gentlemen were lighting their cigars, some of the speculations being offered appeared to be as intimate as those exchanged prior to Mr Lewis's arrival. At one point, Mr Lewis said to the company:

'I agree with you, gentlemen, our M. Dupont can be very unpredictable. But let me tell you, there's one thing you can bet on about him. One thing you can bet on for sure.' He leaned forward and waved his cigar for emphasis. 'Dupont hates Germans. He hated them before the war and he hates them now with a depth you gentlemen here would find hard to understand.' With that, Mr Lewis sat back in his chair again, the genial smile returning fully to his face. 'But tell me, gentlemen,' he continued, 'you can hardly blame a Frenchman for hating the Germans, can you? After all, a Frenchman has good cause to do so, hasn't he?'

There was a moment of slight awkwardness as Mr Lewis glanced around the table. Then Lord Darlington said:

'Naturally, some bitterness is inevitable. But then, of course, we English also fought the Germans long and hard.'

'But the difference with you Englishmen,' Mr Lewis said, 'seems to be that you don't really hate the Germans any more. But the way the French see it, the Germans destroyed civilization here in Europe and no punishment is too bad for them. Of course, that looks an impractical kind of position to us in the United States, but what's always puzzled me is how you English don't seem to share the view of the French. After all, like you say, Britain lost a lot in that war too.'

There was another awkward pause before Sir David said, rather uncertainly:

'We English have often had a different way of looking at such things from the French, Mr Lewis.'

'Ah. A kind of temperamental difference, you might say.' Mr Lewis's smile seemed to broaden slightly as he said this. He nodded to himself, as though many things had now become clear to him, and drew on his cigar. It is possible this is a case of hindsight colouring my memory, but I have a distinct feeling that it was at that moment I first sensed something odd, something duplicitous perhaps, about this apparently charming American gentleman. But if my own suspicions were aroused at that moment, Lord Darlington evidently did not share them. For after another second or two of awkward silence, his lordship seemed to come to a decision.

▷ **3** *unassaulted:* not yet faced or dealt with **11** *supplies* (pl): things (e.g. food) which are needed by a group of people **21** *recollection:* memory **22** *genial* ['dʒiːnɪəl]: cheerful and friendly **23** *inconvenience:* thing that causes difficulty or does not fit into sb.'s plans **24** *reckon on sth.:* expect sth., plan for sth. **25** *engaging* (adj): attractive in a way that wins people over **37** *unpredictable:* unvorhersehbar • *bet on sth.* (infml): be absolutely sure of sth. **40** *depth:* Tiefe **67** *sense sth.:* feel sth. • *duplicitous:* dishonest, intending to deceive

'Mr Lewis,' he said, 'let me put it frankly. Most of us in England find the present French attitude despicable. You may indeed call it a temperamental difference, but I venture we are talking about something rather more. It is unbecoming to go on hating an enemy like this once a conflict is over. Once you've got a man on the canvas, that ought to be the end of it. You don't then proceed to kick him. To us, the French behaviour has become increasingly barbarous.'

This utterance seemed to give Mr Lewis some satisfaction. He muttered something in sympathy and smiled with contentment at his fellow diners through the clouds of tobacco smoke by now hanging thickly across the table.

The next morning brought more early arrivals; namely, the two ladies from Germany – who had travelled together despite what one would have imagined to have been the great contrast in their backgrounds – bringing with them a large team of ladies-in-waiting and footmen, as well as a great many trunks. Then in the afternoon, an Italian gentleman arrived accompanied by a valet, a secretary, an 'expert' and two bodyguards. I cannot imagine what sort of place this gentleman imagined he was coming to in bringing the latter, but I must say it struck something of an odd note to see in Darlington Hall these two large silent men staring suspiciously in all directions a few yards from wherever the Italian gentleman happened to be. Incidentally, the working pattern of these bodyguards, so it transpired over the following days, entailed one or the other of them going up to sleep at unusual hours so as to ensure at least one was on duty throughout the night. But when on first hearing of this arrangement I tried to inform Miss Kenton of it, she once again refused to converse with me, and in order to accomplish matters as quickly as possible I was actually obliged to write a note and put it under the door of her parlour.

The following day brought several more guests and with two days yet to go to the start of the conference, Darlington Hall was filled with people of all nationalities, talking in rooms, or else standing around, apparently aimlessly, in the hall, in corridors and on landings, examining pictures or objects. The guests were never less than courteous to one another, but for all that, a rather tense atmosphere, characterized largely by distrust, seemed to prevail at this stage. And reflecting this unease, the visiting valets and footmen appeared to regard one another with marked coldness and my own staff were rather glad to be too busy to spend much time with them.

It was around this point, in the midst of dealing with the many demands being made on my attention, that I happened to glance out of a window and spotted the figure of the young Mr Cardinal taking some fresh air around the grounds. He was clutching his attaché case as usual and I could see he was strolling slowly along the path that runs the outer perimeter of the lawn, deeply absorbed in thought. I was of course reminded of my mission regarding the young gentleman and it occurred to me that an outdoor setting, with the general proximity of nature, and in particular the example of the geese close at hand, would not be an unsuitable setting at all in which to convey the sort of message I was bearing. I could see, moreover, that if I were quickly to go outside and conceal my person behind the large rhododendron bush beside the path, it would not be long before Mr Cardinal came by. I would then be able to emerge and convey my message to him. It was not, admittedly, the most subtle of strategies, but you will appreciate that this particular task, though no doubt important in its way, hardly took the highest priority at that moment.

There was a light frost covering the ground and much of the foliage, but it was a mild day for that time of the year. I crossed the grass quickly, placed my person behind the bush, and before long heard Mr Cardinal's footsteps approaching. Unfortunately, I misjudged slightly the timing of my emergence. I had intended to emerge while Mr Cardinal was still a reasonable distance away, so that he would see me in good time and suppose I was on my way to the summerhouse, or perhaps to the gardener's lodge. I could then have pretended to notice him for the first time and have engaged him

▷ **1** *frank:* open, honest **2** *despicable:* extremely unpleasant, hateful **4** *unbecoming* (adj): unfitting, unsuitable **5** *get a man on the canvas:* bring a man down (in a boxing match) **8** *utterance:* statement **15** *lady-in-waiting:* lady who accompanies a woman of higher social rank in order to help her **16** *trunk:* very large suitcase **20** *note* (n): Ton **23** *working pattern:* system of doing a job **24** *transpire:* become clear **36** *courteous:* polite **39** *marked* (adj): very clear and easy to notice **43** *spot sb./sth.:* suddenly see sb./sth. **46** *perimeter* [pəˈrɪmɪtə]: border around an enclosed area **48–49** *with the general proximity of nature:* with nature being very close **55** *subtle:* not easy to notice or understand **57** *priority* [praɪˈɒrɪti]: importance **62** *I misjudged … emergence:* I came out at the wrong moment **65** *lodge* (n): small house on the grounds of a large estate

in conversation in an impromptu manner. As it happened, I emerged a little late and I fear I rather startled the young gentleman, who immediately pulled his attaché case away from me and clutched it to his chest with both arms.

'I'm very sorry, sir.'

'My goodness, Stevens. You gave me a shock. I thought things were hotting up a bit there.'

'I'm very sorry, sir. But as it happens, I have something to convey to you.'

'My goodness, yes, you gave me quite a fright.'

'If I may come straight to the point, sir. You will notice the geese not far from us.'

'Geese?' He looked around a little bewildered. 'Oh yes. That's what they are.'

'And likewise the flowers and shrubs. This is not, in fact, the best time of year to see them in their full glory, but you will appreciate, sir, that with the arrival of spring, we will see a change – a very special sort of change – in the surroundings.'

'Yes, I'm sure the grounds are not at their best just now. But to be perfectly frank, Stevens, I wasn't paying much attention to the glories of nature. It's all rather worrying. That M. Dupont's arrived in the foulest mood imaginable. Last thing we wanted really.'

'M. Dupont has arrived here at this house, sir?'

'About half an hour ago. He's in the most foul temper.'

'Excuse me, sir. I must attend to him straight away.'

'Of course, Stevens. Well, kind of you to have come out to talk to me.'

'Please excuse me, sir. As it happened, I had a word or two more to say on the topic of – as you put it yourself – the glories of nature. If you will indulge me by listening, I would be most grateful. But I am afraid this will have to wait for another occasion.'

'Well, I shall look forward to it, Stevens. Though I'm more of a fish man myself. I know all about fish, fresh water and salt.'

'All living creatures will be relevant to our forthcoming discussion, sir. However, you must now please excuse me. I had no idea M. Dupont had arrived.'

I hurried back to the house to be met immediately by the first footman saying: 'We've been looking all over for you, sir. The French gentleman's arrived.'

M. Dupont was a tall, elegant gentleman with a grey beard and a monocle. He had arrived in the sort of clothes one often sees continental gentlemen wearing on their holidays, and indeed, throughout his stay, he was to maintain diligently the appearance of having come to Darlington Hall entirely for pleasure and friendship. As Mr Cardinal had indicated, M. Dupont had not arrived in a good temper; I cannot recall now all the various things that had upset him since his arrival in England a few days previously, but in particular he had obtained some painful sores on his feet while sightseeing around London and these, he feared, were growing septic. I referred his valet to Miss Kenton, but this did not prevent M. Dupont snapping his fingers at me every few hours to say: 'Butler! I am in need of more bandages.'

His mood seemed much lifted on seeing Mr Lewis. He and the American senator greeted each other as old colleagues and they were to be seen together for much of the remainder of the day, laughing over reminiscences. In fact, one could see that Mr Lewis's almost constant proximity to M. Dupont was proving a serious inconvenience to Lord Darlington, who was naturally keen to make close personal contact with this distinguished gentleman before the discussions began. On several occasions I witnessed his lordship make attempts to draw M. Dupont aside for some private conversation, only for Mr Lewis smilingly to impose himself upon them with some remark like: 'Pardon me, gentlemen, but there's something that's been greatly puzzling me,' so that his lordship soon found himself having to listen to some more of Mr Lewis's jovial anecdotes. Mr Lewis apart, however, the other guests, perhaps through awe, perhaps through a sense of antagonism, kept a wary distance from M. Dupont, a fact that was conspicuous even in that generally guarded atmosphere, and which seemed to underline all the more the

▷ **1** *in an impromptu manner:* as if done without any preparation or planning **2** *startle sb.:* surprise sb. **7** *hot up* (infml): become tense **13** *bewildered* [bɪ'wɪldəd] (adj): confused **15** *likewise:* also • *shrub:* small bush **29–30** *if you will indulge me by listening:* if you will be so kind as to listen **43** *diligent:* taking great care and effort **45** *temper:* mood **48** *sore* (n): painful area on the skin caused by a wound **49** *septic* (adj): infected with bacteria **50** *snap your fingers:* move your fingers so that they make a short sharp noise **55** *reminiscence* (n): memory of an event that people shared and later talk about **61** *impose yourself upon sb.:* join sb. even though they do not really want your company **65** *awe* [ɔː]: feeling of great respect **68** *guarded* (adj): cautious

feeling that it was M. Dupont who somehow held the key to the outcome of the following days.

The conference began on a rainy morning during the last week of March 1923 in the somewhat unlikely setting of the drawing room – a venue chosen to accommodate the 'off the record' nature of many of the attendances. In fact, to my eyes, the appearance of informality had been taken to a faintly ludicrous degree. It was odd enough to see that rather feminine room crammed full with so many stern, dark-jacketed gentlemen, sometimes sitting three or four abreast upon a sofa; but such was the determination on the part of some persons to maintain the appearance that this was nothing more than a social event that they had actually gone to the lengths of having journals and newspapers open on their knees.

I was obliged during the course of that first morning to go constantly in and out of the room, and so was unable to follow the proceedings at all fully. But I recall Lord Darlington opening the discussions by formally welcoming the guests, before going on to outline the strong moral case for a relaxing of various aspects of the Versailles treaty, emphasizing the great suffering he had himself witnessed in Germany. Of course, I had heard these same sentiments expressed by his lordship on many occasions before, but such was the depth of conviction with which he spoke in this august setting that I could not help but be moved afresh. Sir David Cardinal spoke next, and though I missed much of his speech, it seemed to be more technical in substance, and quite frankly, rather above my head. But his general gist seemed to be close to his lordship's, concluding with a call for a freezing of German reparation payments and the withdrawal of French troops from the Ruhr region. The German countess then began to speak, but I was at this point, for some reason I do not recollect, obliged to leave the drawing room for an extended period. By the time I re-entered, the guests were in open debate, and the discussion – with much talk of commerce and interest rates – was quite beyond me.

M. Dupont, so far as I could observe, was not contributing to the discussion, and it was hard to tell from his sullen demeanour if he was attending carefully to what was being said or else deeply engrossed in other thoughts. At one stage, when I happened to depart the room in the midst of an address by one of the German gentlemen, M. Dupont suddenly rose and followed me out.

'Butler,' he said, once we were in the hall, 'I wonder if I could have my feet changed. They are giving me so much discomfort now, I can hardly listen to these gentlemen.'

As I recall, I had conveyed a plea to Miss Kenton for assistance – via a messenger, naturally – and had left M. Dupont sitting in the billiard room awaiting his nurse, when the first footman had come hurrying down the staircase in some distress to inform me that my father had been taken ill upstairs.

I hurried up to the first floor and on turning at the landing was met by a strange sight. At the far end of the corridor, almost in front of the large window, at that moment filled with grey light and rain, my father's figure could be seen frozen in a posture that suggested he was taking part in some ceremonial ritual. He had dropped down on to one knee and with head bowed seemed to be pushing at the trolley before him, which for some reason had taken on an obstinate immobility. Two chambermaids were standing at a respectful distance, watching his efforts in some awe. I went to my father and releasing his hands from their grip on the edge of the trolley, eased him down on to the carpet. His eyes were closed, his face was an ashen colour, and there were beads of sweat on his forehead. Further assistance was called, a bath-chair arrived in due course, and my father was transported up to his room.

Once my father had been laid in his bed, I was a little uncertain as to how to proceed; for while it seemed undesirable that I leave my father in such a condition, I did not really have a moment to spare. As I stood hesitating in the doorway, Miss Kenton appeared at my side

▷ **7** *ludicrous:* ridiculous **8** *stern:* unpleasantly strict **9** *abreast:* next to each other **12** *go to the lengths of sth.:* put in too much effort into doing sth. (when it is not necessary) **26** *gist:* idea, main point **27** *freezing* (n): decision which stops sb. from having to pay money to sb. • *reparation payments:* money paid by a country to other countries for damage it has caused (esp. after a war) **28** *withdrawal:* removal • *Ruhr region:* In January 1923 French and Belgian troops occupied the Ruhr region to force Germany to pay reparations. **30** *extended* (adj): quite long **32** *interest rate:* Zinssatz **35** *sullen:* mürrisch, missmutig **41** *discomfort:* feeling of slight pain **43** *plea* (n): urgent request, call for help **46** *distress* (n): feeling of great worry **51** *frozen:* fixed • *posture:* position in which you hold your body **55** *obstinate:* stubborn **58** *ease sb. down:* lay sb. down carefully **64** *a moment to spare:* a free moment

and said: 'Mr Stevens, I have a little more time than you at the moment. I shall, if you wish, attend to your father. I shall show Dr Meredith up and notify you if he has anything noteworthy to say.'

'Thank you, Miss Kenton,' I said, and took my leave.

When I returned to the drawing room, a clergyman was talking about the hardships being suffered by children in Berlin. I immediately found myself more than occupied replenishing the guests with tea and coffee. A few of the gentlemen, I noticed, were drinking spirits, and one or two, despite the presence of the two ladies, had started to smoke. I was, I recall, leaving the drawing room with an empty teapot in my hand when Miss Kenton stopped me and said: 'Mr Stevens, Dr Meredith is just leaving now.'

As she said this, I could see the doctor putting on his mackintosh and hat in the hall and so went to him, the teapot still in my hand. The doctor looked at me with a disgruntled expression. 'Your father's not so good,' he said. 'If he deteriorates, call me again immediately.'

'Yes, sir. Thank you, sir.'

'How old is your father, Stevens?'

'Seventy-two, sir.'

Dr Meredith thought about this, then said again: 'If he deteriorates, call me immediately.'

I thanked the doctor again and showed him out.

It was that evening, shortly before dinner, that I overheard the conversation between Mr Lewis and M. Dupont. I had for some reason gone up to M. Dupont's room and was about to knock, but before doing so, as is my custom, I paused for a second to listen at the door. You may not yourself be in the habit of taking this small precaution to avoid knocking at some highly inappropriate moment, but I always have been and can vouch that it is common practice amongst many professionals. That is to say, there is no subterfuge implied in such an action, and I for one had no intention of overhearing to the extent I did that evening. However, as fortune would have it, when I put my ear to M. Dupont's door, I happened to hear Mr Lewis's voice, and though I cannot recall precisely the actual words I first heard, it was the tone of his voice that raised my suspicions. I was listening to the same genial, slow voice with which the American gentleman had charmed many since his arrival and yet it now contained something unmistakably covert. It was this realization along with the fact that he was in M. Dupont's room, presumably addressing this most crucial personage, that caused me to stop my hand from knocking, and continue to listen instead.

The bedroom doors of Darlington Hall are a certain thickness and I could by no means hear complete exchanges; consequently, it is hard for me now to recall precisely what I overheard, just as, indeed, it was for me later that same evening when I reported to his lordship on the matter. Nevertheless, this is not to say I did not gain a fairly clear impression of what was taking place within the room. In effect, the American gentleman was putting forward the view that M. Dupont was being manipulated by his lordship and other participants at the conference; that M. Dupont had been deliberately invited late to enable the others to discuss important topics in his absence; that even after his arrival, it was to be observed that his lordship was conducting small private discussions with the most important delegates without inviting M. Dupont. Then Mr Lewis began to report certain remarks his lordship and others had made at dinner on that first evening after his arrival.

'To be quite frank, sir,' I heard Mr Lewis say, 'I was appalled at their attitude towards your countrymen. They actually used words like "barbarous" and "despicable". In fact, I noted them in my diary only a few hours afterwards.'

M. Dupont said something briefly which I did not catch, then Mr Lewis said again: 'Let me tell you, sir, I was appalled. Are these words to use about an ally you stood shoulder to shoulder with only a few years back?'

I am not sure now if I ever proceeded to knock; it is quite possible, given the alarming nature of what I heard, that I judged it best to withdraw altogether. In any case, I did not linger long enough – as I was obliged to explain to his lordship shortly afterwards – to hear anything that would give a clue as to M. Dupont's attitude to Mr Lewis's remarks.

▷ **3** *notify sb.:* inform sb. • *noteworthy:* important **6** *hardship:* extreme difficulty **7** *replenish sb. with sth.:* serve sb. with sth. again **9** *spirits* (pl): strong alcoholic drinks **13** *mackintosh:* type of raincoat **15** *disgruntled* (adj): unhappy **16** *deteriorate:* get worse **23** *overhear sth.:* hear sth. accidentally and without being noticed by the people talking **26** *as is sb.'s custom:* like sb. usually does **30** *subterfuge:* secret trick **38** *covert* ['kəʊvɜːt]: secret or hidden **57** *appalled* [ə'pɔːld]: shocked **67** *linger:* stay

The next day, the discussion in the drawing room appeared to reach a new level of intensity and by lunchtime, the exchanges were becoming rather heated. My impression was that utterances were being directed accusingly, and with increasing boldness, towards the armchair where M. Dupont sat fingering his beard, saying little. Whenever the conference adjourned, I noticed, as no doubt his lordship did with some concern, that Mr Lewis would quickly take M. Dupont away to some corner or other where they could confer quietly. Indeed, once, shortly after lunch, I recall I came upon the two gentlemen talking rather furtively just inside the library doorway, and it was my distinct impression they broke off their discussion upon my approach.

In the meantime, my father's condition had grown neither better nor worse. As I understood, he was asleep for much of the time, and indeed, I found him so on the few occasions I had a spare moment to ascend to that little attic room. I did not then have a chance actually to converse with him until that second evening after the return of his illness.

On that occasion, too, my father was sleeping when I entered. But the chambermaid Miss Kenton had left in attendance stood up upon seeing me and began to shake my father's shoulder.

'Foolish girl!' I exclaimed. 'What do you think you are doing?'

'Mr Stevens said to wake him if you returned, sir.'

'Let him sleep. It's exhaustion that's made him ill.'

'He said I had to, sir,' the girl said, and again shook my father's shoulder.

My father opened his eyes, turned his head a little on the pillow, and looked at me.

'I hope Father is feeling better now,' I said.

He went on gazing at me for a moment, then asked: 'Everything in hand downstairs?'

'The situation is rather volatile. It is just after six o'clock, so Father can well imagine the atmosphere in the kitchen at this moment.'

An impatient look crossed my father's face. 'But is everything in hand?' he said again.

'Yes, I dare say you can rest assured on that. I'm very glad Father is feeling better.'

With some deliberation, he withdrew his arms from under the bedclothes and gazed tiredly at the backs of his hands. He continued to do this for some time.

'I'm glad Father is feeling so much better,' I said again eventually. 'Now really, I'd best be getting back. As I say, the situation is rather volatile.'

He went on looking at his hands for a moment. Then he said slowly: 'I hope I've been a good father to you.'

I laughed a little and said: 'I'm so glad you're feeling better now.'

'I'm proud of you. A good son. I hope I've been a good father to you. I suppose I haven't.'

'I'm afraid we're extremely busy now, but we can talk again in the morning.'

My father was still looking at his hands as though he were faintly irritated by them.

'I'm so glad you're feeling better now,' I said and took my leave.

On descending, I found the kitchen on the brink of pandemonium, and in general, an extremely tense atmosphere amongst all levels of staff. However, I am pleased to recall that by the time dinner was served an hour or so later, nothing but efficiency and professional calm was exhibited on the part of my team.

It was always something of a memorable sight to see that magnificent banqueting hall employed to its full capacity and that evening was no exception. Of course, the effect produced by unbroken lines of gentlemen in evening suits, so outnumbering representatives of the fairer sex, was a rather severe one; but then again, in those days, the two large chandeliers that hang over the table still ran on gas – resulting in a subtle, quite soft light pervading the room – and did not produce the dazzling brightness they have done ever since their electrification. On that second and final dinner of the conference – most guests were expected to disperse after lunch the following day –

▷ **4** *boldness:* feeling that you are not afraid to say what you want to **6** *adjourn:* finish or stop for a break, etc. **8** *confer* [- '-]: discuss with the hope of reaching a decision **10** *furtive:* secretive **15** *ascend:* go up **23** *exhaustion:* extreme tiredness **31** *volatile:* likely to change quickly and become dangerous **35** *rest assured on sth.:* be sure of sth. **51** *irritated* (adj): annoyed and impatient **53** *descend:* go down • *on the brink of sth.:* very close to becoming sth. • *pandemonium:* wild and noisy disorder **56** *efficiency:* competence, effectiveness **57** *exhibit sth.:* show sth. **61** *outnumber sb.:* be greater in number than sb. **62** *severe:* lacking in decoration **63** *chandelier:* Kronleuchter **64** *pervade sth.:* spread through every part of sth. **65** *dazzling* (adj): very bright so it is difficult to look at **67** *disperse:* go away to the places they came from

the company had lost much of the reserve that had been noticeable throughout the previous days. Not only was the conversation glowing more freely and loudly, we found ourselves serving out wine at a conspicuously increased rate. At the close of dinner, which from a professional viewpoint had been executed without any significant difficulties, his lordship rose to address his guests.

He opened by expressing his gratitude to all present that the discussions during the previous two days, 'though at times exhilaratingly frank', had been conducted in a spirit of friendship and the desire to see good prevail. The unity witnessed over the two days had been greater than he could ever have hoped for, and the remaining morning's session of 'rounding up' would, he trusted, be rich in commitments on the part of participants concerning action each would be taking before the important international conference in Switzerland. It was around this point – and I have no idea if he had planned to do so beforehand – that his lordship began to reminisce about his late friend, Herr Karl-Heinz Bremann. This was a little unfortunate, the topic being one close to his lordship's heart and one he was inclined to explicate at some length. It should also be said, perhaps, that Lord Darlington was never what might be called a natural public speaker, and soon all those small sounds of restlessness that betray that an audience's attention has been lost grew steadily around the room. Indeed, by the time Lord Darlington had finally come round to bidding his guests rise and drink to 'peace and justice in Europe', the level of such noises – perhaps on account of the liberal amounts of wine that had been consumed – struck me as bordering on the ill-mannered.

The company had seated themselves again, and conversation was just beginning to resume, when there came an authoritative rapping of knuckles upon wood and M. Dupont had risen to his feet. At once, a hush fell over the room. The distinguished gentleman glanced around the table with a look almost of severity. Then he said: 'I hope I am not trespassing over a duty ascribed to someone else present here, but then I had heard no proposals for anyone to give a toast in thanks to our host, the most honourable and kind Lord Darlington.' There was a murmur of approval. M. Dupont went on: 'Many things of interest have been said in this house over the past days. Many important things.' He paused, and there was now utter stillness in the room.

'There has been much', he continued, 'which has implicitly or otherwise *criticized* – it is not so strong a word – *criticized* the foreign policy of my country.' He paused again, looking rather stern. One might even have thought him to be angry. 'We have heard in these two days several thorough and intelligent analyses of the present very complex situation in Europe. But none of them, may I say, has fully comprehended the reasons for the attitude France has adopted towards her neighbour. However,' – he raised a finger – 'this is not the time to enter into such debates. In fact, I deliberately refrained from entering into such debates during these past days because I came principally to listen. And let me say now that I have been impressed by certain of the arguments I have heard here. But how impressed, you may be asking.' M. Dupont took another pause during which his gaze travelled in an almost leisurely manner around all the faces fixed upon him. Then at last he said: 'Gentlemen – and ladies, pardon me – I have given much thought to these matters and I wish to say here in confidence to you, that while there remains between myself and many of those present differences of interpretation as to what is really occurring in Europe at this moment, despite this, as to the main points that have been raised in this house, I am convinced, gentlemen, convinced both of their justice and their practicality.' A murmur which seemed to contain both relief and triumph went round the table, but this time M. Dupont raised his voice slightly and pronounced over it: 'I am happy to assure you all here that I will bring what modest influence I have to encourage certain changes of emphasis in French policy in accordance with much of what has been said here. And I will endeavour to do so in good time for the Swiss conference.'

▷ **1** *reserve* (n): feeling that you cannot express your ideas openly **8–9** *exhilarating:* exciting **10** *prevail* (v): win **13** *commitment:* statement in which sb. promises to do something **16** *beforehand:* before the event • *reminisce:* recount memories **19** *explicate sth.:* talk in much and usu. unnecessary detail about sth. **21–22** *restlessness:* impatience **26** *liberal amounts:* rather large quantity **27** *border on the ill-mannered:* be almost impolite **29–30** *rapping of knuckles:* knocking (on the table) with the middle part of one's fingers **31** *hush* (n): silence (after there has been some noise) **32** *severity:* strictness **33** *trespass over sth.:* (here) wrongfully do sth. which sb. else should do **38** *utter* (adj): absolute, total **43** *thorough:* profound, complete **45** *comprehend sth.:* understand sth. completely **55** *in confidence:* relying on sb.'s trustfulness **59** *practicality:* workability, feasibility **63** *modest influence:* little influence

There was a ripple of applause, and I saw his lordship exchange a look with Sir David. M. Dupont held up his hand, though whether to acknowledge the applause or to stem it was not clear.

'But before I go on to thank our host, Lord Darlington, I have some small thing I would wish to remove from my chest. Some of you may say it is not good manners to be removing such things from one's chest at the dinner table.' This brought enthusiastic laughter. 'However, I am for frankness in these matters. Just as there is an imperative to express gratitude formally and publicly to Lord Darlington, who has brought us here and made possible this present spirit of unity and goodwill, there is, I believe, an imperative to openly condemn any who come here to abuse the hospitality of the host, and to spend his energies solely in trying to sow discontent and suspicion. Such persons are not only socially repugnant, in the climate of our present day they are extremely dangerous.' He paused again and once more there was utter stillness. M. Dupont went on in a calm deliberate voice: 'My only question concerning Mr Lewis is this. To what extent does his abominable behaviour exemplify the attitude of the present American administration? Ladies and gentlemen, let me myself hazard a guess as to the answer, for such a gentleman capable of the levels of deceit he has displayed over these past days should not be relied upon to provide a truthful reply. So I will hazard my guess. Of course, America is concerned about our debt payments to her in the event of a freeze in German reparations. But I have over the last six months had occasion to discuss this very matter with a number of very highly placed Americans, and it seems to me that thinking in that country is much more far-sighted than that represented by their countryman here. All those of us who care for the future well-being of Europe will take comfort from the fact that Mr Lewis is now – how shall we put it? – hardly the influence he once was. Perhaps you think me unduly harsh to express these things so openly. But the reality is, ladies and gentlemen, I am being merciful. You see, I refrain from outlining just what this gentleman has been saying to me – *about you all.* And with a most clumsy technique, the audacity and crudeness of which I could hardly believe. But enough of condemnations. It is time for us to thank. Join me then, please, ladies and gentlemen, in raising your glasses to Lord Darlington.'

M. Dupont had not once looked over in Mr Lewis's direction during the course of this speech, and indeed, once the company had toasted his lordship and were seated again, all those present seemed to be studiously avoiding looking towards the American gentleman. An uneasy silence reigned for a moment, and then finally Mr Lewis rose to his feet. He was smiling pleasantly in his customary manner.

'Well, since everyone's giving speeches, I may as well take a turn,' he said, and it was at once apparent from his voice that he had had a good deal to drink. 'I don't have anything to say to the nonsense our French friend has been uttering. I just dismiss that sort of talk. I've had people try to put one over on me many times, and let me tell you, gentlemen, few people succeeded. Few people succeeded.' Mr Lewis came to a halt and for a moment seemed at a loss as to how he should go on. Eventually he smiled again and said: 'As I say, I'm not going to waste my time on our French friend over there. But as it happens, I do have something to say. Now we're all being so frank, I'll be frank too. You gentlemen here, forgive me, but you are just a bunch of naïve dreamers. And if you didn't insist on meddling in large affairs that affect the globe, you would actually be charming. Let's take our good host here. What is he? He is a gentleman. No one here, I trust, would care to disagree. A classic English gentleman. Decent, honest, well-meaning. But his lordship here is *an amateur*.' He paused at the word and looked around the table. 'He is an amateur and international affairs today are no longer for gentlemen amateurs. The sooner you here in Europe realize that the better. All you decent, well-meaning gentlemen, let me ask you, have you any idea what sort of place the world is becoming all around you? The days when you could act out of your noble instincts are over. Except of course, you here in Europe don't yet seem to know it. Gentlemen like our good host still believe it's their business to meddle in matters they

▷ **1** *ripple* (n): small wave **3** *acknowledge sth.:* show that you have noticed and accepted sth. • *stem sth.:* stop sth. **6** *remove sth. from your chest:* get rid of sth. that is a burden **11** *condemn sb./sth.:* express strong criticism of sb./sth. **12** *abuse sth.* [ə'bju:z]: use sth. for the wrong purpose **13** *solely:* only • *sow sth.* [səʊ]: etwas säen **14** *repugnant:* very unpleasant and offensive **18** *abominable:* extremely unpleasant • *exemplify sth.:* illustrate sth. clearly **23** *debt:* sum of money that sb. owes **29** *comfort:* satisfaction **32** *merciful:* kind and forgiving **34** *clumsy:* lacking in skill • *audacity:* Unverfrorenheit, Dreistigkeit • *crudeness:* rudeness, vulgarity **41** *studiously:* carefully **42** *reign:* dominate **47** *dismiss sth.:* refuse to consider sth. seriously **48** *put one over on sb.* (infml): deceive sb., win against sb. **55** *meddle:* deliberately get involved in a situation that is none of your concern or that you do not understand **56** *affect the globe:* be important for the whole world

don't understand. So much hog-wash has been spoken here these past two days. Well-meaning, naïve hog-wash. You here in Europe need professionals to run your affairs. If you don't realize that soon you're headed for disaster. A toast, gentlemen. Let me make a toast. To professionalism.'

There was a stunned silence and no one moved. Mr Lewis shrugged, raised his glass to all the company, drank and sat back down. Almost immediately, Lord Darlington stood up.

'I have no wish,' his lordship said, 'to enter into a quarrel on this our last evening together which we all deserve to enjoy as a happy and triumphant occasion. But it is out of respect for your views, Mr Lewis, that I feel one should not simply cast them to one side as though they were uttered by some soap-box eccentric. Let me say this. What you describe as "amateurism", sir, is what I think most of us here still prefer to call "honour".'

This brought a loud murmur of assent with several 'hear, hear's and some applause.

'What is more, sir,' his lordship went on, 'I believe I have a good idea of what you mean by "professionalism". It appears to mean getting one's way by cheating and manipulating. It means ordering one's priorities according to greed and advantage rather than the desire to see goodness and justice prevail in the world. If that is the "professionalism" you refer to, sir, I don't much care for it and have no wish to acquire it.'

This was met by the loudest burst of approval yet, followed by warm and sustained applause. I could see Mr Lewis smiling at his wine glass and shaking his head wearily. It was just around this stage that I became aware of the first footman beside me, who whispered: 'Miss Kenton would like a word with you, sir. She's just outside the door.'

I made my exit as discreetly as possible just as his lordship, still on his feet, was embarking on a further point.

Miss Kenton looked rather upset. 'Your father has become very ill, Mr Stevens,' she said. 'I've called for Dr Meredith, but I understand he may be a little delayed.'

I must have looked a little confused, for Miss Kenton then said: 'Mr Stevens, he really is in a poor state. You had better come and see him.'

'I only have a moment. The gentlemen are liable to retire to the smoking room at any moment.'

'Of course. But you must come now, Mr Stevens, or else you may deeply regret it later.'

Miss Kenton was already leading the way, and we hurried through the house up to my father's small attic room. Mrs Mortimer, the cook, was standing over my father's bed, still in her apron.

'Oh, Mr Stevens,' she said upon our entry, 'he's gone very poorly.'

Indeed, my father's face had gone a dull reddish colour, like no colour I had seen on a living being. I heard Miss Kenton say softly behind me: 'His pulse is very weak.' I gazed at my father for a moment, touched his forehead slightly, then withdrew my hand.

'In my opinion,' Mrs Mortimer said, 'he's suffered a stroke. I've seen two in my time and I think he's suffered a stroke.' With that, she began to cry. I noticed she reeked powerfully of fat and roast cooking. I turned away and said to Miss Kenton:

'This is most distressing. Nevertheless, I must now return downstairs.'

'Of course, Mr Stevens. I will tell you when the doctor arrives. Or else when there are any changes.'

'Thank you, Miss Kenton.'

I hurried down the stairs and was in time to see the gentlemen proceeding into the smoking room. The footmen looked relieved to see me, and I immediately signalled them to get to their positions.

Whatever had taken place in the banqueting hall after my departure, there was now a genuinely celebratory atmosphere amongst the guests. All around the smoking room, gentlemen seemed to be standing in clusters laughing and clapping each other on the shoulder. Mr Lewis, so far as I could ascertain, had already retired. I found myself making my way through the guests, a decanter of port upon my tray. I had just finished serving a glass to a gentleman when a voice behind me said: 'Ah. Stevens, you're interested in fish, you say.'

▷ **1** *hog-wash:* stupid talk **4** *head for disaster:* go in a direction that will end up in a catastrophe **6** *stunned* (adj): surprised and shocked **7** *shrug* (v): mit den Achseln zucken **12** *cast sth.:* throw sth. **13** *soap-box eccentric:* person with odd views which they tell people about loudly and forcefully (usu. while standing on a box in order to be visible) **16** *assent* (n): agreement **21** *greed:* Gier **26** *sustained* (adj): that continues for a long time **34** *be delayed:* arrive later than planned **44** *poorly* (infml): ill **49** *stroke* (n): Schlaganfall **51** *reek of sth.:* smell strongly and unpleasantly of sth. **53** *distressing* (adj): unpleasant **64** *cluster:* small group **66** *decanter:* glass container for alcoholic drinks • *port:* strong sweet Portuguese wine

I turned to find the young Mr Cardinal beaming happily at me. I smiled also and said: 'Fish, sir?'

'When I was young, I used to keep all sorts of tropical fish in a tank. Quite a little aquarium it was. I say, Stevens, are you all right?'

I smiled again. 'Quite all right, thank you, sir.'

'As you so rightly pointed out, I really should come back here in spring. Darlington Hall must be rather lovely then. The last time I was here, I think it was winter then too. I say, Stevens, are you sure you're all right there?'

'Perfectly all right, thank you, sir.'

'Not feeling unwell, are you?'

'Not at all, sir. Please excuse me.'

I proceeded to serve port to some other of the guests. There was a loud burst of laughter behind me and I heard the Belgian clergyman exclaim: 'That is really heretical! Positively heretical!' then laugh loudly himself. I felt something touch my elbow and turned to find Lord Darlington.

'Stevens, are you all right?'

'Yes, sir. Perfectly'

'You look as though you're crying.'

I laughed and taking out a handkerchief, quickly wiped my face. 'I'm very sorry, sir. The strains of a hard day.'

'Yes, it's been hard work.'

Someone addressed his lordship and he turned away to reply. I was about to continue further around the room when I caught sight of Miss Kenton through the open doorway, signalling to me. I began to make my way towards the doors, but before I could reach them, M. Dupont touched my arm.

'Butler,' he said, 'I wonder if you would find me some fresh bandages. My feet are unbearable again.'

'Yes, sir.'

As I proceeded towards the doors, I realized M. Dupont was following me. I turned and said: 'I will come and find you, sir, just as soon as I have what is required.'

'Please hurry, butler. I am in some pain.'

'Yes, sir. I'm very sorry, sir.'

Miss Kenton was still standing out in the hall where I had first spotted her. As I emerged, she walked silently towards the staircase, a curious lack of urgency in her manner. Then she turned and said:

'Mr Stevens, I'm very sorry. Your father passed away about four minutes ago.'

'I see.'

She looked at her hands, then up at my face. 'Mr Stevens, I'm very sorry', she said. Then she added: 'I wish there was something I could say.'

'There's no need, Miss Kenton.'

'Dr Meredith has not yet arrived.' Then for a moment she bowed her head and a sob escaped her. But almost immediately, she resumed her composure and asked in a steady voice: 'Will you come up and see him?'

'I'm very busy just now, Miss Kenton. In a little while perhaps.'

'In that case, Mr Stevens, will you permit me to close his eyes?'

'I would be most grateful if you would, Miss Kenton.'

She began to climb the staircase, but I stopped her, saying: 'Miss Kenton, please don't think me unduly improper in not ascending to see my father in his deceased condition just at this moment. You see, I know my father would have wished me to carry on just now.'

'Of course, Mr Stevens.'

'To do otherwise, I feel, would be to let him down.'

'Of course, Mr Stevens.'

I turned away, the decanter of port still on my tray, and re-entered the smoking room. That relatively small room appeared to be a forest of black dinner jackets, grey hair and cigar smoke. I wended my way past the gentlemen, searching for glasses to replenish. M. Dupont tapped my shoulder and said:

'Butler, have you seen to my arrangements?'

'I am very sorry, sir, but assistance is not immediately available at this precise moment.'

'What do you mean, butler? You've run out of basic medical supplies?'

'As it happens, sir, a doctor is on his way.'

'Ah, very good! You called a doctor.'

▷ **1** *beam* (v): smile very happily **3** *tank:* large container for liquid or gas **15** *heretical:* ketzerisch **22** *strain* (n): severe demand on sb.'s mental or physical strength **39** *curious:* strange **48** *sob* (n): Schluchzen **49** *composure:* state of being calm and in control of your feelings **55** *improper:* not doing what should be done **56** *in sb.'s deceased condition:* (here) dead **59** *let sb. down:* disappoint sb. **63** *wend your way:* move slowly in a certain direction

'Yes, sir.'

'Good, good.'

M. Dupont resumed his conversation and I continued my way around the room for some moments. At one point, the German countess emerged from the midst of the gentlemen and before I had had a chance to serve her, began helping herself to some port from my tray.

'You will compliment the cook for me, Stevens,' she said.

'Of course, madam. Thank you, madam.'

'And you and your team did well also.'

'Thank you most kindly, madam.'

'At one point during dinner, Stevens, I would have sworn you were at least three people,' she said and laughed.

I laughed quickly and said: 'I'm delighted to be of service, madam.'

A moment later, I spotted the young Mr Cardinal not far away, still standing on his own, and it struck me the young gentleman might be feeling somewhat overawed in the present company. His glass, in any case, was empty and so I started towards him. He seemed greatly cheered at the prospect of my arrival and held out his glass.

'I think it's admirable that you're a nature-lover, Stevens,' he said, as I served him. 'And I dare say it's a great advantage to Lord Darlington to have someone to keep an expert eye on the activities of the gardener.'

'I'm sorry, sir?'

'Nature, Stevens. We were talking the other day about the wonders of the natural world. And I quite agree with you, we are all much too complacent about the great wonders that surround us.'

'Yes, sir.'

'I mean, all this we've been talking about. Treaties and boundaries and reparations and occupations. But Mother Nature just carries on her own sweet way. Funny to think of it like that, don't you think?'

'Yes, indeed it is, sir.'

'I wonder if it wouldn't have been better if the Almighty had created us all as – well – as sort of plants. You know, firmly embedded in the soil. Then none of this rot about wars and boundaries would have come up in the first place.'

The young gentleman seemed to find this an amusing thought. He gave a laugh, then on further thought laughed some more. I joined him in his laughter. Then he nudged me and said: 'Can you imagine it, Stevens?' and laughed again.

'Yes, sir,' I said, laughing also, 'it would have been a most curious alternative.'

'But we could still have chaps like you taking messages back and forth, bringing tea, that sort of thing. Otherwise, how would we ever get anything done? Can you imagine it, Stevens? All of us rooted in the soil? Just imagine it!'

Just then a footman emerged behind me. 'Miss Kenton is wishing to have a word with you, sir,' he said.

I excused myself from Mr Cardinal and moved towards the doors. I noticed M. Dupont apparently guarding them and as I approached, he said: 'Butler, is the doctor here?'

'I am just going to find out, sir. I won't be a moment.'

'I am in some pain.'

'I'm very sorry, sir. The doctor should not be long now.'

On this occasion, M, Dupont followed me out of the door. Miss Kenton was once more standing out in the hall.

'Mr Stevens,' she said, 'Dr Meredith has arrived and gone upstairs.'

She had spoken in a low voice, but M. Dupont behind me exclaimed immediately: 'Ah, good!'

I turned to him and said: 'If you will perhaps follow me, sir.'

I led him into the billiard room where I stoked the fire while he sat down in one of the leather chairs and began to remove his shoes.

'I'm sorry it is rather cold in here, sir. The doctor will not be long now.'

'Thank you, butler. You've done well.'

Miss Kenton was still waiting for me in the hallway and we ascended through the house in silence. Up in my father's room, Dr Meredith was making some notes and Mrs Mortimer weeping bitterly. She was still wearing her apron, which, evidently, she had been using to wipe away her tears; as a result there were grease marks all over her face, giving her the appearance of a participant in a minstrel show. I had expected the room to smell of death, but on account of Mrs Mortimer – or else her apron – the room was dominated by the smell of roasting.

▷ **16** *overawed* (adj): impressed so that you feel nervous **18** *cheered* (adj): feeling happier than before • *prospect:* Aussicht **26** *complacent* [kəm'pleɪsənt]: gleichgültig **32** *the Almighty:* God **34** *soil:* ground • *rot* (infml): nonsense **60** *stoke the fire:* add more coal or wood to keep the fire going **61** *remove sth.:* take sth. off **68** *grease:* animal fat **70** *minstrel show:* popular type of musical show in the 1920s in which actors painted their faces black

Dr Meredith rose and said: 'My condolences, Stevens. He suffered a severe stroke. If it's any comfort to you, he wouldn't have suffered much pain. There was nothing in the world you could have done to save him.'

'Thank you, sir.'

'I'll be on my way now. You'll see to arrangements?'

'Yes, sir. However, if I may, there is a most distinguished gentleman downstairs in need of your attention.'

'Urgent?'

'He expressed a keen desire to see you, sir.'

I led Dr Meredith downstairs, showed him into the billiard room, then returned quickly to the smoking room where the atmosphere, if anything, had grown even more convivial.

Of course, it is not for me to suggest that I am worthy of ever being placed alongside the likes of the 'great' butlers of our generation, such as Mr Marshall or Mr Lane – though it should be said there are those who, perhaps out of misguided generosity, tend to do just this. Let me make clear that when I say the conference of 1923, and that night in particular, constituted a turning point in my professional development, I am speaking very much in terms of my own more humble standards. Even so, if you consider the pressures contingent on me that night, you may not think I delude myself unduly if I go so far as to suggest that I did perhaps display, in the face of everything, at least in some modest degree a 'dignity' worthy of someone like Mr Marshall – or come to that, my father. Indeed, why should I deny it? For all its sad associations, whenever I recall that evening today, I find I do so with a large sense of triumph.

▷ **1** *condolences* (pl): expressions of sympathy and comfort for sb. who has just lost a family member **13** *convivial:* friendly and pleasantly cheerful **17** *misguided* (adj): wrong, not properly thought out • *generosity:* Großzügigkeit **21** *the pressures contingent on sb.:* (here) the pressures sb. is under **22** *delude sb.:* make sb. think sth. that is not true **26** *for all its sad associations:* (here) in spite of all the sad things connected with it

DAY TWO – AFTERNOON

Mortimer's Pond, Dorset

It would seem there is a whole dimension to the question 'what is a "great" butler?' I have hitherto not properly considered. It is, I must say, a rather unsettling experience to realize this about a matter so close to my heart, particularly one I have given much thought to over the years. But it strikes me I may have been a little hasty before in dismissing certain aspects of the Hayes Society's criteria for membership. I have no wish, let me make clear, to retract any of my ideas on 'dignity' and its crucial link with 'greatness'. But I have been thinking a little more about that other pronouncement made by the Hayes Society – namely the admission that it was a prerequisite for membership of the Society that 'the applicant be attached to a distinguished household'. My feeling remains, no less than before, that this represents a piece of unthinking snobbery on the part of the Society. However, it occurs to me that perhaps what one takes objection to is, specifically, the outmoded understanding of what a 'distinguished household' is, rather than to the general principle being expressed. Indeed, now that I think further on the matter, I believe it may well be true to say it *is* a prerequisite of greatness that one 'be attached to a distinguished household' – so long as one takes 'distinguished' here to have a meaning deeper than that understood by the Hayes Society.

In fact, a comparison of how I might interpret 'a distinguished household' with what the Hayes Society understood by that term illuminates sharply, I believe, the fundamental difference between the values of our generation of butlers and those of the previous generation. When I say this, I am not merely drawing attention to the fact that our generation had a less snobbish attitude as regards which employers were landed gentry and which were 'business'. What I am trying to say – and I do not think this an unfair comment – is that we were a much more idealistic generation. Where our elders might have been concerned with whether or not an employer was titled, or otherwise from one of the 'old' families, we tended to concern ourselves much more with the *moral* status of an employer. I do not mean by this that we were preoccupied with our employers' private

▷ **2** *hitherto:* until now **3** *unsettling* (adj): making sb. feel nervous or upset **6** *dismiss sth.:* reject sth. **7** *retract sth.:* say that sth. you said earlier was not correct **10** *admission:* Zugeständnis **14** *take objection* (usu. *exception*) *to sth.:* object to sth., criticize sth. **15** *outmoded* (adj): no longer up to date, outdated **23** *illuminate sth.:* make sth. clearer **27** *landed gentry:* families that have owned a lot of land for a long time

behaviour. What I mean is that we were ambitious, in a way that would have been unusual a generation before, to serve gentlemen who were, so to speak, furthering the progress of humanity. It would have been seen as a far worthier calling, for instance, to serve a gentleman such as Mr George Ketteridge, who however humble his beginnings, has made an undeniable contribution to the future well-being of the empire, than any gentleman, however aristocratic his origin, who idled away his time in clubs or on golf courses.

In practice, of course, many gentlemen from the noblest families have tended to devote themselves to alleviating the great problems of the day, and so, at a glance, it may have appeared that the ambitions of our generation differed little from those of our predecessors. But I can vouch there was a crucial distinction in attitude, reflected not only in the sorts of things you would hear fellow professionals express to each other, but in the way many of the most able persons of our generation chose to leave one position for another. Such decisions were no longer a matter simply of wages, the size of staff at one's disposal or the splendour of a family name; for our generation, I think it fair to say, professional prestige lay most significantly in the moral worth of one's employer.

I believe I can best highlight the difference between the generations by expressing myself figuratively. Butlers of my father's generation, I would say, tended to see the world in terms of a ladder – the houses of royalty, dukes and the lords from the oldest families placed at the top, those of 'new money' lower down and so on, until one reached a point below which the hierarchy was determined simply by wealth – or the lack of it. Any butler with ambition simply did his best to climb as high up this ladder as possible, and by and large, the higher he went, the greater his professional prestige. Such are, of course, precisely the values embodied in the Hayes Society's idea of a 'distinguished household', and the fact that it was confidently making such pronouncements as late as 1929 shows clearly why the demise of that society was inevitable, if not long overdue. For by that time, such thinking was quite out of step with that of the finest men emerging to the forefront of our profession. For our generation, I believe it is accurate to say, viewed the world not as a ladder, but more as a *wheel*. Perhaps I might explain this further.

It is my impression that our generation was the first to recognize something which had passed the notice of all earlier generations:

namely that the great decisions of the world are not, in fact, arrived at simply in the public chambers, or else during a handful of days given over to an international conference under the full gaze of the public and the press. Rather, debates are conducted, and crucial decisions arrived at, in the privacy and calm of the great houses of this country. What occurs under the public gaze with so much pomp and ceremony is often the conclusion, or mere ratification, of what has taken place over weeks or months within the walls of such houses. To us, then, the world was a wheel, revolving with these great houses at the hub, their mighty decisions emanating out to all else, rich and poor, who revolved around them. It was the aspiration of all those of us with professional ambition to work our way as close to this hub as we were each of us capable. For we were, as I say, an idealistic generation for whom the question was not simply one of how well one practised one's skills, but *to what end* one did so; each of us harboured the desire to make our own small contribution to the creation of a better world, and saw that, as professionals, the surest means of doing so would be to serve the great gentlemen of our times in whose hands civilization had been entrusted.

Of course, I am now speaking in broad generalizations and I would readily admit there were all too many persons of our generation who had no patience for such finer considerations. Conversely, I am sure there were many of my father's generation who recognized instinctively this 'moral' dimension to their work. But by and large, I believe these generalizations to be accurate, and indeed, such 'idealistic' motivations as I have described have played a large part in my own career. I myself moved quite rapidly from employer to employer during my early career – being aware that these situations were incapable of bringing me lasting satisfaction – before being rewarded at last with the opportunity to serve Lord Darlington.

▷ **4** *calling* (n): Berufung **5** *humble* (adj): modest, lowly **6** *undeniable:* obvious, certain **8** *idle away your time:* waste time with trivial things **10** *alleviate sth.:* make sth. less difficult or painful **12** *predecessor:* person who did the same job before **21** *highlight sth.:* show sth. clearly by giving or pointing to an example **22** *figurative:* using images, not literal **33** *long overdue:* that should have occurred much earlier **46** *ratification:* act of making sth. official and public **48** *revolve:* turn **49** *at the hub:* at the centre of the wheel • *emanate:* flow **54** *to what end:* with which aim **55** *harbour the desire:* have the wish **62** *conversely:* on the other hand **69** *reward sb.:* jdn. belohnen

It is curious that I have never until today thought of matters in these terms; indeed, that through all those many hours we spent discussing the nature of 'greatness' by the fire of our servants' hall, the likes of Mr Graham and I never considered this whole dimension to the question. And while I would not retract anything I have previously stated regarding the quality of 'dignity', I must admit there is something to the argument that whatever the degree to which a butler has attained such a quality, if he has failed to find an appropriate outlet for his accomplishments he can hardly expect his fellows to consider him 'great'. Certainly, it is observable that figures like Mr Marshall and Mr Lane have served only gentlemen of indisputable moral stature – Lord Wakeling, Lord Camberley, Sir Leonard Gray – and one cannot help get the impression that they simply would not have offered their talents to gentlemen of lesser calibre. Indeed, the more one considers it, the more obvious it seems: association with a *truly* distinguished household is a prerequisite of 'greatness'. A 'great' butler can only be, surely, one who can point to his years of service and say that he has applied his talents to serving a great gentleman – and through the latter, to serving humanity.

As I say, I have never in all these years thought of the matter in quite this way; but then it is perhaps in the nature of coming away on a trip such as this that one is prompted towards such surprising new perspectives on topics one imagined one had long ago thought through thoroughly. I have also, no doubt, been prompted to think along such lines by the small event that occurred an hour or so ago – which has, I admit, unsettled me somewhat.

Having enjoyed a good morning's motoring in splendid weather, and having lunched well at a country inn, I had just crossed the border into Dorset. It was then I had become aware of a heated smell emanating from the car engine. The thought that I had done some damage to my employer's Ford was, of course, most alarming and I had quickly brought the vehicle to a halt.

I found myself in a narrow lane, hemmed in on either side by foliage so that I could gain little idea of what was around me. Neither could I see far ahead, the lane winding quite sharply twenty yards or so in front. It occurred to me that I could not remain where I was for long without incurring the risk of an oncoming vehicle coming round the same bend and colliding into my employer's Ford. I thus started the engine again and was partially reassured to find that the smell seemed not as powerful as before.

My best course, I could see, was to look for a garage, or else a large house of a gentleman where there would be a good chance I might find a chauffeur who could see what the matter was. But the lane continued to wind for some distance, and the high hedges on either side of me also persisted, obscuring my vision so that though I passed several gates, some of which clearly yielded on to driveways, I was unable to glimpse the houses themselves. I continued for another half-mile or so, the disturbing smell now growing stronger by the moment, until at last I came out on to a stretch of open road. I could now see some distance before me, and indeed, ahead to my left there loomed a tall Victorian house with a substantial front lawn and what was clearly a driveway converted from an old carriage track. As I drew up to it, I was encouraged further to glimpse a Bentley through the open doors of a garage attached to the main house.

The gate too had been left open and so I steered the Ford a little way up the drive, got out and made my way to the back door of the house. This was opened by a man dressed in his shirt sleeves, wearing no tie, but who, upon my asking for the chauffeur of the house, replied cheerfully that I had 'hit the jackpot first time'. On hearing my problem, the man without hesitation came out to the Ford, opened the bonnet and informed me after barely a few seconds' inspection: 'Water, guv. You need some water in your radiator.' He seemed to be rather amused by the situation, but was obliging enough; he returned inside the house and after a few moments emerged again with a jug of water and a funnel. As he filled the radiator, his head bent over the

▷ **9** *an appropriate outlet for his accomplishments:* (here) a suitable position, the right house to serve in **12** *indisputable:* that cannot be argued against, true • *moral stature:* ethical qualities **14–15** *of lesser calibre:* not as great **23** *be prompted towards sth.:* be caused to think about sth. **31** *emanate from sth.:* come out of sth. **34** *be hemmed in:* be closely surrounded **36** *wind* [waɪnd] (adj): move not in a straight line but in curves **38** *incur the risk:* das Risiko eingehen **39** *collide into sth.:* crash into sth. **46** *obscure sb.'s vision:* prevent sb. from seeing clearly **47** *yield on to sth.:* zu etwas führen • *driveway:* Grundstückszufahrt **52** *substantial:* large **53** *convert sth.:* change sth., rebuild sth. as another thing **55** *attached to sth.:* joined to sth. **56** *steer:* drive **60** *hit the jackpot* (infml): find what you need or want **62** *bonnet:* Motorhaube **63** *guv* (infml): lower-class way of addressing a male customer in a shop, taxi, etc. **64** *obliging* (adj): helpful **66** *funnel:* Trichter

engine, he began to chat amiably, and on ascertaining that I was undertaking a motoring tour of the area, recommended I visit a local beauty spot, a certain pond not half a mile away.

I had had in the meantime more opportunity to observe the house; it was taller than it was broad, comprising four floors, with ivy covering much of the front right up to the gables. I could see from its windows, however, that at least half of it was dust-sheeted. I remarked on this to the man once he had finished with the radiator and closed the bonnet.

'A shame really,' he said. 'It's a lovely old house. Truth is, the Colonel's trying to sell the place off. He ain't got much use for a house this size now.'

I could not help inquiring then how many staff were employed there, and I suppose I was hardly surprised to be told there was only himself and a cook who came in each evening. He was, it seemed, butler, valet, chauffeur and general cleaner. He had been the Colonel's batman in the war, he explained; they had been in Belgium together when the Germans had invaded and they had been together again for the Allied landing. Then he regarded me carefully and said:

'Now I got it. I couldn't make you out for a while, but now I got it. You're one of them top-notch butlers. From one of them big posh houses.'

When I told him he was not so far off the mark, he continued:

'Now I got it. Couldn't make you out for a while, see, 'cause you talk almost like a gentleman. And what with you driving an old beauty like this' – he gestured to the Ford – 'I thought at first, here's a really posh geezer. And so you are, guv. Really posh, I mean. I never learnt any of that myself, you see. I'm just a plain old batman gone civvy.'

He then asked me where it was I was employed, and when I told him he leant his head to one side with a quizzical look.

'Darlington Hall,' he said to himself. 'Darlington Hall. Must be a really posh place, it rings a bell even to an idiot like yours truly. Darlington Hall. Hang on, you don't mean *Darlington* Hall, Lord Darlington's place?'

'It was Lord Darlington's residence until his death three years ago,' I informed him. 'The house is now the residence of Mr John Farraday, an American gentleman.'

'You really must be top-notch working in a place like that. Can't be many like you left, eh?' Then his voice changed noticeably as he inquired: 'You mean you actually used to work for that Lord Darlington?'

He was eyeing me carefully again. I said:

'Oh no, I am employed by Mr John Farraday, the American gentleman who bought the house from the Darlington family.'

'Oh, so you wouldn't have known that Lord Darlington. Just that I wondered what he was like. What sort of bloke he was.'

I told the man that I would have to be on my way and thanked him emphatically for his assistance. He was, after all, an amiable fellow, taking the trouble to guide me in reversing out through the gateway, and before I parted, he bent down and recommended again that I visit the local pond, repeating his instructions as to how I would find it.

'It's a beautiful little spot,' he added. 'You'll kick yourself for missing it. In fact, the Colonel's doing a bit of fishing there this minute.'

The Ford seemed to be in fine form again, and since the pond in question was but a small detour off my route, I decided to take up the batman's suggestion. His directions had seemed clear enough, but once I had turned off the main road in an attempt to follow them, I found myself getting lost down narrow, twisting lanes much like the one in which I had first noticed the alarming smell. At times, the foliage on either side became so thick as practically to blot out the sun altogether, and one found one's eyes struggling to cope with the sudden contrasts of bright sunlight and deep shade. Eventually, however, after some searching, I found a signpost to 'Mortimer's Pond', and so it was that I arrived here at this spot a little over half an hour ago.

I now find myself much indebted to the batman, for quite aside from assisting with the Ford, he has allowed me to discover a most charming spot which it is most improbable I would ever have found

▷ **1** *amiable:* friendly, likable **5** *ivy* ['aɪvi]: Efeu **6** *gable* ['geɪbl]: Giebel **11** *colonel* ['kɜ:nl]: Oberst **17** *batman:* personal servant in the British army **19** *the Allied landing:* the landing of Allied troop in Normany, France, in 1944 (usu. called 'D-Day') **20** *I couldn't make you out:* I couldn't figure out who or what you are **21** *top-notch* (infml): excellent, of high quality • *posh:* upper class **23** *not so far off the mark* (infml): not far from the truth **27** *geezer* (infml): man **28** *gone civvy* (infml): (here) turned into a civilian, having taken up a job outside the army **30** *quizzical:* that seems to ask a question **32** *it rings a bell:* it reminds me of sth. • *like yours truly* (infml.): like me **33** *hang on* (infml): used when you suddenly realize sth. **42** *eye sb./sth.:* look at sb./sth. closely **46** *bloke* (infml): man **49** *reverse* (v): drive backwards **50** *part* (v): leave **55** *detour* ['di:tʊə]: Umweg **65** *much indebted to sb.:* having reason to be thankful to sb.

otherwise. The pond is not a large one – a quarter of a mile around its perimeter perhaps – so that by stepping out to any promontory, one can command a view of its entirety. An atmosphere of great calm pervades here. Trees have been planted all around the water just closely enough to give a pleasant shade to the banks, while here and there clusters of tall reeds and bulrushes break the water's surface and its still reflection of the sky. My footwear is not such as to permit me easily to walk around the perimeter – I can see even from where I now sit the path disappearing into areas of deep mud – but I will say that such is the charm of this spot that on first arriving, I was sorely temped to do just that. Only the thought of the possible catastrophes that might befall such an expedition, and of sustaining damage to my travelling suit, persuaded me to content myself with sitting here on this bench. And so I have done for the past half-hour, contemplating the progress of the various figures seated quietly with their fishing rods at various points around the water. At this point, I can see a dozen or so such figures, but the strong lights and shades created by the low-hanging branches prevent me from making any of them out clearly and I have had to forgo the small game I had been anticipating of guessing which of these fishermen is the Colonel at whose house I have just received such useful assistance.

It is no doubt the quiet of these surroundings that has enabled me to ponder all the more thoroughly these thoughts which have entered my mind over this past half-hour or so. Indeed, but for the tranquillity of the present setting, it is possible I would not have thought a great deal further about my behaviour during my encounter with the batman. That is to say, I may not have thought further why it was that I had given the distinct impression I had never been in the employ of Lord Darlington. For surely, there is no real doubt that is what occurred. He had asked: 'You mean you actually worked for that Lord Darlington?' and I had given an answer which could mean little other than that I had not. It could simply be that a meaningless whim had suddenly overtaken me at that moment – but that is hardly a convincing way to account for such distinctly odd behaviour. In any case, I have now come to accept that the incident with the batman is not the first of its kind; there is little doubt it has some connection – though I am not quite clear of the nature of it – with what occurred a few months ago during the visit of the Wakefields.

Mr and Mrs Wakefield are an American couple who have been settled in England – somewhere in Kent, I understand – for some twenty years. Having a number of acquaintances in common with Mr Farraday amidst Boston society, they paid a short visit one day to Darlington Hall, staying for lunch and leaving before tea. I now refer to a time only a few weeks after Mr Farraday had arrived at the house, a time when his enthusiasm for his acquisition was at a height; consequently, much of the Wakefields' visit was taken up with my employer leading them on what might have seemed to some an unnecessarily extensive tour of the premises, including all the dust-sheeted areas. Mr and Mrs Wakefield, however, appeared to be as keen on the inspection as Mr Farraday, and as I went about my business, I would often catch various American exclamations of delight coming from whichever part of the house they had arrived at. Mr Farraday had commenced the tour at the top of the house, and by the time he had brought his guests down to inspect the magnificence of the ground-floor rooms, he seemed to be on an elevated plane, pointing out details on cornicings and window frames, and describing with some flourish 'what the English lords used to do' in each room. Although of course I made no deliberate attempt to overhear, I could not help but get the gist of what was being said, and was surprised by the extent of my employer's knowledge, which, despite the occasional infelicity, betrayed a deep enthusiasm for English ways. It was noticeable, moreover, that the Wakefields – Mrs Wakefield in particular – were themselves by no means ignorant of the traditions of our country, and one gathered from the many remarks they made that they too were owners of an English house of some splendour.

It was at a certain stage during this tour of the premises – I was crossing the hall under the impression that the party had gone out to

▷ **2** *promontory:* a higher piece of ground **3** *command a view of its entirety:* see the whole pond **4** *pervade here:* (here) can be felt all over this place **6** *reed:* Schilf • *bulrush:* Binse **7** *footwear:* shoes **10** *sorely:* very much **12** *befall sth:* (here) happen during sth. **15–16** *fishing rod:* Anglerute **19** *forgo sth.* [- '-]: give sth. up, abandon sth. **32** *whim:* sudden wish to do sth. (usu. unusual) **41** *acquaintance:* person you know **45** *acquisition:* thing that has been bought or acquired **48** *the premises:* the buildings and the land that are part of one property **55** *plane:* level **56** *cornicings:* types of decoration at the top edge of a wall **57** *with some flourish:* with confidence and enthusiasm **60** *extent:* degree, breadth **61** *infelicity:* unsuitable remark, minor error **64** *gather:* conclude

explore the grounds – when I saw that Mrs Wakefield had remained behind and was closely examining the stone arch that frames the doorway into the dining room. As I went past, muttering a quiet 'excuse me, madam,' she turned and said:

'Oh, Stevens, perhaps you're the one to tell me. This arch here *looks* seventeenth century, but isn't it the case that it was built quite recently? Perhaps during Lord Darlington's time?'

'It is possible, madam.'

'It's very beautiful. But it is probably a kind of mock period piece done only a few years ago. Isn't that right?'

'I'm not sure, madam, but that is certainly possible.'

Then, lowering her voice, Mrs Wakefield had said: 'But tell me, Stevens, what was this Lord Darlington like? Presumably you must have worked for him.'

'I didn't, madam, no.'

'Oh, I thought you did. I wonder why I thought that.'

Mrs Wakefield turned back to the arch and putting her hand to it, said: 'So we don't know for certain then. Still, it looks to me like it's mock. Very skilful, but mock.'

It is possible I might have quickly forgotten this exchange; however, following the Wakefields' departure, I took in afternoon tea to Mr Farraday in the drawing room and noticed he was in a rather preoccupied mood. After an initial silence, he said:

'You know, Stevens, Mrs Wakefield wasn't as impressed with this house as I believe she ought to have been.'

'Is that so, sir.'

'In fact, she seemed to think I was exaggerating the pedigree of this place. That I was making it up about all these features going back centuries.'

'Indeed, sir?'

'She kept asserting everything was "mock" this and "mock" that. She even thought you were "mock", Stevens.'

'Indeed, sir?'

'Indeed, Stevens. I'd told her you were the real thing. A real old English butler. That you'd been in this house for over thirty years, serving a real English lord. But Mrs Wakefield contradicted me on this point. In fact, she contradicted me with great confidence.'

'Is that so, sir?'

'Mrs Wakefield, Stevens, was convinced you never worked here until I hired you. In fact, she seemed to be under the impression she'd had that from your own lips. Made me look pretty much a fool, as you can imagine.'

'It's most regrettable, sir.'

'I mean to say, Stevens, this is a genuine grand old English house, isn't it? That's what I paid for. And you're a genuine old-fashioned English butler, not just some waiter pretending to be one. You're the real thing, aren't you? That's what I wanted, isn't that what I have?'

'I venture to say you do, sir.'

'Then can you explain to me what Mrs Wakefield is saying? It's a big mystery to me.'

'It is possible I may well have given the lady a slightly misleading picture concerning my career, sir. I do apologize if this caused embarrassment.'

'I'll say it caused embarrassment. Those people have now got me down for a braggart and a liar. Anyway, what do you mean, you may have given her a "slightly misleading picture"?'

'I'm very sorry, sir. I had no idea I might cause you such embarrassment.'

'But dammit, Stevens, why did you tell her such a tale?'

I considered the situation for a moment, then said; 'I'm very sorry, sir. But it is to do with the ways of this country.'

'What are you talking about, man?'

'I meant to say, sir, that it is not customary in England for an employee to discuss his past employers.'

'OK, Stevens, so you don't wish to divulge past confidences. But does that extend to you actually denying having worked for anyone other than me?'

'It does seem a little extreme when you put it that way, sir. But it has often been considered desirable for employees to give such an impression. If I may put it this way, sir, it is a little akin to the custom as regards marriages. If a divorced lady were present in the company

▷ **1** *explore the grounds:* examine the gardens and outside areas **9** *mock period piece:* thing in the style of a certain period but made much later (*mock:* fake, not authentic) **27** *pedigree:* historic value and importance **28** *make it up about sth.:* lie about sth. **55** *braggart* (infml): Prahler **65** *divulge sth.:* give information about sth. (esp. about sth. secret) • *confidences:* things told secretly and with trust **66** *extend to sth.:* go as far as sth.

of her second husband, it is often thought desirable not to allude to the original marriage at all. There is a similar custom as regards our profession, sir.'

'Well, I only wish I'd known about your custom before, Stevens,' my employer said, leaning back in his chair. 'It certainly made me look like a chump.'

I believe I realized even at the time that my explanation to Mr Farraday – though, of course, not entirely devoid of truth – was woefully inadequate. But when one has so much else to think about, it is easy not to give such matters a great deal of attention, and so I did, indeed, put the whole episode out of my mind for some time. But now, recalling it here in the calm that surrounds this pond, there seems little doubt that my conduct towards Mrs Wakefield that day has an obvious relation to what has just taken place this afternoon.

Of course, there are many people these days who have a lot of foolish things to say about Lord Darlington, and it may be that you are under the impression I am somehow embarrassed or ashamed of my association with his lordship, and it is this that lies behind such conduct. Then let me make it clear that nothing could be further from the truth. The great majority of what one hears said about his lordship today is, in any case, utter nonsense, based on an almost complete ignorance of the facts. Indeed, it seems to me that my odd conduct can be very plausibly explained in terms of my wish to avoid any possibility of hearing any further such nonsense concerning his lordship; that is to say, I have chosen to tell white lies in both instances as the simplest means of avoiding unpleasantness. This does seem a very plausible explanation the more I think about it; for it is true, nothing vexes me more these days than to hear this sort of nonsense being repeated. Let me say that Lord Darlington was a gentleman of great moral stature – a stature to dwarf most of these persons you will find talking this sort of nonsense about him – and I will readily vouch that he remained that to the last. Nothing could be less accurate than to suggest that I regret my association with such a gentleman. Indeed, you will appreciate that to have served his lordship at Darlington Hall during those years was to come as close to the hub of this world's wheel as one such as I could ever have dreamt. I gave thirty-five years' service to Lord Darlington; one would surely not be unjustified in claiming that during those years, one was, in the truest terms, 'attached to a distinguished household'.

In looking back over my career thus far, my chief satisfaction derives from what I achieved during those years, and I am today nothing but proud and grateful to have been given such a privilege.

▷ **6** *chump* (AE infml): stupid person, fool **8** *devoid of sth.:* without sth. **9** *woefully inadequate:* far from accurate, of a very low standard **13** *conduct* ['- -]: behaviour **25** *white lie:* lie that is told for a good reason and with no intention to harm **28** *vex sb.:* make sb. angry **30** *dwarf sb./sth.:* make sb./sth. look very small and unimportant by comparison

DAY THREE – MORNING

Taunton, Somerset

I lodged last night in an inn named the Coach and Horses a little way outside the town of Taunton, Somerset. This being a thatch-roofed cottage by the roadside, it had looked a conspicuously attractive prospect from the Ford as I had approached in the last of the daylight. The landlord led me up a timber stairway to a small room, rather bare, but perfectly decent. When he inquired whether I had dined, I asked him to serve me with a sandwich in my room, which proved a perfectly satisfactory option as far as supper was concerned. But then as the evening drew on, I began to feel a little restless in my room, and in the end decided to descend to the bar below to try a little of the local cider.

There were five or six customers all gathered in a group around the bar – one guessed from their appearance they were agricultural people of one sort or another – but otherwise the room was empty. Acquiring a tankard of cider from the landlord, I seated myself at a table a little way away, intending to relax a little and collect my thoughts concerning the day. It soon became clear, however, that these local people were perturbed by my presence, feeling something of a need to show hospitality. Whenever there was a break in their conversation, one or the other of them would steal a glance in my direction as though trying to find it in himself to approach me. Eventually, one raised his voice and said to me:

'It seems you've let yourself in for a night upstairs here, sir.'

When I told him this was so, the speaker shook his head doubtfully and remarked: 'You won't get much of a sleep up there, sir. Not unless you're fond of the sound of old Bob' – he indicated the landlord – 'banging away down here right the way into the night. And then you'll get woken by his missus shouting at him right from the crack of dawn.'

Despite the landlord's protests, this caused loud laughter all round.

'Is that indeed so?' I said. And as I spoke, I was struck by the thought – the same thought as had struck me on numerous occasions of late in Mr Farraday's presence – that some sort of witty retort was required of me. Indeed, the local people were now observing a polite

▷ **2–3** *thatch-roofed cottage:* small country house with a roof of dried straw **5** *timber:* wooden **11** *cider* ['saɪdə]: alcoholic drink made from apples **15** *tankard:* large metal cup **18** *perturbed* (adj): disquieted, disturbed **20** *steal a glance:* look secretly **28–39** *from the crack of dawn:* from very early in the morning

silence, awaiting my next remark. I thus searched my imagination and eventually declared:

'A local variation on the cock crow, no doubt.'

At first the silence continued, as though the local persons thought I intended to elaborate further. But then noticing the mirthful expression on my face, they broke into a laugh, though in a somewhat bemused fashion. With this, they returned to their previous conversation, and I exchanged no further words with them until exchanging good nights a little while later.

I had been rather pleased with my witticism when it had first come into my head, and I must confess I was slightly disappointed it had not been better received than it was. I was particularly disappointed, I suppose, because I have been devoting some time and effort over recent months to improving my skill in this very area. That is to say, I have been endeavouring to add this skill to my professional armoury so as to fulfil with confidence all Mr Farraday's expectations with respect to bantering.

For instance, I have of late taken to listening to the wireless in my room whenever I find myself with a few spare moments – on those occasions, say, when Mr Farrady is out for the evening. One programme I listen to is called *Twice a Week or More*, which is in fact broadcast three times each week, and basically comprises two persons making humorous comments on a variety of topics raised by readers' letters. I have been studying this programme because the witticisms performed on it are always in the best of taste and, to my mind, of a tone not at all out of keeping with the sort of bantering Mr Farraday might expect on my part. Taking my cue from this programme, I have devised a simple exercise which I try to perform at least once a day; whenever an odd moment presents itself, I attempt to formulate three witticisms based on my immediate surroundings at that moment. Or, as a variation on this same exercise, I may attempt to think of three witticisms based on the events of the past hour.

You will perhaps appreciate then my disappointment concerning my witticism yesterday evening. At first, I had thought it possible its limited success was due to my not having spoken clearly enough. But then the possibility occurred to me, once I had retired, that I might actually have given these people offence. After all, it could easily have been understood that I was suggesting the landlord's wife resembled a cockerel – an intention that had not remotely entered my head at the time. This thought continued to torment me as I tried to sleep, and I had half a mind to make an apology to the landlord this morning. But his mood towards me as he served breakfast seemed perfectly cheerful and in the end I decided to let the matter rest.

But this small episode is as good an illustration as any of the hazards of uttering witticisms. By the very nature of a witticism, one is given very little time to assess its various possible repercussions before one is called to give voice to it, and one gravely risks uttering all manner of unsuitable things if one has not first acquired the necessary skill and experience. There is no reason to suppose this is not an area in which I will become proficient given time and practice, but, such are the dangers, I have decided it best, for the time being at least, not to attempt to discharge this duty in respect of Mr Farraday until I have practised further.

In any case, I am sorry to report that what the local people had themselves offered last night as a witticism of sorts – the prediction that I would not have a good night owing to disturbances from below – proved only too true. The landlord's wife did not actually shout, but one could hear her talking incessantly both late into the night as she and her husband went about their tasks, and again from very early this morning. I was quite prepared to forgive the couple, however, for it was clear they were of diligent hard-working habits, and the noise, I am sure, was all attributable to this fact. Besides, of course, there had been the matter of my unfortunate remark. I thus gave no indication of having had a disturbed night when I thanked the landlord and took my leave to explore the market town of Taunton.

Perhaps I might have done better to have lodged here in this establishment where I now sit enjoying a pleasant mid-morning cup of tea. For indeed, the notice outside advertises not only 'teas, snacks

▷ **5** *elaborate further* [ɪ'læbəreɪt] (v): enlarge on sth., talk more about sth. • *mirthful:* happy, about to laugh **15** *armoury:* arsenal (= place where weapons are stored) **18** *wireless* (old use): radio **27** *take your cue from sth.:* copy what others do in order to behave in the right way **37** *offence:* insult **38** *resemble sth.:* be similar to sth. **39** *cockerel:* young male chicken • *not remotely:* not at all **40** *torment sb.:* trouble sb. **41** *apology:* words expressing that you are sorry **50** *proficient:* competent • *given time and practice:* with enough time and training **55** *a witticism of sorts:* a kind of witticism **58** *incessant:* never stopping

and cakes', but also 'clean, quiet, comfortable rooms'. It is situated on the high street of Taunton, very close to the market square, a somewhat sunken building, its exterior characterized by heavy dark timber beams. I am at present sitting in its spacious tearoom, oak-panelled, with enough tables to accommodate, I would guess, two dozen people without a feeling of crowding. Two cheery young girls serve from behind a counter displaying a good selection of cakes and pastries. All in all, this is an excellent place to partake of morning tea, but surprisingly few of the inhabitants of Taunton seem to wish to avail themselves of it. At present, my only companions are two elderly ladies, sitting abreast one another at a table along the opposite wall, and a man – perhaps a retired farmer – at a table beside one of the large bay windows. I am unable to discern him clearly because the bright morning sunlight has for the moment reduced him to a silhouette. But I can see him studying his newspaper, breaking off regularly to look up at the passers-by on the pavement outside. From the way he does this, I had thought at first that he was waiting for a companion, but it would seem he wishes merely to greet acquaintances as they pass by.

I am myself ensconced almost at the back wall, but even across the distance of this room, I can see clearly out into the sunlit street, and am able to make out on the pavement opposite a signpost pointing out several nearby destinations. One of these destinations is the village of Mursden. Perhaps 'Mursden' will ring a bell for you, as it did for me upon my first spotting it on the road atlas yesterday. In fact, I must say I was even tempted to make a slight detour from my planned route just to see the village. Mursden, Somerset, was where the firm of Giffen and Co. was once situated, and it was to Mursden one was required to dispatch one's order for a supply of Giffen's dark candles of polish, 'to be flaked, mixed into wax and applied by hand'. For some time, Giffen's was undoubtedly the finest silver polish available, and it was only the appearance of new chemical substances on the market shortly before the war that caused demand for this impressive product to decline.

As I remember, Giffen's appeared at the beginning of the twenties, and I am sure I am not alone in closely associating its emergence with that change of mood within our profession – that change which came to push the polishing of silver to the position of central importance it still by and large maintains today. This shift was, I believe, like so many other major shifts around this period, a generational matter; it was during these years that our generation of butlers 'came of age', and figures like Mr Marshall, in particular, played a crucial part in making silver-polishing so central. This is not to suggest, of course, that the polishing of silver – particularly those items that would appear at table – was not always regarded a serious duty. But it would not be unfair to suggest that many butlers of, say, my father's generation did not consider the matter such a key one, and this is evidenced by the fact that in those days, the butler of a household rarely supervized the polishing of silver directly, being content to leave it to, say, the under-butler's whims, carrying out inspections only intermittently. It was Mr Marshall, it is generally agreed, who was the first to recognize the full significance of silver – namely, that no other objects in the house were likely to come under such intimate scrutiny from outsiders as was silver during a meal, and as such, it served as a public index of a house's standards. And Mr Marshall it was who first caused stupefaction amongst ladies and gentlemen visiting Charleville House with displays of silver polished to previously unimagined standards. Very soon, naturally, butlers up and down the country, under pressure from their employers, were focusing their minds on the question of silver-polishing. There quickly sprang up, I recall, various butlers, each claiming to have discovered methods by which they could surpass Mr Marshall – methods they made a great show of keeping secret, as though they were French chefs guarding their recipes. But I am confident – as I was then – that the sorts of elaborate and mysterious processes

▷ **3** *sunken:* built at a lower level than the surrounding ground **4** *beam* (n): long piece of wood that forms the structure of a house or roof • *oak:* Eichenholz **5** *panelled* (adj): getäfelt • *accommodate sb.:* (here) provide enough space for sb. **10** *avail yourself of sth.:* make use of sth. **11** *abreast one another:* next to each other **13** *bay window:* large window that sticks outwards from the wall of a house **20** *ensconced* (adj): nestled, sitting comfortably in a private place **23** *destination:* place (you can go to) **29** *be required to do sth.:* have to do sth. **30** *polish* ['pɒlɪʃ]: Politur • *flake sth.:* break sth. off in small thin pieces • *wax* (n): Wachs **36** *emergence:* appearance **40** *shift* (n): change **48** *evidenced by sth.:* proven by sth. **51** *intermittent:* now and then, not regularly or continuously **54** *scrutiny:* examination **55** *a public index of a house's standards:* a public indication of the social position of a family **56** *stupefaction:* astonishment **60** *focus sth.:* concentrate sth. **62** *surpass sb./sth.:* be even better or greater than sb./sth. **64** *recipe* ['resɪpi]: Rezept

performed by someone like Mr Jack Neighbours had little or no discernible effect on the end result. As far as I was concerned, it was a simple enough matter; one used good polish, and one supervized closely. Giffen's was the polish ordered by all discerning butlers of the time, and if this product was used correctly, one had no fear of one's silver being second best to anybody's.

I am glad to be able to recall numerous occasions when the silver at Darlington Hall had a pleasing impact upon observers. For instance, I recall Lady Astor remarking, not without a certain bitterness, that our silver 'was probably unrivalled'. I recall also watching Mr George Bernard Shaw, the renowned playwright, at dinner one evening, examining closely the dessert spoon before him, holding it up to the light and comparing its surface to that of a nearby platter, quite oblivious to the company around him. But perhaps the instance I recall with most satisfaction today concerns the night that a certain distinguished personage – a cabinet minister, shortly afterwards to become foreign secretary – paid a very 'off the record' visit to the house. In fact, now that the subsequent fruits of those visits have become well documented, there seems little reason not to reveal that I am talking of Lord Halifax.

As things turned out, that particular visit was simply the first of a whole series of such 'unofficial' meetings between Lord Halifax and the German Ambassador of that time, Herr Ribbentrop. But on that first night, Lord Halifax had arrived in a mood of great wariness; virtually his first words on being shown in were: 'Really, Darlington, I don't know what you've put me up to here. I know I shall be sorry.'

Herr Ribbentrop not being expected for a further hour or so, his lordship had suggested to his guest a tour of Darlington Hall – a strategy which had helped many a nervous visitor to relax. However, as I went about my business, all I could hear for some time was Lord Halifax, in various parts of the building, continuing to express his doubts about the evening ahead, and Lord Darlington trying in vain to reassure him. But then at one point I overheard Lord Halifax exclaiming: 'My goodness, Darlington, the silver in this house is a delight.' I was of course very pleased to hear this at the time, but what was for me the truly satisfying corollary to this episode came two or three days later, when Lord Darlington remarked to me: 'By the way, Stevens, Lord Halifax was jolly impressed with the silver the other night. Put him into a different frame of mind altogether.' These

→ p. 77

were – I recollect it clearly – his lordship's actual words and so it is not simply my fantasy that the state of the silver had made a small, but significant contribution towards the easing of relations between Lord Halifax and Herr Ribbentrop that evening.

It is probably apt at this point to say a few words concerning Herr Ribbentrop. It is, of course, generally accepted today that Herr Ribbentrop was a trickster: that it was Hitler's plan throughout those years to deceive England for as long as possible concerning his true intentions, and that Herr Ribbentrop's sole mission in our country was to orchestrate this deception. As I say, this is the commonly held view and I do not wish to differ with it here. It is, however, rather irksome to have to hear people talking today as though they were never for a moment taken in by Herr Ribbentrop – as though Lord Darlington was alone in believing Herr Ribbentrop an honourable gentleman and developing a working relationship with him. The truth is that Herr Ribbentrop was, throughout the thirties, a well-regarded figure, even a glamorous one, in the very best houses. Particularly around 1936 and 1937, I can recall all the talk in the servants' hall from visiting staff revolving around 'the German Ambassador', and it was clear from what was said that many of the most distinguished ladies and gentlemen in this country were quite enamoured of him. It is, as I say, irksome to have to hear the way these same people now talk of those times, and in particular, what some have said concerning his lordship. The great hypocrisy of these

▷ **9** *Lady Astor* (1879–1964): US-born British Conservative MP; the first woman to sit in the House of Commons and a supporter of appeasement towards Germany in the 1930s **10** *unrivalled:* better than any other **14** *platter:* large plate from which food is served **17** *foreign secretary:* Außenminister/in **20** *Lord Halifax* (1881–1959): British Conservative politician and Foreign Secretary (1938–1940) who was an early admirer of Hitler and supporter of appeasement towards Germany in the 1930s **23** *ambassador:* Botschafter/in • *Herr Ribbentrop* = *Joachim von Ribbentrop* (1893–1946): leading Nazi politician and German ambassador to Britain (1936–1938) **24** *wariness* ['weərinəs]: suspicion, watchfulness **32** *ahead:* that was still to come **33** *reassure sb.:* make sb. feel calmer and less worried **36** *corollary:* consequence **39** *altogether:* totally **42** *easing* (n): relaxation **44** *apt:* fitting, appropriate **46** *trickster:* person who deceives or cheats other people **49** *orchestrate sth.:* organize sth. • *deception:* Täuschung **51** *irksome:* annoying **52** *take sb. in:* deceive sb. **56** *glamorous:* very attractive and exciting **58** *revolve around sb./sth.:* deal with sb./sth. **61** *enamoured of sb.:* charmed by sb. **63** *hypocrisy:* Heuchelei

persons would be instantly obvious to you were you to see just a few of their own guest lists from those days; you would see then not only the extent to which Herr Ribbentrop dined at these same persons' tables, but that he often did so as guest of honour.

And then again, you will hear these same persons talking as though Lord Darlington did something unusual in receiving hospitality from the Nazis on the several trips he made to Germany during those years. I do not suppose they would speak quite so readily if, say, *The Times* were to publish even one of the guest lists of the banquets given by the Germans around the time of the Nuremberg Rally. The fact is, the most established, respected ladies and gentlemen in England were availing themselves of the hospitality of the German leaders, and I can vouch at first hand that the great majority of these persons were returning with nothing but praise and admiration for their hosts. Anyone who implies that Lord Darlington was liaising covertly with a known enemy is just conveniently forgetting the true climate of those times.

It needs to be said too what salacious nonsense it is to claim that Lord Darlington was anti-Semitic, or that he had close association with organizations like the British Union of Fascists. Such claims can only arise from complete ignorance of the sort of gentleman his lordship was. Lord Darlington came to abhor anti-Semitism; I heard him express his disgust on several separate occasions when confronted with anti-Semitic sentiments. And the allegation that his lordship never allowed Jewish people to enter the house or any Jewish staff to be employed is utterly unfounded – except, perhaps, in respect to one very minor episode in the thirties which has been blown up out of all proportion. And as for the British Union of Fascists, I can only say that any talk linking his lordship to such people is quite ridiculous. Sir Oswald Mosley, the gentleman who led the 'blackshirts', was a visitor at Darlington Hall on, I would say, three occasions at the most, and these visits all took place during the early days of that organization before it had betrayed its true nature. Once the ugliness of the blackshirts' movement became apparent – and let it be said his lordship was quicker than most in noticing it – Lord Darlington had no further association with such people.

In any case, such organizations were a complete irrelevance to the heart of political life in this country. Lord Darlington, you will understand, was the sort of gentleman who cared to occupy himself only with what was at the true centre of things, and the figures he gathered together in his efforts over those years were as far away from such unpleasant fringe groups as one could imagine. Not only were they eminently respectable, these were figures who held real influence in British life: politicians, diplomats, military men, clergy. Indeed, some of the personages were Jewish, and this fact alone should demonstrate how nonsensical is much of what has been said about his lordship.

But I drift. I was in fact discussing the silver, and how Lord Halifax had been suitably impressed on the evening of his meeting with Herr Ribbentrop at Darlington Hall. Let me make clear, I was not for a moment suggesting that what had initially threatened to be a disappointing evening for my employer had turned into a triumphant one solely on account of the silver. But then, as I indicated, Lord Darlington himself suggested that the silver might have been at least a small factor in the change in his guest's mood that evening, and it is perhaps not absurd to think back to such instances with a glow of satisfaction.

There are certain members of our profession who would have it that it ultimately makes little difference what sort of employer one serves; who believe that the sort of idealism prevalent amongst our generation – namely the notion that we butlers should aspire to serve those great gentlemen who further the cause of humanity – is just high-flown talk with no grounding in reality. It is of course noticeable that the individuals who express such scepticism invariably turn out to be the most mediocre of our profession – those who know they lack

▷ **1** *instantly:* immediately **10–11** *the Nuremberg Rally:* the annual meetings of the National Socialist Party (esp. from 1933–1938) **16** *liaise with sb.* [li'eɪz]: establish a relationship with sb. • *convenient:* useful **18** *salacious:* obscene **20** *the British Union of Fascists:* (also called the 'blackshirts') extreme right-wing political organization formed in 1932 by Sir Oswald Mosley (1896–1980) **22** *abhor sth.:* hate sth. **24** *allegation:* accusation **26** *unfounded:* not based on facts **28** *blow sth. up out of all proportion:* emphasize sth. much more than it deserves **29** *link sb. to sb. else:* make a connection between sb. and sb. else **34** *ugliness:* Hässlichkeit **37** *a complete irrelevance:* a thing that is totally unimportant or insignificant **42** *fringe group:* Randgruppe **43** *eminently:* extremely **48** *drift* (v): move away from your central topic **59** *ultimately:* in the final analysis **60** *prevalent:* common, often found **61** *aspire to sth.:* aim for sth. **63** *high-flown:* too idealistic • *grounding* (n): foundation, basis **65** *mediocre:* second-rate

the ability to progress to any position of note and who aspire only to drag as many down to their own level as possible – and one is hardly tempted to take such opinions seriously. But for all that, it is still satisfying to be able to point to instances in one's career that highlight very clearly how wrong such people are. Of course, one seeks to provide a general, sustained service to one's employer, the value of which could never be reduced to a number of specific instances – such as that concerning Lord Halifax. But what I am saying is that it is these sorts of instances which over time come to symbolize an irrefutable fact; namely that one has had the privilege of practising one's profession at the very fulcrum of great affairs. And one has a right, perhaps, to feel a satisfaction those content to serve mediocre employers will never know – the satisfaction of being able to say with some reason that one's efforts, in however modest a way, comprise a contribution to the course of history.

But perhaps one should not be looking back to the past so much. After all, I still have before me many more years of service I am required to give. And not only is Mr Farraday a most excellent employer, he is an American gentleman to whom, surely, one has a special duty to show all that is best about service in England. It is essential, then, to keep one's attention focused on the present; to guard against any complacency creeping in on account of what one may have achieved in the past. For it has to be admitted, over these last few months, things have not been all they might at Darlington Hall. A number of small errors have surfaced of late, including that incident last April relating to the silver. Most fortunately, it was not an occasion on which Mr Farraday had guests, but even so, it was a moment of genuine embarrassment to me.

It had occurred at breakfast one morning, and for his part, Mr Farraday – either through kindness, or because being an American he failed to recognize the extent of the shortcoming – did not utter one word of complaint to me throughout the whole episode. He had, upon seating himself, simply picked up a fork, examined it for a brief second, touching the prongs with a fingertip, then turned his attention to the morning headlines. The whole gesture had been carried out in an absent-minded sort of way, but of course, I had spotted the occurrence and had advanced swiftly to remove the offending item. I may in fact have done so a little too swiftly on account of my disturbance, for Mr Farraday gave a small start, muttering: 'Ah, Stevens.'

I had continued to proceed swiftly out of the room, returning without undue delay bearing a satisfactory fork. As I advanced upon the table – and a Mr Farraday now apparently absorbed in his newspaper – it occurred to me I might slip the fork on to the tablecloth quietly without disturbing my employer's reading. However, the possibility had already occurred to me that Mr Farraday was simply feigning indifference in order to minimize my embarrassment, and such a surreptitious delivery could be interpreted as complacency on my part towards my error – or worse, an attempt to cover it up. This was why, then, I decided it appropriate to put the fork down on to the table with a certain emphasis, causing my employer to start a second time, look up and mutter again: 'Ah, Stevens.'

Errors such as these which have occurred over the last few months have been, naturally enough, injurious to one's self-respect, but then there is no reason to believe them to be the signs of anything more sinister than a staff shortage. Not that a staff shortage is not significant in itself; but if Miss Kenton were indeed to return to Darlington Hall, such little slips, I am sure, would become a thing of the past. Of course, one has to remember there is nothing stated specifically in Miss Kenton's letter – which, incidentally, I reread last night up in my room before putting out the light – to indicate unambiguously her desire to return to her former position. In fact, one has to accept the distinct possibility that one may have previously – perhaps through wishful thinking of a professional kind – exaggerated what evidence there was regarding such a desire on her part. For I must say I was a little surprised last night at how difficult it was actually to point to any passage which clearly demonstrated her wish to return.

▷ **1** *note:* Bedeutung **2** *drag sb. down:* pull sb. down **6** *provide sth.:* give or supply sth. **10** *irrefutable:* indisputable **11** *fulcrum:* centre **22** *complacency:* self-satisfaction **25** *surface* (v): come to the surface **34** *prong:* (Gabel)zinke **37** *swift:* quick **37–38** *the offending item:* thing that has annoyed or bothered sb. **39** *give a start:* move suddenly, because you are surprised **42** *without undue delay:* not staying away for too long **47** *feign indifference* [feɪn]: pretend not to know or to care • *minimize sth.:* reduce sth. considerably **48** *surreptitious:* secret **49** *cover sth. up:* hide sth. **54** *injurious:* damaging

But then again, it seems hardly worthwhile to speculate greatly on such matters now when one knows one will, in all likelihood, be talking face to face with Miss Kenton within forty-eight hours. Still, I must say, I did spend some long minutes turning those passages over in my mind last night as I lay there in the darkness, listening to the sounds from below of the landlord and his wife clearing up for the night.

▷ **2** *likelihood:* probability

DAY THREE – EVENING

Moscombe, near Tavistock, Devon

I feel I should perhaps return a moment to the question of his lordship's attitude to Jewish persons, since this whole issue of anti-Semitism, I realize, has become a rather sensitive one these days. In particular, let me clear up this matter of a supposed bar against Jewish persons on the staff at Darlington Hall. Since this allegation falls very directly into my own realm, I am able to refute it with absolute authority. There were many Jewish persons on my staff throughout all my years with his lordship, and let me say furthermore that they were never treated in any way differently on account of their race. One really cannot guess the reason for these absurd allegations – unless, quite ludicrously, they originate from that brief, entirely insignificant few weeks in the early thirties when Mrs Carolyn Barnet came to wield an unusual influence over his lordship.

Mrs Barnet, the widow of Mr Charles Barnet, was at that point in her forties – a very handsome, some might say glamorous lady. She had a reputation for being formidably intelligent, and in those days one often tended to hear of how she had humiliated this or that learned gentleman at dinner over some important contemporary issue. For much of the summer of 1932, she was a regular presence at Darlington Hall, she and his lordship often spending hour after hour deep in conversation, typically of a social or political nature. And it was Mrs Barnet, as I recall, who took his lordship on those 'guided inspections' of the poorest areas of London's East End, during which his lordship visited the actual homes of many of the families suffering the desperate plight of those years. That is to say, Mrs Barnet, in all likelihood, made some sort of contribution to Lord Darlington's developing concern for the poor of our country and as such, her influence cannot be said to have been entirely negative. But she was too, of course, a member of Sir Oswald Mosley's 'blackshirts' organization, and the very little contact his lordship ever had with Sir Oswald occurred during those few weeks of that summer. And it was during those same weeks that those entirely untypical incidents took

▷ **4** *supposed* (adj): vermutet, mutmaßlich **4–5** *bar against Jewish persons on the staff:* rule stating that Jews were forbidden to join the staff **6** *refute sth.:* say that sth. is not true **13** *wield sth.:* etwas ausüben **15** *handsome:* attractive **17** *humiliate sb.:* make sb. feel ashamed **18** *learned* ['lɜːnɪd]: having a lot of knowledge • *contemporary:* of that time **25** *plight:* bad condition or situation

place at Darlington Hall which must, one supposes, have provided what flimsy basis exists for these absurd allegations.

I call them 'incidents' but some of these were extremely minor. For instance, I recall overhearing at dinner one evening, when a particular newspaper had been mentioned, his lordship remarking: 'Oh, you mean that Jewish propaganda sheet.' And then on another occasion around that time, I remember his instructing me to cease giving donations to a particular local charity which regularly came to the door on the grounds that the management committee was 'more or less homogeneously Jewish'. I have remembered these remarks because they truly surprised me at the time, his lordship never previously having shown any antagonism whatsoever towards the Jewish race.

Then, of course, came that afternoon his lordship called me into his study. Initially, he made rather general conversation, inquiring if all was well around the house and so on. Then he said:

'I've been doing a great deal of thinking, Stevens. A great deal of thinking. And I've reached my conclusion. We cannot have Jews on the staff here at Darlington Hall.'

'Sir?'

'It's for the good of this house, Stevens. In the interests of the guests we have staying here. I've looked into this carefully, Stevens, and I'm letting you know my conclusion.'

'Very well, sir.'

'Tell me, Stevens, we have a few on the staff at the moment, don't we? Jews, I mean.'

'I believe two of the present staff members would fall into that category, sir.'

'Ah.' His lordship paused for a moment, staring out of this window. 'Of course, you'll have to let them go.'

'I beg your pardon, sir?'

'It's regrettable, Stevens, but we have no choice. There's the safety and well-being of my guests to consider. Let me assure you, I've looked into this matter and thought it through thoroughly. It's all in our best interests.'

The two staff members concerned were, in fact, both housemaids. It would hardly have been proper, then, to have taken action without first informing Miss Kenton of the situation, and I resolved to do just this that same evening when I met her for cocoa in her parlour. I should perhaps say a few words here concerning these meetings in her parlour at the end of each day. These were, let me say, overwhelmingly professional in tone – though naturally we might discuss some informal topics from time to time. Our reason for instituting such meetings was simple: we had found that our respective lives were often so busy, several days could go by without our having an opportunity to exchange even the most basic of information. Such a situation, we recognized, seriously jeopardized the smooth running of operations, and to spend fifteen minutes or so together at the end of the day in the privacy of Miss Kenton's parlour was the most straightforward remedy. I must reiterate, these meetings were predominantly professional in character; that is to say, for instance, we might talk over the plans for a forthcoming event, or else discuss how a new recruit was settling in.

In any case, to return to my thread, you will appreciate I was not unperturbed at the prospect of telling Miss Kenton I was about to dismiss two of her maids. Indeed, the maids had been perfectly satisfactory employees and – I may as well say this since the Jewish issue has become so sensitive of late – my every instinct opposed the idea of their dismissal. Nevertheless, my duty in this instance was quite clear, and as I saw it, there was nothing to be gained at all in irresponsibly displaying such personal doubts. It was a difficult task, but as such, one that demanded to be carried out with dignity. And so it was that when I finally raised the matter towards the end of our conversation that evening, I did so in as concise and businesslike a way as possible, concluding with the words:

'I will speak to the two employees in my pantry tomorrow morning at ten thirty. I would be grateful then, Miss Kenton, if you would send them along. I leave it entirely to yourself whether or not you inform them beforehand as to the nature of what I am going to say to them.'

At this point, Miss Kenton seemed to have nothing to say in response. So I continued: 'Well, Miss Kenton, thank you for the cocoa. It's high time I was turning in. Another busy day tomorrow.'

▷ **2** *flimsy:* not to be taken seriously **8** *donation:* thing (usu. money) given to support charitable or political institutions **9** *on the grounds that:* because **10** *homogeneous* [ˌhɒməˈdʒiːniəs]: consisting of the same kind of people **37** *resolve* (v): decide **43** *institute sth.:* start sth. **43–44** *our respective lives:* her life and my life **49** *the most straightforward remedy:* the easiest way of overcoming that risk **50** *predominantly:* mostly **54** *unperturbed:* not worried **55** *dismiss sb.:* remove sb. from their job **71** *it's high time I was turning in:* it's time for me to go to bed

It was then Miss Kenton said: 'Mr Stevens, I cannot quite believe my ears. Ruth and Sarah have been members of my staff for over six years now. I trust them absolutely and indeed they trust me. They have served this house excellently.'

'I am sure that is so, Miss Kenton. However, we must not allow sentiment to creep into our judgement. Now really, I must bid you good night ...'

'Mr Stevens, I am outraged that you can sit there and utter what you have just done as though you were discussing orders for the larder. I simply cannot believe it. You are saying Ruth and Sarah are to be dismissed on the grounds that they are Jewish?'

'Miss Kenton, I have just this moment explained the situation to you fully. His lordship has made his decision and there is nothing for you and I to debate over.'

'Does it not occur to you, Mr Stevens, that to dismiss Ruth and Sarah on these grounds would be simply – *wrong*? I will not stand for such things. I will not work in a house in which such things can occur.'

'Miss Kenton, I will ask you not to excite yourself and to conduct yourself in a manner befitting your position. This is a very straightforward matter. If his lordship wishes these particular contracts to be discontinued, then there is little more to be said.'

'I am warning you, Mr Stevens, I will not continue to work in such a house. If my girls are dismissed, I will leave also.'

'Miss Kenton, I am surprised to find you reacting in this manner. Surely I don't have to remind you that our professional duty is not to our own foibles and sentiments, but to the wishes of our employer.'

'I am telling you, Mr Stevens, if you dismiss my girls tomorrow, it will be wrong, a sin as any sin ever was one and I will not continue to work in such a house.'

'Miss Kenton, let me suggest to you that you are hardly well placed to be passing judgements of such a high and mighty nature. The fact is, the world of today is a very complicated and treacherous place. There are many things you and I are simply not in a position to understand concerning, say, the nature of Jewry. Whereas his lordship, I might venture, is somewhat better placed to judge what is for the best. Now, Miss Kenton, I really must retire. I thank you again for the cocoa. Ten thirty tomorrow morning. Send the two employees concerned, please.'

It was evident from the moment the two maids stepped into my pantry the following morning that Miss Kenton had already spoken to them, for they both came in sobbing. I explained the situation to them as briefly as possible, underlining that their work had been satisfactory and that they would, accordingly, receive good references. As I recall, neither of them said anything of note throughout the whole interview, which lasted perhaps three or four minutes, and they left sobbing just as they had arrived.

Miss Kenton was extremely cold towards me for some days following the dismissal of the employees. Indeed, at times she was quite rude to me, even in the presence of staff. And although we continued our habit of meeting for cocoa in the evening, the sessions tended to be brief and unfriendly. When there had been no sign of her behaviour abating after a fortnight or so, I think you will understand that I started to become a little impatient. I thus said to her during one of our cocoa sessions, in an ironic tone of voice:

'Miss Kenton, I'd rather expected you to have handed in your notice by now,' accompanying this with a light laugh. I did, I suppose, hope that she might finally relent a little and make some conciliatory response or other, allowing us once and for all to put the whole episode behind us. Miss Kenton, however, simply looked at me sternly and said:

'I still have every intention of handing in my notice, Mr Stevens. It is merely that I have been so busy, I have not had time to see to the matter.'

This did, I must admit, make me a little concerned for a time that she was serious about her threat. But then, as week followed week, it became clear that there was no question of her leaving Darlington

▷ **6** *sentiment:* feeling **8** *outraged* (adj): very angry and shocked **10** *larder:* room or large cupboard for storing food in a house **20** *befitting* (adj): appropriate to **21** *contract:* Arbeitsvertrag **27** *foible:* habit or feature of sb.'s character which is a bit strange or silly **32** *pass judgement:* ein Urteil fällen • *high and mighty* (infml): arrogant **35** *Jewry* ['dʒʊəri]: the Jewish people **45** *references* (pl): documents reporting on the quality of their work **53** *abate:* become less strong or aggressive **56–57** *hand in your notice:* inform your employer that you will be leaving your job soon **58** *relent:* change your attitude and become less severe, cruel or unfriendly to sb. • *conciliatory:* intended to re-establish a friendly relationship **63–64** *see to the matter:* get sth. done about a particular situation

Hall, and as the atmosphere between us gradually thawed, I suppose I tended to tease her every now and again by reminding her of her threatened resignation. For instance, if we were discussing some future large occasion to be held at the house, I might put in: 'That is, Miss Kenton, assuming you are still with us at that stage.' Even months after the event, such remarks still tended to make Miss Kenton go quiet – though by this stage, I fancy, this was due more to embarrassment than anger.

Eventually, of course, the matter came to be, by and large, forgotten. But I remember it coming up one last time well over a year after the dismissal of the two maids.

It was his lordship who initially revived the matter one afternoon when I was serving his tea in the drawing room. By then, Mrs Carolyn Barnet's days of influence over his lordship were well over – indeed, the lady had ceased to be a visitor at Darlington Hall altogether. It is worth pointing out, furthermore, that his lordship had by that time severed all links with the 'blackshirts', having witnessed the true, ugly nature of that organization.

'Oh, Stevens,' he had said to me. 'I've been meaning to say to you. About that business last year. About the Jewish maids. You recall the matter?'

'Indeed, sir.'

'I suppose there's no way of tracing them now, is there? It was wrong what happened and one would like to recompense them somehow.'

'I will certainly look into the matter, sir. But I am not at all certain it will be possible to ascertain their whereabouts at this stage.'

'See what you can do. It was wrong, what occurred.'

I assumed this exchange with his lordship would be of some interest to Miss Kenton, and I decided it only proper to mention it to her – even at the risk of getting her angry again. As it turned out, my doing so on that foggy afternoon I encountered her in the summerhouse produced curious results.

I recall a mist starting to set in as I crossed the lawn that afternoon. I was making my way up to the summerhouse for the purpose of clearing away the remains of his lordship's tea there with some guests a little while earlier. I can recall spotting from some distance – long before reaching the steps where my father had once fallen – Miss Kenton's figure moving about inside the summerhouse. When I entered she had seated herself on one of the wicker chairs scattered around its interior, evidently engaged in some needlework. On closer inspection, I saw she was performing repairs to a cushion. I went about gathering up the various items of crockery from amidst the plants and the cane furniture, and as I did so, I believe we exchanged a few pleasantries, perhaps discussed one or two professional matters. For the truth was, it was extremely refreshing to be out in the summerhouse after many continuous days in the main building and neither of us was inclined to hurry with our tasks. Indeed, although one could not see out far that day on account of the encroaching mist, and the daylight too was rapidly fading by this stage, obliging Miss Kenton to hold her needlework up to the last of it, I remembered our often breaking off from our respective activities simply to gaze out at the views around us. In fact, I was looking out over the lawn to where the mist was thickening down around the poplar trees planted along the cart-track, when I finally introduced the topic of the previous year's dismissals. Perhaps a little predictably, I did so by saying:

'I was just thinking earlier, Miss Kenton. It's rather funny to remember now, but you know, only this time a year ago, you were still insisting you were going to resign. It rather amused me to think of it.' I gave a laugh, but behind me Miss Kenton remained silent. When I finally turned to look at her, she was gazing through the glass at the great expanse of fog outside.

'You probably have no idea, Mr Stevens,' she said eventually, 'how seriously I really thought of leaving this house. I felt so strongly about what happened. Had I been anyone worthy of any respect at all, I dare say I would have left Darlington Hall long ago.' She paused for a while, and I turned my gaze back out to the poplar trees down in the

▷ **1** *gradually:* step by step, slowly • *thaw:* melt; (here) relax **2** *tease sb.:* provoke sb. in a friendly and humorous way **7** *fancy* (v): imagine **12** *revive sth.:* talk about sth. again **17** *sever all links with sb.:* break off all connections with sb. • *witness sth.:* see sth. first-hand **23** *trace sb.:* find out where sb. lives and works **24** *recompense sb.:* give sb. a payment for trouble or losses they have suffered **39** *wicker chair:* Korbstuhl/-sessel **39–40** *scattered around its interior:* standing here and there inside the room **42** *crockery:* cups, plates, etc. **43** *cane:* wicker **44** *pleasantries* (pl): polite small talk **48** *encroach:* slowly begin to cover an area **49** *fade:* disappear slowly **55** *predictable:* vorhersehbar **58** *resign:* tell your boss you are leaving your job **61** *expanse:* very large area of sth.

distance. Then she continued in a tired voice: 'It was cowardice, Mr Stevens. Simple cowardice. Where could I have gone? I have no family. Only my aunt. I love her dearly, but I can't live with her for a day without feeling my whole life is wasting away. I did tell myself, of course, I would soon find myself some new situation. But I was so frightened, Mr Stevens. Whenever I thought of leaving, I just saw myself going out there and finding nobody who knew or cared about me. There, that's all my high principles amount to. I feel so ashamed of myself. But I just couldn't leave, Mr Stevens, I just couldn't bring myself to leave.'

Miss Kenton paused again and seemed to be deep in thought. I thus thought it opportune to relate at this point, as precisely as possible, what had taken place earlier between myself and Lord Darlington. I proceeded to do so and concluded by saying:

'What's done can hardly be undone. But it is at least a great comfort to hear his lordship declare so unequivocally that it was all a terrible misunderstanding. I just thought you'd like to know, Miss Kenton, since I recall you were as distressed by the episode as I was.'

'I'm sorry, Mr Stevens,' Miss Kenton said behind me in an entirely new voice, as though she had just been jolted from a dream, 'I don't understand you.' Then as I turned to her, she went on: 'As I recall, you thought it was only right and proper that Ruth and Sarah be sent packing. You were positively cheerful about it.'

'Now really, Miss Kenton, that is quite incorrect and unfair. The whole matter caused me great concern, great concern indeed. It is hardly the sort of thing I like to see happen in this house.'

'Then why, Mr Stevens, did you not tell me so at the time?'

I gave a laugh, but for a moment was rather at a loss for an answer. Before I could formulate one, Miss Kenton put down her sewing and said:

'Do you realize, Mr Stevens, how much it would have meant to me if you had thought to share your feelings last year? You knew how upset I was when my girls were dismissed. Do you realize how much it would have helped me? Why, Mr Stevens, why, why, why do you always have to *pretend*?'

I gave another laugh at the ridiculous turn the conversation had suddenly taken. 'Really, Miss Kenton,' I said, 'I'm not sure I know what you mean. Pretend? Why, really ...'

'I suffered so much over Ruth and Sarah leaving us. And I suffered all the more because I believed I was alone.'

'Really, Miss Kenton ...' I picked up the tray on which I had gathered together the used crockery. 'Naturally, one disapproved of the dismissals. One would have thought that quite self-evident.'

She did not say anything, and as I was leaving I glanced back towards her. She was again gazing out at the view, but it had by this point grown so dark inside the summerhouse, all I could see of her was her profile outlined against a pale and empty background. I excused myself and proceeded to make my exit.

Now that I have recalled this episode of the dismissing of the Jewish employees, I am reminded of what could, I suppose, be called a curious corollary to that whole affair: namely, the arrival of the housemaid called Lisa. That is to say, we were obliged to find replacements for the two dismissed Jewish maids, and this Lisa turned out to be one of them.

This young woman had applied for the vacancy with the most dubious of references, which spelt out to any experienced butler that she had left her previous situation under something of a cloud. Moreover, when Miss Kenton and I questioned her, it became clear that she had never remained in any position for longer than a few weeks. In general, her whole attitude suggested to me that she was quite unsuitable for employment at Darlington Hall. To my surprise, however, once we had finished interviewing the girl, Miss Kenton began to insist we take her on. 'I see much potential in this girl,' she continued to say in the face of my protests. 'She will be directly under my supervision and I will see to it she proves good.'

I recall we became locked in disagreement for some time, and it was perhaps only the fact that the matter of the dismissed maids

▷ **1** *cowardice:* Feigheit **8** *that's all sth. amounts to:* that's all sth. is worth **12** *opportune:* happening at the right time **16** *unequivocal:* clear, unambiguous, in no uncertain terms **20** *jolt sb. from a dream:* move sb. suddenly and roughly so that they wake up **22–23** *send sb. packing* (infml): dismiss or fire sb. **28** *be at a loss for an answer:* not know what to say in reply **48** *make my exit:* go away **53** *replacement:* person to take the job of sb. else **55** *vacancy* ['veɪkənsi]: job that is available **56** *dubious:* questionable • *spell sth. out to sb.:* mean sth. to sb. **66** *become locked in disagreement:* argue very much about sth.

was so recent in our minds that I did not hold out as strongly as I might against Miss Kenton. In any case, the result was that I finally gave way, albeit by saying:

'Miss Kenton, I hope you realize that the responsibility for taking on this girl rests squarely with yourself. There is no doubt as far as I am concerned that at this present moment she is far from adequate to be a member of our staff. I am only allowing her to join on the understanding that you will personally oversee her development.'

'The girl will turn out well, Mr Stevens. You will see.'

And to my astonishment, during the weeks that followed, the young girl did indeed make progress at a remarkable rate. Her attitude seemed to improve by the day, and even her manner of walking and going about tasks – which during the first days had been so slovenly that one had to avert one's eyes – improved dramatically. As the weeks went on, and the girl appeared miraculously to have been transformed into a useful member of staff, Miss Kenton's triumph was obvious. She seemed to take particular pleasure in assigning Lisa some task or other that required a little extra responsibility, and if I were watching, she would be sure to try and catch my eye with her rather mocking expression. And the exchange we had that night in Miss Kenton's parlour over cocoa was fairly typical of the sort of conversation we tended to have on the topic of Lisa.

'No doubt, Mr Stevens,' she said to me, 'you will be extremely disappointed to hear Lisa has still not made any real mistake worth speaking of.'

'I'm not disappointed at all, Miss Kenton. I'm very pleased for you and for all of us. I will admit, you have had some modest success regarding the girl thus far.'

'Modest success! And look at that smile on your face, Mr Stevens. It always appears when I mention Lisa. That tells an interesting story in itself. A very interesting story indeed.'

'Oh, really, Miss Kenton. And may I ask what exactly?'

'It is very interesting, Mr Stevens. Very interesting you should have been so pessimistic about her. Because Lisa is a pretty girl, no doubt about it. And I've noticed you have a curious aversion to pretty girls being on the staff.'

'You know perfectly well you are talking nonsense, Miss Kenton.'

'Ah. But I've noticed it, Mr Stevens. You do not like pretty girls to be on the staff. Might it be that our Mr Stevens fears distraction? Can it be that our Mr Stevens is flesh and blood after all and cannot fully trust himself?'

'Really, Miss Kenton. If I thought there was one modicum of sense in what you are saying I might bother to engage with you in this discussion. As it is, I think I shall simply place my thoughts elsewhere while you chatter away.'

'Ah, but then why is that guilty smile still on your face, Mr Stevens?'

'It is not a guilty smile at all, Miss Kenton. I am slightly amused by your astonishing capacity to talk nonsense, that is all.'

'It *is* a guilty little smile you have on, Mr Stevens. And I've noticed how you can hardly bear to look at Lisa. Now it is beginning to become very clear why you objected so strongly to her.'

'My objections were extremely solid, Miss Kenton, as you very well know. The girl was completely unsuitable when she first came to us.'

Now of course, you must understand we would never have carried on in such a vein within the hearing of staff members. But just around that time, our cocoa evenings, while maintaining their essentially professional character, often tended to allow room for a little harmless talk of this sort – which did much, one should say, to relieve the many tensions produced by a hard day.

Lisa had been with us for some eight or nine months – and I had largely forgotten her existence by this point – when she vanished from the house together with the second footman. Now, of course, such things are simply part and parcel of life for any butler of a large household. They are intensely irritating, but one learns to accept them. In fact, as far as these sorts of 'moonlight' departures were concerned, this was among the more civilized. Aside from a little food, the couple had taken nothing that belonged to the house, and furthermore, both parties had left letters. The second footman, whose name I no longer recall, left a short note addressed to me, saying

▷ **3** *give way:* agree to sth. more or less against your will • *albeit by saying:* although I did say **5** *squarely:* directly and firmly **12** *by the day:* from day to day **14** *slovenly:* lazily and untidily • *avert your eyes:* look somewhere else **15** *miraculous:* as if by a miracle (= Wunder) **18** *assign sb. sth.*: give sb. sth. to do **20** *mocking* (adj): spöttisch, höhnisch **39** *distraction:* thing that takes your attention away from what you are doing **42** *modicum:* small amount **55** *in such a vein:* in a particular manner **58** *relieve sth.:* make sth. easier to bear or endure **63** *part and parcel of sth.:* a normal or essential part of sth. **65** *'moonlight' departure:* act of leaving without telling anyone beforehand

something like: 'Please do not judge us too harshly. We are in love and are going to be married.' Lisa had written a much longer note addressed to 'the Housekeeper', and it was this letter Miss Kenton brought into my pantry on the morning following their disappearance. There were, as I recall, many misspelt, ill-formed sentences about how much in love the couple were, how wonderful the second footman was, and how marvellous the future was that awaited them both. One line, as I recall it, read something to the effect of: 'We don't have money but who cares we have love and who wants anything else we've got one another that's all anyone can ever want.' Despite the letter being three pages long, there was no mention of any gratitude towards Miss Kenton for the great care she had given the girl, nor was there any note of regret at letting all of us down.

Miss Kenton was noticeably upset. All the while I was running my eye over the young woman's letter, she sat there at the table before me, looking down at her hands. In fact – and this strikes one as rather curious – I cannot really recall seeing her more bereft than on that morning. When I put the letter down on the table, she said:

'So, Mr Stevens, it seems you were right and I was wrong.'

'Miss Kenton, this is nothing to upset yourself over,' I said. 'These things happen. There really is little the likes of us can ever do to prevent these things.'

'I was at fault, Mr Stevens. I accept it. You were right all along, as ever, and I was wrong.'

'Miss Kenton, I really cannot agree with you. You did wonders with that girl. What you managed with her proved many times over that it was in fact I who was in error. Really, Miss Kenton, what has happened now might have happened with any employee. You did remarkably well with her. You may have every reason to feel let down by her, but no reason at all to feel any responsibility on your own part.'

Miss Kenton continued to look very dejected. She said quietly: 'You're very kind to say so, Mr Stevens. I'm very grateful.' Then she sighed tiredly and said: 'She's so foolish. She might have had a real career in front of her. She had ability. So many young women like her throw away their chances, and all for what?'

We both looked at the notepaper on the table between us, and then Miss Kenton turned her gaze away with an air of annoyance.

'Indeed,' I said. 'Such a waste, as you say.'

'So foolish. And the girl is bound to be let down. And she had a good life ahead of her if only she'd persevered. In a year or two, I could have had her ready to take on a housekeeper's post in some small residence. Perhaps you think that far-fetched, Mr Stevens, but then look how far I came with her in a few months. And now she's thrown it all away. All for nothing.'

'It really is most foolish of her.'

I had started to gather up the sheets of notepaper before me, thinking I might file them away for reference. But then as I was doing so, I became a little uncertain as to whether Miss Kenton had intended me to keep the letter, or if she herself wished to do so, and I placed the pages back down on the table between the two of us. Miss Kenton, in any case, seemed far away.

'She's bound to be let down,' she said again. 'So foolish.'

But I see I have become somewhat lost in these old memories. This had never been my intention, but then it is probably no bad thing if in doing so I have at least avoided becoming unduly preoccupied with the events of this evening – which I trust have now finally concluded themselves. For these last few hours, it must be said, have been rather trying ones.

I find myself now in the attic room of this small cottage belonging to Mr and Mrs Taylor. That is to say, this is a private residence; this room, made so kindly available to me tonight by the Taylors, was once occupied by their eldest son now long grown and living in Exeter. It is a room dominated by heavy beams and rafters, and the floorboards have no carpet or rug to cover them, and yet the atmosphere is surprisingly cosy. And it is clear Mrs Taylor has not only made up the bed for me, she has also tidied and cleaned; for aside from a few cobwebs near the rafters, there is little to reveal that this room has been unoccupied for many years. As for Mr and Mrs Taylor them-

▷ **12** *gratitude:* feeling of being thankful **17** *bereft:* feeling very sad and lonely (often due to a loss) **23** *I was at fault:* it was my mistake; I was wrong **31** *dejected* (adj): unhappy, disappointed **39** *the girl is bound to be let down:* she is sure to experience disappointment **42** *far-fetched* (adj): unrealistic **47** *file sth. away for reference:* put sth. in a particular place so it can be found again easily **63** *rafter:* large piece of wood that forms the structure of a house or roof **65** *cosy:* gemütlich, behaglich **67** *cobweb:* net of sticky threads made by a spider

selves, I have ascertained that they ran the village green grocery here from the twenties until their retirement three years ago. They are kind people, and though I have on more than one occasion tonight offered remuneration for their hospitality, they will not hear of it.

The fact that I am now here, the fact I came to be to all intents and purposes at the mercy of Mr and Mrs Taylor's generosity on this night, is attributable to one foolish, infuriatingly simple oversight: namely, I allowed the Ford to run out of petrol. What with this and the trouble yesterday concerning the lack of water in the radiator, it would not be unreasonable for an observer to believe such general disorganization endemic to my nature. It may be pointed out, of course, that as far as long-distance motoring is concerned, I am something of a novice, and such simple oversights are only to be expected. And yet, when one remembers that good organization and foresight are qualities that lie at the very heart of one's profession, it is hard to avoid the feeling that one has, somehow, let oneself down again.

But it is true, I had been considerably distracted during the last hour or so of motoring prior to the petrol running out. I had planned to lodge the night in the town of Tavistock, where I arrived a little before eight o'clock. At the town's main inn, however, I was informed all the rooms were occupied on account of a local agricultural fair. Several other establishments were suggested to me, but though I called at each, I was met every time with the same apology. Finally, at a boarding house on the edge of the town, the landlady suggested I motor on several miles to a roadside inn run by a relative of hers – which, she assured me, was bound to have vacancies, being too far out of Tavistock to be affected by the fair.

She had given me thorough directions, which had seemed clear enough at the time, and it is impossible to say now whose fault it was that I subsequently failed to find any trace of this roadside establishment. Instead, after fifteen minutes or so of motoring, I found myself out on a long road curving across bleak, open moorland. On either side of me were what appeared to be fields of marsh, and a mist was rolling across my path. To my left, I could see the last glow of the sunset. The skyline was broken here and there by the shapes of barns and farmhouses some way away over the fields, but otherwise, I appeared to have left behind all signs of community.

I recall turning the Ford round at about this stage and doubling back some distance in search of a turning I had passed earlier. But when I found it, this new road proved, if anything, more desolate than the one I had left. For a time, I drove in near-darkness between high hedges, then found the road beginning to climb steeply. I had by now given up hope of finding the roadside inn and had set my mind on motoring on till I reached the next town or village and seeking shelter there. It would be easy enough, so I was reasoning to myself, to resume my planned route first thing in the morning. It was at this point, half-way up the hill road, that the engine stuttered and I noticed for the first time that my petrol was gone.

The Ford continued its climb for several yards, then came to a halt. When I got out to assess my situation, I could see I had only a few more minutes of daylight left to me. I was standing on a steep road bound in by trees and hedgerows; much further up the hill, I could see a break in the hedges where a wide barred gate stood outlined against the sky. I began to make my way up to it, supposing that a view from this gate would give me some sense of my bearings; perhaps I had even hoped to see a farmhouse near by where I could gain prompt assistance. I was a little disconcerted then by what eventually greeted my eyes. On the other side of the gate a field sloped down very steeply so that it fell out of vision only twenty yards or so in front of me. Beyond the crest of the field, some way off in the distance – perhaps a good mile or so as the crow would fly – was a small village. I could make out through the mist a church steeple, and around it, clusters of dark-slated roofs; here and there, wisps of white smoke were rising from chimneys. One had to confess, at that moment, to

▷ **1** *green grocery:* shop that sells fruits and vegetables **2** *retirement:* Ausscheiden aus dem Arbeitsleben **4** *remuneration:* payment for help given • *hospitality:* kindness shown to a guest • *they will not hear of it:* they refuse to accept sth. **5–6** *to all intents and purposes:* almost completely **6** *at the mercy of sb./sth.:* dependent on sb./sth. **7** *infuriating* (adj): very annoying • *oversight:* mistake you make by not noticing sth. or by forgetting sth. **11** *endemic:* always present **12** *novice:* person who has no experience, beginner **21** *agricultural fair:* a kind of market for farmers **26** *vacancy:* room that is available **30–31** *this roadside establishment:* the inn mentioned before **32** *bleak:* without any pleasant or attractive features **34** *marsh:* Sumpf **40** *desolate:* empty, lonely, sad **44** *seek shelter:* look for a place to spend the night **47** *stutter:* make little explosive noises **53** *barred:* with bars across it; locked completely **55** *my bearings:* where I was **57** *prompt* (adj): quick • *disconcerted* [- - '- -] (adj): confused, worried, upset **58** *slope down:* form a downhill slope (= Abhang) **60** *crest:* top

being overcome by a certain sense of discouragement. Of course, the situation was not by any means hopeless; the Ford was not damaged, simply out of fuel. A walk down to the village could be accomplished in a half-hour or so and there I could surely find accommodation and a can of petrol. And yet it was not a happy feeling to be up there on a lonely hill, looking over a gate at the lights coming on in a distant village, the daylight all but faded, and the mist growing ever thicker.

There was little to be gained in growing despondent, however. In any case, it would have been foolish to waste the few remaining minutes of daylight. I walked back down to the Ford where I packed a briefcase with some essential items. Then, arming myself with a bicycle lamp, which cast a surprisingly good beam, I went in search of a path by which I could descend to the village. But no such path offered itself, though I went some distance up the hill, a good way past my gate. Then when I sensed that the road had ceased to climb, but was beginning to curve slowly down in a direction *away* from the village – the lights of which I could glimpse regularly through the foliage – I was overcome again by a sense of discouragement. In fact, for a moment I wondered if my best strategy would not be to retrace my steps to the Ford and simply sit in it until another motorist came by. By then, however, it was very close to being dark, and I could see that if one were to attempt to hail a passing vehicle in these circumstances, one might easily be taken for a highwayman or some such. Besides, not a single vehicle had passed since I had got out of the Ford; in fact, I could not really remember having seen another vehicle at all since leaving Tavistock. I resolved then to return as far as the gate, and from there, descend the field, walking in as direct a line as possible towards the lights of the village, regardless of whether or not there was a proper path.

It was not, in the end, too arduous a descent. A series of grazing fields, one after the next, led the way down to the village and by keeping close to the edge of each field as one descended, one could be ensured of reasonable walking. Only once, with the village very close, could I find no obvious way to gain access to the next field down, and I had to shine my bicycle lamp to and fro along the hedgerow obstructing me. Eventually, I discovered a small gap through which I proceeded to squeeze my person, but only at some cost to the shoulder of my jacket and the turn-ups of my trousers. The last few fields, furthermore, became increasingly muddy and I deliberately refrained from shining my lamp on to my shoes and turn-ups for fear of further discouragement.

By and by I found myself on a paved path going down into the village, and it was while descending this path that I met Mr Taylor, my kind host of this evening. He had emerged out of a turning a few yards in front of me, and had courteously waited for me to catch up, whereupon he had touched his cap and asked if he could be of any assistance to me. I had explained my position as succinctly as possible, adding that I would be most gratified to be guided towards a good inn. At this, Mr Taylor had shaken his head, saying: 'I'm afraid there's no inn as such in our village, sir. John Humphreys usually takes in travellers at the Crossed Keys, but he's having work done to the roof at the moment.' Before this distressing piece of information could have its full effect, however, Mr Taylor said: 'If you didn't mind roughing it a little, sir, we could offer you a room and a bed for the night. It's nothing special, but the wife will see to it everything's clean and comfortable enough in a basic sort of way.'

I believe I uttered some words, perhaps in a rather half-hearted way, to the effect that I could not inconvenience them to such an extent. To which Mr Taylor had said: 'I tell you, sir, it would be an honour to have you. It's not often we get the likes of yourself passing through Moscombe. And quite honestly, sir, I don't know what else you could do at this hour. The wife would never forgive me if I were to let you away into the night.'

Thus it was that I came to accept the kind hospitality of Mr and Mrs Taylor. But when I spoke earlier of this evening's events being 'trying', I was not referring simply to the frustrations of running out of

▷ **1** *be overcome by sth.:* von etwas überwältigt werden **8** *despondent:* unhappy and without hope **12** *beam:* Lichtstrahl **19–20** *retrace your steps:* go back the way you came **22** *hail sth.:* ask sth. (esp. a car or taxi) to stop and take you somewhere **23** *highwayman* (old-fashioned): criminal who stops people and carriages on the road and robs them **30** *arduous:* involving a lot of strength and effort • *descent:* act of climbing downwards **30–31** *grazing field:* field used by animals for eating grass **34** *gain access to sth.:* find a way of reaching sth. **36** *obstruct sb.:* prevent sb. from going on **37** *squeeze sth.:* press sth. through a narrow opening **38** *turn-ups:* Hosenaufschläge **44** *turning* (n): side path **45** *catch up:* (jdn.) einholen **46** *whereupon:* and then **47** *succinct:* brief and clear **48** *gratified* (adj): pleased and satisfied **54** *rough it* (infml): live for a short time in conditions that are not very comfortable **58** *inconvenience sb.:* cause sb. problems or difficulty

petrol and of having to make such an uncouth journey down into the village. For what occurred subsequently – what unfolded once I sat down to supper with Mr and Mrs Taylor and their neighbours – proved in its own way far more taxing on one's resources than the essentially physical discomforts I had faced earlier. It was, I can assure you, a relief indeed to be able at last to come up to this room and to spend some moments turning over these memories of Darlington Hall from all those years ago.

The fact is, I have tended increasingly of late to indulge myself in such recollections. And ever since the prospect of seeing Miss Kenton again first arose some weeks ago, I suppose I have tended to spend much time pondering just why it was our relationship underwent such a change. For change it certainly did, around 1935 or 1936, after many years in which we had steadily achieved a fine professional understanding. In fact, by the end, we had even abandoned our routine of meeting over a cup of cocoa at the end of each day. But as to what really caused such changes, just what particular chain of events was responsible, I have never quite been able to decide.

In thinking about this recently, it seems possible that that odd incident the evening Miss Kenton came into my pantry uninvited may have marked a crucial point. Why it was she came to my pantry I cannot remember with certainty. I have a feeling she may have come bearing a vase of flowers 'to brighten things up', but then again, I may be getting confused with the time she attempted the same thing earlier at the start of our acquaintanceship. I know for a fact she tried to introduce flowers to my pantry on at least three occasions over the years, but perhaps I am confused in believing this to have been what brought her that particular evening. I might emphasize, in any case, that notwithstanding our years of good working relations, I had never allowed the situation to slip to one in which the housekeeper was coming and going from my pantry all day. The butler's pantry, as far as I am concerned, is a crucial office, the heart of the house's operations, not unlike a general's headquarters during a battle, and it is imperative that all things in it are ordered – and left ordered – in precisely the way I wish them to be. I have never been that sort of butler who allows all sorts of people to wander in and out with their queries and grumbles. If operations are to be conducted in a smoothly co-ordinated way, it is surely obvious that the butler's pantry must be the one place in the house where privacy and solitude are guaranteed.

As it happened, when she entered my pantry that evening, I was not in fact engaged in professional matters. That is to say, it was towards the end of the day during a quiet week and I had been enjoying a rare hour or so off duty. As I say, I am not certain if Miss Kenton entered with her vase of flowers, but I certainly do recall her saying:

'Mr Stevens, your room looks even less accommodating at night than it does in the day. The electric bulb is too dim, surely, for you to be reading by.'

'It is perfectly adequate, thank you, Miss Kenton.'

'Really, Mr Stevens, this room resembles a prison cell. All one needs is a small bed in the corner and one could well imagine condemned men spending their last hours here.'

Perhaps I said something to this, I do not know. In any case, I did not look up from my reading, and a few moments passed during which I waited for Miss Kenton to excuse herself and leave. But then I heard her say:

'Now I wonder what it could be you are reading there, Mr Stevens.'

'Simply a book, Miss Kenton.'

'I can see that, Mr Stevens. But what sort of book – that is what interests me.'

I looked up to see Miss Kenton advancing towards me. I shut the book, and clutching it to my person, rose to my feet.

'Really, Miss Kenton,' I said, 'I must ask you to respect my privacy.'

'But why are you so shy about your book, Mr Stevens? I rather suspect it may be something rather racy.'

'It is quite out of the question, Miss Kenton, that anything "racy", as you put it, should be found on his lordship's shelves.'

▷ **1** *uncouth* [ʌn'kuːθ]: rough, uncivilized **2** *unfold:* develop, happen **4** *taxing* (adj): needing a lot of effort, demanding, tiring • *on your resources:* (here) on your abilities **5–6** *I can assure you:* I can certainly say **9** *indulge yourself in sth.:* allow yourself the pleasure of sth. **30** *notwithstanding:* in spite of **38** *queries and grumbles:* questions and complaints **46** *accommodating* (adj): comfortable, attractive **47** *dim:* not very bright **52** *condemned* (adj): who are going to be killed or executed as a punishment **61** *advance towards sb./sth.:* approach sb./sth. **66** *racy:* having a certain erotic appeal

'I have heard it said that many learned books contain the most racy of passages, but I have never had the nerve to look. Now Mr Stevens, do please allow me to see what it is you are reading.'

'Miss Kenton, I must ask you to leave me alone. It is quite impossible that you should persist in pursuing me like this during the very few moments of spare time I have to myself.'

But Miss Kenton was continuing to advance and I must say it was a little difficult to assess what my best course of action would be. I was tempted to thrust the book into the drawer of my desk and lock it, but this seemed absurdly dramatic. I took a few paces back, the book still held to my chest.

'Please show me the volume you are holding, Mr Stevens,' Miss Kenton said, continuing her advance, 'and I will leave you to the pleasures of your reading. What on earth can it be you are so anxious to hide?'

'Miss Kenton, whether or not you discover the title of this volume is in itself not of the slightest importance to me. But as a matter of principle, I object to your appearing like this and invading my private moments.'

'I wonder, is it a perfectly respectable volume, Mr Stevens, or are you in fact protecting me from its shocking influences?'

Then she was standing before me, and suddenly the atmosphere underwent a peculiar change – almost as though the two of us had been suddenly thrust on to some other plane of being altogether. I am afraid it is not easy to describe clearly what I mean here. All I can say is that everything around us suddenly became very still; it was my impression that Miss Kenton's manner also underwent a sudden change; there was a strange seriousness in her expression, and it struck me she seemed almost frightened.

'Please, Mr Stevens, let me see your book.'

She reached forward and began gently to release the volume from my grasp. I judged it best to look away while she did so, but with her person positioned so closely, this could only be achieved by my twisting my head away at a somewhat unnatural angle. Miss Kenton continued very gently to prise the book away, practically one finger at a time. The process seemed to take a very long time – throughout which I managed to maintain my posture – until I finally heard her say:

'Good gracious, Mr Stevens, it isn't anything so scandalous at all. Simply a sentimental love story.'

I believe it was around this point that I decided there was no need to tolerate any more. I cannot recall precisely what I said, but I remember showing Miss Kenton out of my pantry quite firmly and the episode was thus brought to a close.

I suppose I should add a few words here concerning the matter of the actual volume around which this small episode revolved. The book was, true enough, what might be described as a 'sentimental romance' – one of a number kept in the library, and also in several of the guest bedrooms, for the entertainment of lady visitors. There was a simple reason for my having taken to perusing such works; it was an extremely efficient way to maintain and develop one's command of the English language. It is my view – I do not know if you will agree – that in so far as our generation is concerned, there had been too much stress placed on the professional desirability of good accent and command of language; that is to say, these elements have been stressed sometimes at the cost of more important professional qualities. For all that, it has never been my position that good accent and command of language are not attractive attributes, and I always considered it my duty to develop them as best I could. One straightforward means of going about this is simply to read a few pages of a well-written book during odd spare moments one may have. This had been my own policy for some years, and I often tended to choose the sort of volume Miss Kenton had found me reading that evening simply because such works tend to be written in good English, with plenty of elegant dialogue of much practical value to me. A weightier book – a scholarly study, say – while it might have been more generally improving would have tended to be couched in terms likely to be of more limited use in the course of one's normal intercourse with ladies and gentlemen.

I rarely had the time or the desire to read any of these romances cover to cover, but so far as I could tell, their plots were invariably absurd – indeed, sentimental – and I would not have wasted one

▷ **5** *pursue sb./sth.:* jdn./etwas verfolgen **8–9** *be tempted to do sth.:* feel a strong urge or desire to do sth. **9** *thrust sb./sth.:* throw sb./sth. violently **14** *anxious to do sth.:* wanting to do sth. very much **18** *invade sth.:* enter into sth. without permission **20** *respectable:* anständig **23** *peculiar:* strange **24** *plane of being:* level of existence **35** *prise sth.:* separate sth. from another thing forcefully **38** *good gracious:* Du meine Güte! **53** *desirability:* erstrebenswerte Eigenschaft **65** *weighty:* serious and demanding **66–67** *couched in terms:* using expressions

moment on them were it not for these aforementioned benefits. Having said that, however, I do not mind confessing today – and I see nothing to be ashamed of in this – that I did at times gain a sort of incidental enjoyment from these stories. I did not perhaps acknowledge this to myself at the time, but as I say, what shame is there in it? Why should one not enjoy in a light-hearted sort of way stories of ladies and gentlemen who fall in love and express their feelings for each other, often in the most elegant phrases?

But when I say this, I do not mean to imply the stance I took over the matter of the book that evening was somehow unwarranted. For you must understand, there was an important principle at issue. The fact was, I had been 'off duty' at that moment Miss Kenton had come marching into my pantry. And of course, any butler who regards his vocation with pride, any butler who aspires at all to a 'dignity in keeping with his position', as the Hayes Society once put it, should never allow himself to be 'off duty' in the presence of others. It really was immaterial whether it was Miss Kenton or a complete stranger who had walked in at that moment. A butler of any quality must be seen to *inhabit* his role, utterly and fully; he cannot be seen casting it aside one moment simply to don it again the next as though it were nothing more than a pantomime costume. There is one situation and one situation only in which a butler who cares about his dignity may feel free to unburden himself of his role; that is to say, when he is entirely alone. You will appreciate then that in the event of Miss Kenton bursting in at a time when I had presumed, not unreasonably, that I was to be alone, it came to be a crucial matter of principle, a matter indeed of dignity, that I did not appear in anything less than my full and proper role.

However, it had not been my intention to analyse here the various facets of this small episode from years ago. The main point about it was that it alerted me to the fact that things between Miss Kenton and myself had reached – no doubts after a gradual process of many months – an inappropriate footing. The fact that she could behave as she had done that evening was rather alarming, and after I had seen her out of my pantry, and had had a chance to gather my thoughts a little, I recall resolving to set about re-establishing our professional relationship on a more proper basis. But as to just how much that incident contributed to the large changes our relationship subsequently underwent, it is very difficult now to say. There may well have been other more fundamental developments to account for what took place. Such as, for instance, the matter of Miss Kenton's days off.

From the time she arrived at Darlington Hall right up until perhaps a month or so before that incident in my pantry, Miss Kenton's days off had followed a predictable pattern. She would, once every six weeks, take two days off to visit her aunt in Southampton; otherwise, following my own example, she would not really take days off as such unless we were going through a particularly quiet time, in which case she might spend a day strolling around the grounds and doing a little reading in her parlour. But then, as I say, the pattern changed. She began suddenly to take full advantage of her contracted time off, disappearing regularly from the house from early in the morning, leaving no information other than the hour she might be expected back that night. Of course, she never took more time than her entitlement, and thus I felt it improper to inquire further concerning these outings of hers. But I suppose that this change did perturb me somewhat, for I remember mentioning it to Mr Graham, valet-butler to Sir James Chambers – a good colleague who, incidentally, I seem now to have lost touch with – as we sat talking by the fire one night during one of his regular visits to Darlington Hall.

In fact, all I had said was something to the effect that the housekeeper had been 'a little moody of late' and so had been rather surprised when Mr Graham nodded, leaned towards me and said knowingly:

'I'd been wondering how much longer it would be.'

When I asked him what he meant, Mr Graham went on:

'Your Miss Kenton. I believe she's now what? Thirty-three? Thirty-four? Missed out on the best of her mothering years, but it's not too late yet.'

'Miss Kenton,' I assured him, 'is a devoted professional. I happen to know for a fact that she has no wish for a family.'

▷ **1** *benefit:* gain, profit, useful aspect **4** *incidental enjoyment:* beiläufiges Vergnügen **5** *acknowledge sth.:* admit sth. **11** *there was an important principle at issue:* es ging um ein wichtiges Prinzip **17** *immaterial:* unimportant **25** *burst in:* come in without warning **33** *footing* (n): basis; relationship **51** *contracted time off:* (here) free time as stated in a work contract **55** *entitlement:* thing that a person has a right to **62** *moody:* having sudden changes of mood

But Mr Graham had smiled and shook his head, saying: 'Never believe a housekeeper who tells you she doesn't want a family. Indeed, Mr Stevens, I should think you and I could sit here now and count up at least dozen between us that once said as much, then got married and left the profession.'

I recall I dismissed Mr Graham's theory with some confidence that evening, but thereafter, I must admit, I found it hard to keep out of my mind the possibility that the purpose of these mysterious outings of Miss Kenton was to meet a suitor. This was indeed a disturbing notion, for it was not hard to see that Miss Kenton's departure would constitute a professional loss of some magnitude, a loss Darlington Hall would have some difficulty recovering from. Furthermore, I was obliged to recognize certain other little signs which tended to support Mr Graham's theory. For instance, the collection of mail being one of my duties, I could not help noticing that Miss Kenton had started to get letters on a fairly regular basis – once a week or so – from the same correspondent, and that these letters bore a local postmark. I should perhaps point out here that it would have been well nigh impossible for me not to have noticed such things, given that throughout all her preceding years at the house, she had received very few letters indeed.

Then there were other more nebulous signs to support Mr Graham's view. For instance, although she continued to discharge her professional duties with all her usual diligence, her general mood tended to undergo swings of a sort I had hitherto never witnessed. In fact the times when she became extremely cheerful for days on end – and for no observable reason – were almost as disturbing to me as her sudden, often prolonged sullen spells. As I say, she remained utterly professional throughout it all, but then again, it was my duty to think about the welfare of the house in the long term, and if indeed these signs tended to support Mr Graham's notion that Miss Kenton was contemplating departing for romantic purposes, I clearly had a responsibility to probe the matter further. I did then venture to ask her one evening during one of our sessions over cocoa:

'And will you be going off again on Thursday, Miss Kenton? On your day off, I mean.'

I had half expected her to be angry at this inquiry, but on the contrary, it was almost as though she had been long awaiting an opportunity to raise the very topic. For she said in something of a relieved way:

'Oh, Mr Stevens, it's just someone I knew once when I was at Granchester Lodge. As a matter of fact, he was the butler there at the time, but now he's left service altogether and is employed by a business near by. He somehow learnt of my being here and started writing to me, suggesting we renew our acquaintance. And that, Mr Stevens, is really the long and short of it.'

'I see, Miss Kenton. No doubt, it is refreshing to leave the house at times.'

'I find it so, Mr Stevens.'

There was a short silence. Then Miss Kenton appeared to make some decision and went on:

'This acquaintance of mine, I remember when he was butler at Granchester Lodge, he was full of the most marvellous ambitions. In fact, I imagine his ultimate dream would have been to become butler of a house like this one. Oh, but when I think now of some of his methods! Really, Mr Stevens, I can just imagine your face if you were to be confronted by them now. It really is no wonder his ambitions remained unfulfilled.'

I gave a small laugh. 'In my experience,' I said, 'too many people believe themselves capable of working at these higher levels without having the least idea of the exacting demands involved. It is certainly not suited to just anybody.'

'So true. Really, Mr Stevens, what would you have said if you had observed him in those days!'

'At these sorts of levels, Miss Kenton, the profession isn't for everybody. It is easy enough to have lofty ambitions, but without certain qualities, a butler will simply not progress beyond a certain point.'

Miss Kenton seemed to ponder this for a moment, then said:

'It occurs to me you must be a well-contented man, Mr Stevens. Here you are, after all, at the top of your profession, every aspect of

▷ **9** *suitor:* man who wants to marry a particular woman **11** *a professional loss of some magnitude:* a considerable loss to the staff **12** *recover from sth.:* sich von etwas erholen **17** *postmark:* Poststempel **18** *well nigh* [naɪ]: almost but not quite **21** *nebulous:* vague, not clear **24** *swings:* noticeable changes in mood **25** *for days on end:* for a lot of days without interruption **27** *prolonged* (adj): that continue for a long time **45** *the long and short of it:* the whole story **60** *exacting* (adj): hard and involving a high level of skill

your domain well under control. I really cannot imagine what more you might wish for in life.'

I could think of no immediate response to this. In the slightly awkward silence that ensued, Miss Kenton turned her gaze down into the depths of her cocoa cup as if she had become engrossed by something she had noticed there. In the end, after some consideration, I said:

'As far as I am concerned, Miss Kenton, my vocation will not be fulfilled until I have done all I can to see his lordship through the great tasks he has set himself. The day his lordship's work is complete, the day *he* is able to rest on his laurels, content in the knowledge that he has done all anyone could ever reasonably ask of him, only on that day, Miss Kenton, will I be able to call myself, as you put it, a well-contented man.'

She may have been a little puzzled by my words; or perhaps it was that they had for some reason displeased her. In any case, her mood seemed to change at that point, and our conversation rapidly lost the rather personal tone it had begun to adopt.

It was not so long afterwards that these meetings over cocoa in her parlour came to an end. In fact, I recall quite clearly the very last time we met like that; I was wishing to discuss with Miss Kenton a forthcoming event – a weekend gathering of distinguished persons from Scotland. It is true the event was still a month or so away, but then it had always been our habit to talk over such events from an early stage. On this particular evening, I had been discussing various aspects of it for a little while when I realized Miss Kenton was contributing very little; indeed, after a time, it became perfectly obvious her thoughts were somewhere else altogether. I did on a few occasions say things like: 'Are you with me, Miss Kenton?' particularly if I had been making a lengthy point, and though whenever I did so she would become a little more alert, within seconds I could see her attention drifting again. After several minutes of my talking and her contributing only statements such as, 'Of course, Mr Stevens,' or, 'I quite agree, Mr Stevens,' I finally said to her:

'I am sorry, Miss Kenton, but I see little point in our continuing. You simply do not seem to appreciate the importance of this discussion.'

'I am sorry, Mr Stevens,' she said, sitting up a little. 'It's simply that I'm rather tired this evening.'

'You are increasingly tired now, Miss Kenton. It used not to be an excuse you needed to resort to.'

To my astonishment, Miss Kenton responded to this in a sudden burst:

'Mr Stevens, I have had a very busy week. I am very tired. In fact I have been wishing for my bed for the last three or four hours. I am very, very tired, Mr Stevens, can you not appreciate that?'

It is not as though I had expected an apology from her, but the stridency of this reply did, I must say, take me aback a little. However, I decided not to get drawn into an unseemly argument with her and made sure to pause for a telling moment or two before saying quite calmly:

'If that is how you feel about it, Miss Kenton, there is no need at all for us to continue with these evening meetings. I am sorry that all this time I had no idea of the extent to which they were inconveniencing you.'

'Mr Stevens, I merely said that I was tired tonight ...'

'No, no, Miss Kenton, it's perfectly understandable. You have a busy life, and these meetings are a quite unnecessary addition to your burden. There are many alternative options for achieving the level of professional communication necessary without our meeting on this basis.'

'Mr Stevens, this is quite unnecessary. I merely said ...'

'I mean it, Miss Kenton. In fact, I had been wondering for some time if we should not discontinue these meetings, given how they prolong our already very busy days. The fact that we have met here now for years is no reason in itself why we should not seek a more convenient arrangement from here on.'

'Mr Stevens, please, I believe these meetings are very useful ...'

'But they are inconvenient for you, Miss Kenton. They tire you out. May I suggest that from now on, we simply make a special point of communicating important information during the course of the normal working day. Should we not be able to find each other readily, I suggest we leave written messages at one another's doors. That seems to me a perfectly fine solution. Now, Miss Kenton, I apologize for keeping you up so long. Thank you very kindly for the cocoa.'

▷ **1** *domain:* area of activity for which a person is responsible **4** *ensue:* follow **11** *rest on your laurels:* be satisfied with what you have achieved **47** *stridency* ['straɪdənsi]: loudness and unpleasantness **62** *prolong sth.:* make sth. longer

Naturally – and why should I not admit this? – I have occasionally wondered to myself how things might have turned out in the long run had I not been so determined over the issue of our evening meetings; that is to say, had I relented on those several occasions over the weeks that followed when Miss Kenton suggested we reinstitute them. I only speculate over this now because in the light of subsequent events, it could well be argued that in making my decision to end those evening meetings once and for all, I was perhaps not entirely aware of the full implications of what I was doing. Indeed, it might even be said that this small decision of mine constituted something of a key turning point; that the decision set things on an inevitable course towards what eventually happened.

But then, I suppose, when with the benefit of hindsight one begins to search one's past for such 'turning points', one is apt to start seeing them everywhere. Not only my decision in respect of our evening meetings, but also that episode in my pantry, if one felt so inclined, could be seen as such a 'turning point'. What would have transpired, one may ask, had one responded slightly differently that evening she came in with her vase of flowers? And perhaps – occurring as it did around the same time as these events – my encounter with Miss Kenton in the dining room the afternoon she received the news of her aunt's death might be seen as yet another 'turning point' of sorts.

News of the death had arrived some hours earlier; indeed, I had myself knocked on the door of her parlour that morning to hand her the letter. I had stepped inside for a brief moment to discuss some professional matter, and I recall we were seated at her table and in mid-conversation at the moment she opened the letter. She became very still, but to her credit she remained composed, reading the letter through at least twice. Then she put the letter carefully back in its envelope and looked across the table to me.

'It is from Mrs Johnson, a companion of my aunt. She says my aunt died the day before yesterday.' She paused a moment, then said: 'The funeral is to take place tomorrow. I wonder if it might be possible for me to take the day off.'

'I am sure that could be arranged, Miss Kenton.'

'Thank you, Mr Stevens. Forgive me, but perhaps I may now have a few moments alone.'

'Of course, Miss Kenton.'

I made my exit, and it was not until after I had done so that it occurred to me I had not actually offered her my condolences. I could well imagine the blow the news would be to her, her aunt having been, to all intents and purposes, like a mother to her, and I paused out in the corridor, wondering if I should go back, knock and make good my omission. But then it occurred to me that if I were to do so, I might easily intrude upon her private grief. Indeed, it was not impossible that Miss Kenton, at that very moment, and only a few feet from me, was actually crying. The thought provoked a strange feeling to rise within me, causing me to stand there hovering in the corridor for some moments. But eventually I judged it best to await another opportunity to express my sympathy and went on my way.

As it turned out, I did not see her again until the afternoon, when, as I say, I came across her in the dining room, replacing crockery into the sideboard. By this point, I had been preoccupied for some hours with the matter of Miss Kenton's sorrow, having given particular thought to the question of what I might best do or say to ease her burden a little. And when I had heard her footsteps entering the dining room – I was busy with some task out in the hall – I had waited a minute or so, then put down what I was doing and followed her in.

'Ah, Miss Kenton,' I said. 'And how might you be this afternoon?'

'Quite well, thank you, Mr Stevens.'

'Is everything in order?'

'Everything is in order, thank you.'

'I had been meaning to ask you if you were experiencing any particular problems with the new recruits.' I gave a small laugh. 'Various small difficulties are apt to arise when so many new recruits arrive all at once. I dare say the best of us can often profit by a little professional discussion at such times.'

'Thank you, Mr Stevens, but the new girls are very satisfactory to me.'

▷ **5** *reinstitute sth.:* take sth. up again **17** *transpire:* happen **28** *to her credit ...:* it speaks in her favour that ... • *composed* (adj): calm, not upset **33** *funeral:* Beerdigung **43–44** *make good my omission:* do what I had forgotten to do **45** *intrude upon her private grief:* go in when she wanted to be alone with her sorrow **48** *hover* ['hɒvə] (v): wait nervously in the same place **53** *sideboard:* long low piece of furniture usu. in a dining room

'You don't consider any changes necessary to the present staff plans on account of the recent arrivals?'

'I don't think any such changes will be necessary, Mr Stevens. However, if I change my view on this, I will let you know immediately.'

She turned her attention back to the sideboard, and for a moment, I thought about leaving the dining room. In fact, I believe I actually took a few steps towards the doorway, but then I turned to her again and said:

'So, Miss Kenton, the new recruits are getting on well, you say.'

'They are both doing very well, I assure you.'

'Ah, that is good to hear.' I gave another short laugh. 'I merely wondered, because we had established that neither girl had worked previously in a house of this size.'

'Indeed, Mr Stevens.'

I watched her filling the sideboard and waited to see if she would say anything further. When after several moments it became clear she would not, I said: 'As a matter of fact, Miss Kenton, I have to say this. I have noticed one or two things have fallen in standard just recently. I do feel you might be a little less complacent as regards new arrivals.'

'Whatever do you mean, Mr Stevens?'

'For my part, Miss Kenton, whenever new recruits arrive, I like to make doubly sure all is well. I check all aspects of their work and try to gauge how they are conducting themselves with other staff members. It is, after all, important to form a clear view of them both technically and in terms of their impact on general morale. I regret to say this, Miss Kenton, but I believe you have been a little remiss in these respects.'

For a second, Miss Kenton looked confused. Then she turned towards me and a certain strain was visible in her face.

'I beg your pardon, Mr Stevens?'

'For instance, Miss Kenton, although the crockery is being washed to as high a standard as ever, I have noticed it is being replaced on the kitchen shelves in a manner which, while not obviously dangerous, would nevertheless over time result in more breakages than necessary.'

'Is that so, Mr Stevens?'

'Yes, Miss Kenton. Furthermore, that little alcove outside the breakfast room has not been dusted for some time. You will excuse me, but there are one or two other small things I might mention.'

'You needn't press your point, Mr Stevens. I will, as you suggest, check the work of the new maids.'

'It is not like you to have overlooked such obvious things, Miss Kenton.'

Miss Kenton looked away from me, and again an expression crossed her face as though she was trying to puzzle out something that had quite confused her. She did not look upset so much as very weary. Then she closed the sideboard, said: 'Please excuse me, Mr Stevens,' and left the room.

But what is the sense in forever speculating what might have happened had such and such a moment turned out differently? One could presumably drive oneself to distraction in this way. In any case, while it is all very well to talk of 'turning points', one can surely only recognize such moments in retrospect. Naturally, when one looks back to such instances today, they may indeed take the appearance of being crucial, precious moments in one's life; but of course, at the time, this was not the impression one had. Rather, it was as though one had available a never-ending number of days, months, years in which to sort out the vagaries of one's relationship with Miss Kenton; an infinite number of further opportunities in which to remedy the effect of this or that misunderstanding. There was surely nothing to indicate at the time that such evidently small incidents would render whole dreams forever irredeemable.

But I see I am becoming unduly introspective, and in a rather morose sort of way at that. No doubt, this has to do with the late hour, and the trying nature of the events I have had to endure this evening. No doubt, too, my present mood is not unconnected with the fact that tomorrow – provided I am supplied with petrol by the local garage, as the Taylors assure me I will be – I should arrive in Little Compton by

▷ **26** *impact* ['- -] (n): effect, influence • *morale* [mə'rɑːl]: (Arbeits)moral **27** *remiss* (adj): careless **30** *strain:* sign of effort, worry or annoyance **37** *alcove:* Nische **40** *press a point:* add further arguments to prove you are right **47** *weary* (adj): tired **51** *drive yourself to distraction:* drive yourself mad, become too preoccupied with sth. **53** *in retrospect:* looking back at past events (often with a different opinion of it from one you had at the time) **58** *vagaries* (pl): unexpected events, changes, etc. that have an effect on sb.'s life **59** *remedy sth.:* make sth. good, correct or improve sth. **61** *render sth.* (+ adj): make sth. (+ adj) **62** *irredeemable:* that can never be realized or fulfilled, lost forever **63** *introspective:* examining your own feelings and mind too much **64** *morose:* depressed, tending to stress the negative aspects • *at that:* what is more

lunch-time and will, presumably, see Miss Kenton again after all these years. There is, of course, no reason at all to suppose our meeting will be anything but cordial. In fact, I would expect our interview – aside from a few informal exchanges quite proper in the circumstances – to be largely professional in character. That is to say, it will be my responsibility to determine whether or not Miss Kenton has any interest, now that her marriage, sadly, appears to have broken down and she is without a home, in returning to her old post at Darlington Hall. I may as well say here that having reread her letter again tonight, I am inclined to believe I may well have read more into certain of her lines than perhaps was wise. But I would still maintain there is more than a hint of nostalgic longing in certain parts of her letter, particularly when she writes such things as: 'I was so fond of that view from the second floor bedrooms overlooking the lawn with the downs visible in the distance.'

But then again, what is the purpose in endlessly speculating as to Miss Kenton's present wishes when I will be able to ascertain these from her own person tomorrow? And in any case, I have drifted considerably from the account I was giving of this evening's events. These last few hours, let me say it, have proved unreasonably taxing ones. One would have thought that having to abandon the Ford on some lonely hill, having to walk down to this village in near-darkness by the unorthodox route one did, would be sufficient inconvenience to befall one for a single evening. And my kind hosts, Mr and Mrs Taylor, would never, I am certain, have knowingly put me through what I have just endured. But the fact is, once I had sat down to supper at their table, once a number of their neighbours had come calling, a most discomforting set of events began to unfold around me.

The room downstairs at the front of this cottage would appear to serve Mr and Mrs Taylor as both dining room and general living quarters. It is a rather cosy room, dominated by a large, roughly hewn table of the sort one might expect to see in a farmhouse kitchen, its surface unvarnished and bearing many small marks left by choppers and breadknives. These latter I could see quite clearly despite the fact that we were sitting in a low yellow light cast by an oil lamp on a shelf in one corner.

'It's not as though we don't have electricity out here, sir,' Mr Taylor remarked to me at one point, nodding towards the lamp. 'But something went wrong with the circuit and we've been without it now for almost two months. To tell you the truth, we don't miss it so much. There's a few houses in the village that's never had electricity at all. Oil gives a warmer light.'

Mrs Taylor had served us with a good broth, which we had eaten with helpings of crusty bread, and at that point, there had been little to suggest the evening held for me anything more daunting than an hour or so of pleasant conversation before retiring to bed. However, just as we had finished supper and Mr Taylor was pouring for me a glass of ale brewed by a neighbour, we heard footsteps approaching on the gravel outside. To my ears, there was something a little sinister in the sound of feet coming ever closer in the darkness up to an isolated cottage, but neither my host nor hostess seemed to anticipate any menace. For it was with curiosity and nothing else in his voice that Mr Taylor said: 'Hello, now who could this be?'

He said this more or less to himself, but then we heard, as though in reply, a voice call outside: 'It's George Andrews. Just happened to be walking by.'

The next moment, Mrs Taylor was showing in a well-built man, perhaps in his fifties, who judging from his dress had spent a day engaged in agricultural work. With a familiarity which suggested he was a regular visitor, he placed himself on a small stool by the entrance and removed his wellington boots with some effort, exchanging a few casual remarks with Mrs Taylor as he did so. Then he came towards the table and stopped, standing to attention before me as though reporting to an officer in the army.

'The name's Andrew, sir,' he said. 'A very good evening to you. I'm very sorry to hear about your mishap, but I hope you're not too put out to be spending the night here in Moscombe.'

I was a little puzzled as to how this Mr Andrews had come to hear of my 'mishap', as he termed it. In any case, I replied with a smile that

▷ **3** *cordial:* friendly **19** *account* (n): report, story **23** *unorthodox* (adj): unusual **28** *discomforting* (adj): unpleasant **33** *unvarnished* (adj): naturbelassen, unbehandelt • *chopper:* Hackbeil **34** *these latter:* (here) the marks left by the knives **39** *circuit* ['sɜːkɪt]: Schaltkreis **43** *broth:* thick soup **44** *helping* (n): portion **48** *ale:* type of beer • *brew sth.:* etwas brauen **49** *gravel:* small stones, used to make a surface for paths, roads etc. • *sinister:* unheimlich **52** *menace* (n): threat, danger **60** *stool:* Hocker **61** *wellington boots:* long rubber boots **63** *stand to attention:* stand up straight (like a soldier) **69** *mishap* ['mɪshæp]: small accident or mistake

far from being 'put out', I felt extremely indebted for the hospitality I was receiving. By this I had of course been referring to Mr and Mrs Taylor's kindness, but Mr Andrew seemed to believe himself included by my expression of gratitude, for he said immediately, holding up defensively his two large hands:

'Oh no, sir, you're most welcome. We're pleased to have you. It's not often the likes of yourself comes through here. We're all very pleased you could stop by.'

The way he said this seemed to suggest the whole village was aware of my 'mishap' and subsequent arrival at this cottage. In fact, as I was soon to discover, this was very close to being the case; I can only imagine that in the several minutes after I had first been shown up to this bedroom – while I was washing my hands and doing what I could to make good the damage inflicted upon my jacket and trouser turn-ups – Mr and Mrs Taylor had conveyed news of me to passers-by. In any case, the next few minutes saw the arrival of another visitor, a man with an appearance much like that of Mr Andrews – that is to say, somewhat broad and agricultural, and wearing muddy wellington boots, which he proceeded to remove in much the way Mr Andrews had just done. Indeed, their similarity was such that I supposed them to be brothers, until the newcomer introduced himself to me as 'Morgan, sir, Trevor Morgan.'

Mr Morgan expressed regret concerning my 'misfortune', assuring me all would be well in the morning, before going on to say how welcome I was in the village. Of course, I had already heard similar sentiments a few moments earlier, but Mr Morgan actually said: 'It's a privilege to have a gentleman like yourself here in Moscombe, sir.'

Before I had had any time to think of a reply to this, there came the sound of more footsteps on the path outside. Soon, a middle-aged couple were shown in, who were introduced to me as Mr and Mrs Harry Smith. These people did not look at all agricultural; she was a large, matronly woman who rather reminded me of Mrs Mortimer, the cook at Darlington Hall through much of the twenties and thirties. In contrast, Mr Harry Smith was a small man with a rather intense expression that furrowed his brow. As they took their places around the table, he said to me: 'Your car would be the vintage Ford up there on Thornley Bush Hill, sir?'

'If that is the hill road overlooking this village,' I said. 'But I'm surprised to hear you've seen it.'

'I've not seen it myself, sir. But Dave Thornton passed it on his tractor a short while ago as he was coming home. He was so surprised to see it sitting there, he actually stopped and got out.' At this point, Mr Harry Smith turned to address the others around the table. 'Absolute beauty, it is. Said he'd never seen anything like it. Put the car Mr Lindsay used to drive completely in the shade!'

This caused laughter around the table, which Mr Taylor explained to me by saying: 'That was a gent used to live in the big house not far from here, sir. He did one or two odd things and wasn't appreciated around here.'

This brought a general murmur of assent. Then someone said: 'Your health, sir,' lifting one of the tankards of ale Mrs Taylor had just finished distributing, and the next moment I was being toasted by the whole company.

I smiled and said: 'I assure you the privilege is all mine.'

'You're very kind, sir,' Mrs Smith said. 'That's the way a real gentleman is. That Mr Lindsay was no gentleman. He may have had a lot of money, but he was never a gentleman.'

Again, there was agreement all round. Then Mrs Taylor whispered something in Mrs Smith's ear, causing the latter to reply: 'He said he'd try to be along as soon as he could.' They both turned towards me with a self-conscious air, then Mrs Smith said: 'We told Dr Carlisle you were here, sir. The doctor would be very pleased to make your acquaintance.'

'I expect he has patients to see,' Mrs Taylor added apologetically, 'I'm afraid we can't say for certain he'll be able to call in before you'd be wanting to retire, sir.'

It was then that Mr Smith, the little man with the furrowed brow, leaned forward again and said: 'That Mr Lindsay, he had it all wrong, see? Acting the way he did. Thought he was so much better than us, and he took us all for fools. Well, I can tell you, sir, he soon learnt otherwise. A lot of hard thinking and talking goes on in this place. There's plenty of good strong opinion around and people here aren't

▷ **1** *put out* (adj): upset **14** *inflicted upon sth.:* caused to sth. **32** *matronly* (adj): fairly fat and no longer young **35** *furrow sb.'s brow:* made deep lines on sb.'s forehead **36** *vintage Ford:* Ford car manufactured between 1917 and 1930 **48** *appreciate sth.:* like sth. **61** *with a self-conscious air:* looking slightly embarrassed **64** *apologetically:* in a way that shows you are sorry **66** *retire:* go to bed

shy about expressing it. That's something your Mr Lindsay learnt quickly enough.'

'He was no gentleman,' Mr Taylor said quietly. 'He was no gentleman, that Mr Lindsay.'

'That's right, sir,' Mr Harry Smith said. 'You could tell just watching him he was no gentleman. All right, he had a fine house and good suits, but somehow you just knew. And so it proved in good time.'

There was a murmur of agreement, and for a moment all present seemed to be considering whether or not it would be proper to divulge to me the tale concerning this local personage. Then Mr Taylor broke the silence by saying:

'That's true what Harry says. You can tell a true gentleman from a false one that's just dressed in finery. Take yourself, sir. It's not just the cut of your clothes, nor is it even the fine way you've got of speaking. There's something else that marks you out as a gentleman. Hard to put your finger on it, but it's plain for all to see that's got eyes.'

This brought more sounds of agreement around the table.

'Dr Carlisle shouldn't be long now, sir,' Mrs Taylor put it. 'You'll enjoy talking with him.'

'Dr Carlisle's got it too,' Mr Taylor said. 'He's got it. He's a true gent, that one.'

Mr Morgan, who had said little since his arrival, bent forward and said to me: 'What do you suppose it is, sir? Maybe one that's got it can better say what it is. Here we are all talking about who's got it and who hasn't, and we're none the wiser about what we're talking about. Perhaps you could enlighten us a bit, sir.'

A silence fell around the table and I could sense all the faces turn to me. I gave a small cough and said:

'It is hardly for me to pronounce upon qualities I may or may not possess. However, as far as this particular question is concerned, one would suspect that the quality being referred to might be most usefully termed "dignity".'

I saw little point in attempting to explain this statement further. Indeed, I had merely given voice to the thoughts running through my mind while listening to the preceding talk and it is doubtful I would have said such a thing had the situation not suddenly demanded it of me. My response, however, seemed to cause much satisfaction.

'There's a lot of truth in what you say there, sir,' Mr Andrews said, nodding, and a number of other voices echoed this.

'That Mr Lindsay could certainly have done with a little more dignity,' Mrs Taylor said. 'The trouble with his sort is they mistake acting high and mighty for dignity.'

'Mind you,' put in Mr Harry Smith, 'with all respect for what you say, sir, it ought to be said. Dignity isn't just something gentlemen have. Dignity's something every man and woman in this country can strive for and get. You'll excuse me, sir, but like I said before, we don't stand on ceremony here when it comes to expressing opinions. And that's my opinion for what it's worth. Dignity's not just something for gentlemen.'

I perceived, of course, that Mr Harry Smith and I were rather at cross purposes on this matter, and that it would be far too complicated a task for me to explain myself more clearly to these people. I thus judged it best simply to smile and say: 'Of course, you're quite correct.'

This had the immediate effect of dispelling the slight tension that had built in the room while Mr Harry Smith had been speaking. And Mr Harry Smith himself seemed to lose all inhibitions, for now he leaned forward and continued:

'That's what we fought Hitler for, after all. If Hitler had had things his way, we'd just be slaves now. The whole world would be a few masters and millions upon millions of slaves. And I don't need to remind anyone here, there's no dignity to be had in being a slave. That's what we fought for and that's what we won. We won the right to be free citizens. And it's one of the privileges of being born English that no matter who you are, no matter if you're rich or poor, you're born free and you're born so that you can express your opinion freely, and vote in your member of parliament or vote him out. That's what dignity's really about, if you'll excuse me, sir.'

'Now now, Harry,' Mrs Taylor said, 'I can see you're warming up to one of your political speeches.'

▷ **13** *finery:* clothes and jewellery that are beautiful or very expensive **26** *enlighten sb.:* explain sth. to sb. **29** *it is hardly for me to …:* I'm not really the right person to … • *pronounce upon sth.:* make statements about sth. **47** *stand on ceremony:* behave in a formal manner; (here) hesitate to say what you think **50** *perceive sth.:* realize sth. **50–51** *be at cross purposes:* (here) not understand the ideas of the other person, have different views **55** *dispel sth.* [-'-]: overcome sth., remove sth. **57** *inhibition:* Hemmung

This brought laughter. Mr Harry Smith smiled a little shyly, but went on:

'I'm not talking politics. I'm just saying, that's all. You can't have dignity if you're a slave. But every Englishman can grasp it if only he cares to. Because we fought for that right.'

'This may seem like a small, out of the way place we have here, sir,' his wife said. 'But we gave more than our share in the war. More than our share.'

A solemnness hung in the air after she said this, until eventually Mr Taylor said to me: 'Harry here does a lot of organizing for our local member. Give him half a chance and he'll tell you everything that's wrong with the way the country's run.'

'Ah, but I was just saying what was *right* about the country this time.'

'Have you had much to do with politics yourself, sir?' Mr Andrew asked.

'Not directly as such,' I said, 'And particularly not these days. More so before the war perhaps.'

'It's just that I seem to remember a Mr Stevens who was a member of parliament a year or two ago. Heard him on the wireless once or twice. Had some very sensible things to say about housing. But that wouldn't be yourself, sir?'

'Oh, no,' I said with a laugh. Now I am not at all sure what made me utter my next statement; all I can say is that it seemed somehow called for in the circumstances in which I found myself. For I then said: 'In fact, I tended to concern myself with international affairs more than domestic ones. Foreign policy, that is to say.'

I was a little taken aback by the effect this seemed to have upon my listeners. That is to say, a sense of awe seemed to descend on them. I added quickly: 'I never held any high office, mind you. Any influence I exerted was in a strictly unofficial capacity.' But the hushed silence remained for several more seconds.

'Excuse me, sir,' Mrs Taylor said eventually, 'but have you ever met Mr Churchill?'

'Mr Churchill? He did come to the house on a number of occasions. But to be quite frank, Mrs Taylor, during the time I was most involved in great affairs, Mr Churchill was not such a key figure and was not really expected to become one. The likes of Mr Eden and Lord Halifax were more frequent visitors in those days.'

'But you have actually met Mr Churchill, sir? What an honour to be able to say that.'

'I don't agree with many things Mr Churchill says,' Mr Harry Smith said, 'but there's no doubt about it, he's a great man. It must be quite something, sir, to be discussing matters with his like.'

'Well, I must reiterate,' I said, 'I didn't have a great deal to do with Mr Churchill. But as you rightly point out it's rather gratifying to have consorted with him. In fact, all in all, I suppose I have been very fortunate, I would be the first to admit that. It has been my good fortune, after all, to have consorted not just with Mr Churchill, but with many other great leaders and men of influence – from America and from Europe. And when you think that it was my good fortune to have had their ear on many great issues of the day, yes, when I think back, I do feel a certain gratitude. It's a great privilege, after all, to have been given a part to play, however small, on the world's stage.'

'Excuse me asking, sir,' Mr Andrews said, 'but what sort of man is Mr Eden? I mean, at the personal level. I've always had the impression he's a jolly decent sort. The sort that can talk to anyone high or low, rich or poor. Am I right, sir?'

'I would say that is, by and large, an accurate picture. But of course I have not seen Mr Eden in recent years, and he may have been much changed by pressures. One thing I have witnessed is that public life can change people unrecognizably in a few short years.'

'I don't doubt that, sir,' said Mr Andrews. 'Even Harry here. Got himself involved with his politics a few years back and he's never been the same man since.'

There was laughter again, while Mr Harry Smith shrugged and allowed a smile to cross his face. Then he said:

'It's true I've put a lot into the campaigning work. It's only at a local level, and I never meet anyone half as grand as the likes you associate with, sir, but in my own small way I believe I'm doing my part. The way I see it, England's a democracy, and we in this village have

▷ **4** *grasp sth.:* understand sth. **9** *solemnness:* mood of seriousness **10–11** *local member:* member of parliament for the area **27** *domestic:* taking place within a country **31** *in a strictly unofficial capacity:* strictly outside of any public office • *hushed* (adj): gedämpft **47** *consort with sb.:* spend some time together with sb. **62** *unrecognizably:* to a such an extent that sb. is no longer the same **68** *campaigning work:* political activities intended to achieve a particular result

suffered as much as anyone fighting to keep it that way. Now it's up to us to exercise our rights, every one of us. Some fine young lads from this village gave their lives to give us that privilege, and the way I see it, each one of us here now owes it to them to play our part. We've all got strong opinions here, and it's our responsibility to get them heard. We're out of the way, all right, a small village, we're none of us getting younger, and the village is getting smaller. But the way I see it we owe it to the lads we lost from this village. That's why, sir, I give so much of my time now to making sure our voice gets heard in high places. And if it changes me, or sends me to an early grave, I don't mind.'

'I did warn you, sir,' Mr Taylor said with a smile. 'There was no way Harry was going to let an influential gentleman like yourself come through the village without giving you his usual earful.'

There was laughter again, but I said almost immediately:

'I think I understand your position very well, Mr Smith. I can well understand that you wish the world to be a better place and that you and your fellow residents here should have an opportunity to contribute to the making of a better world. It is a sentiment to be applauded. I dare say it was a very similar urge which led me to become involved in great affairs before the war. Then, as now, world peace seemed something we had only the most fragile grasp of, and I wished to do my part.'

'Excuse me, sir,' said Mr Harry Smith, 'but my point was a slightly different one. For the likes of yourself, it's always been easy to exert your influence. You can count the most powerful in the land as your friends. But the likes of us here, sir, we can go year in year out and never even lay eyes on a real gentleman – other than maybe Dr Carlisle. He's a first-class doctor, but with all respect, he doesn't have *connections* as such. It gets easy for us here to forget our responsibility as citizens. That's why I work so hard at the campaigning. Whether people agree or disagree – and I know there's not one soul in this room now who'd agree with *every*thing I say – at least I'll get them thinking. At least I'll remind them of their duty. This is as democratic country we're living in. We fought for it. We've all got to play our part.'

'I wonder what could have happened to Dr Carlisle,' Mrs Smith said. 'I'm sure the gentleman could just about use some *educated* talk now.'

This provoked more laughter.

'In fact,' I said, 'although it has been extremely enjoyable to meet you all, I must confess I'm beginning to feel rather exhausted …'

'Of course, sir,' Mr Taylor said, 'you must be very tired. Perhaps I'll fetch another blanket for you. It's getting much chillier at night now.'

'No, I assure you, Mrs Taylor, I'll be most comfortable.'

But before I could rise from the table, Mr Morgan said:

'I just wondered, sir, there's a fellow we like to listen to on the wireless, his name's Leslie Mandrake. I wondered if you'd happened to have met him.'

I replied that I had not, and was about to make another attempt to retire only to find myself detained by further inquiries regarding various persons I may have met. I was, then, still seated at the table when Mrs Smith remarked:

'Ah, there's someone coming. I expect that's the doctor at last.'

'I really ought to be retiring,' I said. 'I feel quite exhausted.'

'But I'm sure this is the doctor now, sir,' said Mrs Smith. 'Do wait a few more minutes.'

Just as she said this, there came a knock and a voice said: 'It's just me, Mrs Taylor.'

The gentleman who was shown in was still fairly young – perhaps around forty or so – tall and thin; tall enough, in fact, that he was obliged to stoop to enter the doorway of the cottage. No sooner had he bade us all a good evening than Mrs Taylor said to him:

'This is our gentleman here, Doctor. His car's stuck up there on Thornley Bush and he's having to endure Harry's speeches as a result.'

The doctor came up to the table and held out his hand to me.

'Richard Carlisle,' he said with a cheerful smile as I rose to shake it. 'Rotten bit of luck about your car. Still, trust you're being well looked after here. Looked after rather too well, I imagine.'

'Thank you,' I replied. 'Everyone has been most kind.'

▷ **2** *lad* (infml): young man **7–8** *owe sth. to sb.:* jdm. etwas schuldig sein **10** *send sb. to an early grave:* lead to sb.'s early death **13** *give sb. an earful* (infml): tell sb. all your opinions **21** *have a fragile grasp of sth.:* not be very sure of sth. **41** *exhausted* (adj): extremely tired **43** *chilly:* cold **50** *detain sb.:* keep sb. back, hold sb. up **61** *stoop* (v): bend your body forward **62** *bid (– bade – bidden;* here incorrectly *'bade') sb. sth.:* wish sb. sth. (esp. good morning/evening) **68** *rotten* (adj; infml): unpleasant

'Well, nice to have you with us.' Dr Carlisle seated himself almost directly across the table from me. 'Which part of the country are you from?'

'Oxfordshire,' I said, and indeed, it was no easy task to suppress the instinct to add 'sir'.

'Fine part of the country. I have an uncle lives just outside Oxford. Fine part of the country.'

'The gentleman was just telling us, Doctor,' Mrs Smith said, 'he knows Mr Churchill.'

'Is that so? I used to know a nephew of his, but I've rather lost touch. Never had the privilege of meeting the great man, though.'

'And not only Mr Churchill,' Mrs Smith went on. 'He knows Mr Eden. And Lord Halifax.'

'Really?'

I could sense the doctor's eyes examining me closely. I was about to make some appropriate remark, but before I could do so, Mr Andrews said to the doctor:

'Gentleman was just telling us he's had a lot to do with foreign affairs in his time.'

'Is that so indeed?'

It seemed to me that Dr Carlisle went on looking at me for an inordinate length of time. Then he regained his cheerful manner and asked:

'Touring around for pleasure?'

'Principally,' I said, and gave a small laugh.

'Plenty of nice country around here. Oh, by the way, Mr Andrews, I'm sorry not to have returned that saw yet.'

For a little time, the focus of attention left me and I was able to remain silent. Then, seizing what seemed a suitable moment, I rose to my feet saying: 'Please excuse me. It has been a most enjoyable evening, but I really must now retire.'

'Such a pity you have to retire already, sir,' Mrs Smith said. 'The doctor's only just arrived.'

Mr Harry Smith leaned across his wife and said to Dr Carlisle: 'I was hoping the gentleman would have a few words to say about your ideas of the Empire, Doctor.' Then turning to me, he went on: 'Our doctor here's for all kinds of little countries going independent. I don't have the learning to prove him wrong, though I know he is. But

I'd have been interested to hear what the likes of yourself would have to say to him on the subject, sir.'

Yet again, Dr Carlisle's gaze seemed to study me. Then he said: 'A pity, but we must let the gentleman go off to bed. Had a tiring day, I expect.'

'Indeed,' I said, and with another small laugh, began to make my way round the table. To my embarrassment, everyone in the room, including Dr Carlisle, rose to their feet.

'Thank you all very much,' I said, smiling. 'Mrs Taylor, I did enjoy a splendid supper. I wish you all a very good night.'

There came a chorus of, 'Good night, sir,' in reply. I had almost left the room when the doctor's voice caused me to halt at the door.

'I say, old chap,' he said, and when I turned, I saw he had remained on his feet. 'I have a visit to make in Stanbury first thing in the morning. I'd be happy to give you a lift up to your car. Save you the walk. And we can pick up a can of petrol from Ted Hardacre's on the way.'

'That is most kind,' I said. 'But I don't wish to put you to any trouble.'

'No trouble at all. Seven thirty all right for you?'

'That would be most helpful indeed.'

'Right then, seven thirty it is. Make sure your guest's up and breakfasted for seven thirty, Mrs Taylor.' Then turning back to me, he added: 'So we can have our talk after all. Though Harry here won't have the satisfaction of witnessing my humiliation.'

There was laughter, and another exchange of good nights before I was at last allowed to ascend to the sanctuary of this room.

I trust I need hardly underline the extent of the discomfort I suffered tonight on account of the unfortunate misunderstanding concerning my person. I can only say now that in all honesty I fail to see how I might reasonably have prevented the situation developing as it did; for by the stage I had become aware of what was occurring, things had gone so far I could not have enlightened these people without

▷ **4** *suppress sth.:* hold sth. back; (here) not say sth. **22** *inordinate* [ɪn'ɔ:dɪnət]: far more than you would reasonably or normally expect **27** *saw:* Säge **29** *seize sth.* [si:z]: (here) take advantage of sth. **51** *I say, old chap:* (of the upper classes) familiar way of addressing sb. who is your social equal **62** *humiliation:* shame and embarrassment (here, because of losing the argument) **64** *sanctuary:* peaceful place that is safe and provides protection

creating much embarrassment all round. In any case, regrettable as the whole business was, I do not see that any real harm has been done. I will, after all, take my leave of these people in the morning and presumably never encounter them again. There seems little point in dwelling on the matter.

However, the unfortunate misunderstanding aside, there are perhaps one or two other aspects to this evening's events which warrant a few moments' thought – if only because otherwise they may come to niggle one throughout the coming days. For instance, there is the matter of Mr Harry Smith's pronouncements on the nature of 'dignity'. There is surely little in his statement that merits serious consideration. Of course, one has to allow that Mr Harry Smith was employing the word 'dignity' in a quite different sense altogether from my own understanding of it. Even so, even taken on their own terms, his statements were, surely, far too idealistic, far too theoretical, to deserve respect. Up to a point, no doubt, there is some truth in what he says: in a country such as ours, people may indeed have a certain duty to think about great affairs and form their opinions. But life being what it is, how can ordinary people truly be expected to have 'strong opinions' on all manner of things – as Mr Harry Smith rather fancifully claims the villagers here do? And not only are these expectations unrealistic, I rather doubt if they are even desirable. There is, after all, a real limit to how much ordinary people can learn and know, and to demand that each and every one of them contribute 'strong opinion' to the great debates of the nation cannot, surely, be wise. It is, in any case, absurd that anyone should presume to define a person's 'dignity' in these terms.

As it happens, there is an instance that comes to mind which I believe illustrates rather well the real limits of whatever truth may be contained in Mr Harry Smith's view. It is, as it happens, an instance from my own experience, an episode that took place before the war, around 1935.

As I recall, I was rung for late one night – it was past midnight – to the drawing room where his lordship had been entertaining three gentlemen since dinner. I had, naturally, been called to the drawing room several times already that night to replenish refreshments, and had observed on these occasions the gentlemen deep in conversation over weighty issues. When I entered the drawing room on this last occasion, however, all the gentlemen stopped talking and looked at me. Then his lordship said:

'Step this way a moment, will you, Stevens? Mr Spencer here wishes a word with you.'

The gentleman in question went on gazing at me for a moment without changing the somewhat languid posture he had adopted in his armchair. Then he said:

'My good man, I have a question for you. We need your help on a certain matter we've been debating. Tell me, do you suppose the debt situation regarding America is a significant factor in the present low levels of trade? Or do you suppose this is a red herring and that the abandonment of the gold standard is at the root of the matter?'

I was naturally a little surprised by this, but then quickly saw the situation for what it was; that is to say, it was clearly expected that I be baffled by the question. Indeed, in the moment or so that it took for me to perceive this and compose a suitable response, I may even have given the outward impression of struggling with the question, for I saw the gentlemen in the room exchange mirthful smiles.

'I'm very sorry, sir,' I said, 'but I am unable to be of assistance on this matter.'

I was by this point well on top of the situation, but the gentlemen went on laughing covertly. Then Mr Spencer said:

'Then perhaps you will help us on another matter. Would you say that the currency problem in Europe would be made better or worse if there were to be an arms agreement between the French and the Bolsheviks?'

'I'm very sorry, sir,' I said, 'but I am unable to be of assistance on this matter.'

'Oh dear,' said Mr Spencer. 'So you can't help us here either.'

There was more suppressed laughter before his lordship said: 'Very well, Stevens. That will be all.'

'Please, Darlington, I have one more question to put to our good man here,' Mr Spencer said. 'I very much wanted his help on the question presently vexing many of us, and which we all realize is

▷ **1** *regrettable:* bedauerlich **5** *dwell on sth.:* think or talk too much about sth. **8** *warrant sth.:* deserve sth., justify sth. **9** *niggle sb.:* bother sb.,annoy sb. **21** *fanciful:* unrealistic **36** *refreshments:* food and drink **44** *languid:* relaxed **49** *red herring:* unimportant fact that takes people's attention away from the important facts **53** *baffle sb.:* confuse sb.

crucial to how we should shape our foreign policy. My good fellow, please come to our assistance. What was M. Laval really intending, by his recent speech on the situation in North Africa? Are you also of the view that it was simply a ruse to scupper the nationalist fringe of his own domestic party?'

'I'm sorry, sir,' I said, 'but I am unable to assist in this matter.'

'You see, gentlemen,' Mr Spencer said, turning to the others, 'our man is unable to assist us in these matters.'

This brought fresh laughter, now barely suppressed.

'And yet,' Mr Spencer went on, 'we still persist with the notion that this nation's decisions be left in the hands of our good man here and to the few million others like him. Is it any wonder, saddled as we are with our present parliamentary system, that we are unable to find any solution to our many difficulties? Why, you may as well ask a committee of the mothers' union to organize a war campaign.'

There was open, hearty laughter at this remark, during which his lordship muttered; 'Thank you, Stevens,' thus enabling me to take my leave.

While of course this was a slightly uncomfortable situation, it was hardly the most difficult, or even an especially unusual one to encounter in the course of one's duties, and you will no doubt agree that any decent professional should expect to take such events in his stride. I had, then, all but forgotten the episode by the following morning, when Lord Darlington came into the billiard room while I was up on a step-ladder dusting portraits, and said:

'Look here, Stevens, it was dreadful. The ordeal we put you through last night.'

I paused in what I was doing and said: 'Not at all, sir. I was only too happy to be of service.'

'It was quite dreadful. We'd all had rather too good a dinner, I fancy. Please accept my apologies.'

'Thank you, sir. But I am happy to assure you I was not unduly inconvenienced.'

His lordship walked over rather wearily to a leather armchair, seated himself and sighed. From my vantage point up on my ladder, I could see practically the whole of his long figure caught in the winter sunshine pouring in through the french window and streaking much of the room. It was, as I recall it, one of those moments that brought home how much the pressures of life had taken their toll on his lordship over a relatively small number of years. His frame, always slender, had become alarmingly thin and somewhat misshapen, his hair prematurely white, his face strained and haggard. For a while, he sat gazing out of the french windows towards the downs, then said again:

'It really was quite dreadful. But you see, Stevens, Mr Spencer had a point to prove to Sir Leonard. In fact, if it's any consolation, you did assist in demonstrating a very important point. Sir Leonard had been talking a lot of the old-fashioned nonsense. About the will of the people being the wisest arbitrator and so on. Would you believe it, Stevens?'

'Indeed, sir.'

'We're really so slow in this country to recognize when a thing's outmoded. Other great nations know full well that to meet the challenges of each new age means discarding old, sometimes well-loved methods. Not so here in Britain. There's still so many talking like Sir Leonard last night. That's why Mr Spencer felt the need to demonstrate his point. And I tell you, Stevens, if the likes of Sir Leonard are made to wake up and think a little, then you can take it from me your ordeal last night was not in vain.'

'Indeed, sir.'

Lord Darlington gave another sigh. 'We're always the last, Stevens. Always the last to be clinging on to outmoded systems. But sooner or later, we'll need to face up to the facts. Democracy is something for a bygone era. The world's far too complicated a place now for universal suffrage and such like. For endless members of parliament debating things to a standstill. All fine a few years ago perhaps, but in today's world? What was it Mr Spencer said last night? He put it rather well.'

▷ **2** *M. Laval* (1883–1945): French premier (1931–1932, 1935–1936) **4** *ruse:* clever trick made to deceive sb. • *scupper sth.:* ruin sb.'s plans or chances of success for sth. • *fringe:* extreme group **12** *saddled* (adj): burdened **22–23** *take sth. in your stride:* not allow yourself to be annoyed, embarrassed or upset by sth. **26** *dreadful:* horrible **32–33** *I was not unduly inconvenienced:* it did not matter much to me **35** *vantage point:* a good position from which you can see sth. **39** *take its toll on sb.:* have a very bad effect on sb. **41** *misshapen* (adj): not of the normal or natural shape **42** *strained* (adj): showing the signs of great effort or too much work • *haggard:* marked by deep lines and dark marks around the eyes **48** *arbitrator* ['ɑːbɪtreɪtə]: person who judges officially how an argument between two opposing sides should be settled **60** *cling on to sth.:* hold fast to sth. **62** *bygone* (adj): past **63** *universal suffrage:* allgemeines Wahlrecht

'I believe, sir, he compared the present parliamentary system to a committee of the mothers' union attempting to organize a war campaign.'

'Exactly, Stevens. Here we are in the midst of a continuing crisis. I've seen it with my own eyes when I went north with Mr Whittaker. People are suffering. Ordinary, decent working people are suffering terribly. Germany and Italy have set their houses in order by acting. And so have the wretched Bolsheviks in their own way, one supposes. Even President Roosevelt, look at him, he's not afraid to take a few bold steps on behalf of his people. But look at us here, Stevens. Year after year goes by, and nothing gets better. All we do is argue and debate and procrastinate. Any decent idea is amended to ineffectuality by the time it's gone half-way through the various committees it's obliged to pass through. The few people qualified to know what's what are talked to a standstill by ignorant people all around them. What do you make of it, Stevens?'

'The nation does seem to be in a regrettable condition, sir.'

'I'll say. Look at Germany and Italy, Stevens. See what strong leadership can do if it's allowed to act. None of this universal suffrage nonsense there. If your house is on fire, you don't call the household into the drawing room and debate the various options for escape for an hour, do you? It may have been all very well once, but the world's a complicated place now. The man in the street can't be expected to know enough about politics, economics, world commerce and what have you. And why should he? In fact, you made a very good reply last night, Stevens. How did you put it? Something to the effect that it was not in your realm? Well, why should it be?'

It occurs to me in recalling these words that, of course, many of Lord Darlington's ideas will seem today rather odd – even, at times, unattractive. But surely it cannot be denied that there is an important element of truth in these things he said to me that morning in the billiard room. Of course, it is quite absurd to expect any butler to be in a position to answer authoritatively questions of the sort Mr Spencer had put to me that night, and the claim of people like Mr Harry Smith that one's 'dignity' is conditional on being able to do so can be seen for the nonsense it is. Let us establish this quite clearly: a butler's duty is to provide good service. It is not to meddle in the great affairs of the nation. The fact is, such great affairs will always be beyond the understanding of those such as you and me, and those of us who wish to make our mark must realize that we best do so by concentrating on what *is* within our realm; that is to say, by devoting our attention to providing the best possible service to those great gentlemen in whose hands the destiny of civilization truly lies. This may seem obvious, but then one can immediately think of too many instances of butlers who, for a time anyway, thought quite differently. Indeed, Mr Harry Smith's words tonight remind me very much of the sort of misguided idealism which beset significant sections of our generation throughout the twenties and thirties. I refer to that strand of opinion in the profession which suggested that any butler with serious aspirations should make it his business to be forever reappraising his employer – scrutinizing the latter's motives, analysing the implications of his views. Only in this way, so the argument ran, could one be sure one's skills were being employed to a desirable end. Although one sympathizes to some extent with the idealism contained in such an argument, there can be little doubt that it is the result, like Mr Smith's sentiments tonight, of misguided thinking. One need only look at the butlers who attempted to put such an approach into practice, and one will see that their careers – and in some cases they were highly promising careers – came to nothing as a direct consequence. I personally knew at least two professionals, both of some ability, who went from one employer to the next, forever dissatisfied, never settling anywhere, until they drifted from view altogether. That this should happen is not in the least surprising. For it is, in practice, simply not possible to adopt such a critical attitude towards an employer and at the same time provide good service. It is not simply that one is unlikely to be able to meet the many demands of service at the higher levels while one's attention is being diverted by such matters; more fundamentally, a butler who is forever attempting to formulate his own 'strong opinions' on his employer's affairs is bound to lack one quality essential in all good professionals: namely, loyalty. Please do not misunderstand me here;

▷ **10** *on behalf of sb.:* in order to help sb. **12** *procrastinate:* aufschieben, zögern, zaudern **12–13** *amended to ineffectuality:* changed so much that it is no longer helpful **33** *authoritatively:* in a way that shows knowledge and self-confidence **35** *be conditional on sth.:* depend on sth. **46** *misguided* (adj): headed in the wrong direction **48** *strand:* one of the different parts of sth. (e.g. an opinion, a story) **50** *reappraise sb.:* examine sb. again and again, pass judgement on sb. on a regular basis **62** *drift from view altogether:* be no longer heard of or of interest

I do not refer to the mindless sort of 'loyalty' that mediocre employers bemoan the lack of when they find themselves unable to retain the services of high-calibre professionals. Indeed, I would be among the last to advocate bestowing one's loyalty carelessly on any lady or gentleman who happens to employ one for a time. However, if a butler is to be of any worth to anything or anybody in life, there must surely come a time when he ceases his searching; a time when he must say to himself: 'This employer embodies all that I find noble and admirable. I will hereafter devote myself to serving him.' This is loyalty intelligently bestowed. What is there 'undignified' in this? One is simply accepting an inescapable truth: That the likes of you and I will never be in a position to comprehend the great affairs of today's world, and our best course will always be to put our trust in an employer we judge to be wise and honourable, and to devote our energies to the task of serving him to the best of our ability. Look at the likes of Mr Marshall, say, or Mr Lane – surely two of the greatest figures in our profession. Can we imagine Mr Marshall arguing with Lord Camberley over the latter's latest dispatch to the Foreign Office? Do we admire Mr Lane any the less because we learn he is not in the habit of challenging Sir Leonard Gray before each speech in the House of Commons? Of course we do not. What is there 'undignified', what is there at all culpable in such an attitude? How can one possibly be held to blame in any sense because say, the passage of time has shown that Lord Darlington's efforts were misguided, even foolish? Throughout the years I served him, it was he and he alone who weighed up evidence and judged it best to proceed in the way he did, while I simply confined myself, quite properly, to affairs within my own professional realm. And as far as I am concerned, I carried out my duties to the best of my abilities, indeed to a standard which many may consider 'first rate'. It is hardly my fault if his lordship's life and work have turned out today to look, at best, a sad waste – and it is quite illogical that I should feel any regret or shame on my own account.

▷ **2** *bemoan sth.:* complain about sth. **4** *bestow sth. on sb.:* give sth. to sb. **18** *dispatch* (n): message sent between officials **22** *culpable:* that deserves blame or criticism **27** *confine yourself to sth.:* concern youself only with sth. **32** *on my own account:* as far as I am concerned

DAY FOUR – AFTERNOON

Little Compton, Cornwall

I have finally arrived at Little Compton, and at this moment, am sitting in the dining hall of the Rose Garden Hotel having recently finished lunch. Outside, the rain is falling steadily.

The Rose Garden Hotel, while hardly luxurious, is certainly homely and comfortable, and one cannot begrudge the extra expense of accommodating oneself here. It is conveniently situated on one corner of the village square, a rather charming ivy-covered manor house capable of housing, I would suppose, thirty or so guests. This 'dining-hall' where I now sit, however, is a modern annexe built to adjoin the main building – a long, flat room characterized by rows of large windows on either side. On one side, the village square is visible; on the other, the rear garden, from which this establishment presumably takes its name. The garden, which seems well sheltered from the wind, has a number of tables arranged about it, and when the weather is fine, I imagine it is a very pleasant place to partake of meals or refreshments. In fact, I know that a little earlier, some guests had actually commenced lunch out there, only to be interrupted by the appearance of ominous storm clouds. When I was first shown in here an hour or so ago, staff were hurriedly stripping down the garden tables – while their recent occupants, including one gentleman with a napkin still tucked into his shirt, were standing about looking rather lost. Then, very soon afterwards, the rain had come down with such ferocity that for a moment all the guests seemed to stop eating just to stare out of the windows.

My own table is on the village square side of the room and I have thus spent much of the past hour watching the rain falling on the square, and upon the Ford and one or two other vehicles stationed outside. The rain has now steadied somewhat, but it is still sufficiently hard as to discourage one from going out and wandering around the village. Of course, the possibility has occurred to me that I might set off now to meet Miss Kenton; but then in my letter, I informed her I would be calling at three o'clock, and I do not think it

▷ **5** *begrudge the extra expense:* be annoyed or unhappy that more money has to be paid **7–8** *manor house:* large old house, which was the most important house in a village **9** *annexe:* separate building that has been added to a larger one **12** *rear* (adj): lying behind the house **13** *sheltered* (adj) protected **18** *ominous:* threatening **20** *occupant:* (here) person sitting at a table **21** *napkin:* Serviette • *tucked into his shirt:* in sein Hemd gesteckt **23** *ferocity* [-'- - -]: violence **28** *steady* (v): remain at about the same (moderate) level

wise to surprise her by arriving any earlier. It would seem quite likely then, if the rain does not cease very shortly, that I will remain here drinking tea until the proper time comes for me to set off. I have ascertained from the young woman who served me lunch that the address where Miss Kenton is presently residing is some fifteen minutes' walk away, which implies I have at least another forty minutes to wait.

I should say, incidentally, that I am not so foolish as to be unprepared for disappointment. I am only too aware that I never received a reply from Miss Kenton confirming she would be happy about a meeting. However, knowing Miss Kenton as I do, I am inclined to think that a lack of any letter can be taken as agreement; were a meeting for any reason inconvenient, I feel sure she would not have hesitated to inform me. Moreover, I had stated in my letter the fact that I had made a reservation at this hotel and that any last-minute message could be left for me here; that no such message was awaiting me can, I believe, be taken as further reason to suppose all is well.

This present downpour is something of a surprise, since the day started with the bright morning sunshine I have been blessed with each morning since leaving Darlington Hall. In fact, the day had generally begun well with a breakfast of fresh farm eggs and toast, provided for me by Mrs Taylor, and with Dr Carlisle calling by at seven thirty as promised, I was able to take my leave of the Taylors – who continued not to hear of remuneration – before any further embarrassing conversations had had a chance to develop.

'I found a can of petrol for you,' Dr Carlisle announced, as he ushered me into the passenger seat of his Rover. I thanked him for his thoughtfulness, but when I made inquiries as to payment, I found that he, too, would hear none of it.

'Nonsense, old boy. It's only a little bit I found at the back of my garage. But it'll be enough for you to reach Crosby Gate and you can fill up good and proper there.'

The village centre of Moscombe, in the morning sunshine, could be seen to be a number of small shops surrounding a church, the steeple of which I had seen from the hill yesterday evening. I had little chance to study the village, however, for Dr Carlisle turned his car briskly into the driveway of a farmyard.

'Just a little short cut,' he said, as we made our way past barns and stationary farm vehicles. There seemed to be no persons present anywhere, and at one point, when we were confronted by a closed gate, the doctor said: 'Sorry, old chap, but if you wouldn't mind doing the honours.'

Getting out, I went to the gate, and as soon as I did so, a furious chorus of barking erupted in one of the barns near by, so that it was with some relief that I rejoined Dr Carlisle again in the front of his Rover.

We exchanged a few pleasantries as we climbed a narrow road between tall trees, he inquiring after how I had slept at the Taylors and so forth. Then he said quite abruptly:

'I say, I hope you don't think me very rude. But you aren't a manservant of some sort, are you?'

I must confess, my overwhelming feeling on hearing this was one of relief.

'I am indeed, sir. In fact, I am the butler of Darlington Hall, near Oxford.'

'Thought so. All that about having met Winston Churchill and so on. I thought to myself, well, either the chap's been lying his head off, or – then it occurred to me, there's one simple explanation.'

Dr Carlisle turned to me with a smile as he continued to steer the car up the steep winding road. I said:

'It wasn't my intention to deceive anyone, sir. However ...'

'Oh, no need to explain, old fellow. I can quite see how it happened. I mean to say, you are a pretty impressive specimen. The likes of the people here, they're bound to take you for at least a lord or a duke.' The doctor gave a hearty laugh. 'It must do one good to be mistaken for a lord every now and then.'

We travelled on in silence for a few moments. Then Dr Carlisle said to me: 'Well, I hope you enjoyed your little stay with us here.'

'I did very much, thank you, sir.'

'And what did you make of the citizens of Moscombe? Not such a bad bunch, are they?'

▷ **13** *inconvenient:* causing troubles or problems **18** *downpour:* a lot of rain that falls in a short time **19** *be blessed with sth.:* have the good fortune of sth. **27** *usher sb. into sth.:* help sb. into sth. **37** *briskly:* quickly **38** *short cut:* shorter way to a destination than the usual one **39** *stationary:* not moving **41–42** *do the honours:* pour the drinks, serve food, etc. at a social occasion; (here) get out and open the gate **44** *chorus of barking:* the barking of many dogs • *erupt:* break out or start with force **45** *rejoin sb.:* come back to sb. **62** *specimen:* example **70** *bunch:* group

'Very engaging, sir. Mr and Mrs Taylor were extremely kind.'

'I wish you wouldn't call me "sir" like that all the time, Mr Stevens. No, they're not such a bad bunch at all around here. As far as I'm concerned, I'd happily spend the rest of my life out here.'

I thought I heard something slightly odd in the way Dr Carlisle said this. There was, too, a curiously deliberate edge to the way he went on to inquire again:

'So you found them an engaging bunch, eh?'

'Indeed, Doctor. Extremely congenial.'

'So what were they all telling you about last night? Hope they didn't bore you silly with all the village gossip.'

'Not at all, Doctor. As a matter of fact, the conversation tended to be rather earnest in tone and some very interesting viewpoints were expressed.'

'Oh, you mean Harry Smith,' the doctor said with a laugh. 'You shouldn't mind him. He's entertaining enough to listen to for a while, but really, he's all in a muddle. At times you'd think he was some sort of Communist, then he comes out with something that makes him sound true blue Tory. Truth is, he's all in a muddle.'

'Ah, that is very interesting to hear.'

'What did he lecture you on last night? The Empire? The National Health?'

'Mr Smith restricted himself to more general topics.'

'Oh? For instance?'

I gave a cough. 'Mr Smith had some thoughts on the nature of dignity.'

'I say. Now that sounds rather philosophical for Harry Smith. How the devil did he get on to that?'

'I believe Mr Smith was stressing the importance of his campaigning work in the village.'

'Ah yes?'

'He was impressing upon me the point that the residents of Moscombe held strong opinions on all manner of great affairs.'

'Ah, yes. Sounds like Harry Smith. As you probably guessed, that's all nonsense, of course. Harry's always going around trying to work everybody up over issues. But the truth is, people are happier left alone.'

We were silent again for a moment or two. Eventually, I said:

'Excuse me for asking, sir. But may I take it Mr Smith is considered something of a comic figure?'

'Hmm. That's taking it a little too far, I'd say. People do have a political conscience of sorts here. They feel they *ought* to have strong feelings on this and that, just as Harry urges them to. But really, they're no different from people anywhere. They want a quiet life. Harry has a lot of ideas about changes to this and that, but really, no one in the village wants upheaval, even if it might benefit them. People here want to be left alone to lead their quiet little lives. They don't want to be bothered with this issue and that issue.'

I was surprised by the tone of disgust that had entered the doctor's voice. But he recovered himself quickly with a short laugh and remarked:

'Nice view of the village on your side.'

Indeed, the village had become visible some way below us. Of course, the morning sunshine gave it a very different aspect, but otherwise it looked much the same view as the one I had first encountered in the evening gloom, and I supposed from this that we were now close to the spot where I had left the Ford.

'Mr Smith seemed to be of the view,' I said, 'that a person's dignity rested on such things. Having strong opinions and such.'

'Ah, yes, dignity. I was forgetting. Yes, so Harry was trying to tackle philosophical definitions. My word. I take it it was a lot of rot.'

'His conclusions were not necessarily those that compelled agreement, sir.'

Dr Carlisle nodded, but seemed to have become immersed in his own thoughts. 'You know, Mr Stevens,' he said, eventually, 'when I first came out here, I was a committed socialist. Believed in the best services for all the people and all the rest of it. First came here in 'forty-nine. Socialism would allow people to live with dignity. That's what I believed when I came out here. Sorry, you don't want to hear all this rot.' He turned to me cheerily. 'What about you, old chap?'

▷ **1** *engaging* (adj): agreeable **6** *edge:* interest, urgency **9** *congenial* [kən'dʒiːniəl]: companionable, friendly **17** *muddle:* confused state **19** *true blue Tory:* supporter of the British Conservative party **21–22** *the National Health (Service):* (in GB) staatlicher Gesundheitsdienst **46** *upheaval:* (usu. violent or significant) change • *benefit sb.:* be of use or help to sb. **50** *recover yourself:* be your normal self again **56** *gloom:* almost complete darkness **60** *tackle sth.:* deal with sth. **61** *my word:* (here) used to express arrogance **64** *immersed in sth.:* occupied with sth.

'I'm sorry, sir?'

'What do you think dignity's all about?'

The directness of this inquiry did, I admit, take me rather by surprise. 'It's rather a hard thing to explain in a few words, sir,' I said. 'But I suspect it comes down to not removing one's clothing in public.'

'Sorry. What does?'

'Dignity, sir.'

'Ah.' The doctor nodded, but looked a little bemused. Then he said: 'Now, this road should be familiar to you. Probably looks rather different in the daylight. Ah, is that it there? My goodness, what a handsome vehicle!'

Dr Carlisle pulled up just behind the Ford, got out and said again: 'My, what a handsome vehicle.' The next moment he had produced a funnel and a can of petrol and was most kindly assisting me in filling the tank of the Ford. Any fears I had that some deeper trouble was afflicting the Ford were laid to rest when I tried the ignition and heard the engine come to life with a healthy murmur. At this point, I thanked Dr Carlisle and we took leave of each other, though I was obliged to follow the back of his Rover along the twisting hill road for a further mile or so before our routes separated.

It was around nine o'clock that I crossed the border into Cornwall. This was at least three hours before the rain began and the clouds were still all of a brilliant white. In fact, many of the sights that greeted me this morning were among the most charming I have so far encountered. It was unfortunate, then, that I could not for much of the time give to them the attention they warranted; for one may as well declare it, one was in a condition of some preoccupation with the thought that – barring some unseen complication – one would be meeting Miss Kenton again before the day's end. So it was, then, that while speeding along between large open fields, no human being or vehicle apparent for miles, or else steering carefully through marvellous little villages, some no more than a cluster of a few stone cottages, I found myself yet again turning over certain recollections from the past. And now, as I sit here in Little Compton, here in the dining room of this pleasant hotel with a little time on my hands, watching the rain splashing on the pavement of the village square outside, I am unable to prevent my mind from continuing to wander along these same tracks.

One memory in particular has preoccupied me all morning – or rather, a fragment of a memory, a moment that has for some reason remained with me vividly through the years. It is a recollection of standing alone in the back corridor before the closed door of Miss Kenton's parlour; I was not actually facing the door, but standing with my person half turned towards it, transfixed by indecision as to whether or not I should knock; for at that moment, as I recall, I had been struck by the conviction that behind that very door, just a few yards from me, Miss Kenton was in fact crying. As I say, this moment has remained firmly embedded in my mind, as has the memory of the peculiar sensation I felt rising within me as I stood there like that. However, I am not at all certain now as to the actual circumstances which had led me to be standing thus in the back corridor. It occurs to me that elsewhere in attempting to gather such recollections, I may well have asserted that this memory derived from the minutes immediately after Miss Kenton's receiving news of her aunt's death; that is to say, the occasion when, having left her to be alone with her grief, I realized out in the corridor that I had not offered her my condolences. But now, having thought further, I believe I may have been a little confused about this matter; that in fact this fragment of memory derives from events that took place on an evening at least a few months after the death of Miss Kenton's aunt – the evening, in fact, when the young Mr Cardinal turned up at Darlington Hall rather unexpectedly.

Mr Cardinal's father, Sir David Cardinal, had been for many years his lordship's close friend and colleague, but had been tragically killed in a riding accident some three or four years prior to the evening I am now recalling. Meanwhile, the young Mr Cardinal had been building something of a name as a columnist, specializing in witty comments on international affairs. Evidently, these columns were rarely to Lord Darlington's liking, for I can recall numerous instances of his looking up from a journal and saying something like: 'Young Reggie writing

▷ **17** *afflict sth.:* make sth. not work well • *ignition:* Zündung **29** *barring some unseen complication:* if nothing unexpected happens **45** *transfixed by indecision:* unable to move because you do not know what to do **50** *sensation:* feeling, emotion **68** *columnist:* person who writes articles that appear regularly in a newspaper or magazine **70** *liking* (n): taste

such nonsense again. Just as well his father's not alive to read this.' But Mr Cardinal's columns did not prevent him being a frequent visitor at the house; indeed, his lordship never forgot that the young man was his godson and always treated him as kin. At the same time, it had never been Mr Cardinal's habit to turn up to dinner without any prior warning, and I was thus a little surprised when on answering the door that evening I found him standing there, his briefcase cradled in both arms.

'Oh, hello, Stevens, how are you?' he said. 'Just happened to be in a bit of a jam tonight and wondered if Lord Darlington would put me up for the night.'

'It's very nice to see you again, sir. I shall tell his lordship you are here.'

'I'd intended to stay at Mr Roland's place, but there seems to have been some misunderstanding and they've gone away somewhere. Hope it's not too inconvenient a time to call. I mean, nothing special on tonight, is there?'

'I believe, sir, his lordship is expecting some gentlemen to call after dinner.'

'Oh, that's bad luck. I seem to have chosen a bad night. I'd better keep my head low. I've got some pieces I have to work on tonight anyway.' Mr Cardinal indicated his briefcase.

'I shall tell his lordship you are here, sir. You are, in any case, in good time to join him for dinner.'

'Jolly good, I was hoping I might have been. But I don't expect Mrs Mortimer's going to be very pleased with me.'

I left Mr Cardinal in the drawing room and made my way to the study, where I found his lordship working through some pages with a look of deep concentration. When I told him of Mr Cardinal's arrival, a look of surprised annoyance crossed his face. Then he leaned back in his chair as though puzzling something out.

'Tell Mr Cardinal I'll be down shortly,' he said finally. 'He can amuse himself for a little while.'

When I returned downstairs, I discovered Mr Cardinal moving rather restlessly around the drawing room examining objects he must long ago have become familiar with. I conveyed his lordship's message and asked him what refreshment I might bring him.

'Oh, just some tea for now, Stevens. Who's his lordship expecting tonight?'

'I'm sorry, sir, I'm afraid I am unable to help you.'

'No idea at all?'

'I'm sorry, sir.'

'Hmm, curious. Oh, well. Better keep my head low tonight.'

It was not long after this, I recall, that I went down to Miss Kenton's parlour. She was sitting at her table, though there was nothing before her and her hands were empty; indeed, something in her demeanour suggested she had been sitting there like that for some time prior to my knocking.

'Mr Cardinal is here, Miss Kenton,' I said. 'He'll be requiring his usual room tonight.'

'Very good, Mr Stevens. I shall see to it before I leave.'

'Ah. You are going out this evening, Miss Kenton?'

'I am indeed, Mr Stevens.'

Perhaps I looked a little surprised, for she went on: 'You will recall, Mr Stevens, we discussed this a fortnight ago.'

'Yes, of course, Miss Kenton. I beg your pardon, it had just slipped my mind for the moment.'

'Is something the matter, Mr Stevens?'

'Not at all, Miss Kenton. Some visitors are expected this evening, but there is no reason why your presence will be required.'

'We did agree to my taking this evening off a fortnight ago, Mr Stevens.'

'Of course, Miss Kenton. I do beg your pardon.'

I turned to leave, but then I was halted at the door by Miss Kenton saying:

'Mr Stevens, I have something to tell you.'

'Yes, Miss Kenton?'

'It concerns my acquaintance. Who I am going to meet tonight.'

'Yes, Miss Kenton.'

'He asked me to marry him. I thought you had a right to know that.'

'Indeed, Miss Kenton. That is very interesting.'

'I am still giving the matter thought.'

'Indeed.'

▷ **4** *kin:* member of a family **10** *jam* (infml): difficult or uncomfortable situation **10–11** *put sb. up:* give sb. a place to sleep **21** *keep your head low:* keep to yourself, not show up too often **30** *annoyance:* anger **31** *puzzle sth. out:* try to solve sth. (esp. a confusing or difficult problem)

She glanced down a second at her hands, but then almost immediately her gaze returned to me. 'My acquaintance is to start a job in the West Country as of next month.'

'Indeed.'

'As I say, Mr Stevens, I am still giving the matter some thought. However, I thought you should be informed of the situation.'

'I'm very grateful, Miss Kenton. I do hope you have a pleasant evening. Now if you will excuse me.'

It must have been twenty minutes or so later that I encountered Miss Kenton again, this time while I was busy with preparations for dinner. In fact, I was half-way up the back staircase, carrying a fully laden tray, when I heard the sound of angry footsteps rattling the floorboards somewhere below me. Turning, I saw Miss Kenton glaring up at me from the foot of the stairs.

'Mr Stevens, so I understand that you are wishing me to remain on duty this evening?'

'Not at all, Miss Kenton. As you pointed out, you did notify me some time ago.'

'But I can see you are very unhappy about my going out tonight.'

'On the contrary, Miss Kenton.'

'Do you imagine that by creating so much commotion in the kitchen and by stamping back and forth like this outside my parlour you will get me to change my mind?'

'Miss Kenton, the slight excitement in the kitchen is solely on account of Mr Cardinal coming to dinner at the last moment. There is absolutely no reason why you should not go out this evening.'

'I intend to go with or without your blessing, Mr Stevens, I with to make this clear. I made arrangements weeks ago.'

'Indeed, Miss Kenton. And once again, I would wish you a very pleasant evening.'

At dinner, an odd atmosphere seemed to hang in the air between the two gentlemen. For long moments, they ate in silence, his lordship in particular seeming very far away. At one point, Mr Cardinal said:

'Something special tonight, sir?'

'Eh?'

'Your visitors this evening. Special?'

'Afraid I can't tell you, my boy. Strictly confidential.'

'Oh dear. I suppose this means I shouldn't sit in on it.'

'Sit in on what, my boy?'

'Whatever it is that's going to take place tonight?'

'Oh, it wouldn't be of any interest to you. In any case, confidentiality is of the utmost. Can't have someone like you around. Oh no, that wouldn't do at all.'

'Oh dear. This does sound very special.'

Mr Cardinal was watching his lordship very keenly, but the latter simply went back to his food without saying anything further.

The gentlemen retired to the smoking room for port and cigars. In the course of clearing the dining room, and also in preparing the drawing room for the arrival of the evening's visitors, I was obliged to walk repeatedly past the smoking-room doors. It was inevitable, then, that I would notice how the gentlemen, in contrast to their quiet mood at dinner, had begun to exchange words with some urgency. A quarter of an hour later, angry voices were being raised. Of course, I did not stop to listen, but I could not avoid hearing his lordship shouting: 'But that's not your business, my boy! That's not your business!'

I was in the dining room when the gentlemen eventually came out. They seemed to have calmed themselves, and the only words exchanged as they walked across the hall were his lordship's: 'Now remember, my boy. I'm trusting you.' To which Mr Cardinal muttered with irritation: 'Yes, yes, you have my word.' Then their footsteps separated, his lordship's going towards his study, Mr Cardinal's towards the library.

At almost precisely eight thirty, there came the sound of motor cars pulling up in the courtyard. I opened the door to a chauffeur, and past his shoulder I could see some police constables dispersing to various points of the grounds. The next moment, I was showing in two very distinguished gentlemen, who were met by his lordship in the hall and ushered quickly into the drawing room. Ten minutes or so later came the sound of another car and I opened the door to Herr Ribbentrop, the German Ambassador, by now no

▷ **12–13** *rattle the floorboards:* (here) make a loud noise on the wooden floor **14** *glare at sb.:* look at sb. angrily **21** *commotion:* sudden noisy activity **22** *stamp* (v): walk noisily **27** *blessing* (n): approval **38** *confidential:* intended to be or remain secret **62** *irritation:* anger, displeasure **67** *disperse:* go away in different directions

stranger to Darlington Hall. His lordship emerged to meet him and the two gentlemen appeared to exchange complicit glances before disappearing together into the drawing room. When a few minutes later I was called in to provide refreshments, the four gentlemen were discussing the relative merits of different sorts of sausage, and the atmosphere seemed on the surface at least quite convivial.

Thereafter I took my position out in the hall – the position near the entrance arch that I customarily took up during important meetings – and was not obliged to move from it again until some two hours later, when the back door bell was rung. On descending, I discovered a police constable standing there with Miss Kenton, requesting that I verify the latter's identity.

'Just security, miss, no offence meant,' the officer muttered as he wandered off again into the night.

As I was bolting the door, I noticed Miss Kenton waiting for me, and said:

'I trust you had a pleasant evening, Miss Kenton.'

She made no reply, so I said again, as we were making our way across the darkened expanse of the kitchen floor: 'I trust you had a pleasant evening, Miss Kenton.'

'I did, thank you, Mr Stevens.'

'I'm pleased to hear that.'

Behind me, Miss Kenton's footsteps came to a sudden halt, and I heard her say:

'Are you not in the least interested in what took place tonight between my acquaintance and I, Mr Stevens?'

'I do not mean to be rude, Miss Kenton, but I really must return upstairs without further delay. The fact is, events of a global significance are taking place in this house at this very moment.'

'When are they not, Mr Stevens? Very well, if you must be rushing off, I shall just tell you that I accepted my acquaintance's proposal.'

'I beg your pardon, Miss Kenton?'

'His proposal of marriage.'

'Ah, is that so, Miss Kenton? Then may I offer you my congratulations.'

'Thank you, Mr Stevens. Of course, I will be happy to serve out my notice. However, should it be that you are able to release me earlier, we would be very grateful. My acquaintance begins his new job in the West Country in two weeks' time.

'I will do my best to secure a replacement at the earliest opportunity, Miss Kenton. Now if you will excuse me, I must return upstairs.'

I started to walk away again, but then when I had all but reached the doors out to the corridor, I heard Miss Kenton say: 'Mr Stevens,' and thus turned once more. She had not moved, and consequently she was obliged to raise her voice slightly in addressing me, so that it resonated rather oddly in the cavernous spaces of the dark and empty kitchen.

'Am I to take it,' she said, 'that after the many years of service I have given in this house, you have no more words to greet the news of my possible departure than those you have just uttered?'

'Miss Kenton, you have my warmest congratulations. But I repeat, there are matters of global significance taking place upstairs and I must return to my post.'

'Did you know, Mr Stevens, that you have been a very important figure for my acquaintance and I?'

'Really, Miss Kenton?'

'Yes, Mr Stevens. We often pass the time amusing ourselves with anecdotes about you. For instance, my acquaintance is always wanting me to show him the way you pinch your nostrils together when you put pepper on your food. That always gets him laughing.'

'Indeed.'

'He's also rather fond of your staff "pep-talks". I must say, I've become quite expert in re-creating them. I only have to do a few lines to have the pair of us in stitches.'

'Indeed, Miss Kenton. Now you will please excuse me.'

I ascended to the hall and took up my position again. However, before five minutes had passed, Mr Cardinal appeared in the doorway of the library and beckoned me over.

'Hate to bother you, Stevens,' he said. 'But I couldn't trouble you to fetch a little more brandy, could I? The bottle you brought in earlier appears to be finished.'

▷ **2** *complicit:* as if involved in something secret or criminal **12** *verify sth.:* confirm sth. **28** *without further delay:* immediately **36–37** *serve out your notice:* continue working until you can legally leave **40** *secure a replacement:* find a substitute **45** *raise your voice:* speak louder **46** *resonate:* echo • *cavernous:* very large and deep **59** *pinch sth.:* press sth. together • *nostril:* Nasenloch **64** *in stitches* (infml): laughing uncontrollably **68** *beckon sb.:* wave to sb. to do sth.

pep talk - Motivationsgespräch
to give sb a pep talk: to work harder, to have more confid.

'You are very welcome to whatever refreshments you care for, sir. However, in view of the fact that you have your column to complete, I wonder if it is entirely wise to partake further.'

'My column will be fine, Stevens. Do get me a little more brandy, there's a good fellow.'

'Very well, sir.'

When I returned to the library a moment later, Mr Cardinal was wandering around the shelves, scrutinizing spines. I could see papers scattered untidily over one of the writing desks nearby. As I approached, Mr Cardinal made an appreciative sound and slumped down into a leather armchair. I went over to him, poured a little brandy and handed it to him.

'You know, Stevens,' he said, 'we've been friends for some time now, haven't we?'

'Indeed, sir.'

'I always look forward to a little chat with you whenever I come here.'

'Yes, sir.'

'Won't you care to join me in a little drink?'

'That's very kind of you, sir. But no, thank you, I won't.'

'I say, Stevens, are you all right there?'

'Perfectly all right, thank you, sir,' I said with a small laugh.

'Not feeling unwell, are you?'

'A little tired, perhaps, but I'm perfectly fine, thank you, sir.'

'Well then, you should sit down. Anyway, as I was saying. We've been friends for some time. So I really ought to be truthful with you. As you no doubt guessed, I didn't happen by tonight just by accident. I had a tip-off, you see. About what's going on. Over there across the hall at this very moment.'

'Yes, sir.'

'I do wish you'd sit down, Stevens. I want us to talk as friends, and you're standing there holding that blasted tray looking like you're about to wander off any second.'

'I'm sorry, sir.'

I put down my tray and seated myself – in an appropriate posture – on the armchair Mr Cardinal was indicating.

'That's better,' Mr Cardinal said. 'Now, Stevens, I don't suppose the Prime Minister is presently in the drawing room, is he?'

'The Prime Minister, sir?'

'Oh, it's all right, you don't have to tell me. I understand you're in a tricky position.' Mr Cardinal heaved a sigh, and looked wearily towards his papers scattered over the desk. Then he said:

'I hardly need to tell you, do I, Stevens, what I feel towards his lordship. I mean to say, he's been like a second father to me. I hardly need to tell you, Stevens.'

'No, sir.'

'I care deeply for him.'

'Yes, sir.'

'And I know you do too. Care deeply for him. Don't you, Stevens?'

'I do indeed, sir.'

'Good. So we both know where we stand, But let's face facts. His lordship is in deep waters. I've watched him swimming further and further out and let me tell you, I'm getting very anxious. He's out of his depth, you see, Stevens.'

'Is that so, sir?'

'Stevens, do you know what is happening at this very moment as we sit here talking? What's happening just several yards from us? Over in that room – and I don't need you to confirm it – there is gathered at this moment the British Prime Minister, the Foreign Secretary and the German Ambassador. His lordship has worked wonders to bring this meeting about, and he believes – faithfully believes – he's doing something good and honourable. Do you know why his lordship has brought these gentlemen here tonight? Do you know, Stevens, what is going on here?'

'I'm afraid not, sir.'

'You're afraid not. Tell me, Stevens, don't you care at all? Aren't you curious? Good God, man, something very crucial is going on in this house. Aren't you at all curious?'

'It is not my place to be curious about such matters, sir.'

▷ **5** *there's a good fellow* (infml): slightly patronizing way of asking sb. to do sth. **10** *appreciative* [ə'pri:ʃətɪv]: showing thanks • *slump* (v): sit with your body hanging loosely as if exhausted **28** *tip-off:* warning that sth. is going to happen **32** *blasted* (infml): term used when you are very annoyed **38** *the Prime Minister = Stanley Baldwin* (1867–1947): Conservative prime minister (1923–1929, 1935–1937) **41** *heave a sigh:* breathe out noisily and slowly **53–54** *out of his depth:* involved in a situation that is too difficult for him **59–60** *the Foreign Secretary = Anthony Eden* (1897–1977): Secretary of State for Foreign Affairs (1935–1938, 1940–1945), prime minister (1955–1957)

that you cannot control

'But you care about his lordship. You care deeply, you just told me that. If you care about his lordship, shouldn't you be concerned? At least a little curious? The British Prime Minister and the German Ambassador are brought together by your employer for secret talks in the night, and you're not even curious?'

'I would not say I am not curious, sir. However, it is not my position to display curiosity about such matters.'

'It's not your position? Ah, I suppose you believe that to be loyalty. Do you? Do you think that's being loyal? To his lordship? Or to the Crown, come to that?'

'I'm sorry sir, I fail to see what it is you are proposing.'

Mr Cardinal sighed again and shook his head. 'I'm not proposing anything, Stevens. Quite frankly, I don't know what's to be done. But you might at least be curious.'

He was silent for a moment, during which time he seemed to be gazing emptily at the area of carpet around my feet.

'Sure you won't join me in a drink, Stevens?' he said eventually.

'No, thank you, sir.'

'I'll tell you this, Stevens. His lordship is being made a fool of. I've done a lot of investigating, I know the situation in Germany now as well as anyone in this country, and I tell you, his lordship is being made a fool of.'

I gave no reply, and Mr Cardinal went on gazing emptily at the floor. After a while, he continued:

'His lordship is a dear, dear man. But the fact is, he is out of his depth. He is being manoeuvred. The Nazis are manoeuvring him like a pawn. Have you noticed this, Stevens? Have you noticed this is what has been happening for the last three or four years at least?'

'I'm sorry, sir, I have failed to notice any such development.'

'Haven't you ever had a suspicion? The smallest suspicion that Herr Hitler, through our dear friend Herr Ribbentrop, has been manoeuvring his lordship like a pawn, just as easily as he manoeuvres any of his other pawns back in Berlin?'

'I'm sorry, sir, I'm afraid I have not noticed any such development.'

'But I suppose you wouldn't, Stevens, because you're not curious. You just let all this go on before you and you never think to look at it for what it is.'

Mr Cardinal adjusted his position in the armchair so that he was a little more upright, and for a moment he seemed to be contemplating his unfinished work on the desk near by. Then he said:

'His lordship is a gentleman. That's what's at the root of it. He's a gentleman, and he fought a war with the Germans, and it's his instinct to offer generosity and friendship to a defeated foe. It's his instinct. Because he's a gentleman, a true old English gentleman. And you must have seen it, Stevens. How could you not have seen it? The way they've used it, manipulated it, turned something fine and noble into something else – something they can use for their own foul ends? You must have seen it, Stevens.'

Mr Cardinal was once again staring at the floor. He remained silent for a few moments, then he said:

'I remember coming here years ago, and there was this American chap here. We were having a big conference, my father was involved in organizing it. I remember this American chap, even drunker than I am now, he got up at the dinner table in front of the whole company. And he pointed at his lordship and called him an amateur. Called him a bungling amateur and said he was out of his depth. Well, I have to say, Stevens, that American chap was quite right. It's a fact of life. Today's world is too foul a place for fine and noble instincts. You've seen it yourself, haven't you, Stevens? The way they've manipulated something fine and noble. You've seen it yourself, haven't you?'

'I'm sorry, sir, but I can't say I have.'

'You can't say you have. Well, I don't know about you, but I'm going to do something about it. If Father were alive, he would do something to stop it.'

Mr Cardinal fell silent again and for a moment – perhaps it was to do with his having evoked memories of his late father – he looked extremely melancholy. 'Are you content, Stevens,' he said finally, 'to watch his lordship go over the precipice just like that?'

'I'm sorry, sir, I don't fully understand what it is you're referring to.'

▷ **10** *come to that:* übrigens **20** *investigate:* examine (sth.), look closely into (sth.) **26** *manoeuvre sb.* [mə'nuːvə]: manipulate sb. **27** *pawn:* person who is being manipulated but does not know it **47** *foul:* evil **56** *bungling* (adj): unsuccessful due to foolishness **66** *evoke sth.:* bring sth. (e.g. a feeling or memory) to mind **68** *precipice* ['presəpɪs]: Abgrund

'You don't understand, Stevens. Well, we're friends and so I'll put it to you frankly. Over the last few years, his lordship has probably been the single most useful pawn Herr Hitler has had in this country for his propaganda tricks. All the better because he's sincere and honourable and doesn't recognize the true nature of what he's doing. During the last three years alone, his lordship has been crucially instrumental in establishing links between Berlin and over sixty of the most influential citizens of this country. It's worked beautifully for them. Herr Ribbentrop's been able virtually to bypass our foreign office altogether. And as if their wretched Rally and their wretched Olympic Games weren't enough, do you know what they've got his lordship working on now? Do you have any idea what is being discussed now?'

'I'm afraid not, sir.'

'His lordship has been trying to persuade the Prime Minister himself to accept an invitation to visit Herr Hitler. He really believes there's a terrible misunderstanding on the Prime Minister's part concerning the present German regime.'

'I cannot see what there is to object to in that, sir. His lordship has always striven to aid better understanding between nations.'

'And that's not all, Stevens. At this very moment, unless I am very much mistaken, at this very moment, his lordship is discussing the idea of His Majesty himself visiting Herr Hitler. It's hardly a secret our new king has always been an enthusiast for the Nazis. Well, apparently he's now keen to accept Herr Hitler's invitation. At this very moment, Stevens, his lordship is doing what he can to remove Foreign Office objections to this appalling idea.'

'I'm sorry, sir, but I cannot see that his lordship is doing anything other than that which is highest and noblest. He is doing what he can, after all, to ensure that peace will continue to prevail in Europe.'

'Tell me, Stevens, aren't you struck by even the remote possibility that I am correct? Are you not, at least, curious about what I am saying?'

'I'm sorry sir, but I have to say that I have every trust in his lordship's good judgement.'

'No one with good judgement could persist in believing anything Herr Hitler says after the Rhineland, Stevens. His lordship is out of his depth. Oh dear, now I've really offended you.'

'Not at all, sir,' I said, for I had risen on hearing the bell from the drawing room. 'I appear to be required by the gentlemen. Please excuse me.'

In the drawing room, the air was thick with tobacco smoke. Indeed, the distinguished gentlemen continued to smoke their cigars, solemn expressions on their faces, not uttering a word, while his lordship instructed me to bring up a certain exceptionally fine bottle of port from the cellar.

At such a time of night, one's footsteps descending the back staircase are bound to be conspicuous and no doubt they were responsible for arousing Miss Kenton. For as I was making my way along the darkness of the corridor, the door to her parlour opened and she appeared at the threshold, illuminated by the light from within.

'I am surprised to find you still down here, Miss Kenton,' I said as I approached.

'Mr Stevens, I was very foolish earlier on.'

'Excuse me, Miss Kenton, but I have not time to talk just now.'

'Mr Stevens, you mustn't take anything I said earlier to heart. I was simply being foolish.'

'I have not taken anything you have said to heart, Miss Kenton. In fact, I cannot recall what it is you might be referring to. Events of great importance are unfolding upstairs and I can hardly stop to exchange pleasantries with you. I would suggest you retire for the night.'

With that I hurried on, and it was not until I had all but reached the kitchen doors that the darkness falling again in the corridor told me Miss Kenton had closed her parlour door.

It did not take me long to locate the bottle in question down in the cellar and to make the necessary preparations for its serving. It was, then, only a few minutes after my short encounter with Miss Kenton that I found myself walking down the corridor again on my return

▷ **9** *bypass sb./sth.:* get past sb./sth., avoid contacting or dealing with sb./sth. **11** *Olympic Games:* the Berlin Olympic Games of 1936, which were used for propaganda purposes **20** *strive (– strove – striven):* make an effort, work towards a goal **23** *His Majesty:* Edward VIII (1894–1972), king of Great Britain and Northern Ireland (1936) **36** *persist in sth.:* go on with sth. **37** *Rhineland:* in 1936 Germany moved troops into the Rhineland, which was against the Treaty of Versailles **44** *solemn:* serious, grave **49** *arouse sb.:* (here) make sb. wake up or (here) get up

journey, this time bearing a tray. As I approached Miss Kenton's door, I saw from the light seeping around its edges that she was still within. And that was the moment, I am now sure, that has remained so persistently lodged in my memory – that moment as I paused in the dimness of the corridor, the tray in my hands, an ever-growing conviction mounting within me that just a few yards away, on the other side of that door, Miss Kenton was at the moment crying. As I recall, there was no real evidence to account for this conviction – I had certainly not heard any sounds of crying – and yet I remember being quite certain that were I to knock and enter, I would discover her in tears. I do not know how long I remained standing there; at the time it seemed a significant period, but in reality, I suspect, it was only a matter of a few seconds. For, of course, I was required to hurry upstairs to serve some of the most distinguished gentlemen of the land and I cannot imagine I would have delayed unduly.

When I returned to the drawing room, I saw that the gentlemen were still in a rather serious mood. Beyond this, however, I had little chance to gain any impression of the atmosphere, for no sooner had I entered that his lordship was taking the tray from me, saying: 'Thank you, Stevens, I'll see to it. That'll be all.'

Crossing the hall again, I took up my usual position beneath the arch, and for the next hour or so, until, that is, the gentlemen finally departed, no event occurred which obliged me to move from my spot. Nevertheless, that hour I spent standing there has stayed very vividly in my mind throughout the years. At first, my mood was – I do not mind admitting it – somewhat downcast. But then as I continued to stand there, a curious thing began to take place; that is to say, a deep feeling of triumph started to well up within me. I cannot remember to what extent I analysed this feeling at the time, but today, looking back on it, it does not seem so difficult to account for. I had, after all, just come through an extremely trying evening, throughout which I had managed to preserve a 'dignity in keeping with my position' – and had done so, moreover, in a manner even my father might have been proud of. And there across the hall, behind the very doors upon which my gaze was then resting, within the very room where I had just executed my duties, the most powerful gentlemen of Europe were conferring over the fate of our continent. Who would doubt at that moment that I had indeed come as close to the great hub of things as any butler could wish? I would suppose, then, that as I stood there pondering the events of the evening – those that had unfolded and those still in the process of doing so – they appeared to me a sort of summary of all that I had come to achieve thus far in my life. I can see few other explanations for that sense of triumph I came to be uplifted by that night.

▷ **2** *seep:* flow **4** *persistently:* permanently, continually • *lodged:* placed, fixed **5** *dimness:* the state of being fairly dark **8** *account for sth.:* explain sth., support the idea of sth. **26** *downcast:* depressed **28** *well up* (v): rise, get stronger **36** *execute sth.:* carry out sth., perform sth.

DAY SIX – EVENING

Weymouth

This seaside town is a place I have thought of coming to for many years. I have heard various people talk of having spent a pleasant holiday here, and Mrs Symons too, in *The Wonder of England*, calls it a 'town that can keep the visitor fully entertained for many days on end'. In fact, she makes special mention of this pier, upon which I have been promenading for the past half-hour, recommending particularly that it be visited in the evening when it becomes lit up with bulbs of various colours. A moment ago, I learnt from an official that the lights would be switched on 'fairly soon', and so I have decided to sit down here on this bench and await the event. I have a good view from here of the sun setting over the sea, and though there is still plenty of daylight left – it has been a splendid day – I can see, here and there, lights starting to come on all along the shore. Meanwhile, the pier remains busy with people; behind me, the drumming of numerous footsteps upon these boards continues without interruption.

I arrived in this town yesterday afternoon, and have decided to remain a second night here so as to allow myself this whole day to spend in a leisurely manner. And I must say, it has been something of a relief not to be motoring; for enjoyable though the activity can be, one can also get a little weary of it after a while. In any case, I can well afford the time to remain this further day here; an early start tomorrow will ensure that I am back at Darlington Hall by teatime.

It is now fully two days since my meeting with Miss Kenton in the tea lounge of the Rose Garden Hotel in Little Compton. For indeed, that was where we met, Miss Kenton surprising me by coming to the hotel. I had been whiling away some time after finishing my lunch – I was, I believe, simply staring at the rain from the window by my table – when a member of the hotel staff had come to inform me that a lady was wishing to see me at the reception. I rose and went out into the lobby, where I could see no one I recognized. But then the receptionist had said from behind her counter: 'The lady's in the tea lounge, sir.'

Going in through the door indicated, I discovered a room filled with ill-matching armchairs and occasional tables. There was no one

▷ **5** *pier* ['pɪə]: Pier, Hafenmole, Landungsbrücke **8** *bulb:* Glühbirne **27** *while away some time:* spend some time in a pleasant and lazy way **35** *ill-matching* (adj): not fitting very well together

else present other than Miss Kenton, who rose as I entered, smiled and held out her hand to me.

'Ah, Mr Stevens. How nice to see you again.'

'Mrs Benn, how lovely.'

The light in the room was extremely gloomy on account of the rain, and so we moved two armchairs up close to the bay window. And that was how Miss Kenton and I talked for the next two hours or so, there in the pool of grey light while the rain continued to fall steadily on the square outside.

She had, naturally, aged somewhat, but to my eyes at least, she seemed to have done so very gracefully. Her figure remained slim, her posture as upright as ever. She had maintained, too, her old way of holding her head in a manner that verged on the defiant. Of course, with the bleak light falling on her face, I could hardly help but notice the lines that had appeared here and there. But by and large the Miss Kenton I saw before me looked surprisingly similar to the person who had inhabited my memory over these years. That is to say, it was, on the whole, extremely pleasing to see her again.

For the first twenty or so minutes, I would say we exchanged the sort of remarks strangers might; she inquired politely about my journey thus far, how I was enjoying my holiday, which towns and landmarks I had visited and so on. As we continued to talk, I must say I thought I began to notice further, more subtle changes which the years had wrought on her. For instance, Miss Kenton appeared, somehow, slower. It is possible this was simply the calmness that comes with age, and I did try hard for some time to see it as such. But I could not escape the feeling that what I was really seeing was a weariness with life; the spark which had once made her such a lively, and at times volatile person seemed now to have gone. In fact, every now and then, when she was not speaking, when her face was in repose, I thought I glimpsed something like sadness in her expression. But then again, I may well have been mistaken about this.

After a little while, what little awkwardness as existed during the initial minutes of our meeting had dissipated completely, and our conversation took a more personal turn. We spent some time reminiscing about various persons from the past, or else exchanging any news we had concerning them, and this was, I must say, most enjoyable. But it was not so much the content of our conversation as the little smiles she gave at the end of utterances, her small ironic inflexions here and there, certain gestures with her shoulders or her hands, which began to recall unmistakably the rhythms and habits of our conversations from all those years ago.

It was around this point, also, that I was able to establish some facts concerning her present circumstances. For instance, I learnt that her marriage was not in quite as parlous a state as might have been supposed from her letter; that although she had indeed left her home for a period of four or five days – during which time the letter I had received had been composed – she had returned home and Mr Benn had been very pleased to have her back. 'It's just as well one of us is sensible about these things,' she said with a smile.

I am aware, of course, that such matters were hardly any of my business, and I should make clear I would not have dreamt of prying into these areas were it not that I did have, you might recall, important professional reasons for doing so; that is to say, in respect to the present staffing problems at Darlington Hall. In any case, Miss Kenton did not seem to mind at all confiding in me over these matters and I took this as a pleasing testimony to the strength of the close working relationship we had once had.

For a little while after that, I recall, Miss Kenton went on talking more generally about her husband, who is to retire soon, a little early on account of poor health, and of her daughter, who is now married and expecting a child in the autumn. In fact, Miss Kenton gave me her daughter's address in Dorset, and I must say, I was rather flattered to see how keen she was that I call in on my return journey. Although I explained that it was unlikely I would pass through that part of Dorset, Miss Kenton continued to press me, saying: 'Catherine's heard all about you, Mr Stevens. She'd be so thrilled to meet you.'

For my own part, I tried to describe to her as best I could the Darlington Hall of today. I attempted to convey to her what a genial employer Mr Farraday is; and I described the changes to the house

▷ **13** *verge on sth.:* be very close to sth. • *defiant* [dɪˈfaɪənt]: refusing to do what sb. tells you to do **24** *wrought:* caused, produced **28** *spark:* Funke **30–31** *in repose:* at rest **34** *dissipate:* disappear **40** *inflexion:* the way the sound of a voice goes up and down when sb. is speaking **45** *parlous:* in a very bad or uncertain condition **52–53** *pry into sth.:* try to find out details about sth. (that does not concern you) **56** *confide in sb.:* tell sb. about personal things **57** *testimony to:* proof of **63** *be flattered:* be pleased because sb. has made you feel important or special **67** *thrilled* (adj): excited

itself, the alterations and the dust-sheetings, as well as the present staffing arrangements. Miss Kenton, I thought, became visibly happier when I talked about the house and soon we were recollecting together various old memories, frequently laughing over them.

Only once do I recall our touching upon Lord Darlington. We had been enjoying some recollection or other concerning the young Mr Cardinal, so that I was then obliged to go on to inform Miss Kenton of the gentleman's being killed in Belgium during the war. And I had gone on to say: 'Of course, his lordship was very fond of Mr Cardinal and took it very badly.'

I did not wish to spoil the pleasant atmosphere with unhappy talk, so tried to leave the topic again almost immediately. But as I had feared, Miss Kenton had read of the unsuccessful libel action, and inevitably, took the opportunity to probe me a little. As I recall, I rather resisted being drawn in, thought in the end I did say to her:

'The fact is, Mrs Benn, throughout the war, some truly terrible things had been said about his lordship – and by that newspaper in particular. He bore it all while the country remained in peril, but once the war was over, and the insinuations simply continued, well, his lordship saw no reason to go on suffering in silence. It's easy enough to see now, perhaps, all the dangers of going to court just at that time, what with the climate as it was. But there you are. His lordship sincerely believed he would get justice. Instead, of course, the newspaper simply increased its circulation. And his lordship's good name was destroyed for ever. Really, Mrs Benn, afterwards, well his lordship was virtually an invalid. And the house became so quiet. I would take him tea in the drawing room and, well … It really was most tragic to see.'

'I'm very sorry, Mr Stevens. I had no idea things had been so bad.'

'Oh yes, Mrs Benn. But enough of this. I know you remember Darlington Hall in the days when there were great gatherings, when it was filled with distinguished visitors. Now that's the way his lordship deserves to be remembered.'

As I say, that was the only time we mentioned Lord Darlington. Predominantly, we concerned ourselves with very happy memories, and those two hours we spent together in the tea lounge were, I would say, extremely pleasant ones. I seem to remember various other guests coming in while we were talking, sitting down for a few moments and leaving again, but they did not distract us in any way at all. Indeed, one could hardly believe two whole hours had elapsed when Miss Kenton looked up at the clock on the mantelshelf and said she would have to be returning home. On establishing that she would have to walk in the rain to the bus stop a little way out of the village, I insisted on running her there in the Ford, and so it was that after obtaining an umbrella from the reception desk, we stepped outside together.

Large puddles had formed on the ground around where I had left the Ford, obliging me to assist Miss Kenton a little to allow her to reach the passenger door. Soon, however, we were motoring down the village high street, and then the shops had gone and we found ourselves in open country. Miss Kenton, who had been sitting quietly watching the passing view, turned to me at this point, saying:

'What are you smiling to yourself about like that, Mr Stevens?'

'Oh … you must excuse me, Mrs Benn, but I was just recalling certain things you wrote in your letter. I was a little worried when I read them, but I see now I had little reason to be.'

'Oh? What things in particular do you mean, Mr Stevens?'

'Oh, nothing in particular, Mrs Benn.'

'Oh, Mr Stevens, you really must tell me.'

'Well, for instance, Mrs Benn,' I said with a laugh, 'at one point in your letter, you write – now let me see – "the rest of my life stretches out like an emptiness before me". Some words to that effect.'

'Really, Mr Stevens,' she said, also laughing a little. 'I couldn't have written any such thing.'

'Oh, I assure you you did, Mrs Benn. I recall it very clearly.'

'Oh dear. Well, perhaps there are some days when I feel like that. But they pass quickly enough. Let me assure you, Mr Stevens, my life does not stretch out emptily before me. For one thing, we are looking forward to the grandchild. The first of a few perhaps.'

'Yes, indeed. That will be splendid for you.'

We drove on quietly for a few further moments. Then Miss Kenton said:

▷ **13** *unsuccessful libel action:* Lord Darlington evidently accused a newspaper of libel, i.e. of making false and damaging statements about him, and took legal action against the paper (= verklagte sie), but was unsuccessful. **18** *peril:* danger **24** *circulation:* the average number of copies sold a day **40** *elapse:* go by **41** *mantelshelf:* long shelf above a fireplace

'And what about you, Mr Stevens? What does the future hold for you back at Darlington Hall?'

'Well, whatever awaits me, Mrs Benn, I know I'm not awaited by emptiness. If only I were. But oh no, there's work, work and more work.'

We both laughed at this. Then Miss Kenton pointed out a bus shelter visible further up the road. As we approached it, she said:

'Will you wait with me, Mr Stevens? The bus will only be a few minutes.'

The rain was still falling steadily as we got out of the car and hurried towards the shelter. This latter – a stone construct complete with a tiled roof – looked very sturdy, as indeed it needed to be, standing as it did in a highly exposed position against a background of empty fields. Inside, the paint was peeling everywhere, but the place was clean enough. Miss Kenton seated herself on the bench provided, while I remained on my feet where I could command a view of the approaching bus. On the other side of the road, all I could see were more farm fields; a line of telegraph poles led my eye over them into the far distance.

After we had been waiting in silence for a few minutes, I finally brought myself to say:

'Excuse me, Mrs Benn. But the fact is we may not meet again for a long time. I wonder if you would perhaps permit me to ask you something of a rather personal order. It is something that has been troubling me for some time.'

'Certainly, Mr Stevens. We are old friends after all.'

'Indeed, as you say, we are old friends. I simply wished to ask you, Mrs Benn. Please do not reply if you feel you shouldn't. But the fact is, the letters I have had from you over the years, and in particular the last letter, have tended to suggest that you are – how might one put it? – rather unhappy. I simply wondered if you were being ill-treated in some way. Forgive me, but as I say, it is something that has worried me for some time. I would feel foolish had I come all this way and seen you and not at least asked you.'

'Mr Stevens, there's no need to be so embarrassed. We're old friends, after all, are we not? In fact, I'm very touched you should be so concerned. And I can put your mind at rest on this matter absolutely. My husband does not mistreat me at all in any way. He is not in the least a cruel or ill-tempered man.'

'I must say, Mrs Benn, that does take a load from my mind.'

I leaned forward into the rain, looking for signs of the bus.

'I can see you are not very satisfied, Mr Stevens,' Miss Kenton said. 'Do you not believe me?'

'Oh, it's not that, Mrs Benn, not that at all. It's just that the fact remains, you do not seem to have been happy over the years. That is to say – forgive me – you have taken it on yourself to leave your husband on a number of occasions. If he does not mistreat you, then, well ... one is rather mystified as to the cause of your unhappiness.'

I looked out into the drizzle again. Eventually, I heard Miss Kenton say behind me: 'Mr Stevens, how can I explain? I hardly know myself why I do such things. But it's true, I've left three times now.' She paused a moment, during which time I continued to gaze out towards the fields on the other side of the road. Then she said: 'I suppose, Mr Stevens, you're asking whether or not I love my husband.'

'Really, Mrs Benn, I would hardly presume ...'

'I feel I should answer you, Mr Stevens. As you say, we may not meet again for many years. Yes, I do love my husband. I didn't at first. I didn't at first for a long time. When I left Darlington Hall all those years ago, I never realized I was really, truly leaving. I believe I thought of it as simply another ruse, Mr Stevens, to annoy you. It was a shock to come out here and find myself married. For a long time, I was very unhappy, very unhappy indeed. But then year after year went by, there was the war, Catherine grew up, and one day I realized I loved my husband. You spend so much time with someone, you find you get used to him. He's a kind, steady man, and yes, Mr Stevens, I've grown to love him.'

Miss Kenton fell silent again for a moment. Then she went on:

'But that doesn't mean to say, of course, there aren't occasions now and then – extremely desolate occasions – when you think to yourself: "What a terrible mistake I've made with my life." And you get to thinking about a different life, a *better* life you might have had. For instance, I get to thinking about a life I might have had with you, Mr Stevens. And I suppose that's when I get angry over some trivial

▷ **5–6** *bus shelter:* small open building with a roof where people can wait for a bus **11** *sturdy:* solidly built **13** *peel:* come off **30** *ill-treat sb.*: treat sb. badly **36** *put sb.'s mind at rest:* calm sb., end sb.'s worries **39** *load* (n): burden **47** *mystified* (adj): puzzled, confused **48** *drizzle* (n): light, steady rain

little thing and leave. But each time I do so, I realize before long – my rightful place is with my husband. After all, there's no turning back the clock now. One can't be forever dwelling on what might have been. One should realize one has as good as most, perhaps better, and be grateful.'

I do not think I responded immediately, for it took me a moment or two to fully digest these words of Miss Kenton. Moreover, as you might appreciate, their implications were such as to provoke a certain degree of sorrow within me. Indeed – why should I not admit it? – at that moment, my heart was breaking. Before long, however, I turned to her and said with a smile:

'You're very correct, Mrs Benn. As you say, it is too late to turn back the clock. Indeed, I would not be able to rest if I thought such ideas were the cause of unhappiness for you and your husband. We must each of us, as you point out, be grateful for what we *do* have. And from what you tell me, Mrs Benn, you have reason to be contented. In fact I would venture, what with Mr Benn retiring, and with grandchildren on the way, that you and Mr Benn have some extremely happy years before you. You really mustn't let any more foolish ideas come between yourself and the happiness you deserve.'

'Of course, you're right, Mr Stevens. You're so kind.'

'Ah, Mrs Benn, that appears to be the bus coming now.'

I stepped outside and signalled, while Miss Kenton rose and came to the edge of the shelter. Only as the bus pulled up did I glance to Miss Kenton and perceived that her eyes had filled with tears. I smiled and said:

'Now, Mrs Benn, you must take good care of yourself. Many say retirement is the best part of life for a married couple. You must do all you can to make these years happy ones for yourself and your husband. We may never meet again, Mrs Benn, so I would ask you to take good heed of what I am saying.'

'I will, Mr Stevens, thank you. And thank you for the lift. It was so very kind of you. It was so nice to see you again.'

'It was a great pleasure to see you again, Mrs Benn.'

The pier lights have been switched on and behind me a crowd of people have just given a loud cheer to greet this event. There is still plenty of daylight left – the sky over the sea has turned a pale red – but it would seem that all these people who have been gathering on this pier for the past half-hour are now willing night to fall. This confirms very aptly, I suppose, the point made by the man who until a little while ago was sitting here beside me on this bench, and with whom I had my curious discussion. His claim was that for a great many people, the evening was the best part of the day, the part they most looked forward to. And as I say, there would appear to be some truth in this assertion, for why else would all these people give a spontaneous cheer simply because the pier lights have come on?

Of course, the man had been speaking figuratively, but it is rather interesting to see his words borne out so immediately at the literal level. I would suppose he had been sitting here next to me for some minutes without my noticing him, so absorbed had I become with my recollections of meeting Miss Kenton two days ago. In fact, I do not think I registered his presence on the bench at all until he declared out loud:

'Sea air does you a lot of good.'

I looked up and saw a heavily built man, probably in his late sixties, wearing a rather tired tweed jacket, his shirt open at the neck. He was gazing out over the water, perhaps at some seagulls in the far distance, and so it was not at all clear that he had been talking to me. But since no one else responded, and since I could see other obvious persons close by who might do so, I eventually said:

'Yes, I'm sure it does.'

'The doctor says it does you good. So I come up here as much as the weather will let me.'

The man went on to tell me about his various ailments, only very occasionally turning his eyes away from the sunset in order to give me a nod or a grin. I really only started to pay any attention at all when he happened to mention that until his retirement three years ago, he had been a butler of a nearby house. On inquiring further, I ascertained that the house had been a very small one in which he had been the only full-time employee. When I asked him if he had ever worked with a proper staff under him, perhaps before the war, he replied:

▷ **7** *digest sth.* [daɪ'dʒest]: take sth. in, think about and understand sth. **31** *take good heed of sth.:* pay attention to and follow sth. (e.g. advice) **39** *will sth. to happen:* want sth. very much to happen **48** *borne out:* proved, shown to be true **52** *register sth.:* notice sth. **57** *seagull:* Möwe

'Oh, in those days, I was just a footman. I wouldn't have had the know-how to be a butler in *those* days. You'd be surprised what it involved when you had those big houses you had then.'

At this point, I thought it appropriate to reveal my identity, and although I am not sure 'Darlington Hall' meant anything to him, my companion seemed suitably impressed.

'And here I was trying to explain it all to you,' he said with a laugh. 'Good job you told me when you did before I made a right fool of myself. Just shows you never know who you're addressing when you start talking to a stranger. So you had a big staff, I suppose. Before the war, I mean.'

He was a cheerful fellow and seemed genuinely interested, so I confess I did spend a little time telling him about Darlington Hall in former days. In the main, I tried to convey to him some of the 'know-how', as he put it, involved in overseeing large events of the sort we used often to have. Indeed, I believe I even revealed to him several of my professional 'secrets' designed to bring that extra bit out of staff, as well as the various 'sleights-of-hand' – the equivalent of a conjuror's – by which a butler could cause a thing to occur at just the right time and place without guests even glimpsing the often large and complicated manoeuvre behind the operation. As I say, my companion seemed genuinely interested, but after a time I felt I had revealed enough and so concluded by saying:

'Of course, things are quite different today under my present employer. An American gentleman.'

'American, eh? Well, they're the only ones can afford it now. So you stayed on with the house. Part of the package.' He turned and gave me a grin.

'Yes,' I said, laughing a little. 'As you say, part of the package.'

The man turned his gaze back to the sea again, took a deep breath and sighed contentedly. We then proceeded to sit there together quietly for several moments.

'The fact is, of course,' I said after a while, 'I gave my best to Lord Darlington. I gave him the very best I had to give, and now – well – I find I do not have a great deal more left to give.'

The man said nothing, but nodded, so I went on:

'Since my new employer Mr Farraday arrived, I've tried very hard, very hard indeed, to provide the sort of service I would like him to have. I've tried and tried, but whatever I do I find I am far from reaching the standards I once set myself. More and more errors are appearing in my work. Quite trivial in themselves – at least so far. But they're of the sort I would never have made before, and I know what they signify. Goodness knows, I've tried and tried, but it's no use. I've given what I had to give. I gave it all to Lord Darlington.'

'Oh dear, mate. Here, you want a hankie? I've got one somewhere. Here we are. It's fairly clean. Just blew my nose once this morning, that's all. Have a go, mate.'

'Oh dear, no, thank you, it's quite all right. I'm very sorry, I'm afraid the travelling has tired me. I'm very sorry.'

'You must have been very attached to this Lord whatever. And it's three years since he passed away, you say? I can see you were very attached to him, mate.'

'Lord Darlington wasn't a bad man. He wasn't a bad man at all. And at least he had the privilege of being able to say at the end of his life that he made his own mistakes. His lordship was a courageous man. He chose a certain path in life, it proved to be a misguided one, but there, he chose it, he can say that at least. As for myself, I cannot even claim that. You see, I *trusted*. I trusted in his lordship's wisdom. All those years I served him, I trusted I was doing something worthwhile. I can't even say I made my own mistakes. Really – one has to ask oneself – what dignity is there in that?'

'Now, look, mate, I'm not sure I follow everything you're saying. But if you ask me, your attitude's all wrong, see? Don't keep looking back all the time, you're bound to get depressed. And all right, you can't do your job as well as you used to. But it's the same for all of us, see? We've all got to put our feet up at some point. Look at me. Been happy as a lark since the day I retired. All right, so neither of us are exactly in our first flush of youth, but you've got to keep looking forward.' And I believe it was then that he said: 'You've got to enjoy yourself. The evening's the best part of the day. You've done your day's work. Now you can put your feet up and enjoy it. That's how I look at

▷ **18** 'sleight-of-hand' [slaɪt]: clever trick **19** *conjuror:* person who entertains other people by performing tricks in which things appear, disappear, or change as if by magic **45** *hankie* (infml): handkerchief **50** *you must have been very attached to (him):* you must have liked (him) a lot **67** *happy as a lark:* very happy (lark = Lerche) **68** *in your first flush of youth:* young

it. Ask anybody, they'll all tell you. The evening's the best part of the day.'

'I'm sure you're quite correct,' I said. 'I'm so sorry, this is so unseemly. I suspect I'm over-tired. I've been travelling rather a lot, you see.'

It is now some twenty minutes since the man left, but I have remained here on this bench to await the event that has just taken place – namely, the switching on of the pier lights. As I say, the happiness with which the pleasure-seekers gathering on this pier greeted this small event would tend to vouch for the correctness of my companion's words; for a great many people, the evening is the most enjoyable part of the day. Perhaps, then, there is something to his advice that I should cease looking back so much, that I should adopt a more positive outlook and try to make the best of what remains of my day. After all, what can we ever gain in forever looking back and blaming ourselves if our lives have not turned out quite as we might have wished? The hard reality is, surely, that for the likes of you and me, there is little choice other than to leave our fate, ultimately, in the hands of those great gentlemen at the hub of this world who employ our services. What is the point in worrying oneself too much about what one could or could not have done to control the course one's life took? Surely it is enough that the likes of you and me at least *try* to make our small contribution count for something true and worthy. And if some of us are prepared to sacrifice much in life in order to pursue such aspirations, surely that is in itself, whatever the outcome, cause for pride and contentment.

A few minutes ago, incidentally, shortly after the lights came on, I did turn on my bench a moment to study more closely these throngs of people laughing and chatting behind me. There are people of all ages strolling around this pier: families with children; couples, young and elderly, walking arm in arm. There is a group of six or seven people gathered just a little way behind me who have aroused my curiosity a little. I naturally assumed at first that they were a group of friends out together for the evening. But as I listened to their exchanges, it became apparent they were strangers who had just happened upon one another here on this spot behind me. Evidently, they had all paused a moment for the lights coming on, and then proceeded to fall into conversation with one another. As I watch them now, they are laughing together merrily. It is curious how people can build such warmth among themselves so swiftly. It is possible these particular persons are simply united by the anticipation of the evening ahead. But, then, I rather fancy it has more to do with this skill of bantering. Listening to them now, I can hear them exchanging one bantering remark after another. It is, I would suppose, the way many people like to proceed. In fact, it is possible my bench companion of a while ago expected me to banter with him – in which case, I suppose I was something of a sorry disappointment. Perhaps it is indeed time I began to look at this whole matter of bantering more enthusiastically. After all, when one thinks about it, it is not such a foolish thing to indulge in – particularly if it is the case that in bantering lies the key to human warmth.

It occurs to me, furthermore, that bantering is hardly an unreasonable duty for an employer to expect a professional to perform. I have of course already devoted much time to developing my bantering skills, but it is possible I have never previously approached the task with the commitment I might have done. Perhaps, then, when I return to Darlington Hall tomorrow – Mr Farraday will not himself be back for a further week – I will begin practising with renewed effort. I should hope, then, that by the time of my employer's return, I shall be in a position to pleasantly surprise him.

▷ **28** *throng:* large group, crowd **47** *sorry:* sad or bad

THE AUTHOR

© Touhig Sion/Corbis Sygma

Born in Nagasaki in 1954, Kazuo Ishiguro moved with his parents to Britain in 1960. After studying English and Philosophy at the University of Kent, he received his MA at the University of East Anglia. He did some social work in the 1980s, during which he met his wife Lorna Anne MacDougal, whom he married in 1986.

Ishiguro has published five novels, and a sixth one (*Never Let Me Go*) is scheduled to appear in 2005. His first and second novels, *A Pale View of Hills* (1982) and *An Artist of the Floating World* (1986) are both retrospectives concerned with the Japanese experience of the Second World War. His third and best-known novel, *The Remains of the Day* (1989), won the prestigious Booker Prize and was adapted as a film in 1993. *The Unconsoled*, the emotional journey of a famous pianist, followed in 1995. In 2000 Ishiguro published *When We Were Orphans*, an intriguing detective and quest story set in both England and China. He has also written short stories, two television dramas and a screenplay.

Ishiguro's novels offer subtle explorations of human relationships against the background of world history, involving characters who are trying to come to terms with their haunting and often repressed memories. The author focuses on what can be called 'inauthentic existence', with protagonists unsteadily poised between a fundamental blindness and a growing awareness of who they are.